THE SLAYING OF SOULS
Teresa Murray

What if the true battle in life is to keep
our souls intact?

This Book is for the true heroes of life, not those with hundreds of thousands of followers on social media. Not those who are famous or rich, or held up and revered for their feats of grandeur. I have written this book for those who suffer terrible things in silence, those who remain invisible most of the time.
I hope that this book makes them a little bit less invisible.

Ria sat at the back of the house scrolling through her phone notifications. It was getting close to dinner time. She could hear her mother's raised voice as she argued with Jamil, Ria's older brother. She heard his voice, low, tense, on the defensive. Alana, the girl he was bringing to stay the night was going to be an important speaker at tomorrow's big protest at their university campus. The source of the argument between her mother and brother was Alana staying the night. It had been going on for a few days now.

Ria sighed and turned her face up to the sun, enjoying the warm feeling. She was usually the sibling her mother argued with the most. Jamil was the only male and also the eldest and could do no wrong in his mother's eyes. That however had all changed when he had started to get more and more involved in the student protests.

Ria took a sip of her tea. It was nice and strong with plenty of sugar and mint. She smiled. Life was good. She had achieved better examination results than she had hoped for in her first year of university and was meeting her friends after dinner to celebrate. She felt excited about the big protest that Alana was speaking at. It had been a lot of work and because Alana would be there, attendance would be huge. Alana was well known all across the region for her leadership of the student rebellion and admired by many students and youth, she was a role model for many. Ria had worked non-stop with Jamil these last few weeks, printing leaflets and informing as many students and young people across the region as possible about the protest, all while juggling her exams.

"I am sick of this. She never listens to what I have to say!" Jamil complained to Ria as he stormed out of the back door and stood over her, fuming. "She still treats me like a child. I am a grown man!"

"She's just worried. You know about what the neighbours will think if Alana stays the night here. You know what she's like about her morals. That's all she's worried about."

"It's not that. It's about the work. The work I'm doing. The work Alana is doing." Jamil said and ran a flustered hand through his thick hair. "She thinks it's dangerous for us all that Alana stays here tonight."

"And what about the work I'm doing!" Ria said, not liking him discarding her after all the hours she had spent doing things for him. "What does she mean, dangerous? It's just another student protest." Ria sighed. She felt Jamil's stare on her and looked up at him. He looked angry. At her!

"What! What is it, Jamil?" Ria asked. "She's wrong, isn't she? To be worried? It's not dangerous, is it?"

He sat down next to her and looked at her, his face serious. "Just another student protest! Ria, it is hard to believe that still, after all this time, you haven't understood what is happening in our country at the moment. What does this all mean for you? Just something exciting for you to do other than chatter with your silly friends?"

"They are not silly!" Ria said angrily. "That's not it. It's just what she said about danger. Why is she saying that? Why is she saying that about Alana? What is dangerous about what we are doing?"

"Ria, this is serious. We live where we live. We are not allowed to protest, do you understand? It is forbidden by the state. Do you not understand what happened to our father? It was because he said and did things the regime didn't approve of! He spoke out and died for it. That is what she means by dangerous, and she's right!"

Ria was silent. No-one had ever talked about her father, so she knew very little about him. She didn't believe what Jamil was saying about what had happened to him, that's not what her mother had told them. But she held her tongue. Her mother had not told them much about how her father had died now that she thought about it.

"Ria, there will come a time, when these protests we are organising, these flyers we are printing, everything we are doing now, will not be enough. Not enough to bring change. For change, there must be a revolution, we will have to fight. Soon, very soon, what is happening in other countries like ours will happen here. We will have our own revolution. It is going to happen soon, whether we want it or not, it has to happen. You must get ready for it, we all must, our mother too. The regime here will not go quietly like in some of the other countries where young people have demonstrated. Here those in power will cling to it like a drowning man clings to a piece of floating wood. We will have to fight soon. It is inevitable."

"What are you talking about Jamil? We are protesting peacefully just like they are doing in other countries. It has worked elsewhere, and it will work here, there will be no need to fight. It is great that Alana is coming to speak, it will be our biggest protest yet. You should be happy and excited. It is a great honour for our university. Why do you always have to be so angry and dramatic about everything!" Ria said, turning to him, exasperated.

"Because there is a lot to be angry about Ria! Stop being so naïve. Listen to what Alana says tomorrow and speak to her tonight after dinner instead of going out dancing with your friends. We can all go for a walk after dinner. She can tell you about what is happening in other places. It will help you to understand."

"No Jamil. I have helped you enough already with the organisation. I will be here when she comes and I'll help you with Mama later, but as soon as we finish dinner, I am going out to celebrate my exam result with my friends. I can enjoy myself for once can I not? There's nothing to worry about. All this talk about fighting and revolution makes no sense Jamil. You said it would be peaceful protesting. If not, I want no part of it."

Jamil stood up abruptly and looked down at her, frowning. She couldn't help feeling he was disappointed with her.

"Ria, if that is how you feel, then you are not really a part of this movement, and it means that you have understood very little about everything we've been saying these last few months."

Ria opened her mouth to appease him, but his phone rang breaking the tense silence between them. He shot her a cold look, then turned his back on her and walked away now fully focused now on his phone conversation. She felt deflated. Jamil was her older brother, someone she looked up to and admired. She did not want to disappoint him, but he was being ungrateful and surely, he was blowing things out of proportion. She had helped and done what he had asked. She had even helped him convince her mother that Alana could come and stay the night. She and her sister Hana had even agreed to let Alana stay in their room!

Jamil made her so mad sometimes. Calling her friends 'silly'. He was so serious about everything. He was only two years older than her, but he acted like he was her father!

Ria sighed again, her enjoyment of the early evening sun and the glow of her academic success had now faded after her conversation with her brother. She got up and went inside to help her mother with dinner and to smooth things over with her mother to make sure she behaved herself when Alana arrived.

2

The next day was hot and humid. Ria watched the growing crowd of students jostled under the glaring sun from just in front of the main entrance of the university. A tattered white bed sheet hung across the main entrance flapping gently in the breeze, a slogan painted clumsily across it in red paint. A popular song blasted from the two loudspeakers that were balanced on top of flimsy cardboard boxes. The crowd was singing and jumping up and down to the music, some even dancing. Spirits were high, the academic year had ended. Ria smiled when the mass of students cheered even louder as three students climbed up the university steps and onto a makeshift stage. They waved to the crowd.

The hairs on Ria's arm stood up from the intensity of the atmosphere, and she felt a glow of pride as she watched her brother pick up a loud hailer to address the crowd. He pumped his fist in the air several times and then smiled. The crowd cheered even more. He signalled with his hand for quiet, and the crowd settled, waiting. Alana stood beside him.

Ria noticed that Jamil's white t-shirt was as smudged as usual and his jeans and boots were covered in dust, but he looked cool to her. She could see he was a bit nervous, but she knew that no-one else would notice.

"Friends!" Jamil began. "You know the challenges we face. How we live, oppressed and persecuted by this violent regime. We already know there are no jobs waiting for us. There is no future for us where we can be free and live a decent life. Not unless things change. But you know the regime will do anything to stop change! They are so desperate to hang on to their power. You have all heard the rumours of the terrible things happening to other students across the country. They are all true, we know that. But now is our time. We have seen the possibilities of what could be from the inspiring acts of other students and young people who have demonstrated against their dictators and succeeded! Students and young people just like us have shown their old governments that they HAVE HAD ENOUGH."

The crowd cheered. Ria cheered too. Jamil's expression changed now, becoming more solemn.

"But friends, the state has seen what has happened to those leaders in other countries. It is afraid and it is reacting quickly, frightened it will meet the same fate. We see how it threatens us all, our families and friends, and how it viciously silences anyone who speaks out against it. You know it does that with no mercy!"

The crowd jeered.

"Enough is enough!" Jamil shouted, louder now. "The time has come for change. If we don't free ourselves from this regime that oppresses us what is the point of studying or even living? Our regime rules by fear alone. Our leaders have sacrificed generation after generation to preserve itself. But it falls to us to finally stop it. If we fail, we will have no future. You have seen news of how young people in other countries like ours have overthrown their ageing dictators. They succeeded because they had had nothing left to lose but their fear. If we unite, we are strong and we can win. There are more of us than them. But, if we choose to do nothing, our fate is already sealed. Nothing will change and damned we will be." Jamil paused and looked out over the faces. "It is time. "Are you ready to fight for a better future? A different future?" he shouted.

"Yes, Yes, Yes!" The crowd cheered and jumped in time with each *yes*.

"Enough is enough!" Jamil ended with those words, fist-punching the air on each last word.

The crowd of students chanted the words '*Enough is Enough*' over and over and with each repetition their chants got louder and louder. Ria felt the atmosphere become more charged with excitement and anticipation, but she also noticed a hint of anger in the chants. This was by far the biggest protest yet, there were many more students here than they had thought would come. For the first time since she had become involved, she felt the strong sense of unity and a spirit of hope and solidarity. It was a powerful and intoxicating feeling.

Jamil put up his hand to silence the crowd and continued.

"Today, you have come to hear Alana speak, not me! Alana is a great leader and was the one who organised one of the first-ever student protests. In that protest three students were beaten to death and more than forty others were arrested by the military. Of those forty students, still today nothing is known. We will read out each of their names at the end. We will never forget them." He said.

Jamil passed the loudspeaker to Alana. Ria could see by the crowd's reaction just how much they admired her.

Alana took the loudhailer, smiled at Jamil, and greeted the crowd. She was tall and strong looking, dressed in black jeans and a black t-shirt. Her long black hair was tied back off her face. The dinner the evening before had been without tension thanks to Alana's engaging and respectful demeanour. Ria could tell that her mother, in spite of herself, had really liked Alana. Ria had felt drawn to her as well. She was charismatic, kind, and fun, and she saw how her brother looked at her. So did her mother, who missed nothing. Any talk of the protest had been avoided at all costs.

Ria heard a very loud noise whipped round to look in the direction it had come from. From where she stood on the steps below Jamil and Alana, she could make no sense of what she was seeing. A long line of armoured military vehicles, too many to count, were filing into the campus grounds at high speed, raising a lot of dust and their tyres spitting up gravel as each vehicle stopped and turned to position itself in a formation that seemed to be surrounding the crowd of students.

Ria watched as huge machine guns mounted on the vehicles were moved, clicking as they did so, and were trained on the students. What was going on? All of her attention was on the vehicles now and silence fell as the students turned towards the military vehicles. Ria stood there transfixed, staring in confusion at the soldiers standing behind the guns. They were all wearing black face masks, only their eyes and mouths visible. Surely by now there was not one student left who had not noticed the trucks. The music blared out strangely out of place now in the tense silence.

Ria turned around to look up at where Jamil and Alana had just been, but they were no longer there.

Then suddenly several sharp bursts of a machine gun fire broke the uneasy silence. Ria didn't register the sounds as machine gun fire at first because of all the screaming. Such terrible screams! She stood there on the step rooted to the spot hearing soft thudding sounds all around her. She heard herself scream but wasn't really sure if it had been her or somebody else. What the hell was happening? She crouched down instinctively. To her left, a young male student lay on the step below her writhing, blood pouring from his stomach, she urinated. She understood now what was happening.

People started running in all directions, trying to get away from the vehicles, but the high campus walls blocked their way. Horrified, Ria watched as one of those white walls quickly turned red from all the blood and saw a mound of unmoving students form along the base of the walls. Ria couldn't move, she felt frozen to the spot. She put her hands over her ears to block out the terrifying sound of the loud guns.

Someone grabbed her arm. She saw a face flash in front of her, someone's mouth moving. She uncovered her ears. It was Jamil pulling at her arm, Alana was crouched down next to him.

"Ria, come on, we've got to go." He shouted at her.

11

She just stared back at him.

He jerked her arm harder, and they half-stumbled, half-ran past the stage and towards the main university entrance. She could see the door ahead. Other students were running off to her right, away from the entrance, trying to get behind the university walls for protection. Ria tried to side-step the many blood-spattered people on the ground as she was pulled along by Jamil, but it was impossible to avoid trampling over them, there were just too many. She felt horrified as she felt the bodies under her sandals, stifling a scream. A sea of panic propelled the still-living forward. Jamil suddenly veered away from the main running group and entered a small side door further down along the wall pulling her with him.

"Come on, we have to move fast." he shouted at Ria. He sounded too loud. Why was he shouting? Alana was still beside him.

"How could they do this?" Ria cried.

"Ria come on!" Alana shouted at Ria. "We have to hurry."

But Ria's legs had stopped working. Despite her efforts she could not make them move fast enough so she began to lag behind Jamil and Alana. Jamil stopped, turned and sprinted back towards her. She caught the blur of a movement before suddenly feeling a sudden hot sting on her cheek. Jamil had hit her! She stared at him, eyes wide, but then started to run faster behind him.

They ran, her sandals flip-flopping along the empty corridor right down to the end where there was a back exit.

"Wait!" Alana said and moved slowly to check outside. "It's okay, they're not here yet. Let's go but keep very low."

The three of them edged their way outside and ran crab-like across the sand and into a narrow side street that was part of the market. Ria could still hear the guns firing, and the screams, but noticed there were fewer and fewer screams and more gun sounds. As they picked their way past the market stalls that lined the narrow streets, the sellers were frantically packing up their goods.

Without warning, Jamil ducked behind a fruit stall, dragging Ria with him, Alana now beside Ria. He shouldered open a narrow wooden door that opened into a narrow passageway. It was very dark in there and so quiet that their ragged breathing sounded so loud that Ria was convinced the soldiers would hear them.

No-one said a word. Ria started to sob.

"Shut up Ria", said Jamil, so she did.

They waited, straining to hear. Ria heard a lot of shouting and then a deadly quiet.

"Jamil, we have to go now." said Alana. "They'll go onto the streets next."

"Maybe they won't." Jamil said. "Maybe it was just about the protest, the students."

Ria noticed his voice was trembling.

"Jamil, what are you saying? Why did they do this? I don't understand." cried Ria.

"It's simple, Ria. They are killing us before we start, they don't want us to protest. It's a warning." Alana said.

13

Ria saw anger in her eyes.

Alana continued. "They are afraid so they must put us down, like rabid dogs before we can bite. This is an example to others of what will happen if they do the same. This will create even more fear."

"This is not the time to talk!" Jamil said. "Ria, listen to Alana, she has more experience, and she knows what they are capable of doing. We have to go."

"Mama was right Jamil about all this being too dangerous. I never imagined anything like this could happen. You never said anything! We should have listened to our mother! All those students, they're our friends Jamil! We have to get help for them, some might still be alive." Ria was talking very quickly, her words tumbling one over another.

"Ria, it is too late for them now. There's nothing we can do for them." Alana took her by the shoulders.

Ria pulled away. "You don't know that, Alana! You don't know. They can't have killed us all!"
Ria saw Alana's eyes fill with tears, but she did not shed them.

"Ria, we have to run now so we can fight another day! To fight for those, they have killed today. We are no good to anyone dead!" Alana said.

"Ria, I have to get Alana out now and make sure she gets away safely. They might be looking for her. Go home and make sure our mother and Hana are safe. Tell our mother what has happened, she will know what to do. I'll call you when it's safe. I promise. Now go!" Jamil said.

14

"No, Jamil! Please, don't go. Come home with me, please, don't go now. Bring Alana home, she can stay with us. Just don't leave me here alone!" Ria shouted.

"No, Ria, our home will be the first place they will look for her. Go! Now, before it's too late!" he shouted back at her.

Alana had already opened the door a little and was checking the street. She left the passageway, turned and nodded to Jamil. Jamil looked back at Ria for a moment, their eyes met, then he turned and followed Alana out into the street. Ria stood alone in the dark, damp passageway, tears streaming down her face, but she dared not make a sound with her crying.

3

Ria stood there staring at the door, which was still swinging back and forth on its hinges. She felt lightheaded, as if she were about to fall. Her heart was pounding so hard it sounded loud in her chest.

'Run! Run! Move!' A voice inside her urged.

But she couldn't. Her feet felt like they had heavy weights attached to them and her legs were trembling. She could not trust her limbs and she didn't want to leave that dark passageway. It felt safer there and she was finding it hard to think. All her mind seemed to be doing was mixing up fleeting images of her mother, Hana, and Jamil with the terrible images of what she had just witnessed in the campus.

Why had Jamil left? Why hadn't he taken her with him? How could he just leave her here like this and tell her to go home on her own after what had just happened? Had Alana not said the soldiers would go onto the streets next. She was sure that was what Alana had said. Her brother was supposed to look after her, and his family! Was Alana more important to him than his own family?

Anger stirred and fused with her rising panic. What the hell was she supposed to do now?

Surely it was better to stay where she was until she knew for sure that it was safe to leave. Yes, that would be better. No point trying to get home. If they were on the street and saw her, they would kill her just like all the others. Surely by now they were already patrolling. Yes, better to stay here. That was a better plan than her brother's. It was too dangerous to go outside. What the hell had he been thinking? Her mother would know what to do without her. She'd take care of Hana. There wasn't much Ria could do. Her mother was older and more experienced.

To ease the trembling in her thighs and the feeling of light-headedness, she sat down on the dusty ground and pressed her back against the cold, damp wall of the passageway. A wave of nausea surged, and she turned her head to one side and gagged. Nothing came up, but the scent of vomit filled her nostrils. She spat on the ground a few times and tried to muster enough saliva to swallow but every time she tried, she felt like gagging again.

She heard some men shouting in the distance. She crawled forward to the battered door and pushed it firmly shut. She pressed the side of her head against the door and strained to hear. The shouting was indistinct and faint and soon replaced with the same deadly quiet as before. The thunderous beating of her heart filled the vacuum where normal sounds should be.

What if they were patrolling the streets? Going from door to door? What if they found her? Surely, they would find her any minute. They would kill her on the spot.

She peered through the tiny cracks in the door but could see nothing. Nobody. No boots creeping along the stones, no uniform flapping by. She stood up and shook out her legs in front of her one at a time. Then she moved her arms up and down as if warming up for a workout, careful not to make a sound.

She opened the door slowly and looked up and down the street. What had been alien to her before was now familiar once again. She knew where she was. The normally busy market street was empty except for the hastily abandoned stalls. She saw some fruit squashed into the cobbled flagstones.

Maybe it was better to run for home and do what Jamil had told her to do than stay there alone. He was more experienced after all in all this. It was fifteen minutes to her house if she ran very fast. She could stick to the narrow back streets. It would be safer that way. But she was too afraid. Fifteen minutes seemed a long time to be out there alone and exposed amongst soldiers who would her shoot on sight.

But then with no conscious thought it seemed, she slipped out from her hiding place and onto the street. She looked around and then turned and stepped forward in the opposite direction to her home, back towards the campus. She pressed her body tightly against the wall as she moved, the sleeves of her shirt snagging now and again on the sharp edges of the stones as she edged her way along the walls of the old buildings.

Where was everybody? As she got nearer to the campus walls, she heard men shouting, then heard a distinct shout of "Move out!". She stopped, heart racing. If someone came out of the side door now, they would see her. Instinctively she made herself as small as possible as she strained to hear, her eyes trained on the campus side door, completely still. Good hearing had quickly become an existential necessity.

She heard the sound of engines revving hard and of tyres spinning on gravel. They must be leaving. There was only one way in for vehicles, so just one way out. But what if they had left some behind to stop people going in? She waited until the sound of the engines was further away and reinitiated her slow advance towards the campus. She felt detached, not herself, yet alert, as if on autopilot. She arrived opposite the side door, the same exit she had escaped through with Jamil and Alana.

She couldn't hear anything. How could there be no sound with the thousands of students in there? Maybe the soldiers were still there, that's why no one was speaking. She half walked, half couched down a long corridor lined with lecture room doors trying not to make a sound with her sandals on the tiles, but they squeaked loudly anyway. She crept out of the large door that opened onto the sandy expanse at the front side of the campus, edging forward towards where she had been before, eyes scanning left and right.

She stopped and stood up straight, body tense. There were no soldiers there. She thought she heard a strange gurgling sound coming from inside her. She stared around her but could not understand what she was seeing. Laid out in all sorts of strange positions in front of her were hundreds of red-streaked bodies.

Somewhere in her mind, her senses registered small movements, and the eery sound that many quiet moans make all together. Was she hearing things or was it the sound of the dying? She started as she heard someone sobbing and looked out in front of her. She saw two students; one lay on top of the other. She saw the dark red stains splashed across their faces, legs, arms, and heads. Both student's eyes were Even though some part of her knew that what she was seeing was real and she knew that all of these bodies were real, she could not accept it as the real. open, unmoving, fixed in a deathly stare.

Everywhere she looked there were blood-streaked students piled on top of each other, most at the main entrance. There were other bodies strewn around in strange positions, laying where and how they had fallen as they tried to get away. There was so much blood that Ria could not see anyone she recognised. Was she the only person alive standing there amid thousands of dead students? No, that was not possible. Ria saw large red criss-crossing patterns all over the pale sand and long smears of red. She knew what those red patterns were. She looked down at her feet. They were covered in the same red spatters.

She doubled over and gagged. Again, nothing but bile. She spat it out and turned back in the direction she had come running faster than she had ever run in all her life.

Ria ran and ran, no longer worried about stealth as she fled through the labyrinth of empty, shadowy, streets, streets she knew like the back of her hand. Streets her mother had dragged her through on countless market days. Streets that were now deserted. She wasn't running to anything. She was running away from everything.

A sudden wave of light-headedness forced her to slow down, and then feeling nauseous again, she stopped to bend over and gagged until she managed to rid herself of a thin spiral of bile caught in the back of her throat. She spat it out again, and again. A slithery film of cold sweat covered her face and arms, despite the intense heat. Her jeans were sticking to her.

She looked around to get her bearings and was able to make out the long familiar lines of olive trees in the distance. Her home was at the end of that line of trees where the grove ended. Ria turned left and ran towards them, grateful for the protection of the leafy trees as she arrived at the first crop. She was surprised that there was no-one there, it was normally such a hive of activity. The trucks that moved constantly between the groves and the towns were not there now. Nobody was tending to their trees either. No one greeting her with a wave.

As she approached her house, she saw that the shutters were pulled firmly shut, just like all of the other houses she had passed on her way home. The green door, always left open during the day, was shut too. It was as if no one was home, but she knew her mother was there. Her mother knew what had happened.

Ria searched for her long-forgotten phone and called her mother. Her mother answered straight away.

"I'm outside. Let me in." Ria said.

Her mother hung up without saying a word. Ria swore but then she saw the front door open just a crack and caught a glimpse of Hana's head as she opened the door slightly. Ria pushed the door open, ran in, and slammed it shut and just stood there trying to get her breath back.

Her mother was standing by the kitchen table, the same one at which they had all eaten and joked the night before. The night Alana had stayed.

"I thought you were dead." her mother said.
Hana hugged Ria tightly. Ria saw how pale both of them looked.

"Where is Jamil, Ria?" her mother asked.

"I don't know." Ria said.

"Is he dead?" Her mother asked. Shaky strength threaded her voice.

"No, he was the one who got me out and Alana. But..."

"But what, where is he now? Why isn't he with you?" her mother's voice was low, but firm.
Ria stared at her mother, no words coming.

"I told you not to get involved in those student activities. I told Jamil to stop those protests. Is it not enough what happened to your father?" her mother said, tense, then turned away.
Ria stared at the floor, feeling the tug of tears, but before she could cry, she felt a sharp, intense pain in her stomach and ran to the bathroom. She barely made it in time and in seconds it felt as if the entire contents of her bowels had just fallen out of her, leaving her stomach cramped and her body weak.
Pale and dry-mouthed, she walked jaded back to the kitchen. Her mother was making tea, a stern frown on her face.

"Tell me what happened, Ria. Now." her mother said, turning to face her, hands on hips.

Ria hesitated glancing at Hana. Why was her mother acting like this?

"Ria! Now!" her mother snapped.

Her mother turned back again and handed her a glass of water.

"We were all at the campus, all the students, we weren't doing anything wrong. Then, out of nowhere, the campus started filling up with soldiers on top of trucks with huge machine guns. Then, then... they just started shooting at everyone. At all of us. Everyone was screaming and running everywhere, trying to get away. Jamil came and got me. He was with Alana. We ran out the back door of the campus into the market and hid in a passageway. I think they are all dead Mama. All of the students. I saw them." Ria said. She wanted to cry but could not. What was wrong with her?

Hana began to cry. Her mother placed the pot of tea on the table, sat down and gestured to the girls to do the same. She poured the tea into three small glasses.

"Drink, both of you." Ria's mother said, frowning at Ria across the table.

"It's not my fault Mama," Ria said. "It's not Jamil's either."

Ria's mother looked at her but said nothing.

Her mother picked up her phone and dialled a number. Ria heard it go to voice mail. After the tone, her mother said, "Jamil. This is your mother. Ria is home. Call me now." She put the phone back down, took a long sip of tea and looked at her daughters.

23

"Finish your tea quickly, then go upstairs and pack your backpacks with just one change of clothes, some underwear, and your passports. Nothing more. We must leave. Put on good shoes for walking. No sandals. Wear dark clothes."

"What? What for? Where are we going? No, Mama. What are you talking about? I don't understand." Hana said. She looked dismayed.

"Mama. What is this? We have to stay here!" Ria said. "What about Jamil? He said to wait here for him! That is what he said. We can't just leave. Not without him!" Ria said, her tone rising. "And why? To go where? For what? Passports! What for?" Ria said. "You don't know what you are saying. It is crazy!"

"Ria do not speak to me like that. You forget yourself. Calm yourself. You will both do as I say. This is not a time for discussion. Now Ria, take your sister upstairs and go and pack like I said. Be back down here in ten minutes! There is no time to explain things to you. No time. Ria. Is what you have just witnessed not enough explanation for you?" Her mother said.

Ria glared at her mother, her words stinging. Ria got up from the table. Hana pushed her cup of tea away from her, her defiant gesture spilling the tea over the wooden table. Her mother picked up a cloth and just wiped it up.

"Go and do what I told you to do." her mother said.

Ria saw the look in her mother's eyes and took to the stairs. Hana followed her upstairs, and Ria heard her mother came up soon after.

24

"Why is she making us do this?" Hana asked, sitting on the end of her bed, shoulders hunched. "It's terrible what happened at the campus. I can't believe such a thing could happen here. Are you okay?" Hana looked up at Ria frowning.

Ria said nothing. Her mind was blank. She could not think. Was she okay? No idea. Not important, people were dead, people she knew. At a protest that she had helped organise. She got out their backpacks, handed Hana hers and started to pack underwear and t-shirts, the odd sweater. She searched in their shared wardrobe for footwear.

"Hana, just do as she says! Now. Come on. Hurry." Ria said. "We can talk later. She will explain after."

Hana got up from the bed reluctantly and started searching through her drawers. "Can I bring a book?"

"Just a small one. Come on. It will be fine Hana. We'll be back soon. It's just temporary. Don't worry." Ria said and touched her sister gently on her arm, realising that her own agitation was causing Hana even more distress.

Ria could hear her mother talking to someone on her phone as her mother moved around in her bedroom banging cupboard doors. Ria stopped to listen, but she couldn't make out what her mother was saying or who she was talking to. Ria strode out of their bedroom and stood in the doorway of her mother's room watching her mother pack a small backpack, phone held in place by her shoulder and neck as she moved around.

"Are you talking to Jamil?" Ria said.

Her mother started at Ria's voice, said something into the phone, hung up and turned to Ria.

"No. Ria, it's not your brother. Why are you just standing there? Have you finished packing? There is no time to explain Ria. They will be here soon. They will come for Jamil, for Alana, for all of us. Do you not understand? There is no time!"

"They?" Then it clicked and Ria nodded. She rushed back to help Hana finish, and they both went downstairs.
Their mother was already waiting, standing by the window looking out through the lats of the window shutters.

"It's time to go. Come on!" Her mother said, picked up her rucksack and turned towards the back door. They slipped out and walked quickly over to the fields of olive trees.

"Stay close to the trees and keep on this side where the shade is" her mother whispered. "Move quickly, and no talking!"

The three of them moved quickly from tree to tree, Ria and Hana mirroring their mother's movements and timings. The afternoon heat was searing and within seconds Ria's black t-shirt was soaking.

Then without warning her mother stopped, bent down and cocked her head. She motioned them to crouch down next to her against a large tree, finger to her lips. Ria strained hearing nothing at first, but then she heard it. The terrifyingly familiar sound of military vehicle motors and men shouting.

The military had arrived. They were at their house! Her mother was right. How had she known?

4

"Run!" her mother said and took off in full sprint, Ria and Hana struggling to keep up, their feet sinking in the soft soil of the olive grove. By the time their mother finally stopped Ria and Hana's breathing was ragged. Ria was surprised to see that her mother's was not. She seemed fine except for the sweat running down her face. Ria followed her mother's gaze as she looked back in the direction of their home and saw what her mother saw. Thick, angry-looking billows of black smoke were spiralling up into the clear blue sky.

"No!" Ria said shaking her head.

Ria met her mother's eyes and saw a wet gleam in them. Hana was sitting on the ground, frantically swiping through her phone, oblivious.

"Hana, turn your phone off now!" her mother shouted. "Let's go. No more phones on. We must save the batteries and make sure the location device is off in your phones!"

Hana pouted but did as her mother said, put her phone in her bag and then she stood up. It was only then that Hana noticed the smoke. She looked at her mother wide-eyed, then at Ria as if expecting an explanation. Her mother said nothing, and Ria didn't know what to say. Hana just stood there staring at their burning home not saying a word, tears streaming down her face.

Ria couldn't bear it. She took out her phone and scrolled quickly through her messages and the newspaper headlines searching to see if there was anything about the campus. Nothing.

"Turn it off now, Ria. Let's go. We must get to the border before they find us." Her mother said.

Reality hit Ria hard now as she heard her mother's words. The border? Of course. They were being chased. Hunted. But why?

The sun had begun its slow late afternoon descent by now, so the heat was a little more bearable. Ria felt the sweat on her back turn slightly cooler and felt a shiver run down her spine. She felt panicked and disconnected at the same time. Her mind churned out random images that melted away before she could see any of them clearly enough to make any sense of them. She felt a heaviness tightening in her chest and suddenly there was not enough air for her to breathe. All she could think about was Jamil. Were they hunting for him or them? Where was he?

They kept on going, slower now but steady. Soon, the sun dropped, and day became dusk. Soon it would be dark.

"Mama, I'm tired and thirsty." Hana said "I have to stop. I need some water. I want to go home. We haven't done anything wrong. Why are we running? Who burned our house? Why? I don't understand...Mama!" Hana said, pleading.

Her mother said nothing, she just kept moving forward.

Hana stopped and stared defiantly at her mother's back. Ria stopped too and her mother turned around to face them. Her mother's face was tense as she looked at Hana. Ria swallowed. No one defied her mother.

Her mother strode back to where Hana was standing, grabbed her by the shoulders and shook her hard.

"Hana, you will do as I tell you if you want to stay alive. Now keep moving. You can drink later, not know." Her mother said in a low voice, but her tone had the same effect as if she had shouted. "Home? There is no home to go back to child!"

Hana started to cry.

"Mama, stop it, you're frightening her. Calm down." Ria said to her mother sharply.

"Calm down? Calm down, she says!" Her mother snapped keeping her voice low. "I told Jamil this would happen! You are both children still, and believe me when I say this, neither of you understand this, and that is because I have protected you both. You don't know the things that happen because I don't tell you. I protect you from all of it, or at least I have tried. Our generation know how things work in this country from experience! I warned your brother that things would get bad for him if he got involved with these protests. I warned you too Ria about going to the protests at the campus, do you remember? I told your brother last night that all this protesting put us all at risk. But no, your brother knows everything. He is too stubborn to listen to me. And you are both young and naïve. Now look at us! We have all lived through things you young people know nothing about. Do you think I am surprised by what happened at the campus today, Ria? Well, I am not! I wish I was. Do you think I am surprised they burned down our house? I am not!" Her mother was fuming. Ria felt attacked, and angry.

"What happened to your father was no accident. You are too naïve Ria, and your brother is a danger to himself in his youthful arrogance. He has brought this danger to our doorstep. Now that is it, once they start, they never stop."

Hana started to cry.

"Listen to me both of you. Hana! Stop your snivelling. Understand this. If they find us, they will take us and they will do things to us to make us talk, to make us tell them where your brother is, and then they will kill us. That is what they do to people who go against them. Do you still not understand anything?" her mother said, now sounding to Ria less angry and more frustrated.

"Why did you never explain then!" Ria said to her mother angrily. "How are we supposed to know things when all you older people do is whisper amongst yourselves?"

Her mother walked up to Ria and slapped her across the face, the sound echoing in the silence. Ria raised her hand to her face in shock, quietened now, abstractly remembering Jamil doing the same to her only hours before.

"To talk of those things Ria is a death sentence." Her mother said quietly. "That is what you and your brother have never understood. You think it is all an exciting game. You think here is like those other countries.

But Ria, you saw it with your own eyes today at your university. They don't play games here."

Panic and shame welled up in Ria as she heard her mother's words. She knew her mother was right. Images of the piles of bloodied bodies at the campus flitted in and out of her mind, images that were stuck on a constant loop. Hana started to cry more loudly. Ria nodded at her mother and took Hana's hand, smiling at her sister briefly and stroking her hair.

"Come Hana, we have to go." Ria said to her sister, and holding Hana's hand, they followed their fast-moving mother.

As it got darker it became harder to see, there was only a sliver of a moon, so it was harder to be seen too. The terrain had changed from soft soil to a gravellier surface allowing them to move more quickly at first but then they reached some low hills, and the surface became more slippery, slowing them down as they had to take more care to avoid tripping and falling. Hana had tripped once already and gashed her elbow and knee and had made a lot of noise as she fell. Ria's legs were heavy from all the effort, but she felt very awake, not tired at all. Her mother was slowing down up ahead, then she stopped gesturing for the girls to crouch down like her. She put her fingers on her lips. Silence!

Ria dropped down, pulling Hana down with her. She could see nothing but the shadowy silhouettes of trees and just hills. But then she heard it. She strained. Engines in the distance, but different engines to the ones earlier.

She glanced at her mother, craning her neck toward the sound.

"Generators." whispered her mother.

"Are you sure?" Ria asked.

"Yes. It must be from one of the border checkpoints. There are many near this border. They move them all the time, so no-one ever knows exactly where they are."

"What do we do now?" Hana asked.

"We will have to go around it, far around it. Sometimes they have dogs, and they patrol often especially after dark." her mother said.

"Dogs?" Hana replied. "For what?

"Don't worry Hana. Just follow Mama." Ria said, trying to reassure her sister.

Her mother gestured again, pointing for them to go back the same way they had come. Crouching, and going very slowly, they circled back and away until the engines sounded further away. Then they proceeded forward like before but even more cautiously now.

Ria felt the ground shift under her feet. It felt like gravelly sand. She bent down to take a handful. It was sand. She looked up and saw there were no more trees. All she could make out ahead was groups of bare mounds not big enough to be hills.

"Those sand hills mean we are near the border, we are close." Her mother said. "No-one plants anything here because of the sand and the patrols so there's nothing to protect us from sight now, but we have to try to cross the border while it's still dark. We are lucky there is no moon. If there are no patrols or dogs, we will get through easily.

But as there is no cover at all on those hills, we must crouch down very low to the ground. Move like this, look. We move, we stop, we listen, then we move again. It will be much slower now and it will take longer, but it is the best way to avoid being seen from lookout towers. We will be easy to see on these hills so we must become as small as possible and move as slowly as possible. It's dark so we have a good chance. It's a risk, but we have no choice. There's nowhere to hide, so, let's go." Her mother said, her voice less harsh than before.

Her mother began moving forward, crouching down and like a crab she moved forward a few metres, then stopped to listen before moving forward again. Ria stifled a strange urge to giggle at her mother's strange posture.

"Hana, are you ok?" Ria asked looking back at her sister. "Come up into the middle," Ria said and gestured for Hana to get between her and her mother. Hana crawled up, making awkward, strange movements, trying to imitate her mother. Ria caught a glimpse of Hana's face as she passed by her. Terror was all she could see. Ria felt the cool sand on her hands as she moved to crouch. It felt calming, though her thighs protested at the posture.

"Come on!", her mother whispered. On moved the caravan of three, crab-walking their way painstakingly up the side of the first sandy hill.

After what felt like hours Ria thought she could see lights in the distance. It looked like a town. Her mother turned and smiled in the dark, her white teeth glowing strangely. She nodded. Perhaps they were almost there. Ria's spirits lifted ever so slightly.

Then, all at the same time, the three of them froze in mid-crawl as they heard the excited barking and whimpering of dogs. Dogs who did not seem to be very far away.

Ria thought they were getting closer, but she was disoriented so it was hard to tell from which direction the sounds were even coming from. Her fear was not helping. She couldn't judge how far away they were from the lights of the town either. She was close enough now to her mother to see that she was tense. She saw worry all over her mother's face, and perhaps a little fear too. Ria had never seen her mother show fear to anyone.

"Have the dogs found us?" Hana asked the question going through all of their heads.

"Come on, don't worry about the dogs. But we will have to move faster now." Her mother said. There was urgency in her voice now.

"Let's run, not crawl," Ria said. "It's faster."

"Yes, but it will be easier for them to see us." Her mother said.

"I know, but if the dogs already have our scent, it won't matter, it will be too late. It's better to go faster now and try to make it to the border before they catch up with us."

"I don't know, maybe the dogs haven't sensed us yet. It's a risk, but I suppose you are right. But we will have to run very fast. It looks as if it is only a couple of kilometres away but that's far on sand. Hana, get ready to run, as fast as you can, just run, even if you are tired. Keep close to each other. Watch out for small rocks and those small bushes see them there, they are all over the place, and try not to fall. Ria, you go first, then you Hana, I'll come behind." Her mother said as she glanced back in the direction of the barking sounds.

Ria sprang into the lead surprising herself with newfound speed, Hana ran just behind her, her mother to her right. Ria was surprised at how fast and strong her mother was. The way her mother had behaved these last few hours had thrown Ria. She had been so used to seeing her mother do 'mother things' like cooking, cleaning, going to the market and chatting with her friends, that this side of her mother was a discovery. Ria felt a surge of some sort pumping through her, making her legs work faster, pushing more air into her lungs to drive her up the slope of the sand hill which was quite steep. It was a very sandy, and even though the sand was packed quite hard there were lots of those treacherously low bushes scattered all over the hills and nothing to cast a protective shadow over them. It all fed their fear.

Ria could hear that Hana was breathing much too fast. Hana hated any form of physical activity, preferring to spend her time with books or drawing. Ria knew Hana was struggling. "You can do it, Hana. Just a little further to go." Ria offered up some breathless motivation.

They made it to the top of the first sand hill. Both Hana and Ria were gasping for breath. Ria looked at the slope down, surely it would be much faster to run down. Her mother stopped and listened for the dogs. Ria's eyes searched the dark hills.

"They seem further away now." Her mother said, turning to eye the steep descent. "Be careful here. It's dusty and stony, stones moving make noise, and a twisted ankle would be a disaster."

Ria noticed that Hana was not even bothering to look down at where she was placing her feet. Hana looked very frightened which only made Ria feel her own panic grow. Keep moving. Focus. Don't think.

"Hana, just have faith, keep alert and just keep moving," Ria said to her sister. "You can do it, we're nearly there, look at the lights!"

Hana looked, but then looked down at the steep incline and looked back at Ria with heart-wrenching self-doubt. But she nodded and Ria sprung forward and down.

They ran zigzagging down the slope as fast as they could. Ria had found a narrow path, and they were now following it. She could smell goat excrement and was sure she had stepped in a substantial amount. Shit on her shoes was a minor issue.

Hana crashed into Ria as Ria stopped without warning. Their mother, in an effort to avoid colliding into Hana, skid and fell heavily, grazing her arm badly on some stones. As Ria watched her mother pull herself up from the ground, elbow bleeding, Ria was suddenly blinded by a large circle of light. That was why she had stopped. She had seen that light moving below her. All she could see now was the light. She raised her hand to cover her eyes and soon saw more moving circles of light coming quickly towards them. She heard the shouts of men now. She stared at them, confused.

"They've found us," her mother said. Ria noticed her defeated tone.

Ria felt herself pulled by strong arms and then pushed forward. Dazed, she fell forward onto the ground with the force of the push only to be roughly pulled up again and pushed towards another blinding light. She could hear her mother speaking but she couldn't hear what she was saying. Then, she heard a sharp, crisp sound echo out in the night and a brief gasp from what sounded like her mother. Ria couldn't see a thing, but she recognised that sound. Her eyes hurt. Would they die now as her mother had said?

She felt her arms being pulled back as someone tied them behind her, then she was grabbed by the arm and pushed forward again, past the figures with torches. Relieved that the blinding glare had ceased, she saw a man in uniform who was gesturing for her to get into one of three military vehicles waiting there at the bottom of the hill. Ria was finding it difficult to move with her cardboard-feeling legs, and bound arms, but she managed to get into the back of the vehicle slowly. She half lay there until she mustered enough energy to push herself up into a seated position using her elbows. She was shaking inside, that internal trembling again.

She searched for her mother and Hana. She thought she could make out her mother's head in the back of the vehicle in front of her. There was no sign of Hana. Ria's mind went blank again. She felt exhausted and now perhaps beyond fear. Now what? What were they going to do to them? Surely her mother had exaggerated. They would just ask them some questions and then take them home. Home? The smoke, she remembered it now. There was no home. They could find somewhere.

She heard more shouting, and then her vehicle pulled up behind the others. It was pitch black apart from the shadowy images cast by the headlights of the vehicle up ahead of her lighting up the empty sides of the dusty track. Two men got into the back with her, one on each side, one of them pushing her over roughly to make room for him.

Ria sat there squeezed between two heavy men. She felt their bodies pushed up against her, their thick legs pressing against hers. She could smell their sweat and the smell of their unwashed clothes. She could also smell the goat shit that was on her shoes. She kept her eyes looking forward, fixed on the vehicle in front, where she thought her mother must surely be. She tried to breathe but there was no air to breathe. She pressed her palms against her jeans. Calm down.

No-one said anything.

5

After a while, Ria could made out bright lights in the distance. They weren't like any kind of lights she'd seen before. The lights weren't like the lights of the town she had seen from further away. These lights were so bright they blazed a beam of light into the desert of darkness. She sat up straighter now, more alert. She sensed danger. The men seemed to tense too.

As they drew nearer, she saw that the bright lights were mounted on very high, grey walls that had coiled wire all around them. It was then that she understood where they were being taken. She could not bring herself to accept it. She felt a sudden need to urinate. She tried to think when she had last gone to the toilet. She couldn't remember. Everything was suspended in some sort of timeless existence. This day felt eternal. All normal time references of no use. She knew that the incident at the campus had happened hours ago, but it felt like weeks had passed.

The vehicles stopped outside a heavy, metal gate. Ria heard men shouting and watched as the heavy-looking gate was pulled open and the convoy of military vehicles slowly entered a large, flood-lit compound.

The two men sitting next to her jumped out of the vehicle before it had even stopped.

"Get out," one of them shouted at her.

She tried to but only managed it with some rough pulling from one of the men. She was dazed by the contrast between the dark hills and tracks and these dazzling

40

lights. As she half closed her eyes, she sought out her mother and her sister. Hana was standing over near their mother who had blood trickling down her chin from her lip. Her mother looked back at Ria. When their eyes met, her mother nodded in the direction of Hana. What was that supposed to mean? Ria did not understand and looked at her mother in confusion.

Her mother turned away, her attention now fully on the soldiers at her side. The soldiers stood stiff, unmoving, heads fixed and forward. Ria thought they looked like they were waiting for something, or someone.
She was right. A door squeaked loudly on its hinges and Ria looked across to the other side of the yard. Two uniformed men were striding towards them. The taller of the two went up to her mother and said something that Ria couldn't hear, her mother muttered something back and then to Ria's shock, the man suddenly slapped her mother hard across the face. Hana began to cry.
Ria's fists clenched tight as she tried to deal with the same surge of deep, contained anger she had felt after the campus.

"Where is he?" The man asked, louder enough now for Ria to hear. His voice sounded strangely quiet after the sudden aggression before.

"Where is who?" Ria's mother replied.

"You know who. Your son Jamil. We know that he was with Alana Bigrat at the campus, where are they now?"

"How should I know? These kids. They do what they want these days. I haven't seen him since last night."

His response this time was a fist to her mother's stomach. Her mother doubled over, but stood back up straight in an instant, glaring at the soldier.

"He is your son. Where is he? If it is just about being kids, why were you running away?" The man said calmly and hit her across the face again. Ria wanted to do something, anything. She could hear Hana crying in the background, she wished she'd stop.

"I told you, I don't know", her mother stood tall and stared at the man as blood ran down her chin from her split lip and nose.

Hana's crying got louder, almost hysterical, making things worse. How could they think?

"Hana, stop, it will be okay," Ria said, knowing that if she did not stop, the next person to receive a blow would be her crying sister.

"Who said you could speak?" a soldier said to her. He lashed out and slapped Ria across the face. It hurt, a lot, but better it was her than Hana. To Ria's relief, Hana stopped crying as soon as she saw the soldier hit Ria. Her mother needed to concentrate and so did she.

Ria finally understood what this was all about. It was not about them. It was just as her mother had said. It was all about Jamil and Alana. But all this for a simple protest? Ria didn't understand. It was hardly a revolution!

The soldier who had hit her mother turned to one of the soldiers who had been in the vehicle next to Ria.

"Get me their phones." he snapped.

The soldier collected the three phones and handed them to him.

"Which one is yours?" he asked Ria's mother.

Her mother pointed to her phone.

"Turn it on and call your son. Tell him what is happening now. Tell him that we have you all here. Tell him to call you back. We will be waiting for his call." The taller man said.

Ria saw her mother's hand trembling slightly as she tried to enter the passcode. It didn't work the first time. She tried again, but again the same thing happened. Was she doing this deliberately Ria wondered? It did not seem good to anger the man who had already hit her more than once!

"Give it to me." The man snapped. "What's the code?" the man snatched the phone from her mother's hands, entered the code her mother gave him. He was silent for a while as he scrolled through the phone's messages.

Once he had finished his scrolling, he held the phone out towards her mother. The phone was ringing. The dial tone was on speaker mode and sounded very loud in the silence. Then, jarringly, they all listened to Jamil's tinny, chirpy voicemail-recorded message. It was his 'protest' voicemail. Ria's heart sank. Such a stupid message Ria thought given the situation now. She had thought the message cool before.

The man scoffed at Jamil's voicemail message.

"Leave him the message," the man said. "Tell him what I told you."

Before her mother could refuse, the man thrust the phone up in front of her mother's mouth.

43

"Do it!" he commanded.

"Jamil. The military has taken us to a base. Call back, it's urgent. They want to speak to you. Please, my son, call." Her mother said, voice strong.

The man smiled, put the phone in his pocket and handed the other two phones back to the soldier.

"Take them inside. Keep them all in separate cells!" He commanded and walked off, the other soldier following him back to where they had come from.

A soldier grabbed Ria's arm and push-marched her roughly towards the other side of the compound. Ria couldn't see her mother or Hana anymore, but she could hear them behind her. Her mother was silent, and so was Hana. Ria's body felt wooden as they pushed her along. The soldier's disgusting breath wafted across her face as he leaned and pushed.

The soldier shoved Ria roughly into a wide, stone corridor, cool in contrast to the heat outside. Dimmed lights lined the corridor walls, spaced at such long intervals that they gave the corridor a ghostly atmosphere. The soldier stopped, opened a heavy metal door with a large key and pushed Ria inside. The door slammed shut and Ria heard them lock the door and then the sound of the soldier's steps moving away and then nothing except the same sounds repeated, she assumed, for her sister and her mother. The place Ria was in complete darkness, so dark she could not see a thing. She had never experienced such absence of light where her sight could not function. It panicked her. She could smell the damp air that hung there and stood rooted to the spot. Was she even alone?

As she stood there, she felt the trickle of warm liquid running down the insides of her thigh. She moved her hand down to touch the inside of her thigh. She had wet herself. She hadn't even felt her bladder's urge. She felt a scream build in her throat, but if it was indeed a scream, she knew that it would have to remain unscreamed, for now, at least.

Standing still, alone in the dark, images of the dead and dying students came and went. Images too of what or who could be in here with her, hidden in the absolute darkness, filled her mind. Her mind went back to the scenes of the campus too. She saw the odd familiar face laid out, a bloody leg, all the unmoving open eyes, someone she thought she knew but could not place exactly. Blood of all shades and patterns. She felt the darkness of where she was, the darkness of the dead bodies, and the horror of it all. She saw her mother being hit over and over in her head. She touched her cheek with her hand where the soldier had hit her. What was going to happen to them in here? They were going to die.

She staggered a little, about to fall but managed to steady herself despite having no visual fixing points. She waited for her eyes to adjust to the darkness and see, but they did not. She shuffled forward slowly, arms stretched out, groping the air like a blind person. Now she knew what it must be like. She felt a fleeting compassion for the blind.

After a few shuffles forward her hands came up against a rough surface that felt like stone. Real stone, not brick. Placing her right hand on the stone wall she turned to face forward and moved slowly along the wall counting the corners. From what she could tell, the room was square and very small. Then she crisscrossed it, fumbling with her hands and feet to feel what might be there, in the middle. There was nothing.

She was the only thing in that cell, apart from those stone walls.

Ria had never been one to be afraid of the dark even when she was a child but there was something so completely terrifying about such depth of darkness and the situation, they were in that it was all just too much. She pushed her back against one of the walls and slowly lowered herself down to sit on the ground. She rested her hands on the cold stone surface feeling the uncomfortable pressure of her wet panties and jeans rub against her. She felt disgusted at herself.

She listened but could only hear distant clanking sounds and occasional footsteps. Now and again, she heard the sound of muffled voices, the occasional shout and the odd crackle and burst of the radios the soldiers used. Nothing more. She felt tempted to shout out her mother's name, Hana's too, but she did not dare.

Hana must be terrified, and her mother must be in pain and worried. Her mother knew much more about these people than she did, but Ria was rapidly understanding the reality of things.

But what good were they to the military? They were nobody important, they knew nothing. If it was Jamil and Alana they were after, why capture them? Was it to use them as bait to get him to come? She knew he would come, but he had done nothing wrong so why such a hunt? Maybe it was about Alana. Maybe she had done something bad. Maybe Jamil had done something bad with Alana. Jamil always took instructions from her, about everything. What would happen if Jamil didn't call back? Were there rats here in the cell?

Hana was terrified of rats, and though she would never admit it to Hana, so was she. She tensed even more. She could hear nothing. What was the sound that rats made? She rubbed her bare arms and brought her knees up to touch her chest and clasped them tightly. She didn't want anything running up her leg in the dark.

Ria turned all of her questions over and over in her mind, but she was too afraid to entertain any possible answers.

As she sat on the hard floor, her breathing eventually slowed down, she took stock of her body and situation. She noticed how raw her throat felt, her dry mouth. She needed water. Her eyes were sore and grainy from all the dust. She rubbed them but that only made them worse. She tried to summon saliva to her mouth, but there was none to be had. Water, all she could think about was water. The thing you want the most is always the thing you can't have. All that sweating and running, if they gave her no water, she could die of thirst quite quickly she thought. How long would that take?

She tried to change the track of her thinking and her mind led her back to this morning before she had left for the campus. She had gone out with her friends to celebrate the night before, much to Jamil's annoyance. They had gone out to eat locally and then onto a club further away. She replayed the night in her mind watching her friends laughing, teasing, flirting. They were all smiling. How innocent and stupid that whole night felt now. Jamil was right. She and her friends were silly.

Just before Ria had gone to the campus for the protest, she had met the friends she'd been out with the night before for a quick coffee. They always did after going out to autopsy the night. Most of her friends had no interest in what they called 'that boring political stuff'. Ria hadn't been that interested either, not at first, but she looked up to Jamil and wanted him to approve of her, so she had responded to all his pestering to watch videos and read stuff online. After a while, it no longer bored her, she had become genuinely interested, then a little more than interested. She studied what was happening in other countries like theirs and it all started to resonate with her. But now, sitting here in the dark, she realised she had not understood what was really happening. Jamil was right about her, and so was her mother.

    The first time she had gone to a campus protest with Jamil, she had felt so electrified and swept away by the atmosphere and the promise of new ideas and was that there was a real sense of momentum and the possibility of a better life. It was exciting. Gradually, she had got more and more involved, but always under Jamil's guidance. Jamil had become more and more committed to the whole thing and had made the protest movement his priority to the detriment of his studies. She admired his dedication and passion, though what he did exactly was unclear to her. He was always a bit vague when she pressed him for details, especially when he spent long periods away. He must have been with Alana.

Ria started as a door slammed nearby. She heard heavy footsteps approaching, a key turned in a lock nearby, and a door creaked opened. The footsteps sounded very near. At first, she thought it was her cell, but it wasn't. She was still alone. Not long afterwards, she heard some muffled shouts, but then she heard something that chilled her to the bone. It was Hana screaming.

6

Ria woke with a start. It took her a few seconds to remember where she was, the unchanged darkness a stark reminder. She must have dozed off. How could she have? After the way Hana had been screaming! It had broken her heart. Those had been no ordinary screams, if there was such a thing as an ordinary scream. They had been screams of real terror. She stood up carefully, and rolled her stiff neck from side to side, stretching her aching body a little at a time. She wiped off the slick film of sweat on her skin. It was so much hotter in the cell. It must be daytime. Her mouth was sticky, and her breath reeked.

She shuffled around the small space again, groping blindly to make sure she hadn't missed anything the last time. She hadn't. She pulled down her jeans, urinated near a corner, and then moved back to the opposite side of the cell. She pressed her hot forehead against the cool stone wall and just leaned there, in timeless dark space.

Loud voices and steps jolted her back to the present. People seemed to be coming nearer to her cell. Another key turned, a door opened, and she reeled as a blinding light flooded in. She shrank back against the wall, hands up against the light, seeing nothing.

It didn't take long. It was over almost before she realised it had happened. Mere seconds for him to roughly pull off her jeans, rip off her panties, and pull her forward along the ground scraping her back against the rough stone floor. Then the brief but unbearable pain as the faceless man violated her. She heard him pant and grunt, then the heavy weight moved off her, the sound of clothing, footsteps and the door slammed closed, and the key turned in the lock again. The bright light now gone. She lay there, legs open, her jeans jamming her thighs together. She was in shock and in pain. It had happened so quickly it barely seemed to have happened at all, but she could not deny what had happened. She slowly moved her trembling hand down to her vagina and felt the thick, sticky liquid that covered the insides of her thighs and pubic hair. Was it blood? She smelled it. It was not blood. She recoiled. She could not bring herself to cry. She hadn't seen anything happen. Her hand moved to search for her panties. She found them by her feet, they felt ripped, she wiped herself clean with them and then flung them across the cell as if contaminated. With great difficulty, she pulled up her jeans, leaving them unfastened at the top, lacking the strength to fasten them. What did it matter? There was a terrible stabbing pain at the entrance of her vagina, and it cut like a knife. But it was the shame and horror of what had happened that was worse than her physical pain. She turned on her side, drew her knees up to her chest and lay there in that foetal position just staring into the dark. No thoughts at all.

She remained like that for a long time and would have remained there for the rest of her life. Nothing mattered to her anymore. Nothing. She had been transformed from one person into another in mere seconds.

All her body could feel now was the imprint of that heavy, faceless body on top of hers in the darkness.

Her body tensed as she heard the same sounds again, they were coming back to do it again. Her door opened and the same light blasted in. She turned away. No, not again. No. She made herself smaller, curling into a ball and tensed.

Terrified, she sensed someone approach and then she was grabbed by the arms and pulled to her feet. She was pushed out into the corridor. Her eyes adjusted to the new shade slowly, and she saw she was with two soldiers, one on each side of her. Had it been one of them? They half-carried, half-shoved her along the corridor until they stopped outside a door. One of the men knocked and waited.

"Come in." A voice answered.

The soldiers dragged her in. She offered no resistance, there was no point. She looked to where the voice had come from. It was the soldier who had hit her mother when they had first arrived. He was sitting at a desk, a small pile of brown files stacked in front of him. The room was very brightly lit in contrast to where she had been, and the glare hurt her eyes. She kept her gaze on the floor, averted from them all. Ashamed. Embarrassed. So many feelings.

Together, the soldiers put her in a chair that was pushed up against a smooth grey wall. They tied each of her feet to something on the ground. Each arm was pulled back against the wall and attached to it. The unnatural position of her arms caused such excruciating pain in her shoulders. She winced. She looked forward and saw another man leaning against the side wall a few metres away. He was dressed differently to the seated man. He wore just a black t-shirt and khaki shorts. The soldiers that had brought her from her cell took up positions one on each side of her and stood stiff to attention.

No-one said anything at first. She could feel the soldiers in front of her staring at her. She felt the urge to look up, to check for her own safety but could not bring herself to. She knew they knew what had happened in her cell. She tried to swallow but couldn't, there was no saliva.

"Water!" She mumbled without planning to.

"You were at the protest at the campus yesterday afternoon." said the man sitting at the table.

It did not sound to Ria like a question, so she said nothing.

"We know what you have been doing all this time with the rest of those insurgents, led by your traitor brother and his girlfriend Alana Bigrat, the insurgent leader. I am sure you are aware that what you have been doing is forbidden. You knew but you did it anyway. I suppose you thought there would be no consequences, or that we didn't know. Did you think it was just an adventure? Your generation and all your whining! What would you know about the history of this great country? What have you got to protest about?"

He didn't need to raise his voice for Ria to hear his anger.

Ria instinctively tried to move her legs but could not, they were tied together very tight, and any movement of her leg caused a sharp pain in her bruised vagina.

The man in the black t-shirt stepped a little closer. Had it been him Ria wondered?

"Where did your brother go after the protest? We know you were with him and that insurgent whore Alana Bigrat." The same man asked.

Ria moved her lips to reply, but only a raspy sound came out.

"Water." She managed.

The man in the t-shirt moved closer. She was aware of him in her peripheral vision, but she kept her focus on the soldier asking the questions, he seemed to be the one in charge. She kept her eyes down. She didn't want him to see her.

She attempted once more to speak. It didn't look like she was going to get any water.

"I don't know." She said. "He left." She said, her voice sounded unlike her own. "He told me to go home." She finished. Such pain in her throat.

"And did you?" The man asked.

"Yes," Ria whispered. "Where if not home?"

The man nodded and Ria felt an intense stab of pain in the side of her head. The man in the black t-shirt had moved fast and hit her so hard that the force had caused her neck to snap over to the other side. The pain was intense.

"Where did he go?" The man asked again.

"I don't know. He just left. I haven't seen him since." she said.

The pain had cured her voice problem somewhat and she had woken up fast. She was ashamed of this new pleading, desperate voice that was coming out of her. She sounded like a child. If her mother saw her like this! But her mother didn't know what had happened to her in the cell. She quickly put that thought out of her head. Focus.

Again, she felt that same intense pain as she received another blow to her head, this time from the other side. Her neck screamed with the pain. What the hell did he want? Whatever she knew she would tell him.

"Do you know what we did to your sister, Hana, last night, Ria?" The man asked. "You must have heard her screaming, there wasn't a man here who didn't. She was in the cell right next to you. Such a young and pretty girl, and so innocent. Such a pity. She didn't even take part in any subversive activity. She respected the law. She's a good girl, a good citizen. Just unlucky to come from a bad family. What happened to her was because of what you and your brother have been doing. Let's not forget your mother or, your father either, Ria? You and your brother are following in the family's footsteps. What your mother must have gone through last night hearing her own daughter scream in that terrible way! All this pain for your sister just because of you and your brother's stupidity. Such a shame. Those not at fault always end up paying the price for the ones who are guilty. Do you think we did to Hana what we did to you? No, no. You were lucky. Your sister, however, was not."

He sounded like a father chastising an errant daughter to Ria. What the hell had they done to Hana and why? Ria frowned in worry.

The man continued. "Then, Ria, all those students at the campus. Protesting! About what? Look where they are now. All dead. They could all still be alive had they simply respected the laws of their country! Such simple rules. How stupid you young people are! All day on your phones sucking in all those Western lies and not appreciating what you have already in this great nation! You are all so immature compared to how we were when we were your age. You are always complaining about this or that, always wanting more and more shiny things from the west. But what is it that your generation is giving back to your country, Ria? Nothing! Just problems! This freedom you all chant for and demand. You don't even know what freedom means." he sneered. "Do you think they are free in the West?" He paused. "If so, you are a silly girl."

Ria felt the pain in her neck and head, a wave of nausea rose, and she turned her head to the side just in time to vomit, the soldier moved his foot out of the way just in time.

The man in the t-shirt flashed in front of her again and like lightning struck yet another blow, this time to her face with his fist. She heard the crunching sound of bone, that was no slap. Then, another, and another. He kept hitting her until she no longer felt anything, she could just hear the sound of his fists on her face and feel them, but she had stopped caring. Let him continue. She hoped he would kill her.

"That's enough for now. Give her some water." The soldier in charge said.

Disappointed, Ria felt the cool touch of something metal pushed up against her bleeding lips. Water. A thick globule of blood slipped back down her throat as she tried to gulp down some of the water, her lips clumsy and uncoordinated from the swelling. She gulped down water and blood. She didn't care about the blood, after all, it was mostly her own, as long as she had the water. She was somewhere else now, in a state of no pain.

The soldier began again "Where did your brother and Alana go, Ria? Where is he now? He has not even called in response to the message your mother left yesterday. Imagine that. He does not care about any of you. His own mother and sisters. So, you know what we did to motivate him to come? We recorded Hana's screams for him and sent them to his phone, but still, he did not come. It is almost unbelievable, isn't it Ria? But it is not surprising to us. These insurgents are cowards deep down. Saving himself is more important to him than saving his poor sister, his mother or even you. But even I am surprised that he would ignore those terrible screams of his own sister. And what kind of son leaves his mother alone in a place like this? A coward that is the kind of boy your brother is." The soldier said, his questions requiring no answer.

Ria heard every word but could not make much sense of what he was saying. Jamil? Messages. All she registered was what he had said about Hana and her mother. What had they done to them? What had they done to Hana? The screams replayed in her head. She felt the terror of all the possibilities her mind contemplated, after all, he had said they had done worse to Hana than to her. What could be worse Ria wondered.

The commanding soldier turned to the soldier in the shorts.

"Take some photos of her now looking like this and send them to my phone straight away. I will send them to her brother's phone. He might have destroyed his phone. Keep her here. No more water. Make sure she stays awake." the man said and got up and left the room.
Ria had not looked at him the whole time.
Ria felt the flash of a camera which hurt her swollen eyes as the man in the shorts took photos of her. She closed her eyes. She felt dizzy. She vomited again, this time onto her shirt. It was less effort.
The man in the shorts left the room and she remained alone slumped in the hard chair with two soldiers.

7

Ria was neither asleep nor awake. Every so often she would receive a sharp clip on her head from one of the soldiers. She felt like she was dreaming. It was a strange mix of daydreams and memories. She felt no pain, but she remembered the sounds of her beating all too well and she could still feel exactly how his fists had felt on her face. She remembered what had happened in the cell as well. More than remembered, she felt it.

However, it was the intense discomfort of her dry mouth that was bothering her the most. It just got drier and drier as every last drop of her saliva slowly dripped down from the side of her mouth onto the floor. Her head was tilted to one side, and her neck was in too much pain to hold it up straight. Her lips must be far too swollen to trap her precious saliva before it was lost to the floor. The soldiers floated in and out of her line of vision, stiff and still, moving now and again like robots to deliver quick whacks to the side of her head to keep her awake. She longed for unconsciousness but to her dismay, her daydreams became less nebulous, and her memory clearer.

She remembered it now clearly. That conversation with Jamil the night before the campus protest. In her mind's eye Ria saw the beautiful red hue form over the olive trees as the sun began its descent. She tried to remember what he had said. About the need to fight, about their father, about her innocence and how naïve she was. How he'd talked of the danger. That soon there would be a revolution. He was angry and passionate, she remembered that, and she remembered his disappointment in her.

She remembered every word he had said as she sat there. She wished she had listened to him more carefully and had gone to speak with Alana as he had urged her to do instead of going out with her friends. But that would have changed nothing that had happened yesterday.

It was just that now she understood what he had meant by it all. Sitting there in that chair, raped and badly beaten, she understood it all perfectly well. He had been right about everything but so had their mother. She was just a silly girl, not listening, not understanding.

She felt the soldier's hand whack her again but this time she looked up, instantly regretting the movement as she felt the sharp jolt of pain in her neck. Pain, she realised did not dull the senses, but remembering Jamil's words had caused a shift in her. His words had been prophetic in a way, and there had been advice in them, advice she had not heeded. But she would heed it now. Fight he had said. She was just giving up, feeling sorry for herself. Enough of that! Her eyes swept the room, and she studied the layout for the first time. It was brightly lit, small and bare. All she could see was a bucket, and a couple of chairs and the table. She noticed the glimmer of light from the corridor that filtered through the bottom of the door.

How long had it been since they had brought her here? She had no idea, hours, minutes? Hours she decided. One night had passed since the campus incident, she was sure of that so this must be the next day.

Jamil must have been doing a lot more than protesting she now realised. She had been so naïve! Maybe they believed that she was mixed up in whatever Jamil and Alana were doing. Had he joined an armed group, was that what all this was about? Had he been serious about a revolution? What was her brother involved in? Why hadn't he told her? Jamil and her mother had seemed to know about what went on in places like these. She had heard talk, of course, all the rumours, but she had never really thought much about them. She had never asked either. Her heart began to pound faster and faster as her thoughts raced, and she realised that it didn't even matter whether she had done anything wrong or not. Hana's screams proved that innocence did not matter at all. Ria had been involved in work that was forbidden so she would pay for that like the man had said. She had paid already, had she not? She had not even thought of the protest work as forbidden and had certainly never thought of it as dangerous. Now it was too late. It did not even matter what the soldiers believed. The state just wanted people like Jamil and Alana so they could make examples of them and create so much terror that all the protests and resistance would stop. So why hadn't they killed Jamil and Alana, and even her at the campus? Surely it was no coincidence that all three of them had survived. It made no sense.

She glanced at the soldiers' feet. They were wearing dusty, sand-coloured boots. She needed a plan and fast, she needed something to say when that man came back, she could not face another beating, but she knew that another beating or worse was what she would get. She was certain of that. She tried to push down her fear. What was more important now was what she could say to protect her mother and Hana? They weren't involved in anything. Maybe the military had been watching Jamil and Ria for a while. If so, they would know who had done what! She couldn't answer their questions about where Jamil or Alana were or what they were involved in. She didn't know anything, but her instinct told her they wouldn't care. They were just using them as bait to get Jamil, and once they got Jamil, they would make him tell them about Alana. But they weren't just bait, Ria felt it was about punishment too. Her mother was right when she said all this was their fault. So now it was up to her to do something. Jamil was not here, but Ria was.

Ria tried but she couldn't stop thinking about what they might have done to Hana. She couldn't rid her mind of those terrible screams. Had they done the same thing to Hana as they had done to her in her cell? The man had said they hadn't, but why should she believe anything he said. He had said they had done worse. What could be worse? What about her mother? Surely, they would show more respect to her mother, she was older. But why would they? They were clearly not respectful in any way. Her mother was the wife of a man considered an enemy of the state, someone they had murdered. A so-called 'dissident' just like his son and daughter. Ria regretted never really asking her mother questions about her father. She barely remembered him; he was just a face in a photo. She had only been four and Hana two when he was killed. She had felt the emptiness of not having a father like her friends more than any pain of grief or loss. Her mother must have supported her father and agreed with his views. Could that be true? Ria now searched her mind for clues about her mother, she went back over old conversations and stories her mother had told, comments she'd made, searching for any indication of what her mother might have said about the regime. Nothing sprang to mind, except... that phone call her mother had made before they had left their home to run for the border. Who had she been talking to?

Unfortunately, feeling was returning to her body and the pain was distracting her from her thoughts. Her head emitted stabs of intense pain at increasingly shorter intervals. The pain in her shoulder sockets and arms, still pulled back against the wall, was becoming unbearable. Her lower legs felt trembly and ached, and her toes had started to cramp painfully downward.

She felt the soldiers stiffen at her side at the sound of quick steps and loud voices. The door swung open, and three people strode into the room.
Ria recognised the man who had asked her the questions before. He was with another soldier she had not seen yet. But Ria's gaze swept swiftly over these two men to lock on to the tall blond woman in uniform who was staring right at her, a slight smile on her lips.

8

The woman's eyes moved away from Ria when one of the men spoke to her. The uniform the woman was wearing was not a uniform that Ria had ever seen in her country, and it was very different to the ones the other soldiers were wearing. The woman looked foreign. She was foreign. She was white, had short blond hair and very blue eyes. Maybe she would help them! Hope surged through Ria at this prospect. The other man who had come in was in the same uniform as the woman, he was dark and could be taken as a local, but Ria saw there was something foreign about him.

The men and the woman were speaking too low for Ria to hear anything they were saying, but it looked like the foreign man was interpreting between the man who had questioned her before and the blond woman.
After a while, they suddenly stopped talking and they all turned to face Ria. She felt the soldiers at her side stiffen to attention. The small room seemed overcrowded now. The blond woman took a couple of quick steps forward and stood right in front of Ria, towering over her. She was close enough to touch. Ria looked up at her, hope in her eyes.

"Do you speak any English?" The woman asked Ria.
Ria was so caught off guard by this question that no words surfaced. As she looked up at the woman standing over her, Ria caught a glimpse of something in the woman's expression that made her body feel uncomfortable and

tense. Ria lowered her gaze back. The soldier who had been interpreting moved up beside the woman.

"They say she speaks English. They checked her file." He said in English.

The woman nodded curtly.

"Ria. Am I pronouncing your name correctly? I hope so. Details matter." The woman smiled.

Ria said nothing.

"It seems Ria here doesn't want to speak!" the woman's smile was more of a sneer now as she turned to look at the soldier beside her.

"Ria, do you know what your brother is? Do you understand why you are here? Perhaps you think it is about those silly student protests?" the woman laughed.

Not a real laugh. It sounded hollow and full of contempt. Ria's chest tightened and she felt winded, all hope of help gone. She had seen something sinister in the woman's expression.

"Ria, your brother is a terrorist. A terrorist! That is the worst kind of criminal because terrorists are the worst cowards. Terrorists do not fight with honour like soldiers. They don't even fight!" She said and bent down to look closer at Ria.

"What about you Ria? Are you also a terrorist? We know you were working with him, but was it just the protests or was it more than that? That is the question that concerns us now. Both are serious matters of course to your people, but to us, we do not care about your protests. We only care about terrorists - catching them and stopping them. In our minds, those who work or live with terrorists are terrorists too, by association. Did you know that?" the woman asked as if genuinely curious to hear Ria's response.

Ria was confused and her heart had skipped a beat at hearing the word 'terrorist' and her brother's name mentioned in the same sentence. Jamil was no terrorist, and she was certainly no terrorist, not by association not by any means. This foreigner had got her information wrong. What was she doing here anyway? She didn't sound American, Ria knew that accent well, she had a different accent, more European maybe. What did it matter?

Ria was keeping her eyes averted, so she didn't see it coming. The interpreter soldier smashed his boot cap into her leg, just under her knee joint. Ria cried out in pain from the force of impact from the man's boot delivered in such a sensitive place. Her body had recoiled with the force of the blow causing even more strain on her shoulder sockets and arms. Surely her shoulders had come out of their sockets! She placed all of her attention on the foreign soldier now. He was the immediate threat.

"Look at me Ria!" The woman commanded sharply. But Ria did not. The interpreter kicked her other knee, harder this time. Ria started to cry. The pain was just too much now. Crying was not how she wanted to react, but it was just too much.

"The pain will not stop until you do as I say. My soldier knows exactly how to deliver the most pain with the least effort. It is one of his many talents. Is it more pain that you want Ria? From what I can see from your face, you seem to have already experienced quite a lot already." The woman feigned concern.

Ria stared at her but said nothing.

"Ria, I am certain you do not want to be slowly kicked to death. Believe me no-one here wants that to happen either. But it would be so easy for my soldier to do that Ria, he has done it countless times and he enjoys it. But just in case the prospect of death does tempt you, it is important that you know that there are far worse things than being kicked to death. Trust me when I tell you that. Now, look at me." The woman had spoken the words so very softly, so terrifyingly soft.

Ria looked up at the woman, the pain in both of her knees so intense now that she felt her stomach lurch with nausea again.

"Where is your terrorist brother Jamil hiding Ria? He must have friends who would help him to hide. All those rats have networks, special houses, and collaborators. It doesn't matter what the country, it always works the same way. Who do you think would help him to hide? Not everyone would. It's a risk nowadays. I mean knowing what your government does to people who do that sort of thing I am sure the list of people he can turn to is very short. I am going to assume you know some of the people on that list Ria. I am going to stay here with you until you give me their names. We will find your brother one way or another. You can count on that. No one stays hidden from me. But if you give me the names now, fewer people will end up like you." The woman smiled.

Up until now, Ria had barely managed to keep her fear in check but now it took over. She felt the trembling start deep within, and then spread through her whole body. She managed to remain silent. A tiny victory. She knew there was nothing she could say or do to improve her situation.

"Let me make everything crystal clear for you, Ria. Your brother has done some terrible things. Things that affect me and my men. If you don't help us, that will be not only be very bad for you but also for your sweet little sister, who is, they tell me, actually innocent unlike you or your mother. Would you see your sister hurt even more just to save your terrorist brother who has murdered innocent people?"

Ria flinched. Her mother? What did she mean about her mother? What had Jamil done? He would not kill anyone. Ria was sure of that.

"What people?" Ria mumbled, her swollen lips making it hard to speak.

"She speaks!" the woman threw her hands up dramatically. "So, you are going to help us, Ria then. Excellent!" the woman clapped and smiled but her eyes remained stone cold.

"You're lying. Jamil would never hurt anyone. I know him. He would not." Ria said.

Ria's words were barely comprehensible with her swollen lips, but she spoke slowly enough to be understood.

The woman laughed out loud. She seemed genuinely amused, which confused Ria even more. The man who had administered the kicks started to laugh as well but a withering glare from the woman quickly silenced him.

"Listen to me carefully Ria. A few weeks ago, before this campus nonsense, and before they found you in those hills, your brother and his terrorist friends attacked a small military base in a town about forty kilometres from here. Your brother's group killed five of your soldiers. But that's not all. There were other people there who were not military. There was a cleaner and a cook who worked in the kitchen. They were both killed. That is what terrorists do Ria, they kill and maim innocent people and attack soldiers and police who are simply carrying out their duty. That poor cleaner Ria, just imagine! A poor woman working hard to make some money to feed her children but then brutally murdered by her one of her own. I mean. It's shocking when you think about it." the woman paused, eyes drilling into Ria.

"So, Ria tell me, what do you think of your terrorist brother now? I would bet that none of what I just told you comes as a surprise to you. I have no doubt that you already know what he is. How could you not? All that time spent together, planning, organising, you helped him with everything. It's all there in the files." She smiled gesturing to the papers on the table.

Ria could not grasp what the woman was saying. Jamil would never. Would he? Files? What files? Files about them? Were they being watched? No, surely not. They were not doing anything worth watching. Well, she hadn't been at least. About Jamil she was now less sure.

Ria's head was spinning. She could not think so she decided that the best course of action was to not react. To just sit there and say nothing until she had time to think. She pursed her swollen lips as best she could and braced for the inevitable attack from the man, but none came. She looked warily at him out of the corner of her eye, frightened. She could feel the woman's cold stare. She shuddered.

"Ria, this is not going to end well for you and your family." Her tone sounded bored to Ria now. "I promise you that. You can deny that your brother is a terrorist all you want, to me, even to yourself. It makes no difference to me because we already know the facts. Do you know why I am here today, Ria? You can see that I am not a soldier from your country? I don't really care about the cleaner." The woman said pleasantly.

Ria looked up at the woman, unable to resist knowing the answer and shook her head.

"Do you know who else got murdered during your brother's attack on the military base I just told you about? One of *my* men. He was a good man and a great soldier. He had three little children under the age of ten back home. He came here to help your shitty little country be better. He had been in my unit for five years. Five years Ria. That is a long time to serve together! Not that you would know anything about that. Now, he is dead because of *your* brother. He was at the base training your country's soldiers. Just helping when he was gunned down in cold blood by your brother's men." The woman said, her eyes trying to burrow their way into Ria's mind.

Ria could sense her anger, but the woman hid it well.

Ria's heart began to pound again, faster now. This was bad. If this is what this woman believed, then there was no hope for her, Hana or her mother. No hope for any of them. She knew that was true as soon as the words were out of the woman's mouth. This was all about one of her soldiers. She tried to get some more control over her lips and mumbled slowly and deliberately back to the woman. She had nothing to lose now, because all was lost.

"Even if what you say is true, and I am sure it is not, it is not my mother, my sister, or even me who has done what you accuse my brother of. We are innocent. All of us! My mother is innocent. My sister is innocent, and *I* am innocent. I am no terrorist. I don't even know what a terrorist is. No-one I know is a terrorist. You *know* that so why are we here? What do you want from us? I don't understand. We have no information to give you about where Jamil is."

Ria's tone had changed, no longer quiet and trembling, but growing more defiant with each word.

She paused. "If I had any information to give, I would have given it by now. My brother is not worth protecting more than my mother and sister!"

Again, the woman laughed contemptuously. She seemed riled by Ria's response.

"You don't understand?" She said. "Did I not just explain it to you? The situation could not be clearer. This is not about innocence. Someone must *pay* for what your brother did. Someone must pay for murdering *my* soldier. I don't care about your family. My unit will find Jamil sooner or later. It is inevitable. We are very good at hunting terrorists. It's our job. Also, Ria, remember, Jamil knows we have you. Everyone in your village will know too no doubt. Your house was burned down. Yet, still, a day later, he has does nothing to help you."

She paused and raised her eyes in pretend shock, then continued.

"He has not given himself up even though the Commander here has taken the trouble to send messages to his phone. He told him if he came to us, we would free you, but still, he has not come. You see Ria, all terrorists are cowards, you are just collateral damage to him. Your brother will do anything to save himself for his cause. The only thing terrorists care about is their cause. Fanatics! He doesn't care about you, or Hana, or your mother. I have known more terrorists than you Ria. They tell themselves that their cause justifies their means, justifies all the violence. Don't forget Ria that your brother will murder more innocent people and honourable serving soldiers if I don't stop him. Your country's intelligence service, pathetic as it is, has managed to watch him for the last few months, but still, they have allowed him to walk around a free man, allowed him to act. But I am not as stupid as that so do not be a naïve, Ria." The woman said.

Ria saw her arrogance in full show.

"My brother is not a terrorist! That is not true! You're lying!", Ria screamed at her, surprised at the venom in her voice.

The woman turned to the foreign man at her side

"Tell them to take her to the bigger room. When she's there, let me know. When I get there tell them to bring in the mother and sister." The woman said to the foreign soldier who nodded and then saluted.

She nodded back to him and turned to look at Ria again and then left the room with the commanding soldier who had questioned her before the woman. The foreign soldier translated the woman's instructions for the two soldiers they began to untie Ria.

The foreign soldier watched on, and Ria saw the look in his eyes, and it chilled her to the bone.

The soldiers dragged Ria down the corridor and into a very different room. The room was much bigger, and colder, but it was still brightly lit. Unlike the other room, this one was clearly not used as an office. Ria took in with growing horror all of the rings on the walls to attach people to. The line of chairs pushed under each set of rings. Ria saw buckets strewn everywhere. But nothing prepared her for the stench. It was like nothing she had ever smelt before, a strange mix of stale urine, excrement and antiseptics. There was a large table in the centre and a couple of chairs next to it.

The soldiers pushed her down on one of the chairs and tied her up the same way as before. Then, the foreign soldier told them to go and get Hana and Ria's mother. He left but quickly returned, the woman just behind him. She was still smiling that sinister smile as she strode in. She walked over to the table and leaned against it facing Ria. The woman crossed her arms and fixed Ria with that cold stare again, the smirk still playing on her lips. She looked as if she was enjoying herself and that was the most terrifying thing for Ria. Ria averted her eyes again and kept them locked onto the grey flagstones of the floor noting her hairs stand on end and the chill that ran along the back of her neck.

9

The chance of seeing Hana and her mother again filled Ria with joy and terror in equal measure. Ria had understood enough by now to know that there was no hope of getting out of this situation, especially since the woman had arrived on the scene. But maybe there was hope for her sister. Even the woman had admitted that Hana was innocent. For some strange reason, not her mother. Why? Her mother had done nothing but warn them of the danger of protesting.

    Ria's mind raced for a solution, some kind of explanation. It was obviously impossible that Jamil was involved in this attack the woman was talking about. No way. The woman was lying to frighten her, to turn her against Jamil and to force her to give her information about her brother and his friends. That is how the state got information she had heard, with lies and mind games. Ria knew enough about her own country's state apparatus to know something about this. She had heard things whispered. Everyone had. Ria knew her brother well and she knew he was incapable of hurting innocent people. His struggle was against all the violence the state waged against innocent people. It was true that he had been talking about fighting and revolution, but Ria had understood that he had been talking about the future. But what if it had been his way of telling Ria that he was already involved? No! This woman was making all this up. But what if it wasn't true but she believed it was? What if the military had deliberately given her incorrect information just so she would be motivated to get Jamil and Alana?

Either way for Ria it changed nothing. Whatever the woman planned to do with her, she would do regardless. If Jamil wasn't even responding to the military's messages and their threat tactics by sending the recordings of Hana screaming and photos of Ria beaten, then Ria was as good as dead. But surely Jamil wouldn't let that happen. He would give himself up, especially if he had heard Hana's screams. That's what Ria would do if she was in Jamil's situation, so where the hell was he? Maybe they already had him, and this was all about the woman's need for revenge.

It hadn't been the beating that made Ria lose all hope, it hadn't even been that terrible rape in the dark cell the night before. It was what she had seen in the woman's eyes. Whatever it was, it was indefinably disturbing, and Ria had felt its presence in a way she didn't understand. It had to be her instinct warning her about this woman. She could not explain how she knew but she knew beyond any doubt that this woman was the most dangerous person in this place.

Ria knew her death was more a question of how and when. Was she afraid of dying? She couldn't tell. She didn't feel much outside of her physical pain and her all-consuming terror of the woman. But in her terror, there was too a certain detachment. She felt the presence of terror and a disconnection from it at the same time.

She shouldn't be surprised really at what was happening. Jamil had warned her, and it wasn't as if she was completely oblivious to how her country functioned. Growing up Ria and everyone around her had just learned from each other how things worked. No explicit explanations were ever given. You just saw what your elders did and followed the instructions you were given at home. The rules. The spoken ones and the unspoken ones too. No-one she knew had ever spoken outright about anything until the protests had started, but everyone knew something. Ria saw now just how subtle it all was. Everyone's behaviour controlled by the implicit, unspoken threat wielded by a brutal, unforgiving state apparatus.

Violence had always been there, but she had never witnessed any and now she knew why. It happened out of sight in these places, behind closed doors. The massacre at the campus yesterday an anomaly or perhaps a new pattern of state violence. Up until yesterday violence was something spoken of only in hushed whispers usually when someone disappeared never to be seen again. The disappearance would not be talked of just acknowledged by meaningful looks and nods. Ria had not noticed the violent calm that had reigned over them for years, silently keeping them all in check. She had chosen not to see it. But her brother had seen it all and so had her mother.

Ria understood now what Jamil had meant about their father, but what about their mother? Since Ria had got back from the campus, her mother had been acting like someone else. There was her sudden decision to run for the border as if she already knew what was going to happen if they stayed. But it was not just that, it was the way she had moved out there in the hills, and how she had behaved once captured, her defiance to the soldier when they had arrived and the things she knew how to do. Ria knew now that Jamil had been wrong about their mother. He had always criticised her as being too passive - a sheep. Ria had seen no trace of a compliant sheep in her mother since yesterday. Instead, what she had seen was a courageous woman who knew exactly how to handle herself in dangerous situations. Someone who knew exactly what to do and say. Her mother been hit hard and had barely flinched! Ria was sad that Jamil would never know this side of his mother. He would be proud, Ria thought. Ria was proud of her mother and wished she had spent time getting to know her better, the real version.

She wished she could take back all her stupid arguments with her mother. Ria had seen her mother as a controlling, annoying, preaching adult whose function was to cook, clean and make money for her children. Ria had never reflected on how difficult all that must have been for her mother with no husband. If anyone could get Hana out of here alive it was her mother.

The clutter of steps and soft muffled sounds snapped Ria out of her thoughts. They were getting nearer and nearer. The door was pushed open. The woman turned away from Ria to look at the people coming into the room.

Ria stared down at the ground, suddenly ashamed. Her mother was going to see her like this! Looking like an animal. Dirty, beaten, rank, torn open. Ria could even smell her own shit. What would her mother think? Also, Ria was terrified to look at them, frightened of seeing what harm had been inflicted on them, knowing it would hurt her too much to see it. Hana's screams had not been as bloodcurdling as they had been for something small, she knew that, and the man had confirmed it. She wanted to know what had happened to her but was terrified of knowing it. Once you know things, you cannot unknow them, unsee them. If it was bad, and Ria suspected it was, she knew she could not handle it, not in her current state, not in any state.

There was a lot of commotion now, much scraping of chairs, a lot of people moving around, talking, ordering, but then gradually things settled, and it was the woman who spoke.

"So, you must be Alina, and you must be Hana." Ria heard the woman say in English.
Her mother didn't speak English, but Hana did, and very well too, but Hana did not reply. Ria still had not looked up at them. She could hear the woman pacing back and forth as the man translated, pressing them for a response. Ria didn't hear her mother say anything either.

"Bring them over here, closer to Ria. Ria, why are you looking down at the floor, do you not want to see your family?" The woman asked slyly.

79

Ria kept her head down, but then she heard the clank of chains, shuffled steps, and soft whimpering and finally she looked up, dread filling her but unable to resist. Her heart lurched as she took in the sight before her. Hana's face was turned downwards, facing the ground, like Ria's had been, so Ria couldn't see it properly. Yet, it was obvious there was something wrong with Hana's face.

Hana no longer wore the clothes she had on when they were captured but now stood only partially covered by a dirty-looking blanket. Hana was mumbling to herself. It was too indistinct for Ria to understand what she was saying. Ria looked over at her mother quizzically, but her mother was looking straight at her, mouth drawn in a tight line, face impassive, giving nothing away. Ria was relieved to see that she was still wearing her own clothes, and Ria couldn't see signs of any beating. But the doubt remained. Ria's heart fluttered as she caught something, an emotion perhaps, flash across her mother's face as their eyes met. It certainly was not a look of compassion that Ria saw in her mother's eyes. It was not fear either. It was much worse. Ria was sure she had seen shame or had it been anger? Surely her mother didn't blame Ria for all this. But that *was* what she had said before they had got caught. Her fault. Jamil's fault. That's what her mother had said and that is what her mother's expression was now expressing to Ria.

Ria was devastated. Whatever they had done to Hana, her mother blamed Ria. So now, so did she.

"Alina, Ria here refuses to tell us where your son Jamil and his terrorist friends might be hiding. We know

Hana was not involved in your son's terrorist activity. She is just a child. But your other daughter, Ria, now that is a different thing, isn't it? And you Alina? Well, you are no angel now, are you? You're not a terrorist like your son either but what an interesting life you have led! But that is more a matter for your own state to deal with, not me. I have ample evidence that your son Jamil is a very active terrorist and your daughter a terrorist collaborator. You must be so proud! Do you know that your son has already murdered dozens of innocent people, including one of *my* men?"

The foreign soldier stumbled over his own words in his haste to translate, and Ria watched her mother's face as he translated what the woman had said. Not an eyebrow did her mother raise. This seemed to irritate the woman.

"You know Alina, we came to your country to train your soldiers to protect you against these terrorists because they don't know how. Look how your people show their gratitude to us, biting the hands that feed them! Your son knows that you are all in here. We sent him messages last night and today, including, well, some photos of what has happened here..." she nodded towards Hana and then to Ria. "But, despite all that, still no Jamil. Will he come, Alina? Or will he sacrifice you all to save himself?" The woman said sounding as she genuinely wanted an answer.

The man translated for Ria's mother again.

Alina, Ria's mother, faced the woman squarely. She squared her shoulders back and held her head even higher. She looked tired but strong. She took an audible breath.

"Who do you think you are to call my son and daughter terrorists? You are not even a real soldier, where is your country's flag? You are just a foreigner in a uniform that you purchased yourself, someone who murders for money. It does not matter to you who you murder if the price is high enough. You are not here to help us. We know that" Her mother spoke scornfully. "We know why you are really here. We may be a lot of things, but we are not stupid. My son is no terrorist and never will be. My daughter is no terrorist, she wouldn't even know how to become one. I know that for a fact. It is of no matter to me what our little state spies might tell you. They will tell you what you want to hear if it serves their interests."

Ria flinched at what her mother said about her but was proud of her mother's courage. Her mother was not frightened of this woman, not like Ria.

As he finished translating what Ria's mother had said back to the woman, the woman nodded and the same foreign soldier who had beaten Ria, smashed his fist into her mother's stomach. Even Ria could see that he had not held back. Her mother gasped and doubled over at once but just like before she immediately stood back up straight, expressionless, as if nothing had happened. Ria twisted her wrists against her restraints. She glanced at Hana who was standing near but who continued to stare at the ground mumbling. What the hell had they done to her?

"Alina, If I say your son is a terrorist, your son is a terrorist. If I say Ria is a terrorist, she is a terrorist. Do you understand?'" The man translated back the woman's words to Alina.

Alina spat on the floor right in front of the woman narrowly missing the woman's boot.

A tense silence ensued.

Ria braced herself in her chair, shocked at the audacity of her mother's reaction, but proud too. Holding her breath she waited for the woman's reaction.

The woman strode over to Hana and grabbed her roughly under the chin to pull up her face as if to show it to Ria and her mother.

Ria felt sick. Hana's left eye was completely closed, and her lip was split open so badly that Ria could see that she was missing some teeth. Her face was so badly beaten that she was barely recognisable as her sister. Ria could not avert her gaze from the horror. Did *she* look like that as well?

The woman grabbed one of Hana's arms and pulled it upwards towards Ria, and then she grabbed Hana's hand and held it out in front of Ria's face.

Ria had no time. She was not prepared for what she saw and vomited.

Two of Hana's fingers were missing. There were only blackened stubs where Hana's fingers used to be. Ria heard her own screams as Hana rambled on incoherently, oblivious.

10

Ria recoiled instinctively, repulsed at the mutilated hand still thrust out there in front of her. Not just any hand. Hana's hand, her sister's hand. Nausea and horror, not compassion, was all she could feel.

Ria looked down at the vomit stains on her jeans and felt her revulsion ebb, and rage replace it. This was her fault. This was Jamil's fault. Hana, what she must have gone through! The screams, now she understood but still the horror was unimaginable.

The woman as if reading her mind said. "You see, Ria, this is your brother's fault, yours too, and even your mother's. Did you think your mother was just a simple woman Ria? You really are very naïve. Oh, to be so naïve again! But now you have entered the world of adults Ria. We have only taken two fingers, for now. A small price all things considered. But I don't think that is all we will take from her." The woman smiled.

Ria could not think. What the hell was wrong with her? She heard every word the woman said, she felt her rage, her disgust, but she could not summon up even one ounce of defiance. Why could she not defy this woman like her mother? Was it fear? If so, she was the worst kind of coward if she said nothing about this horrible thing they had done to Hana. She looked at the woman and then she studied Hana. Hana was not really there. It was as if she had gone to hide somewhere in her own mind. She was still mumbling to herself incoherently and had begun to sway back and forth, her good eye fixed on some unseen point. The woman released Hana's hand and wiping her own hand on her uniform with a look of disgust as Hana's arm flopped doll-like to her side.

She had to do something, say something. Why was her mother not saying anything? Had she not seen Hana's hand? She must have.

Ria stared at the woman again and said. "Let Hana and my mother go! You can do whatever you want to me. Hana did not deserve this, this terrible thing you have done to her. You used her as bait for my brother. You know she does not know anything. You have done that to her just to get a reaction from Jamil. What kind of a monster are you?" Ria said looking at the woman in disgust.

"I don't know where Jamil is. I told you already. I was not participating in his activities. I just made the flyers and helped organise the protests at my university. NOTHING MORE!" Ria shouted now feeling close to losing herself in her rage. "My brother Jamil was away most of the time. I don't know where. Who knows! He is a grown man! He certainly gives no explanations to me, and I ask for none. He's older than me. I don't know about anything he did, he rarely spoke to me. We do not ask these things of adult men and we only met Alana once! The night before the military massacred all those students protesting peacefully at the campus! All those innocent students, just slaughtered like they were nothing! Why are you doing this? You're not even from here! Are you so afraid of us that you have to do these sick things?" Ria screamed the last part, trying to scream away the horrors from her mind, she felt unhinged now. It was all too much, all the bodies at the campus, what they'd done to Hana, to her, to her mother... what more?

But the woman seemed to relish seeing her so angry, so Ria stopped screaming. She took a deep breath and changed tack.

"Look, please! I don't know anything. I swear. If I did, I would tell you. Let my mother and sister go, please. You can keep me. Cut off all *my* fingers, do whatever terrible things you want to me. Jamil will come only if you let them go. I know him well. If he finds out you have harmed any of us, he will not come. I promise you that. You do not know my brother. You have played the wrong game by sending those photos and those recordings. He will assume we are already dead. You have already made it known that you have us, and you have hurt us, he will know, he is not stupid. Why would he come? Would you? He knows you'll kill us all anyway. Let them go, offer them to Jamil in exchange for him and you have me, if you don't you will NEVER find him." Ria said.

"Ria!" her mother snapped sharply as she heard the translation.

It sounded like a warning to Ria. She looked at her mother in surprise. Irritated.

The woman smiled.

"How could you do that to a young girl? You animal!" Ria said.

Ria had begun coldly, but rage again took a firm hold and she was soon screaming so loudly at the woman that she urinated with the sheer physical force of her rage. She felt it abstractly, but she didn't care, she was getting used to it, and what did it matter anyway? It was the way the woman smiled that incensed her.

For her screaming, she received another crushing blow to the side of her head. Her ears rang with the pain. It had been a much harder blow this time. Her head lolled to one side. She closed her eyes. Give up, give in.

"Ria!" her mother said again, louder this time.

Ria heard her but did not want to open her eyes ever again. But her mother was her mother and her tone commanded. Somehow, she found the will to open her eyes. She straightened her head wincing with the sharp pain and turned carefully to look at her mother. Her mother was shaking her head. What was that supposed to mean? She closed her eyes again.

She heard her mother's voice

"Pay no attention to my daughter. She is young and stupid and doesn't understand the way of things. Please, I beg you, let Hana go. She is so young. She is good. You have damaged her enough, look at her! That is not a thing someone normal does to someone so young. It says much about what you are. You are a monster as my daughter correctly says. But you don't scare me, we are used to monsters here." her mother paused to let the translator catch up.

Her mother continued. "You know that Hana is of no use to you. If my son was going to come, he would have by now. You have enough with me and Ria, we will be your sacrificial lambs. You can take out your revenge for your one little mercenary boy on us. You do not need all three of us. If you let Hana go, Jamil will find her, see her and she will tell him what you have done. Then, as my daughter said, he will come. I know my son. He is neither a terrorist nor a coward. But he knows how things work in this country. I taught him that though he thinks I am too weak. You are in a different country now, a country you do not understand. It is dangerous to come to a country without understanding how things work. Bad things will happen to you here, believe me they will. You come from your little mercenary world, from the west and you do here as you would in your other wars, but you understand nothing at all about us." Her mother paused, drew in a breath, and let it out.

Ria felt the sting of her mother's rejection again. Was she not good too? Why was it just Hana her mother was trying to save? She felt hurt. She wanted her mother to try to save her too, but instead she had offered her up in sacrifice.

Her mother continued using a similar, icy tone as the woman. "You think you are better than us, you think you can teach us better ways, but look at your ways!" her mother said pointing at Hana and Ria. "These are not better ways, just the same ways as always. You pretend to look for terrorists. You people are so afraid of terrorist you can't sleep at night yet there are so few of them. There are more of your kind of monster who just does terrible things like this for the pleasure you get from doing it. Terrorists are not the only ones who hate your kind. There are so many more of us than you imagine. At least our leaders do not pretend to be civilised or democratic. They are what they are, and they are monsters too. But you people, you are the worst hypocrites!"

Her mother stopped and laughed scornfully. "There is nothing to be learnt from you. You came to train us you say? In what? Look at you, a young woman, choosing to be a paid, pretend-soldier, playing war games in a country you know nothing about and spending your time mutilating a young, innocent girl. Why? Are you so desperately unhappy that this the best use of your life?" her mother laughed coldly, "Could you not get into the real army of your country? I am sure they looked at you and thought, no, this one is sick in the head. Then rejected you find a way to the violence as a mercenary, and you kill and torture for pleasure and money. Don't talk to us about honour. You pretend that your work is for the good, finding and killing terrorists! Pathetic!" Her mother sneered and then paused and stared at the woman.

Ria opened her eyes now. Surely her mother had gone too far. Her mother glared at the woman who still wore that cold smile that seemed fixed on her face, her mother's emotion contrasting with the lack of emotion in the woman.

Her mother continued, taking advantage of the woman's silence and the translation lag.

"Yes, only a sick person can do things like this. There is no hope for your soul. I am sure you never got one. Some people are born without one. I feel sorry for you." Her mother stopped as if to measure the woman's reaction. Ria thought she had finished but to her surprise, her mother kept on talking, and the woman had not stopped her yet.

"Do whatever sick thing you want little blond monster... Jamil will not come if you do not let one of us go. He is not stupid. In this country, we may not speak about the past, but we never forget. Never. And we never forgive. One day, when you are safe in your western home far away from the terrible things you have done to people like us, the things you call 'work'. you will see. Now, listen carefully foreign woman, because what I am going to say is important, it is a warning for you. I swear to you that one day, one of us will hunt you down in your own country. That is a fact. So, know that. Sleep on that. Because every night you sleep you will be one night closer to your last day, the day that one of us finds you and puts an end to your life." her mother said.

Her mother had said all of this with so much contempt in her voice Ria was sure she was going to receive yet another blow to her head. Maybe after all the things her mother had just said, they would do something terrible to her mother. It took time for her mother's words to be translated. Ria noticed he omitted some of the things her mother had said. He was wiser than he looked. Ria felt pride at her mother's words and understood her message in the threat. This was the side of her mother that Ria wished she had known better. She had taken their mother for granted and now it was too late.

Ria had understood her mother's message despite her hurt at her mother's rejection. They were not to submit to these people no matter what. Ria raised her head again and nodded when her mother looked over at her. Her mother smiled briefly and nodded back. She then turned to watch the woman's face as she listened to the man translate her mother's words. The man translated the last words almost exactly as her mother had said them, that threat. Ria felt sure she saw anger flash across the woman's face, it was barely perceptible, but Ria saw it in the imperceptible tightening of her mouth, the slight squint of her eyes, the sudden reddening of her pale face. Ria saw her clench her fists by her side. Ria enjoyed every millisecond of the woman's reaction. Her mother's words had affected her.

The woman stood there staring coldly at Ria's mother for a long while, perhaps lost for words, but her mother held the stare effortlessly. Ria felt a smile inside as she watched the two women confront each other. After a while, the woman broke the staring match and glanced at Hana. She frowned, then smiled and turned to Ria.

"Hana must be a virgin, Ria, surely?" the woman asked. "After all, she is only 15, so she must be."
That smirk had returned to her face. Ria tensed.

"Your mother is not. She was married, but now she is a widow, on paper anyway. Who knows what she gets up to!" the woman laughed at her own joke. A weird, strange laugh. It was as if she didn't quite know how to laugh.

"How long do you think it has been for your mother, Ria? Maybe not as long as you think. What about you? Well, we all know Ria that you are no longer a virgin..."
The woman looked meaningfully at Ria's mother, who looked sadly at Ria. Now she knew.

"If you were in my country, there would be no virgins in this room. But here... well things are different. They say that a woman must wait until marriage. Is that true? So old-fashioned and archaic don't you think? You haven't caught up to modern times yet, I suppose. Before you came here Ria, were you waiting for the right man?" the woman enquired.

Ria stared at her, shame washing over her, her anger neutralised by this new and dangerous line of questioning. She was ashamed now that her mother knew she had been raped and she felt ashamed by the way the woman was talking about it. She could feel the soldiers at her side tense even more now as the man translated the last part of what the woman had said for Ria's mother's benefit and the soldiers' too perhaps. The other foreign soldier, the translator, looked over at Ria with interest and moved closer. Ria looked away. It was hard for her to understand that he could be aroused as disgusting as she must look now.

"So, Ria, what do you say? You can tell me. We won't translate. Your mother won't hear. Is Hana a virgin or not?" The woman asked, still smirking.

Ria stared back at the woman as defiantly as she could, but her head was splitting, and the pain was too overwhelming for defiance. All she wanted to do was to close her eyes and just disappear. She said nothing. She could not play this woman's game. She was too tired.

"I'll take that to be a yes then," the woman said. "Hana is still a virgin, but you Ria are not. Soldier, make sure that is clear to Ria's mother. So, Ria, now you must choose, as you are no longer a virgin. You must choose either your mother or your sister."

The man translated and Ria opened her eyes again, attention firmly on the woman. This was a new game the woman was playing, and she needed to pay attention.

Ria tensed. What did she mean? No. Surely not. She tensed in the chair, her eyes wide open and alert now.

"Let my sister go. Let my mother go. Do what you want with me." Ria rasped at the woman in resignation.

"Choose. Choose now." The woman replied.

Ria noticed the subtle change in the tone of the woman's voice. No more sarcasm. Her tone was icy, and her body language looked more dangerous now. Ria recognised the shift, damn her mother. The implicit threat of what was to come hung there unambiguous in the rancid, stale room. It felt to Ria like everyone was holding their breath, but perhaps it was only her.

11

Ria could hear screams in the distance, they mustn't be the only ones being held here. She heard the echo of doors slamming shut so hard that every time it made her jump. She heard that horrible clanking sound that she now knew was the sound of humans trying to walk with chains around their ankles just like Hana's. There were so many new sounds, sounds she never thought she would hear.

Ria looked back at the woman, she was barely able to keep one heavy eyelid open, she did everything in her power to keep her face expressionless. She would not let the woman see her fear of her. Was the woman bluffing? Ria didn't think so given what had already happened.

"Well Ria?" the woman said in that bored tone again. "I don't have all day! Who do you choose?" she asked as she moved closer to Ria, bending down again so that she was on the same level as Ria's eyes.

Ria didn't manage to stop herself from instinctively cowering away from the woman. She was annoyed at herself, she so desperately wanted to be like her mother and resist. But her terror had a will of its own she was quickly learning.

"What is the choice you ask me to make?" Ria asked. "How can I choose if I do not know why?"

"But you do know Ria, whoever you choose will suffer the same fate as you did last night in your cell, but with some differences." The woman said softly so that only Ria could hear, and Hana, if Hana was still able to hear anything from this world.

A chill ran down Ria's back as she watched the woman watch her. Was this just some psychological tactic so the woman could get information, or was it real? It was as real as real could get Ria decided. This woman had already demonstrated that she did what she said she would do. This 'choice' thing was designed to make everything more enjoyable for her. Ria knew her insight to be true. This was no bluff.

"Is it to be your mother or your sister?" she asked Ria again, politely.

"What is the decision for?" Ria said out loud now, buying time. "How can I choose if I do not know why I am choosing?" she said again. "Is it for which of them should go free, is that it?" Ria said knowing full well that was not it at all. "Is it to choose whether my mother or my sister gets to stay here with me and face our fate together? Is that your 'choice'? Or is it something else?" Ria said trying to test this woman, doing everything she could with her voice to convey hatred, not fear.

She wanted to hear the woman say it so that the others could hear it. So that her mother could hear it. She was trying to buy time at any cost. Time for what, though? Jamil was not coming, Ria knew that. No one was. But it was time for Ria to step up and show this woman that her family was strong like her mother had said and did not simply submit to any oppressor, foreign or local. She knew the woman was serious about her threat but failed to understand what she would gain from it.

"Yes, Ria, but not *just* that. I think you and your mother and everyone here in the room, except your poor sister, know exactly what I mean. Whoever you choose *will* go free, I promise you that. I am a woman of my word. But freedom comes with at a price. Do you not agree Ria? As a so-called 'freedom-fighting terrorist' what do you think about that? Anyway, you must choose between the virgin or the widow! Decide now! My patience is running out." The woman said, looking at her watch and frowning.

The woman then smiled and moved back a little to stand next to Hana. Ria could see that the woman was taunting her.

"And if I refuse?" Ria asked. "If I refuse to choose? What then?"

"That's a good question, Ria! If that is what you choose Ria, then I will leave the room for a while, well for more than a while, for a couple of hours. I need a break. This is such tiring work. And well, I'll just leave all these men here with you three women and let them do whatever they want to you. Have no doubt! T*hey* will have no problem choosing, they will choose you all. Each one of them will take their turn with each of you many times during the time I am away. Over and over. Two hours is a very long time to endure that kind of thing don't you think, Ria? I know I couldn't!" She paused for the man to translate.

Ria watched her mother, who looked furious.

Her mother's expression only seemed to satisfy the woman more judging by the expression on her face.

Ria thought her own heart had stopped because she could no longer hear it thudding in her chest. She just wanted this nightmare to end. She couldn't take any more.

"But, Ria, if you make the choice and stop wasting my time, you will save yourself and one other from all of that. Imagine! Such a noble deed! But before you ask, no, you cannot choose yourself to be the one I gift to the men. It is either your mother or your sister. That is the choice, so choose or I'll choose for you, and you may not like my choice." The woman looked at her sternly. "Ria, I really am losing my patience here."

It did not look as if she was losing her patience at all. She glanced at the translator standing behind Hana. He was staring at Hana in such a way that it disgusted her. She couldn't see the soldiers by her side, but she could only imagine. She turned desperately to her mother, but her mother just stood there, listening to the interpreter, her stare on the woman, a stare of pure hatred.

"You are a cruel woman." Ria screamed. "I will not choose between my mother and my sister. I'd rather die."

"Death, my dear Ria, is not an option here... not yet and certainly not for you. Don't you understand? Death is easy. No, this is how *you* pay for *your* terrorist acts. This is how *your* brother pays for his atrocities. There is no way out but to choose Ria or.... as I said, I can leave for a few hours and well you know...."

The woman gestured to the two soldiers by Ria's side. One of them went and stood behind her mother, grabbing her by the arms and the other soldier went and stood next to Hana. They were all staring at Hana, clearly, they had made their choice. Ria was shaking her head because she could find no words.

The woman stepped towards Hana and carefully removed the dirty blanket that covered her shoulders and chest. She rolled down the front piece of the dirty piece of clothing, exposing Hana's breasts, shoulders, and stomach. Ria's eyes widened when she saw the amount of bruising and deep gashes that covered her torso and each one seeping a mixture of blood and pus.

The woman spoke to her soldier interpreter, who told one of the soldiers to remove her mother's headscarf and take off her black sweater. Her mother struggled against the soldier's attempts to carry out the woman's orders. Ria watched as if it were not happening. Hana just stood there shuffling, mumbling, oblivious. Ria hoped she was oblivious.

"Ria!" Her mother said sharply "You know what to do."

"Yes, Ria, you know what to do." The woman sneered mimicking her mother's voice but in English.

Ria did not know what to do. How could her mother say that? What did she mean? Now was not the time for innuendo!

Ria was about to faint. She felt dizzy, her back was covered in cold sweat and her heart was now beating so fast she couldn't breathe. These were now all too familiar sensations. Ria could no longer feel any pain in her head or arms. She yearned to faint, or better still to die and disappear.

"My mother." Ria whispered.

"What's that? Speak up Ria, I can't hear you." said the woman.

Ria looked at the woman and said defiantly. "I choose my mother, now let Hana go."

Ria felt the hot tears of sadness, betrayal and rage stream down her face. She could not bear to look at her mother.

"Well done, Ria!" The woman said.

The woman turned to one of her men and spat out orders.

"Tie up the mother, arms and legs and put her in that seat next to Ria so they can both watch. Bring the girl over to the table. You know what to do, I don't have to spell it out for you." The woman said and the men sprang into action.

The foreign soldier pushed her mother forward very roughly, no respect whatsoever, and pushed her onto the chair next to Ria. He tied her hands behind her back, not to the wall, and then her feet. Ria now looked to see her mother's reaction to what the woman had said and saw her mother's face was a picture of desolation. But as she watched her Ria saw that her mother's expression shifted back and forth between her despair and her rage, her mother's face mirrored Ria's own emotions. The terror of what was about to happen and their powerlessness to stop it. Ria felt a small part of her waiting, hoping the woman would call it off at the last minute, praying that it was all just a bluff. She saw Hana's face as she was ushered forward, shuffling, half-naked. The soldier ripped off the rest of Hana's clothing. Ria felt dirty and ashamed of the sight and very angry. She pulled against her restraints. Say something!

"I said my mother, you sick monster! I chose, you made me choose, I chose my mother. What the hell are you doing with my sister!" Ria screamed at the woman. "Not Hana. No, not Hana. You lied to me. You are the devil! I chose my mother. Not Hana. A woman of your word you said, you fucking sick bitch." Ria felt pure, white-hot rage towards the woman. "Take me. Do it to me. Please." Ria was sobbing now, untethered, overwhelmed.

As Ria watched the monstrous scene shaping before her very eyes, to her horror Hana seemed to snap out of whatever trance-like state she had been in. No, not now Hana, Ria muttered. But Hana seemed to wake up. She looked terrified. Slowly turning around, she saw Ria and her mother, and looked confused. Then Ria watched as her sister looked down at herself, raised her hand and saw what was not there. Her eyes opened wide, and she uttered a piercing sound that Ria had never before heard a human being make. Her mother started screaming oaths and threats at the woman and the men, but the woman just stood there, impassive.

The foreign soldier slid Hana forward along the table by her legs. Hana was trying to resist now but she looked weak. He shoved her back down on her back, then as Ria and her mother watched, both silent now, the man loosened the belt of his khaki shorts, keeping Hana's head and torso immobilised with his forearm.

12

When he had finished with her, one of the other soldiers took his place. He pushed Hana back down onto the table when she tried to sit up and lash out. She was screaming the whole time. He pushed her legs apart. Ria watched but then could watch no more. It was all happening so very quickly that she could not fully comprehend it. Hana's resistance eventually became more and more subdued. It was the turn of the other soldier now. The one who had just finished moved to the other end of the table to hold Hana down on the table, freeing the other soldier from having to control Hana. Hana, perhaps now realising that struggle was futile, stopped, laid still and screamed no more. One after another, each of them took their turn. Ria turned to her mother who was as white as a sheet, tears rolling down her face.

"Mama, mama, we have to stop this." Ria whispered urgently to her mother sitting right by her. The woman stood back against the wall watching it all with a bored expression, but from time to time she would look over at Ria and her mother, seeming more interested in them. This was her revenge for her mother's words, this had nothing to do with terrorists.

Ria's mother suddenly crashed forward onto the hard stone floor, seat and all.

"Get her up." The woman snapped one of the soldiers.

Her mother resisted by doing nothing and making herself heavier, and with her arms tied, the soldier couldn't lift her. Ria saw blood seep from a large gash on her mother's forehead.

"Get her up NOW! Do I have to do everything myself?" The woman shouted at the soldier who didn't understand so the foreign soldier translated.

Ria registered this tiny fissure in the woman's composure. Why now?

The soldier looked increasingly nervous as the woman shouted at him, then the foreign soldier was shouting the translation at him, but try as he might, he could not lift the dead weight of her mother. The woman sighed in exasperation and gestured to one of the other soldiers holding Hana down to help him.

"Let her stand but hold her arm. Do not let her fall again! She must watch." The woman said.

"Mama, no. Mama no. Don't look, Mama. Get away from me!" Hana screamed.

Hana, her torso now freed began to scream louder and louder as another soldier began his second assault on her body.

"Please. No." Hana was sobbing now.

Ria's heart was breaking, and she was sure her mother's was too. Ria could not look, but she couldn't block out the sounds either. The man's heavy breathing, the grunting, Hana's screams, the sound of flesh slapping against flesh, his finishing and gasping. She felt something indescribable inside her. Was it shame? What was it? Ria did not know where to look so she looked at the woman, but she could still see everything that was happening to Hana in her peripheral vision.

Ria forced herself to look at her sister, who had stopped screaming again. She was flat out on the table, her dirty hands hanging onto the side of it as if clinging onto life itself. She saw Hana's ragged hair, the length of her bruised and bedraggled body, now fully unclothed, stretched out on the table, blood dripping down onto the floor from between her legs. The other soldier pulled his trousers down to his ankles. Hana again realising it was going to happen again reacted by struggling as best she could and again began screaming 'NO' over and over. She struggled, but as the man entered her, he leaned forward and over her, pinning her shoulders down, his forearm pressing against Hana's throat. Hana screamed in pain as the man forced himself into her with much more aggression this time it seemed to Ria. The sound Hana made was less of a scream and more of a gurgle because of the man's hold on her throat. She had thought it could not get any worse, but it could. Her own silent rape in her cell seemed insignificant now compared to all this.

Ria forced herself not to not look away. It was out of some sort of warped solidarity that she felt she too had to witness what her sister was being put through. She cast a glance at her mother, she was doing the same but the expression on her mother's face was really something Ria could not bear to see, and she quickly turned back to what was happening to Hana.

Ria's mother began muttering, quietly under her breath, Ria couldn't hear what she was saying over Hana's screaming, but she could see her mother's mouth moving as she looked at her again. Perhaps her mother was praying. Perhaps that was at least something she felt she could do. Ria had never felt so utterly incapable as she now. But she must not remain silent. Why was she so silent? Why was Hana the only one still resisting?

Ria did the only thing she could do. She struggled against all her restraints and began to scream insults at them all, but especially at the woman in English. But as the next soldier stepped up to Hana, Hana had become quiet, and it seemed strangely inappropriate for Ria to continue screaming. She knew it would happen again and she would stay with Hana in spirit, she would not look away again. Her mother's words were now more audible, in the quiet she seemed to intentionally increase the volume. Perhaps her mother wanted Hana to hear what she was saying because they were words of comfort. Ria wanted to cry but could not, how could she cry when her own sister was about to get raped yet again?

To keep looking at someone she loved as they are being broken was the most difficult thing Ria had ever had to do, but it would be worse to turn away and leave her sister alone or to leave this crime unwitnessed. Her mother and Ria were with Hana in the only way they could be, sharing in some of her horror, and letting Hana know that they were there, that they were not abandoning her, that she was not facing this alone. Ria also took comfort from her mother's words and joined her mother in saying them as loudly as she could.

The soldier finished and pulled up his trousers. Hana was silent now. How long had it been? Minutes? Longer? Surely now the nightmare was over.

The foreign soldier walked back up to Hana.

"Please, no, please." Ria pleaded now with the woman. "Please, stop this now. Please!" Ria screamed at the woman.

Then, getting no reaction, she tried to calm her tone and said

"I'll tell you whatever you want. Just leave her alone. You have already broken her, please no more."

Ria repeated, desperate to negotiate anything just to have this stop.

"Yes, Ria, you will tell me everything, with time." The woman replied but she was looking at Ria's mother. Slowly the woman turned her gaze on Ria and smiled.

"Ria, my dear, we are just getting started." She said.

Ria was speechless. She could not comprehend this woman, these men. Hana was barely fifteen. She screamed in rage, horror, desperation, and exhaustion, her emotions in total chaos.

The foreign soldier pulled Hana up to face him, half sitting up, her bare torso battered and bruised, barely conscious. Then, he began hitting her over and over across her face. He was vicious. Then he pulled down his shorts again, put on a condom and raped her again. This time he took his time and held Hana up so that she could see his face. But Hana seemed to have lost consciousness after all his blows, and he had trouble keeping her upright. Her head lolled forward against her chest, she no longer screamed, and she no longer struggled. She was completely limp, half draped over the man who was raping her. It was a terrible sight to witness, and Ria knew she would never be able to erase it from her mind. Ria prayed that Hana was indeed unconscious. This woman was evil, there was no other word to describe her. How could another woman enjoy watching men rape a young girl? Not just enjoy it, order it. Not to mention the men. What kind of man did something like this? Ria's hatred of the woman and these soldiers became all-consuming, a channel for her horror and helplessness.

After a while though, she began to worry. Hana looked strange. Maybe the soldier's blows had killed her? Maybe that would be the best thing. What was she thinking? How could that be the best thing? Her mother was getting louder and louder, she seemed to be trying to wake Hana. Why? Was it not better that she stayed unconscious? Was it not better that she did not come to know any more horror than she had already experienced?
They would kill them all eventually Ria thought. She relished the thought. After what they had done to Hana, what would life for her be like if she was set free? For any of them? No one could get over that, certainly not without her family near, especially her mother. Ria knew that she would be next, but she thought that they would not do that to her mother, not the soldiers from here. They wouldn't dare. She looked at her mother again, worried.

Ria's mother was no longer looking at Hana or the men. She was no longer watching this ultimate horror going on at the table. No, now she was watching the woman as she spoke in her own language. The soldiers were looking at her mother and frowning, casting nervous

107

glances now and again at the woman. As Ria listened more carefully to the words her mother was saying, she noticed it was the same phrase repeated over and over again, louder and louder each time. The woman caught Ria's mother staring at her and stared back with a smirk, but she could not understand what Ria's mother was saying. Maybe she thought her mother was praying.

Her mother was certainly not praying now. There was no translation because the foreign soldier was still busy with Hana.

"You have taken my child, and you have hurt my children. You have done terrible things for no reason. I know we will not leave here alive. What you have done here will be known of by many of our people. Even if it takes a lifetime, we will find you and take those you love most from you. You will pay for this one day."

That was what her mother was saying over and over again. Ria joined her mother and said it too, but Ria repeated the words in English so that the woman would understand. Her mother glared at the woman no longer with a look of despair, now she looked smug and knowing, almost smug. The woman listened to Ria's repetition of the words, rolled her eyes and looked away.

"There's too much blood." The foreign soldier said, looking disgusted, as he buttoned up his shorts and stepped away.

"That's enough now. Stop. Leave her there on the table. Shut them up. No more chanting. I have to go now, but I'll be back soon. Watch them. No water. No food. Nothing." the woman said.

She looked with disdain at Ria's mother and turned and left the room. The man in the khaki shorts followed her out as did the taller man in the uniform, leaving just the two soldiers behind who took up their original positions flanking Ria and now her mother. Hana lay sprawled on the table, head turned away from them, calves dangling off the end of the table. Ria stared at her bare feet. It was such a terrible sight, Ria had to look away.

Ria saw her mother look up at the soldier standing beside her.

Then her mother said. "You call yourself a soldier? You should be ashamed of yourself for following a foreign woman's orders to defile a young girl. Does it give you pleasure to beat and rape a young girl? She is barely fifteen. Maybe you have a daughter, a sister, or a niece who is the same age or younger. Is there something wrong with your head? It is the only explanation. Your mother must hate the sight of you." her mother said and spat at the ground in front of him.

The soldier's neck reddened, and he moved forward quickly, fist raised, poised to strike her.

"Go on. Hit me. That is all you are good for, raping young girls and beating defenceless women. You call yourself a man? A soldier? You are a disgrace to your country." Her mother spat again, directly onto the soldier's boots this time.

Ria tensed as she waited for the inevitable battering her mother would receive. But none came.

The soldier lowered his fist, turned, hunched his shoulders, and walked over to the table where Hana lay, still limp, and before Ria could even process what he was doing he had lifted Hana up into a half and had started slapping her face repeatedly with the back of his hand. All Ria could hear was the crisp slap of his hand against Hana's cheeks as Hana's head snapped right and left with each crack of the soldier's hand. Ria's mother gasped and she began to sob. Her mother had broken.

Eventually, he stopped and turned to look at Ria's mother. His hand was covered in Hana's blood. He smiled at her mother. Ria's mother, in tears now, hurled insults at him, but then broke down and began to emit an eerie howl that Ria could not bear. Hana lay on the table, her face covered in blood. Surely, she was dead now. Ria too began to cry, long sobs that racked every part of her body.

13

Time just passed. Ria and her mother said nothing to each other. It was better to leave the question of whether Hana was alive unasked. They both kept their eyes trained on her, looking for signs. Sometimes her mother would moan, sometimes she would mumble under her breath, sometimes they were silent, spent.
Ria did not know how much time had passed since the woman had left. Her experience of time had become a series of horrific events with no end in sight, and she so desperately desired the end.

    The door swung open and a short, fat man walked in. He was wearing a different type of uniform with a white armband with a red cross on his right arm. He was carrying a large red bag with a cross marked on it. Ria knew it was a medical bag. He must be some kind of doctor. Relief washed over her. He would save Hana. She felt her mother stir, she inhaled deeply but did not exhale.

    He walked over to the table, set the bag down on the table beside Hana and began to examine her. Hana was completely still. She had not moved in a long time. Ria was sure she was dead. She looked again at the pool of blood that had formed on the floor from the dripping of Hana's blood. At first, it had been bright red but now it looked less red and browner. Ria felt as if her heart had exploded into tiny pieces, split forever. All she could do now was stare at Hana on the table, hoping. Hoping for what? She did not know whether she hoped her sister was alive or dead. She did however know what she wanted for herself. Ria's eyes were fixed on the swollen, bleeding pulp that was now Hana's face. She was even more unrecognisable than before. Ria felt sick.

The man put his hand gently on the side of Hana's neck and looked at his watch. Then he moved to where all the blood had flowed from between Hana's legs and pulled on some gloves.

"Bring me some hot water and towels. Now." The man barked at one of the soldiers. "Be quick about it." he looked at them with contempt.

Then while he waited, slowly he moved his hands up and down the body, gently pressing and examining each part. When he got to her face, he frowned. He examined her nose and every inch of her face and head. He bent down, opened his bag, and took out a few tiny bottles and syringes.

"What are you doing to her? Is she, is she alive?" Ria asked.

"Shut up! You will not speak!" said the soldier who had just beaten Hana.

The man ignored her question. Ria watched as he filled a syringe with something from a tiny bottle and injected it into Hana's thigh.

Ria's mother shot a look at her, and Ria understood she was to shut up for Hana's sake. For Hana's life.

The soldier returned carrying a bucket of steaming water and several dark-coloured towels.

The man soaked the towels in the steaming water and began to clean Hana, wiping between her legs first, then doing the same for her face and her whole body. He was gentle, which was confusing for Ria.

He injected her a few times in different places. She, her mother, and the soldiers watched as the tall man stitched up Hana. He started between her legs, then on a few places on her face, on her stomach, and he spent a long time on her head. They watched as he then placed large compresses over different-sized gashes and seemed to do something to her nose, and then he taped it down.

He then took out a very new-looking grey overall, gestured to the two soldiers to help him and together they lifted Hana up while the man dressed her limp body in the grey overall. It was a strange thing to see. He laid her back on the table again, packed up his bag and turned to the soldier beside Ria's mother.

"I will be back. Do not touch her again. Those are direct orders from the captain." He said and left as if in a hurry.

Ria looked at her mother. She could see the wet tracks of tears on the side of her mother's dusty face, but her mother was smiling because Hana was alive. Ria could not find even the glimmer of a genuine smile to match her mother's.

Ria was in a great amount of pain. Now that the events on the table had ceased for the time being, her physical pain had returned with more force. Her arms had been pulled back against the wall for so long now that every nerve, muscle, and tendon was stretched to breaking point. Every few minutes, she suffered excruciating cramping spasms in her arms, fingers, feet, calves, and thighs. Everything was so worn down from being tied in the same position for so long. But the thirst, that overwhelming thirst! She must be very dehydrated by now she thought. As she could not move, she could do nothing about the cramping. Her body felt so tense and despite trying to consciously relax her muscles, it was impossible, they cramped anyway. Some cramps were so painful that she cried out involuntarily, then dreaded the next one. She silenced herself quickly after each cramp fearing another blow to the head from the soldier at her side because she knew her head and neck could not withstand any more blows. But Ria was also aware of how bad she felt inside. Not just the pain from her injuries, there was the pain in her heart, in her soul and there was nothing to be done about that.

Her mother did not even look at her, which hurt her much more than pain. Why was her mother acting like this to her? It must be because she thought Ria was so weak and pathetic, and blamed her. Ria's pain was nothing compared to what Hana had endured and she felt ashamed of her own self-pity, so she gritted her teeth and tried to ignore her physical pain. But she could not ignore this strange but terrifying sensation inside her that she could not identify or name. It was a new feeling, so strong it stood out from all other sensation and feeling. She felt it as it spread into every cell in her body, a sickening, deadening feeling far worse than her physical pain.
The door opened again, and a different soldier came in.

"The foreign captain sent me. She says to untie the girl from the wall. Someone will bring water and food in a few minutes, and she will return in an hour. Your shift will change when they bring the food. Understood?" He asked.

The soldiers saluted and immediately one moved towards Ria to untie her arms. They flopped down by her side, limp and useless. She massaged them to try to get the blood flowing again, first one, then the other. Then he untied her feet.

"Can I stand up? Can I walk a little? The cramps..." She asked him.

"No." He said.

She flexed her legs out from her seat, crossed her arms over and out, and stretched everything possible from the chair. It felt better.

Her mother was a mere arm's length away, but it felt like they were separated by a mighty chasm. Ria looked over at her mother, willing her to look back at her, to see her. Ria's eyes filled with tears and then her mother finally looked at her and nodded almost imperceptibly before turning away again but it was long enough for Ria to see her mother's face. Ria was shocked by the depth of sadness and distress she saw there. They said nothing to each other, there were no words that would do.

"I suppose now you think this is over because they will feed you and untie you or because they sent the doctor. That is what you think, isn't it?" The soldier said to Ria's mother. "If you think that, then you are a really stupid old woman."

Ria's mother turned to look at the soldier. She looked him up and down millimetre by millimetre, taking her time to stare at every part of him. Ria was surprised at the intensity of hatred she saw on her mother's face. Her mother raised her gaze to meet his and spoke. Her voice was strong and as cold as ice.

"You little sick boy. I know it is not over. I know more about these kinds of places than you do. Sleep well while you can. The day will come when all the inhuman things that you have done to your own people in places like these will haunt you and you'll never sleep again. You'll have such terrible nightmares you will stop going to bed. You'll look at yourself in the mirror and wish you were dead but be too much of a coward to end your life. But don't worry, your death will not be long in coming and when it comes, I take comfort knowing it will be a horrible death. Mark my words. You are cursed." her mother said and then looked away.
Ria shuddered.
The soldier attempted a laugh, but it came out forced and betrayed his fear. His mother seemed to have unsettled him, He seemed less sure of himself. Her mother had got inside his head.

The door opened again, and they all turned towards it. A small, slightly stooped man with slightly greying hair entered. He was wearing ordinary clothes and was followed by two older-looking soldiers who seemed to be supervising him. The man was carrying a large tray.

"You can both go now." one of the soldiers said to the others. "Your shift is over." He saluted.

Ria's mother stared at the soldier she had just spoken to. "Run little animal, it won't be long before the nightmares start." She said.

He left quickly without another word.

The man with the tray walked over slowly as if pained by movement. With difficulty, he set the tray down in front of Ria and her mother. The soldiers gestured for them to sit on the ground to eat. Her mother sat cross-legged, and Ria tried to do the same but could not manage to cross her injured limbs. There was a basket of flatbread and a large bowl of muhammara. There was also a jug of cloudy water and two small glasses of steaming tea.

The soldiers took up their positions by the chairs. Ria paid them no attention, driven now by her overwhelming thirst worsened at the sight of the water. She grabbed the jug with trembling hands and tried to lift it to drink from it but could not. It was too heavy for her. Some of the water spilled. Her mother reached over and took the jug from her.

"Ria don't do that. You'll be sick. Drink it slowly, and from the glass not the jug and leave some for me." Her mother said and pointed to two empty glasses on the tray.

Ria felt ashamed. She watched her mother, steady of hand as usual, pour out two glasses of water. She handed Ria a glass.

"Drink it slowly." She said gently.

Ria drank the water. It was the best water she had ever had in her life.

"Now, Ria, eat and drink the tea. Eat as much as you can Ria. But slowly."

"What about Hana?" Ria asked looking up at her still lying there on the table.

"They have drugged her Ria, or worse, I don't know. We can do nothing for her. She sleeps. Just eat, and drink Ria. We must eat while we can. Hana can't eat. Anyway, Hana is gone" her mother said.

Gone? Ria flinched at her mother's words. Her mother's words were tender in tone, but the meaning was harsh. Ria did not understand what her mother meant and opened her mouth to ask, but her mother shot her a look that silenced any questions and then said.

"No talk Ria. Just eat and drink. Do not look at Hana. Do as I do." her mother said.

Ria watched her mother take some bread, break off a piece, scoop up some dip, and chew on it slowly, staring down at the ground. Ria reached out for the bread, feeling sick and guilty as she did so.

14

Ria did as her mother said, or at least she tried. It was the water she needed the most, and there wasn't enough for both of them in the jug. She had no appetite for food. The tea helped but there was a lot of sugar in it, so it just made her even more thirsty. Her thirst took over, it was insatiable and not helped by the room being so hot and stale. She was still finding it hard to breathe. All she could think about was how to get more water. When she put the bread and dip into her mouth, it felt like gritty sand in her dry mouth, and it was agonising to chew anything with her battered jaw and mouth. She tried to swallow the food chewing it as little as possible but when it came to swallowing it was too hard and she gagged and spat it out.

"What the hell are you doing?" one of the soldiers shouted, coming round to stand in front of her. He bent down and slapped her hard across the face. "Eat the food and be grateful, you slut. Wasting our food!" He stood there looking disgusted.

Ria looked at her mother, tears welling. Her mother reached forward, dipped a very small piece of the bread and handed it to Ria. It was such a gentle gesture after the soldier's slap that Ria felt she would lose any control she had left over her emotions. She took the bread and looked down at the ground. She dipped it again to make it even wetter and put it in her mouth, this time she chewed even less and forced herself to swallow it. Knowing what would happen if she didn't swallow the food only increased her anxiety. The soldier stood there hand at the ready waiting, watching.

Ria managed to get it down with great difficulty and though she still felt the gagging sensation as she swallowed, she managed to suppress it, the extra moisture of the dip helped a little.

"Again!" The soldier commanded.

Ria picked up another piece of the flatbread, scooped up a good amount of the dip again and put it into her mouth. As she chewed, she looked up at the soldier, veiled defiance now in her expression. Not enough to get hit, just enough to not submit. He looked very young, perhaps even around her age. What had made him choose to do this? Except for the uniform he wore, he looked just like any other student sitting in the university canteen. She realised she had swallowed without gagging, distracted by her thoughts her body had functioned. He walked away to stand behind them again. She took up another piece of bread. The sensation of thirst worsened with the spicy dip.

"Can we have more water?" Ria asked the soldier.

"No. What you have been brought is more than enough." The soldier responded.

Just then the door swung open again, and the stooped-over man entered again. He made his way over to where Ria and her mother sat and bent over with evident difficulty, groaning a little as he went to pick up the tray. As he stood up, the tray slipped out of his hands. The sudden crash of the tray, glasses, and bowls smashing into the hard stone floor startled Ria and her mother.

"You stupid old man. Clean that up fast and get out." the soldier shouted at him.

"I have to get the brush." The man replied, cowering a little.

"Then, go and get it you clumsy old cripple! And quickly." The soldier shouted at him.

The man scuttled away as fast as his body let him and was back a few minutes later with a sweeping brush much taller than himself and a large piece of cardboard. He bent down and started sweeping the remnants of the glasses, the jug, and the clay bowls onto the cardboard. Ria and her mother sat watching him. As he swept close to her mother, Ria noticed that his mouth seemed to move, and he seemed to say something very brief to her mother and a barely perceptible look was exchanged between the two. Ria thought she had imagined it, but then she saw her mother place one of her hands on the ground beside her and watched her as she covered a sharp piece of glass with her hand. Her mother looked at Ria, then down at the ground near Ria. Ria looked down, saw, and understood and did the same with a large piece of jagged ceramic the man must have swept over to her. Her heart raced as she covered it. Surely the soldiers would see them. But they didn't.

The man finished and shuffled off.

Her mother stuck the piece of glass into one of the pockets of her trousers. Ria nervously put her piece, which was very small, into her jeans pocket, taking care to position it so it couldn't cut into her.

What good would this do? Was it to hurt the soldiers? The soldiers were armed, her mother knew that and so did the old man. Maybe it was for themselves? Ria didn't know, but somehow, she felt a little bit stronger knowing she had that tiny piece of sharp ceramic.

A sudden extremely loud noise shook the ground beneath them. It had been so loud that even after the noise had passed Ria could still feel the vibration coming up from under the stones. What the hell was that? The soldiers' radios burst into life, and a voice uttered a string of meaningless words interjected with some sort of code language that Ria could not understand.

A siren came on, it was so piercing that Ria flung up her hands to cover her ears. Then they heard what sounded like multiple yet distant explosions, each one sending another tremor up through the ground. She looked over at her mother. Her mother looked back, shrugging, but more alert now.

One of the soldiers left the room immediately while the other one ran over to the door to switch off the lights. He turned on his torch at a dim setting and shone it downwards towards the ground just in front of the women. He stood a couple of meters away from them, facing them. It was a good time to use their 'weapons' Ria thought. Two against one. She looked at her mother. No signals.

The soldier with the torch was the same soldier who had just hit her and forced her to eat. She could barely see him in the shadowy light, but she thought he looked unsure of himself now. All alone in the dark with those explosions going off not so far away. He kept glancing anxiously at the door and the window high up on the outer wall.

"They have come." Ria's mother said, taunting him. "They always come."

The soldier looked at her, visibly nervous now, confused even.

"Who has come?" he asked. "Who?" he asked impatiently.

"Does it matter? What does it matter whether it's the Turks, the Americans, the Russians, the French, the British, terrorists, or someone else? While we fight amongst ourselves like children over a worthless toy, others will play their power games in our country. And we will let them because we are weak. Instead of building our country into something we can be proud of, you and those like you, destroy it. You destroy your own people, and you make our country weak."

"You don't know what you are talking about." He snapped.

"I don't know what I am talking about you say." Ria's mother snorted. "You are just a boy. You can't be much older than Ria here. You will see I am right in time boy. Your commanders will tell you that this is your country and that you must fight for your country, die for your country if necessary to keep our enemies away. You wear your country's uniform. But who do you spend your days fighting? Your own people. You are at war with your own people, who just want to live in peace. You are not even fighting another nation. But other nations will come. You are fighting only so that the same men can take from us, that is what you wear the uniform for, to protect the few against the many. Our leaders don't care about you or your family. They only care about money and power. You are just one of the many who does their dirty work for a pittance." she paused.

"You torture and kill us as if *we* were your enemy. Look what has been done to my daughter there, a child, one of your own people! What has she done to become your enemy? You are not a soldier but a thug. You think foreigners will help us, do you?" She looked at him, and he stared, listening.

"Listen to those explosions. Does that sound like help? Yes, they will talk of peace, of democracy, of humanity, of what is right and what is wrong while they rape our women and children and destroy our towns and villages with their bombs. That will come soon. They are not fighting about us or even for us. They are fighting each other. Do you believe you are an honourable soldier boy?"

He said nothing but Ria saw him redden. He looked very uncomfortable, and Ria saw that he was afraid of her mother, now alone in the room.

Her mother laughed in scorn.

Ria stared at her mother. Ria had never heard her mother speak about anything else but the importance of studying and eating well or repeating boring local news. She never let them discuss the protests, the state, the disappearances of neighbours or anything like that. She only warned that ears were everywhere. Ria had thought that was why Jamil spent so much time away from home, but now she questioned that. Her mother knew a lot of things. She spoke like Jamil.

There were no more explosions. The soldier's radio came on again, breaking the tense silence. Ria watched the soldier relax at what he heard, but he didn't turn the lights back on.

Then Ria heard a strange sound. She could have sworn it was coming from near the table where Hana lay. Was Hana trying to speak? Was Hana awake?

Ria looked with hope towards her mother, but her mother was looking towards the table where Hana lay, barely visible in the dark. Her mother looked troubled.

"Mama is here, Hana. It's ok. Your sister is here too. Just rest now. Go back to sleep." Her mother said.

"Shut up!" The soldier said and kicked her mother's leg hard. Ria's mother did not even cry out in pain just stared up at the soldier.

The mumbling on the table seemed to stop. Ria could see Hana twitching as if she were dreaming. As Ria looked at the outline of her sister laid out on the table, she felt a strong feeling of disconnection with Hana and a sense that it was no longer Hana who was lying there. As soon as she thought that she felt ashamed of herself for even thinking such a thing. Of course, it was Hana. Who else would it be? But was it? She couldn't shake the feeling, that as her mother had put it, 'Hana had gone'. She felt that way too now.

There was a lot of shouting now coming from outside. Then they heard the now-familiar rumble of vehicle engines and tyre rubber screeching to a halt. It sounded like a lot of vehicles had arrived, it reminded her of that day at the campus, it had been a while since she had thought about all that. Was it not just yesterday? Ria couldn't remember. She felt her palms become clammy. Was it the woman returning?

The soldier seemed to stand to attention, ready and waiting, eyes fixed on that door.

Ria's mother looked over at her mother.

"Prepare yourself, Ria" she whispered.

"For what Mama?" Ria asked heart pounding.

"For the worst." Her mother whispered and Ria put her hand over her jeans pocket and felt the jagged piece of ceramic.

15

The door opened and Ria and her mother looked up. This time felt different. Now, two other foreign men Ria had not seen before entered, led by the woman. The same foreign translator came in as well. They were all wearing the same uniform as the woman. There was no identifying country flag on any of the uniforms. The soldiers all looked physically different, some dark, some blond, all from different parts of the world it seemed. But something was wrong. This entourage didn't simply walk into the room, they stormed in and were all very heavily armed. Ria looked warily at the woman, who was rapidly approaching her mother and saw that there was a look of barely contained fury on the woman's face. Her whole body was rigid with tension. No longer was she her cold, composed self, instead another, much more dangerous version of this woman now filled the room.

"Your terrorist son is responsible for the deaths of three more of my men Alina!" She was shouting right up into Ria's mother's face. "Do you know what that means for you now? For you and your daughters?"
Ria's mother said nothing, but she met the woman's fury with a defiant look.

"Get the girl off the table and bring her to the chair here in front." The woman said.

"My son would never hurt innocent people, so if it *is* him, your men must not be innocent." Ria's mother said quietly.

"What did she say?" the woman asked the same foreign soldier who translated back.

The woman's expression turned dark, her eyes as cold as steel, but when she spoke to her mother, her voice was like silk, and it did not match her expression. This mismatch caused Ria to feel that strange sensation of the urge to pee again. Fear.

"Alina dear. You are a very silly woman. *Your* son is part of one of the biggest terrorist groups operating in this area. Did you know that? Do you expect me to believe that you really have no idea who or what your son is or what he has been up to these last few months?" The woman paused and stood upright. She looked as if she was thinking "Or maybe you don't know? Either way, we will find him. Then, we will find every member of his group of crazed fanatics and then their families and anyone else who helped them in any way, even if it was just selling them food in the market. They will all pay. We will have our day with them, just like today we will have our day with you three. It is just a question of time, Alina. Soon your family will be gone. Wiped out, no-one left. But first, meet some of my men. They are very angry at losing their friends!"

The soldier translated the woman's words back to Alina. He did so in a sneering tone, smirking as he did. Ria studied her men. They all looked strong, muscular, and dangerous looking. The woman was right, they did look angry and menacing, but they did not have the same sinister look the woman had.

As Ria watched, one of them grabbed her by the arm and pulled her roughly to her feet. It felt like every bone and muscle in her body was being pulled apart. Drinking and eating something had helped but her light-headedness had not gone. Her mother had also been brought to her feet and the others were dragging Hana over to a chair the woman had placed in front of Ria and her mother.

Hana looked as if she was still unconscious, her legs dragged along the stone floor, her head flopping against her chest as they hauled her over. But she was alive. Ria could see her breathing, though it looked shallow. Given the situation now she wished Hana was not alive. What else could this woman do to her?

Ria noticed something strange about the way she was feeling, it was not like the feeling from before. She felt very on edge, as if her body was absorbing all of the tension in the room. She sensed something very bad was about to happen, something much worse than before. This was it. This was the end for the three of them, and it would not be fast. Ria was certain of that terrifying fact. Was she ready to die? She didn't know but death wasn't what she feared. What terrified her was how they were going to die. She was terrified of not dying first and being forced to see her sister suffer even more than she had already or see her mother die in some horrible way. A part of her longed to die, just to get all of this horror over and done with. She knew she would not be released, and she did not expect to live. She was sick of the constant terror, the exhaustion, the pain, and the horror of everything that had happened.

She had not been prepared for the massacre at the campus, she had not been prepared for what they had done to her, and nothing could ever have prepared her for what they had done to Hana. She knew she could not live with it all.

She had had time to accept the situation they were in, it hadn't taken her long, she hadn't even had to think about it that much, it was just something she had known from that first moment she had set eyes on this woman. She had known that this would be the last place she would ever see. She prayed it would be over quickly for all of them. Selfishly she hoped she would be the first to go but was scared about how they would kill her. Would it be brutal and long, like what they had done to Hana? Was there some plan worse than that? Ria felt a sickening feeling in the pit of her stomach, her legs trembled uncontrollably, her jaw ached and the urge to urinate was almost uncontrollable.

"Hurry up! I told you. The air strikes could start over here in a couple of hours. We need to be gone in an hour" The woman said to the soldiers trying to get Hana seated in the chair. Ria registered how long their death would take. An hour was a very long time, but she knew it could well have been longer! Whatever the woman meant by airstrikes, Ria was grateful.

"Ria, your brother *will* pay, just not today. But you, especially you must also pay because you worked with your brother, you supported his terrorist activity, and so did your mother. The only person who truly knew nothing is

Hana. Yet, it is you Ria who will leave this place. I am going to let you go." The woman said.

Ria stared at the woman. What was she talking about? Let her go? Why? To lead them to Jamil? That was not going to happen. Maybe she thought he would come to Ria for information about what had happened. She was probably right. He would.

The woman laughed. "You are surprised. You didn't think we were going to kill you, did you? No, we are not fanatical psychos like your brother and his friends. Anyway, as I said before, death is not the worst thing that can happen to someone, remember? I would have given my life to save my men your brother murdered. That is the honour of a soldier." She looked away in disgust.

Ria felt angry, she had seen no honour in this woman or any of her men.

The woman barked orders to her men "You, keep hold of the mother, and you keep the girl in check. You, wait outside and monitor the channels for any intel on any air strikes."

One of the men grabbed hold of her mother while the one next to her placed his enormous arm on Ria's. The other one left. These men were so tall and big, so different from their own soldiers. She felt it become harder to breathe, there seemed to be even less air now in the room. Ria noticed a pleasant smell of soap from the soldier standing next to her, and she was strangely embarrassed by her own contrasting stench. The foreign soldiers wore heavy looking machine guns slung across their backs, and there were smaller guns tucked in their belts, and long-looking knives in sheaths attached to their thighs. The woman had a longish gun in a leather holster strapped to her leg. Ria had never really noticed guns before but now felt an odd curiosity about them and a very strong desire to have one.

Ria wondered how her mother was feeling. Was she afraid too? Ria didn't think so, her mother was no coward, she was much stronger than Ria. Ria's heartbeat had increased, and she could feel her heart pounding in her chest. To her embarrassment she started to sweat even more profusely. She wished her heart would just stop working. Ria forced herself to look at Hana slumped in the chair, head on her chest. As she was looking at her sister, she jumped as Hana's head suddenly snapped up. The soldier had injected her with something. She now saw the syringe as he laid it down on the table. Hana looked around slowly, looking dazed and out of it, but then it was as if a curtain was suddenly raised in Hana's mind, and the Hana she had always known appeared before her, wide-eyed and alert.

Her face was a mess, but she was no longer mumbling to herself, shut off in that world of her own. She said nothing, but it was clear to Ria that she was unfortunately very present. She looked at Ria. Ria looked back at her sister. She saw Hana's familiar expression amid the swelling, cuts, bruises and gashes. Ria tried to smile at her but, to her shame, found she could not. Hana's face and body were one big bloody mess, the bandages already soaked by the blood. Hana looked very weak and pale. Ria glanced down to Hana's lap where the hand with the missing fingers lay and noticed the yellowish liquid that seeped from where her fingers had been. Ria frowned at her own feelings of disgust, she was simply unable to feel the love she wanted to show Hana, so she looked away, ashamed of herself, and turned her head towards her mother instead, seeking guidance, or perhaps absolution. She did not know which.

Her mother was looking at Hana but not with disgust. Ria could see her mother's love for Hana pouring out through the silent tears streaming down her dirty face and the expression on her face. Her mother seemed to be willing Hana to look at her, but Hana could not see all this love pouring out for her from her mother because she just kept on staring at Ria. Was Hana too ashamed to look at her mother after what had happened? Or was it the horror of everything that was just too much for her?

"It's not your fault Hana!" Ria cried out trying to look at her sister with compassion, feeling tears fall as she spoke. She could not bear the thought that with everything else Hana had gone through, Hana might feel ashamed. But she understood why she would, after all, Ria felt like that.

As indignant rage displaced her own shame Ria looked at Hana and nodded in their mother's direction, urging Hana to look that way. Hana shook her head slowly and continued to stare at Ria.

"Hana?" her mother said. "Hana, look at me please."

Ria saw Hana flinch, and move her head slightly, but it was to look down at the ground. She heard her mother sob.

The woman laughed again. Another cold, hollow laugh that stopped as suddenly as it had started.

"Your sister is alive, Ria. You should be grateful. If I hadn't sent the doctor in, she would be dead by now. Are you not going to thank me? And you, Alina, where is your gratitude?" she said to her Ria's mother.

Her mother though sobbing in despair still managed to spit on the ground again as near to the woman as she could get.

"Gratitude? Only you would expect me to show gratitude. You are sick, do you not realise it? For what you have done to my daughters, I would rather kill you." Her mother shouted.

The soldier translated and again, the woman laughed. "You want to kill me. I'm hurt. What about you Ria? Do you want to kill me too, Ria? Your mother has it in her I am sure, but you, I don't think you have the stomach for it. You are just a frightened little girl. But soon we will see what you are made of?" The woman said briskly and checked her watch.

"Ria?" Ria was startled by the clear sound of her sister's voice and turned away from the woman to look at Hana. "If the time comes, you know what to do. I am already dead. Your sister is dead Ria, gone. Do you understand? I love you both." Hana said and looked at Ria. Ria stared at her. She understood but felt confused. She shook her head firmly at Hana, tears filling her eyes, she felt it now strong and clear, her love for her sister, her pain at her suffering. She clenched her fists at her side and tried with every muscle in her face and body to show her sister her love for her. This time it came easy.

Hana continued to speak. "Mama. I am sorry you had to see all that, no mother should see that. Soon it will be over. Forgive me." Hana said without looking at her mother.

What was happening? Ria could not understand.

"Hana, my dear daughter. My strong child. I am so proud of you. You have nothing to be sorry for. These animals will pay. Jamil will make them pay, and if not Jamil, then someone else. Be at peace Hana, you have done nothing that needs forgiveness. We love you." Her mother said almost pleading with Hana to look at her.

But Hana kept her eyes firmly fixed on the floor.

Ria, tears blurring her vision but still unable to fully cry, heard a clipping noise and turned towards the woman. The woman must have opened the gun holster on her thigh and was now pointing a large gun at Ria's head.

"Enough of this emotional drama!" she snapped. "Soldier, hand me your side-arm. Come on, hurry up" the woman instructed the soldier nearest her. "We don't have much time."

The soldier handed the woman his gun. She took it from him, and they all watched as the woman removed a long piece and removed a lot of bullets. She showed Ria the one remaining bullet before closing it and clicking it back into the gun.

"We only need one bullet, Ria." The woman said as she looked up at Ria.

16

The woman looked at her watch again, moved closer to Ria and turned to the soldier next to her.

"Hold out her arm and keep it held up. When I give her the gun. Keep a strong grip on her arm so she cannot move it herself." The woman instructed the soldier.

The soldier put one arm on Ria just below her elbow and placed his other hand nearer her wrist. His hand was huge and felt very strong. Ria was sure he could have broken her arm like a twig. The woman held out the gun with the sole bullet in it to Ria.

"Take it" she ordered.

Ria shook her head. "No."

"No? You defy me? Take the gun now. Do it now or your sister and your mother will die, your mother first." the woman said.

"We will all die anyway." Ria replied.

"You can't be sure of that Ria." The woman replied.

Ria hesitated, then held out her trembling hand, palm turned upwards. The woman placed the gun on it. Immediately Ria felt the weight of the gun on her hand and would have let it fall had the soldier not been as quick to support her hand. The gun felt cold, heavy, and alien.

"Now Ria, take it and hold it like this." The woman demonstrated with her own gun, and the soldier helped Ria grip the gun correctly and hold it steady.

Ria could not hold it up on her own. It was too heavy, or she was too weak.

"Help her." The woman said impatiently to the soldier who placed his hand under Ria's.

"Now put your finger on the trigger, like this." The woman said to Ria, stepping out of her line of sight. "Soldier. Keep her arm up and your hand on her gun hand." she commanded. "We don't want any accidents!"

"Ria dear, we don't have time for a full class on guns. Remember I gave you a choice to make before, and you chose. Now, you just have to make one more. The last one I promise, but also the most important choice you'll ever make. You get to play God for a few minutes. There is only one bullet left in that gun. You saw me take all the other bullets out. I told you that I would let you go. I know you don't believe me, but it is true. You are of no use to me now. I will let you go, and one other member of your family. But only one. You must choose whether it is your mother or your sister who leaves with you. But I told you before. There is a price for freedom, and s*omeone* must pay for what your brother has done. So, you, and only you, must put a bullet in the head of the person you choose to leave behind." She smiled and continued "If you do not do as I say, my men will kill all three of you, slowly, we still have 45 minutes or so before we have to leave. My men can do a lot in that time. Now, Ria, what would be the point of that? Why let the three of you die when only one of you needs to?"

She stopped. "Translate for the mother."

Ria struggled to take in what she was saying. It was too much. She understood the woman's words but not what she was asking her to do. She looked at her mother. Her mother's face was white. She looked shocked and angry.

"No!" Ria said.

Her legs were shaking. Her arm was shaking even more, the exhaustion and pain from being tied and now this heavy, metal weight. She stared back at the woman. She could feel the soldier's body pressing into her.

"You are a liar. I chose before and you did the opposite." Ria said. "Why should I believe you now?"

Ria tried to move her arm to point the gun at the woman, but the soldier easily stopped her from moving, her arm like a feather in his.

The woman laughed again. "Really Ria? Do you take me for a fool? You will not decide, is that what you are saying? Then, you are still deciding. By not choosing, you still choose. You choose that all three of you die. That will be your choice, Ria. You are a coward, like your terrorist brother, who we *will* find." The woman said.

"I will not do it." Ria said slowly. Everything seemed slowed down now. "You will kill us all anyway and if you think I would kill my mother or my sister, then as my mother says, you are a sick and evil woman. No, you are crazy!" Ria spat.

Ria noticed that being called sick bothered the woman somehow. But the woman was right. If she chose not to pull the trigger, it was still a choice, and they would all die.

139

Her mother spoke. "Ria, do as she says. Choose to take Hana out of here with you. Maybe she is lying, and if so, we will all die. But you have nothing to lose by trying. We will die anyway. I have lived a good life and a much longer one than you both. I will gladly give up my life for just the smallest of chances that this evil viper will let you and your sister go. Do what she says to me. I love you both so much. If there is a chance, no matter how small that she lets you go, you must take it. It is a terrible choice she forces on you, so it is not a choice my child. She knows that. But you know her by now. Remember, you will be doing it for me because I want you to. I will die happy knowing that you and Hana may live. If one of you died, I would not want to live. Do you understand that my brave daughter? I will go in the comfort that Jamil will avenge my death for everything she has done to you both today." Her mother said, eyes pleading with Ria.

Ria turned to face her. "No, Mama. No. I cannot do that. Jamil? This is all his fault. If he was here now, this would be easy! I would choose *him*. NO. I cannot shoot you. I would rather die. I will not murder my own *mother or my sister*."

Ria was crying now, and her hand holding the gun was shaking so much that soldier had to work to steady it.

"Enough of this childish snivelling, and all this emotional bullshit. Ria, this is adult time. You know what to do. I give you my word that I will let two of you go, you are of no use to us, and we have to go. I can't speak for your friends in the military, however. My man will point the gun first at your mother, then at your sister, but you must pull the trigger yourself and shoot one of them. It has to be you. My man will not. If you do not shoot one of them, you know what will happen." She nodded at the soldier. "Do it."

Ria looked at Hana, Hana nodded to Ria. Ria let her bladder go and felt the sudden warm, damp between her legs.

The soldier effortlessly moved Ria's arm to point the gun at her mother, she tried to resist the movement, but he was so strong it was pointless. Her mother was almost close enough to touch with the gun. He positioned Ria's arm so that the gun barrel pointed directly at her mother's head. It was only Ria's finger on the trigger though.

"Do it Ria!" Her mother commanded fiercely.

Ria just stared at her shaking her head, tears streaming down her face.

"Well, not your mother then. Are you sure, Ria?" The woman sneered. "Change!" she instructed the soldier.

The soldier edged her forward, closer to where Hana was. This was the closest she had been to Hana since they had been running terrified across the dusty hills. Her mind was filled with nothing as she looked at her young sister, but her heart broke at what she saw, and then rage surged through her. She felt a deep sadness within for her sister and that rage that had been building up in her from her hatred of the woman and the men who had raped and beaten Hana.

Could she let them all die? The woman had not respected her 'choice' before so why should she believe her? The woman had no reason to release any of them and even if she did, the military would kill them, or worse. Ria knew they were all going to die. She was not going to kill her own family. Let the soldiers kill them. But they wouldn't just kill them, they would rape them first. They would rape her. They would rape her mother and maybe even Hana again. No way. She could not let that happen. They would rape them, beat them, then finally kill them. As the woman had said forty-five minutes was a long time. She could not let Hana go through all that again, or her own mother, she herself did not have the strength to go through it, she knew that. But she could not pull the trigger either. She felt as if the gun was about to slide out of her clammy hand.

"Hurry up!" The woman said, startling her and making her jerk the gun.
The soldier pulled her arm up until the gun was trained on Hana's head, mere inches away.

"Ria." Hana said. "I know this is an impossible situation for you, but I cannot take any more. Please, Ria. Do it. I do not want to live, even if she is not lying, and believe me she is lying. She will not let us go and I cannot... you know, I just cannot take any more of this." Hana said calmly. Ria saw her sister's despair and fear.

"No, Ria!" her mother shouted in warning.

"Ria. Do it or you all die!" shouted the woman. "That I guarantee you. Slowly and horribly too, I assure you!"

Then all the voices dulled and became distant and muffled. Ria's mind emptied and all she could hear was a loud ringing sound in her ears. She felt a fog-like feeling

fill her mind. She was frozen in time, standing there all alone, just her and this heavy gun. So heavy. She could see someone there in front of her. No-one else was in the room now. Her finger tightened around the trigger. It was cold and stiff, and she was weak, but she gritted her teeth and with all her strength managed to pull the trigger in all the way. A loud blast burst in her eardrums, and she felt a sharp pain shoot up her arm to her shoulder, knocking her backwards into the soldier's body. She watched in slow motion as her sister's face exploded open, her blood splatter out in all directions, she felt a sticky wetness like drops of rain hit her face. Then the blood stopped spouting and turned into a slow, steady drip that began to form a pool of blood on the floor. Ria stared at it, not comprehending what had happened but knowing that Hana was now gone.
No-one moved or said a word.
The soldier took the gun from Ria. Her trembling arm dropped down by her side. She couldn't take her eyes off the pool of Hana's blood. She didn't want to look at her sister. She heard sounds in the distance though the blast of the gun was still pounding in her ears drowning out everything else.

"Ria, Ria, RIA!" She heard someone calling and looked up. She saw the woman standing there opening and closing her mouth.

"RIA!" the woman shouted, and Ria felt a slap across her face. The sound in her ears stopped and Ria turned towards the woman who had just hit her and stared at her.

The woman hesitated. The room was silent. Ria stared at her. She could hear her mother screaming at her behind her. She would not look at her, but she could hear her mother's words. She flinched at them. The woman was about to say something, her mouth opened but she was interrupted by a very high-pitched siren sounding.

"The air strikes, they must be early. We have to go. Leave them here. Come on!" The woman shouted and turned to run.

The sound was so loud that it was unbearable. Instinctively she put her arm over her face to protect herself as she a large orange and black fireball blast in through the outer wall. She felt herself being propelled backwards and was briefly aware of her body hitting something hard.

Then nothing.

17

The rain was belting down so hard now that Ria could barely even look up to check where she was without it blasting into her eyes. She knew where she was going but the pavements were crowded, and navigating her way was made more difficult by this dark, moonless evening. It was a bad thunderstorm. The weather in this place felt so alien to her. She could not remember a day when she had seen the sun. It was all just constant greyness and cold.

She pushed on forward through the crowd, drenched. Her socks squelched in her boots, but she didn't care. The people she passed in the street wielded their umbrellas against the wind like shields as they rushed in and out of buildings, shops, cafés, cars and buses. People here were always rushing.

The crowd of people thinned as she crossed to the other side of the busy road. She walked briskly towards the bridge. It was the only place she liked in this unfamiliar city. There were no lovers embracing on the bridge this evening. As she moved across it, she smiled as the wind howled and swirled around her, it made her feel alive. She walked to her favourite spot near the centre of the bridge and beside one of the large stone columns. There was always some shelter there, though not much. Anyway, it was not shelter she sought. The rain came down even harder, but it didn't matter.

She turned to face out from the bridge, her fingers spread out over the cold, wet stone. She steadied herself, bracing against the strong headwind. She stared out into the darkness at nothing and just let herself feel the full force of the ice-cold rain and wind on her face. It was a feeling, fleeting but real.

She looked down. The bridge stood high above the river. She knew the river was very deep and fast-moving, even though she could not see it now in the dark. The bridge was lit up to look enhance its beauty, but the water below her always felt dark and ominous. She came here every evening at the same time, just before she had to return to the centre. She never missed a night. She would often come during the daytime as well. There wasn't much else for her to do in this city. But boredom was not the reason she came here. Each night she would stand in the exact same spot on the bridge and let herself feel the elements. She would feel herself drawn to the water below but feel no fear of its pull on her. She looked down at it now, barely able to make out the dark moving mass of water far below her. It sounded gorged by the rain and ran fierce under the bridge. Such power.

146

Do it. It was never a voice she heard in her head, and more like an urge than a thought. It will be quick tonight. It's dark, no-one will see. The usual urge seemed stronger tonight than other nights. She wondered why. She leaned a bit over the wall of the bridge. It would be so simple to just let herself fall over and be swept away. That is what she wanted, to just disappear and exist no more. She wanted that more than anything so why did she not do it then? It was never the right night. Excuses she told herself.

She spent a long time staring down into the darkness, then sighed and looked up. She was such a coward. She stood there aware now that she was shivering from the wet and cold. She checked her phone and saw it was time to go. She turned back with that same feeling of dread she had every evening and walked slowly off the bridge and headed back towards the centre. It was almost time for curfew, and this was no night to get into trouble.
She quickened her pace and arrived at the main gate of the detention centre five minutes before it would close until the next morning.

"You are very wet!" The security guard said to her in his strongly accented English.
She ignored him and pushed the reception control doors open. Stating the obvious was not worthy of any vocal effort on her part. She was blinded by the fluorescent lighting, sharply contrasting with the darkness outside. She could never get used to everything being so brightly lit, and it was as if these bright lights tugged at something in her memory.

"Ria, you almost didn't make the curfew again. You have to be more careful. You know what happens if you miss it." The thin man dressed in a green shirt and white trousers behind the glass reception counter said in a disapproving tone. "Don't cut it so fine again. You can't afford to."

She threw him a withering stare and waited to sign in while he noted her arrival time and name on the reception computer. Control was everything to them.

"Naira was taken to the hospital while you were gone, so she won't be in your room." He said.

"What happened?" Ria asked, alarmed.

"You know. The same as usual." He replied.

No, she didn't know.

"You can go." He said, dismissing her coldly.

Ria walked down the long corridor, hurrying now after the news about Naira. She stopped outside the door marked number seventy-seven, hesitated, then opened it and went in. The room was brightly lit by two fluorescent strips on the ceiling. No matter how many times she entered, she was always struck by the strange smell of the room. A smell she could never quite place. Perhaps it was the smell of too many humans packed together too tightly. Or more likely it was the smell of the collective suffering the detention centre held, and not just her room.

Ria looked over the room, at the two sets of bunk beds one set on each side of the small room, the tiny sink, and the cheap wooden table and four matching chairs. There was barely enough space to move around when she was alone, let alone when all four of them were in there. There were no windows, just a very small vent at the top of the wall. She could never manage to breathe properly in this room, her chest always tightened up as soon as she entered, and she would not feel better until she left again. Every night she would count down the hours until she could leave the next morning.

Two women were sitting on the floor. One of them was feeding a young baby. It was Naira's baby Khal.

"What happened to Naira?" Ria asked as she took off her wet boots, shed her drenched outer clothing and changed into a dry tracksuit.

She absently watched the puddle of water quickly form on the dark green painted floor and went to get a cloth.

Fatima looked up and made a cutting gesture on her wrists. Ria was shocked, she felt sad but was surprised that she felt angry too.

"What do you mean?" Ria said knowing what she meant.

"She did the same thing as the last time. The ambulance came and the medical people bandaged her up and then they took her away. The cleaners came after to clean up all the blood." Fatima said nodding towards Naira's empty bunk.

"What do you mean?" Ria asked. "The same as last time?"

Ria looked at Fatima, who started to cry. "It is the second time she has tried. The first time was before you came."

"Fatima, stop it." Ria snapped. Fatima looked up her eyes filled with tears, looking hurt.

149

"What are you crying for? It is Naira that is hurt." Ria said.

"Ria, stop!" the other woman Adela said. "Fatima is upset. It is normal to cry."

"I know, but just stop, please Fatima. Crying won't do anyone any good here." Ria said harshly and climbed up onto the top bunk.

Hers was the one furthest away from the door and against the wall. Her bunk was over Naira's. She lay there tense, eyes wide open. As usual, she felt no tiredness at all, but her body felt heavy. She stared up at the grey ceiling, seeing it but not seeing it, waiting for the long night to begin.

Why the hell couldn't Naira get it right? Twice she had tried. Ria had had no idea. Why couldn't Ria let herself go over the bridge into the river? At least Naira had the courage to try. Ria hoped she was okay but knew that if she had tried to kill herself, she couldn't be. How could Ria not have noticed that something was wrong? Naira had seemed fine when she had last seen her that morning.

The black river came back into her mind with more force. She tried to focus on it to shut out the chatter of the women and the squealing baby.

Ria had been in the detention centre for two long months by now.

18

Naira's child cried all night despite the efforts of the other women in the room to soothe him. Maybe he needed his mother. Ria didn't care about not sleeping. She never slept. It was the relentless screaming that riled her. At last, it was morning. Ria got up, changed, put on her boots, picked up her battered rucksack and jacket and left the room without saying a word to the others. As she walked along the corridor towards the exit of the detention centre, she felt her body grow tense as the sounds of the centre's morning activity assaulted her senses. Crying children, mothers shouting over them, the loud hum of a lot of people talking at once in a million different languages and the slam of pots and plates as breakfast was prepared in the canteen. It was all too much. She quickened her step. As she neared the reception control area, she passed an open room and caught a glimpse of a young girl aged about six or seven sitting on a bottom bunk just staring into space. Ria saw the girl's expression and flinched.

"What, no breakfast again? Is our food not good enough for you?" Karine, the woman at the control desk, said sarcastically to Ria as soon as she saw her.

Ria picked up the grimy pen attached to the desk by a dirty chord and signed her name and the time in the 'out' column. All of the 'ins and 'outs' of everybody in the detention centre were monitored. You did not have to account for what you did between those two points of time, but every single coming and going was recorded. Why they did that Ria did not know, they were not prisoners. Or were they? From some of the stories she had heard from the women who had been in the centre longer than her, most of the people here had risked life and limb to get here so why would they leave? It seemed like a stupid system. And so what if they did leave?

Karine was unpleasant and downright mean to everyone, but Ria had observed her enough about her by now to have noticed that the amount of cruelty she dished out was based on skin colour tone. It did not matter if the darkest woman in the centre was the nicest, most compliant woman of all. That was immaterial to Karine. The darkest-coloured women in the centre received the worst treatment and deprivations for no other reason than the insolence of their blackness. Ria was dark, but not like the women from African countries. They really got treated badly by Karine and many others on the staff too. But the African women were fierce and most of them could give back as good as they got without jeopardising their status. Why they had put an outright racist like Karine in a centre like this was beyond Ria.

When Ria was first brought here to the detention centre two months ago, a man who had not bothered to introduce himself to her had carried out what he had called her 'initial intake assessment'. He had informed her that she would be staying in the detention centre while her 'case was being reviewed.' The intake process had taken half a day and involved him filling out endless forms and her having to respond to a battery of questions that ranged from the obscure to the extremely personal. There were strange questions too about her family and friends and her life before.

No matter what the question, or the answer she gave, Ria noticed that the man's tone never once changed, and he never really looked at her. His tone was cold and dispassionate. Ria had felt extremely uncomfortable throughout the whole process, and strangely ashamed. The room she had been questioned in had been small and brightly lit. What had affected Ria most apart from his tone was his body language. It was the body language of boredom, distaste, and indifference. At times, he reacted with an ever so slight raising of an eyebrow that communicated disbelief. At each raised eyebrow, she would make her answers shorter or more ambiguous or she would get flustered. She felt as if she were on trial. She had not even come her herself so that irony was not lost on her. She told him very little, mainly because she didn't know much herself.

After her first few weeks in this migrant detention centre, she had found out from speaking to other women that this 'intake process' was far worse for the women coming from some of the African countries than for people like Ria. This man, Karine, and so many others on the staff, were convinced that if they were from any African country, then that meant that they were here for jobs, not fleeing a war or worse. The staff believed that these women should not have come, should not be there and they were afforded no benefit of the doubt whatsoever. No one was really unless they were fleeing a 'good' war. A 'good' war, Ria had come to understand was one that the West was sympathetic to, not the ones they caused. Of those, Ria saw, nothing was said.

One Congolese woman told Ria that Karine had referred to 'her kind' as swarming rats, bringing their disgusting diseases and dirty habits into their fine country, bringing down the level. It wasn't just Karine either. A lot of the staff working in the centre referred to the African women as parasites. The women heard the staff saying these kinds of things when they talked amongst themselves in their own language thinking that the women didn't understand them. Ria had seen that these women were machines with languages. In a very short time, Ria did not understand how, they would master the language of this country easily and spoke many other languages too, but they would never let on to the staff or authorities that they spoke it. Ria did not bother with this language; it was of no use to her. She would not be here long.

Ria was categorised as being 'from the Middle East' which put Ria in an extremely broad category that existed she imagined only to make things easier for Europeans. That way they did not have to make the effort to understand the huge differences between one country and another. Easier, just like they did with Africa to lump all the different countries and cultures together as if they were one and the same. Ria's category of course meant that she was placed in the "potential terrorist" category by Karine and many others, something which was fed by the constant reports of terrorist attacks fed to the west by the media. The only advantage of that category for Ria was that Karine was more scared of Ria than of the African women. Ria found that mildly amusing and used it to her advantage to punish Karine for her treatment of the others.

Ria threw the pen on the clipboard after signing out and left the building. It was raining yet again but today at least there was less wind, and the rain was lighter. How she missed the sun and the warmth of her own country. Ria did not understand how anyone could be happy in this constant greyness. She walked for about an hour, crossing the city, taking her time. She had so much time on her hands now and so little to do with it that it was frustrating. The migrant detention centre was on the outskirts of the city. Ria guessed it was deliberate. She couldn't imagine people from this city wanting it anywhere near where they lived. Out of sight was out of mind, Ria thought. Despite the distance, and the dismal weather, she always enjoyed this walk. It was the only time she felt a little lighter, freer, and she relished being alone.

She stopped in front of a large block of apartments and pressed a button on the intercom panel. The front door buzzed open in response. There was a lift, but she opted for the stairs as usual. She did not like the panicked feeling she experienced in lifts. There was a slight smell of dampness in the stairwell contrasting with the freshness of the air during her walk and the damp tickled the back of her throat. When she got to the fourth floor, slightly out of breath, one of the four doors was slightly ajar, so she pushed it open and walked in.

She was met by the familiar smell of strong coffee and warmth. She smiled slightly to herself as she took off her wet coat and hung it to dry.

"Wet again I'm sorry." Ria said to the dark-haired woman who had got up from the table and come to kiss Ria on both cheeks.

"Of course. Every day here rain, then more rain. Do they even have a sun?" Shabana asked laughing and threw her hands up in the air dramatically. "Come. The coffee is just about ready, and we've got fresh bread. Omar will be ready soon. I hope." She joked. "Now, Ria, get out of those wet boots and socks, I'll put them to dry while we have breakfast. I'll get you some dry socks."

Ria took off her wet boots and socks and put on the thick pair of socks Shabana handed her. They felt warm and comforting. She sat down opposite Shabana at the table. Shabana poured her some coffee. Ria cupped the hot coffee in her hands and sipped it. She almost felt good.

Shabana gestured to the basket of bread. "Eat!" It was a command.

Ria didn't feel hungry but took a piece of the bread rather than hear another sermon and spread one of the pastes on it.

"Naira tried to kill herself yesterday before I got back." Ria said after her first piece of bread.

She was hungry after all. She took another piece.

Shabana picked up her pack of cigarettes, sighed and lit one. "The poor thing. Is she okay? Where did they take her?"

"I don't know how to find out. Do you know? They left her child with the women." Ria said.

"I'll help you. I know my way around the hospitals." Shabana said. "And I'm not working today."

"When is your next appointment with your case officer?" Shabana asked.

"On Monday. I hope he has news. It's so slow. I just want to go home. Why is that so difficult? I am not their prisoner, but they act like I am. They complain that we are here, but then won't let me go back!" Ria said.

"Yes, I know, it must be frustrating. My family and I arrived in different times. Times when there were fewer migrants and a lot more compassion. It was an awful time though. Not just the waiting for the outcome of the asylum process so much, but more the way the bureaucrats here behaved, how they treated us. I was young but I still remember that. But it's worse now, sadly. Today, their default position is to not believe what the refugees and asylum seekers tell them. They make them repeat their stories so many times and you know people do not want to talk about the terrible things they've been through, over and over to people who don't believe them. People who think they are lying and press them for even more details. It is very traumatising for people coming from terrible situations to be met with such cold distrust." She paused and seemed to go briefly to another place.

"They make them prove over and over that they have been through enough horror to deserve the privilege of being allowed to stay in their precious country. The people here in Europe just can't understand what it is like to have to leave your own country. Worse still they don't even try to understand. There is no curiosity about other countries or cultures. We are all assumed to be ignorant. Our education and qualifications are considered inferior or invalid and our work experience doesn't count. My father always used to say that in his case they were never searching for the truth, it was always the lie they wanted to find. I think today that is even more true." Shabana sighed and picked up another cigarette and lit it.

"Yes, that is it exactly." Ria said nodding. She had been so lucky to have met Shabana and Omar. They were her salvation, her only escape from the misery of the detention centre.

Ria had noticed the flash of pain that had darkened Shabana's expression as she spoke, but Ria did not want to probe, unsure whether Shabana wanted to speak to her about her past. Shabana brightened as Omar burst into the room, all energy and noise, as was Omar.

Ria started in her seat. She never got used to how dramatically he entered rooms. Her heartbeat quickened. Omar came up to the table and hugged Ria, beaming. Ria tensed. She hated hugs.

"Ria! You are here, my dear. I was making myself handsome for work. You know how it is. Any sight of even a little hair on my face and the people from here get frightened." He laughed and Ria smiled.

Shabana got up and went over to straighten his shirt, which looked creased over his shoulders.

"You dress like a teenager, not a man." Shabana said laughing.

"That is because you make me feel like a teenager my love." He joked back. "Now Ria, tell me, is it my fault if this woman makes me feel like a crazy teenager?"

Ria smiled again. "Of course not, Omar! The state of your shirt is Shabana's fault!"

"Omar, go. You cannot be late again. You must go. You know what they are like if you are late. They like to give out warnings and we need this job. Now go!" Shabana said making sweeping gestures with her hands as if shooing a cat.

Omar kissed her on the lips, waved to Ria and left, leaving a wave of turbulence in his wake. Shabana tutted in disapproval, but Ria could see the smile in her eyes. It always made Ria happy to see them together.

"Now that he has finally left the bathroom, it's all yours Ria. Take your time. Every day you rush. Why? You must take this time for yourself away from that place. The shower can be a way of cleansing it from you, for a few hours at least. It is important to take some space and time for yourself. You are still recovering from your injury. I'll be here cleaning up the dishes and reading so don't rush. Then we can go and look for Naira if you want. If they have taken her to hospital she is being looked after so there is no rush. We are not her family so it will not be possible to see her, but maybe we can get some information. I know you are worried, but another hour will not make any difference."

"You and Omar ... you know... I'm so grateful... I..." Ria felt tears hover dangerously, so she quickly picked up her coffee cup and put it on the counter, her back turned to Shabana. Then she walked quickly into the bathroom.

The bathroom was old, but it smelled good, Omar's aftershave lingered, and she loved the smell of soap and different scents that Shabana kept. She undressed, making sure her back was turned to the long mirror that stood propped up in the corner of the bathroom and stepped into the shower as she had done every morning except Sundays for the last two months.

19

A few hours later Ria and Shabana stood in front of a busy hospital reception desk. It was the third and last emergency ward left to check in the city. The phones were constantly ringing.

Finally, the tall, brown-haired woman turned to them. "Can I help you?" she asked. She was unsmiling, and looked stern and flustered, and from her expression it was clear to Ria that the last thing she wanted to do was deal with them.

"We are looking for a friend. We share a room with her at one of the migrant centres. She attempted suicide last night. She has no family here. She is not from here. Her name is Naira Milna." Ria said quickly but smoothly, it was the third time she'd repeated it.

"I don't know if that person is in this hospital, and I cannot tell you even if she was. If you are not family, we cannot give out confidential information about patients to non-authorised family. It is the law." The woman said tersely as she shuffled some papers and looked agitated as the phone started ringing again.

"Look, if your friend survived, and she is in this hospital, only authorised family members can visit, and even then, in those cases, sometimes not even the family can get information unless the patient authorises it." She turned away from them, dismissing them with a sweep of her hand as she poised to answer one of the phones.

Ria felt angry. Shabana seemed to sense her anger and stepped over moving Ria gently away from the window and leaned against the smudged plastic wall with its small hole to speak through.

"Madam, excuse me. We have already been to all of the other hospitals." Shabana's voice sounded so calm and authoritative. "We are just so worried about her. She is a migrant. She has no family here, but she has a young child. He needs to know his mother is okay. Wouldn't you want him to know that his mother was okay, that she was well, and where she was?" Shabana was appealing to the woman's compassion.

The woman kept on staring at the screen in front of her, juggling screens and phones.

"I cannot help you. There are rules, and the rules are stricter in cases like these. If your friend cared so much about the boy... well... " the woman said staring at Shabana.

Ria fuming and pushed her way back in front of the glass panel

"Rules? Since I have been here, I have seen but all your rules and regulations. But what I haven't seem much of is compassion." Ria said, voice raised now.

Shabana drew Ria aside and whispered.

"Ria, people are staring. I know you're angry and worried, but shouting at this woman is not going to get us anywhere. It will just make her more angry and less likely to help. Why don't you go outside. You can call Fatima and see if there is any news back at the centre and while you are out there, please go and get us some coffee. Here. Take this." She handed Ria some money. "I'll try to speak to this woman while you are gone."

Ria hesitated "No. I'm not leaving. Fatima will not know anything. They won't tell her anything. Anyway, she would have phoned me by now if she knew anything." Ria stopped. "But okay, I get your point." Ria stared at the woman behind the desk and took the money from Shabana.

"Please, Ria. Let me do this." Shabana's tone was firm, but not angry.

Ria nodded, smiled briefly and strode off still fuming but knowing that Shabana was right. She went outside and looked around for a café. There were as usual a lot of places, so she called Fatima first.

Fatima answered straight away. Ria could hear the baby screaming in the background.

"Fatima! I'm at one of the hospitals. Have you heard anything?"

"Have you found her? Is she okay?" Fatima asked.

"No, not yet. You know what they are like. I am at the last hospital now. They won't give out any details because I am not family. I am here with my friend Shabana. She knows the system so she will try to at least find out if she is here. Have you heard anything? Fatima, why did you not call me yesterday to tell me about Naira?"

Fatima was silent for a while and then spoke.

"Adela saw her case worker this morning so she asked her if she could find out something about Naira. The case worker called one of her doctor friends from the centre who said she didn't know much but that what she had heard was not good. She said she'd heard that Naira was alive, and that she will live. Khal will not stop screaming Ria, it is as if he knows something is wrong. We have tried everything. He needs her. We had no credit on the phones to call you yesterday Ria and there was no time. I am sorry. It all happened so fast and then I had to take care of Khal, the police came then and the state of the place… there was no time. And anyway, what could you have done? We knew you'd be back."

Ria sighed.

"But Ria, there is more information. Someone came about an hour ago. it's not good. You know one of those authorities, a social worker or something similar, I think. They were talking with one of the staff and one of my friends overheard them saying they would come to take the baby away later on today. Then, then one of the staff came about an hour ago and told us to get Khal ready. They said to gather all his stuff, and make sure that he was clean. As if he was dirty! He is not dirty. Just sad and angry."

"Take him? Take him where? Why?" Ria asked, anger increasing.

"Well, they did not explain that to us, did they? But one of the women heard one of the staff say that it was because his mother could not take care of him, that this was the second time she had tried to kill herself, so that meant they had to take him. We would take care of him, Ria. They don't need to take him. I told the staff that after they came to tell us to get him ready, but they just said to have him ready by five this afternoon. I don't know, maybe it is better Ria, better for him. She will try to do it again. I know she will."

"You don't know that. We need to speak to Naira. I didn't know she had done it before. You should have told me. She seemed okay. I don't understand. I'll be back before they come. I promise." Ria hung up and went towards the café to get the coffees.

Ria pushed open the door. It was full of people sitting around at tables, busy on their phones or on computers, all tapping frantically away. What were they all doing on here at this time of the day? What were they tapping about? Why weren't they at work?
She joined the long queue, her rage simmering at this news about Naira's baby. The server was extremely slow, and she felt like screaming at him. She tried to do what Shabana kept telling her to do, count backwards from ten and breathe in deeper breaths. It never worked. She had never once made it back from ten or been able to breathe deep breaths. She hated the exercise.
Eventually, it was her turn.

The man-boy who served her made her repeat her order several times as he seemed incapable of understanding her English. She didn't speak the language here. He hadn't had any problem with the tourists in front of her who had ordered in English. He had understood them perfectly well. Her order was hardly complicated. When she spoke English, she had an accent, of course, but Shabana understood her perfectly, and so did everyone in the centre. She had done well at English at university, she remembered that much, and it had improved with practice since she had been here. The man looked at her as if she were a lower life form or maybe she was imagining that.

Shabana said she had to get used to that look and that there was no point in reacting to it. But she could not get used to it.

Finally, her name was shouted out and she took the two very hot take-away cups back towards the main entrance to the hospital, pushing the doors open carefully with her shoulder, trying not to spill any of the hot liquid over her.

Shabana was deep in conversation with the woman behind the desk who to Ria's amazement was smiling. Ria stood there in awe and then approached.

"Here you go," said Ria.

"Here, we got you a coffee. We thought maybe with all your hard work, you have not yet had time for a break. And it is, of course, coffee time!"

"Oh, you are a lifesaver. Thank you so much. Is it not always coffee time?" the woman joked. "That's so kind of you, Shabana, thank you. We are always so short on staff, there's too much to do." She said.

Ria, not for the first time, marvelled at Shabana. What the hell had she said? She had only left her for twenty minutes.

"Well, we will let you enjoy the coffee and be off. Take care." Shabana said cheerily, waving as she ushered Ria outside.

"Come on, there's a park over there, let's go and drink our coffee there. It's not raining for once and the fresh air will do us good." Shabana said. "But we need to get another coffee first."

Ria looked up and saw the park across the road. Everything was so glaringly green here, almost too green for the eyes. All this green growth was so effortless here. Not like home.

"It's okay, I don't want one. Let's just go. What did you find out?" Ria answered.

They walked over to the park and sat on the first unoccupied bench. Ria still found it strange that people here sat in parks despite the freezing cold.

"Well? Did your new friend at reception give you any information about Naira?" Ria asked her.

"Not much, but she did confirm that she was there. She's alive she said she would be okay. She is still in intensive care. It was a close call though she said. Her friend, who is a nurse, was on the emergency shift when they brought Naira in. Her friend said that normally in those cases Naira will have to a psychiatric evaluation and depending on that she could be kept in a psychiatric hospital under observation. Especially if it's not her first time. She said they wouldn't let her go back to the centre until they were sure she wouldn't do it again. She told me they get someone like Naira almost every night coming in from the different centres. It's terrible." Shabana finished and sipped her coffee looking very sad.

Ria said nothing, staring ahead at nothing. She understood perfectly well why they would get people like Naira in every night from the centres.

"Well? You don't sound very happy. That is what you wanted to hear, isn't it? We found her and she is alive." Shabana touched her gently on the shoulder. "She will get help now."

"Of course, it's just that... I don't know. I know Naira is complicated but, in the centre, she is my only real friend. If she does not return....I suppose I am just worried and being selfish. But mostly worried. Then there is the matter of her baby." Ria said.

"I called Fatima. She told me that the social worker people are going to take her child away today. They say Naira is not a good mother for him. Fatima said she would look after him until Naira got back, but they refused." Ria said.

"Well, at least they won't be sent back Ria, and I suppose legally they can't just leave a child alone in the centre without his mother," Shabana said softly.

"What's that supposed to mean? He's not alone!" Ria asked a bit sharply. "Sent back? Having a child has not stopped them from sending people back before. I have heard terrible stories, and I doubt that will be any consolation for Naira, Shabana. She will just be in one prison, and her son in another. That is what this means, does it not?"

Shabana looked unsure of what to say. An awkward silence now between them.

"They might let you visit her when she is feeling better. Look, I understand that you are sad and worried."

"Better? Ria snapped "Shabana, you are starting to sound like them. How could anyone *feel* better here?"

"Omar and I are better here, Ria. The boy will be better here too Ria, he's still so young. Do you think it is good for children to grow up in wars, around bombs and death or worse? He will not remember this part of his life much. There are plenty good women here who would adopt the boy. Young babies always get adopted fast, even if they are not white. He could go to a really good home and have a good future here. Surely a better one than Naira can offer him. I am not speaking badly of Naira, just thinking of what is best for the baby. He is only nine months old Ria and Naira has attempted suicide twice already you say, and this time...well she was almost succeeded. What sort of life is that for a baby?"

Ria regretted snapping at Shabana, but she couldn't apologise.

"He might not remember, Shabana, but Naira will. How could *she* forget? What if taking her child away from her makes her want to do it again even more!" Ria said looking off into the distance.

Shabana said nothing more and they sat there in silence.

20

"Ria?" Shabana said.

"Yes, sorry. What did you say?" Ria asked her neck feeling hot.

"Where did you go just now?" Shabana asked gently.

"Go? What do you mean? No. I'm just a little tired you know and thinking about Naira." Ria replied.

"I was asking how you've been sleeping and what you have been doing?" Shabana said.

"Nothing, there is nothing to do in the centre, I find every day endless you know, just waiting and waiting." Ria said.

"What are you waiting for?" Shabana asked.

"You know what. I'm waiting to be released from the centre so I can finally go home. I don't understand why they are keeping me here. What right to they have?" Ria said. "I just want to go home." Ria paused to calm herself. "Shabana, I am not like the other women in the centre who want to stay here or move on to some other country. I want to leave here and go back home. That is also what the authorities and the people here all want us to do – go back. I don't get it." Ria said.

"Yes, I have to admit it is strange that it is taking so long." Shabana said. "But getting frustrated isn't going to help anything."

"Would it not make you frustrated to be held prisoner against your will?" Ria asked.

"It would. Has anything else happened in the centre apart from Naira to upset you?" Shabana asked.

"No. I am always upset am I not?" Ria replied.

"Not always, but yes, mostly." Shabana joked, but then her expression changed. "It's terrible don't you think what that receptionist said about the hospital receiving attempted suicides from the detention centres every night. People have been through such terrible things but still that amount of people trying to kill themselves, now that's worrying" Shabana said. "Do they offer mental health services at your centre?"

"Some people go I think, if you have a mental illness or something. I don't know. I have never asked, and I have never been offered any. No-one speaks of such things. We just get a doctor if we are sick and our case worker."

"I think that everyone in these centres should have access to a therapist. No-one has come here without something bad happening to them."

"Except me." Ria said.

"Well, you don't know that. You only remember waking up in the hospital and then being taken to the centre a month after. So, you don't know what happened to you. Is your head injury not bad enough by itself not to mention your memory loss from the injury? How is it now? Any change?" Shabana asked.

"No," said Ria shaking her head. "But I feel really bad inside all the time, it's not my head and I can never sleep."

"When you say you feel bad, what do you mean?" Shabana asked, turning to look at Ria beside her on the bench.

"Bad, inside. I feel... it's hard to describe, it's a strange feeling, but not a good one. Like how you feel when you've done something wrong. Then, I always feel you know too awake all the time and very irritable. I am not a nice person to the other women in the centre." Ria hung her head in shame. "I just feel annoyed all the time at everyone, everything."

"Why?" Shabana asked.

"They just all make too much noise, and try to speak to me," Ria replied. "All the noise at the centre makes me feel... especially angry, then all those bright lights and having to sleep all of us together in those small rooms with no privacy and nothing to do."

Shabana nodded. "Are you still getting those bad headaches and nausea from your head injury?" Shabana asked.

"Some days yes, some days no. Sometimes the headaches get very bad. I have had weekly check-ups with the neurologist at the hospital where I woke up. But that's not what worries me. I don't care about my head injury or the headaches. What I want to know is how I got here. I want to know who brought me here and why. If I was in a bombing, I would not have been brought here, would I? I would have been taken to a hospital in my city, and anyway the war hadn't started by then. It makes no sense. I don't understand either where my family is. I'm really worried. It's like they have disappeared off the face of the earth. Just gone. I just can't stop thinking that something really bad has happened to them. All that stuff that we see every day on TV from home wasn't happening when I was there, I am sure of that much. I know I keep repeating the same thing over and over Shabana, but I have to go home." Ria looked up now, tone agitated.

"I understand Ria that you are worried about them. I am so sorry. It must be terrible not remembering, not knowing the answers to your questions but I think you have to be patient, the more you put pressure on yourself to remember, the longer it will take. That is what your doctor said wasn't it?" Shabana said.

"Yes." Ria answered. "She said that my scans are fine and that my memory loss is normal with such a traumatic head injury, but that I am young, and I will get stronger, and in time my memory will return," Ria said. "That's what she says. Time."

Ria continued. "You say there is no point in getting frustrated, but that's hard because I know that someone here knows the truth about how and why I came to be here. Why won't they tell me? I keep asking my case officer and writing letters to the Foreign Office but nothing." Ria said her tone rising a few notches higher. "I can't just have suddenly appeared in a hospital bed in this country. I was moved. There must be paperwork. I shouldn't have to wait for my memory to come back. Who knows how long that might take! They should tell me what they know. It is my right!" Ria said, face red now with indignation.

Shabana looked at her and touched her arm.

"Ria, I agree it is strange. But maybe they are protecting you." She said.

"Protecting me?" Ria retorted her eyebrows raised.

"Well, sometimes knowing too much too soon can be too much." Shabana said gently.

"Why?" Ria said. "What do you mean? Do you think something bad happened to me apart from my head injury?"

"How would I know?" But your country is at war and it's a terrible war, so it is possible. But, as you don't have any more information for now, just focus on getting as strong as you can." Shabana said.

"How? I am worried about my mother, my sister, and my brother. My friends. I watch the news, I see what is happening in my city, in my region. It is too horrible to watch. I cannot think of myself. Safe here, while I see what is happening in my home. It feels wrong and selfish." Ria said, hearing her irritable tone.

"You are not a prisoner here Ria, you know that. You are free to leave the centre all day. It is a migrant processing centre as you know. There are so many people coming from your own country and many other countries. I know everything is slow and frustrating. I understand." Shabana paused as if in thought. "It must be horrible, the waiting, and especially not knowing how you got here."

Then she said. "Look Ria, I know it is nearly an impossible task, but maybe it would be better if you stopped watching the news for a while and stopped checking social media on your phone. I know it's hard because news about the war in your country is everywhere, all day long. But it isn't doing you any good to think about all that now and it could be making things worse. You can't do anything about the war, and here you are safer. It is not selfish to want to feel safe, it is human. I understand how difficult it must be to not remember what happened to you but think of it as a sort of self-protection bubble. Ria, take it from me, remembering can be a terrible thing" Shabana said and paused.

Ria looked up at Shabana feeling that she hadn't yet finished. Shabana rarely spoke in this way. Remembering she supposed could be a terrible thing for some, but not for her. For Ria, not remembering was the problem.

Shabana cleared her throat. "When I first came here, I was much younger than you. I remembered everything from my country that I had to leave, my friends, neighbours, school, and I also remembered the terrible journey to get here. I wished I could forget all the bad things I witnessed, but it's impossible. Even though many years have passed, I still can't forget. I saw things a child of my age should never have seen, and those things stay with you for life." Shabana paused.

She sounded a little emotional which made Ria feel uncomfortable. Ria said nothing.

"Ria, you have been through a lot already just from what you do know! Never mind what else you might or might not have gone through or seen. Your injuries were very serious and from what they told you, it sounds like you are lucky to be alive. Did the neurologist not say it was a miracle that you survived? Is that not an amazing thing in itself, Ria?" Shabana asked turning to look at Ria. "You could have died, but against all odds, you lived." Shabana smiled.

Ria kept her gaze down, staring at her shoes.

"Shabana, I understand what you are saying, and it must have been terrible what you went through.... but I must be as honest with you as you have been with me. I do not feel lucky, and I certainly don't feel happy to have survived. I don't feel anything at all, and that's the problem." Ria said. "Nothing good anyway." Ria looked up. "It's not lucky to be kept in that dirty, crowded centre, or to be fed foreign food to a bell, like some animal. I have nothing of my own, nowhere to go and there is nothing to do all day. Then there is the curfew at night that controls us all. I would prefer to be at home, war or not, but at least back with my family and my people. There, maybe I can feel something, there I would be free."

"You may hate that centre, who wouldn't! But there are no bombs falling here every day. You are alive, and even if you say you don't *feel* alive, you are. You know better than I do that too many people in your country have not been so lucky." Shabana paused. "You could be dead Ria. What good would that do anyone?"

"You have applied for political asylum here, Ria," Shabana said. "Like we did a long time ago. Why don't you just wait and see if you get it. Be patient with yourself and the system and focus on recovering."

"You know I only put in that application because my case worker told me I had no choice as I had to have some application in to have some processing status which makes no sense as I am not allowed to leave the country.

When I ask him why I could not go back, he just says he doesn't know, but then he says it will be easy. He says it's easier to go back than to stay. I've told you this already." Ria said wearily.

"I know. So, you must accept that you can't go back…. yet… but that someday you will be able to, and when that day comes you must be well, and you must be strong. Wars are terrible things. I know you are angry, but things are nicer here in the spring, even the people, and Spring is not far off, a couple more months. The system in this country is better than in others. It could always be worse. You could be in one of the Greek Island camps, you know that. You said so yourself the last time." Shabana said and smiled.

Ria had heard some of the women telling stories in the centre about the refugee camps in Greece. She shuddered at the memories.

"You are right," Ria said, nodding slowly. "That would be much worse" She paused. "You know sometimes I can see my mother in my mind giving one of her sermons to us, and I feel happy just for a brief moment. But then, it feels dark and sometimes I see my brother and sister talking but I can't hear what they are saying…" Ria paused again unsure of whether to say it or not. She took a deep breath. "I know this sounds strange, Shabana, but I feel certain they're trying to say something to me, no, not to me, they're saying something bad *about* me, but I can't hear it. It's a feeling but this same thing has happened many times."

Ria paused and stared down at her glass feeling that all-consuming unpleasant feeling creep through her body.
Shabana took her hand, but Ria pulled it away gently.

"Why don't you ask your doctor for something to help you sleep?" Shabana said
Ria felt irritated. This was not the first time Shabana had brought this up.

"I told you. I don't want to take them. I've seen what happens to the women who take those kinds of pills. They end up needing more and more to sleep or to forget. I see them walking around half awake, half asleep. I suppose that is what they want, to forget, and the pills help. But I am trying to remember so I want to stay alert. I don't want to walk around half awake and half asleep, even more confused than I am already." Ria said, strong now, almost proud that she could do without sleep. *She had a mission.*

"Maybe you *think* you want to remember, but maybe you don't." Shabana changed the subject. "Let me ask you a question. Imagine that there *is* some bad news in your past that you can't remember. Now, imagine you have a choice to know it or not. Which would you choose?
Ria looked up at Shabana frowning. *Choice.* That word hit a chord somewhere. A long time passed. Ria said nothing. She could feel Shabana looking at her. Ria felt her chest tighten, and a strong urge to leave.

"I'd rather know it," Ria answered finally, but she was not convinced that her answer was truthful.

"No matter what it was?" Shabana asked, eyebrows raised, half-smiling. "Are you sure about that Ria?"

"Yes, I'm sure. There is nothing worse than not knowing." Ria said.

"There is Ria. Believe me, there is." Shabana said.

Ria shook her head and looked away from Shabana's sad expression. She felt increasingly anxious and panicked. She had to go but just as she opened her mouth to make an excuse to leave Shabana spoke again.

"I know it's hard in the centre Ria. Those places should not even exist, and neither should those terrible camps. Refugees and migrants are increasingly being treated like criminals and denied basic universal rights. They don't want us here, but we have rights which they cannot deny. However, they do not give us those rights easily, and the more who come, the harder it becomes. The fight to make sure those rights are not taken away is an important one. Look at all the people allowed to drown because politicians decide they are not worth saving, and few seem to care. It makes me so sad. I feel that our very humanity is in danger."

Ria looked at Shabana and felt her sadness. But Shabana seemed to shake it off and stood up.

"Look. I have to go Ria. I'll see you tomorrow, same time?"

"Yes, thank you so much for helping me with Naira and the hospital."

They hugged briefly and Shabana walked off across the park.

Ria stood there trying to compose herself. Why had she become so anxious? She did not understand. It was just a conversation! Yet Ria noticed how her body had gone completely rigid and how much she was sweating. She tried to improve her breathing by walking around the park a few times and after an hour or so she managed to breathe more easily.

As Ria circled the park once again, she checked the time. They would be serving lunch at the centre soon. She was too late to get there in time, and she felt too drained now for group eating. It was raining lightly so she walked towards one of the shopping centres to kill some time.

After an hour or so spent browsing shop windows her phone rang. It was Shabana. Ria was surprised, she had just left her.

"Where are you?" Shabana asked. She sounded strange.

"Just walking round the shopping centre. Why? Is something wrong? Are you okay?"

"I can't say over the phone. Can you come over to the flat now? I know it is a long walk to do again, but you can have a late lunch with us as I am sure you have not gone to eat at the centre as usual. You'll have plenty of time to get back before curfew and you said you had nothing to do."

"Shabana. It's past three already and it's a long walk to your house. I am looking outside and it's raining really hard. I'm tired and I have to be back before they come for Naira's baby by five. I promised Fatima."

"I understand and I know you promised. Look Ria, I don't want to tell you over the phone but believe me it is something you will want to know. Come, please. I have made your favourite lunch." Shabana hung up.

Ria stared at the screen. What the hell could be so important that Shabana had to tell her that she couldn't tell her over the phone? Was it about Naira? No. She would have told her over the phone if it was that.

She stood there for a while debating what to do. Shabana's flat was about an hour's walk from where she was. Shabana wouldn't make her walk an hour in the rain for nothing. She went down the shopping centre escalator and out onto the street. There was no way she would get back in time to be with Fatima when they took Naira's baby. Fatima would not be happy, and Ria felt bad. She had promised.

21

When Shabana opened the door, Ria stood there frozen to the bone. The weather had taken a turn for the worse which was a feat in itself just as she had started out. Ria noticed that Shabana was not her usual bubbly self as she greeted her at the door. Omar was pacing back and forth in front of the sofa, frowning.

"What's wrong?" Ria asked. "Has something happened? Omar, what is it?"

"Why don't we all sit down first? Lunch is ready." Shabana said gesturing towards the old wooden table.

"Omar! Sit." Shabana said sharply. He seemed to snap out of whatever was going on with him.

"Hello Ria," Omar said as he sat down. Omar was usually a very effusive man, yet now his greeting was quiet and subdued. He looked nervous. Ria had never seen him like this.

Shabana entered with three small glasses of tea on a tray and sat down at the table which was already laid out with food. It smelled great. Ria looked away from both of them feeling her palms turn clammy with sweat, fighting a strong urge to leave. It rarely happened to her here. If she trusted anyone even just a little in this country, it was Shabana and Omar.

"Omar," Shabana said softly.

Omar took a sip of his tea and stared down at his hands cusping the glass of tea.

"Ria, I have something to tell you." He said quietly.

Ria said nothing, her heart speeded up, beating faster now. This must be about Naira, bad news. No, Shabana would be the one to tell her that, not Omar. This was something else.

"This morning, I was at one of the male processing centres over near one of the crossing points. I was working at the registration table when a young man I was registering said he was from your town. I filled out all the forms for him and then he moved on to the next desk and I continued working as it was a busy morning. I said nothing to him when he mentioned your town. As we were really busy, I could not leave the table to talk to him and then well, by the time I was free he had already been moved into the facility. But I couldn't get him out of my head. I kept thinking of you, and… you know your memory… so…well…. I know your city is quite big, but I thought …you know, maybe, this person knows someone who knows someone… you know how it works. The world is always smaller than we think. And I know how worried you are about your family so I thought maybe this man might know something. Especially as he had just arrived here."

Ria sat still listening to Omar's voice, fully focused on what was coming next. From the way he was acting, it could not be good.

"So, when my lunch break came, I checked which sleeping area he had been assigned to and went to look for him. I didn't think too much about what I was doing, I was... I don't know... so enthusiastic. I was thinking If I could bring you good news... so anyway I just went. I had no difficulty getting in, I know all the guards, we all smoke together. When I got to the man's cubicle, he was sitting there on his bunk just staring into space." Omar paused as if seeing the scene in his head.

"He did not even look up at me standing there so I said. 'Hello, my name is Omar. I registered you before. I think I know someone here from your town.'

Omar paused, took a breath, and then continued. "He seemed very wary and tense, and of course, I saw immediately that he did not trust me, but that is the same with everyone who comes in from the migrant routes, so I didn't think much of it. But still he said nothing. I didn't know what to do so I just stood there and waited for a while. Then the silence became so uncomfortable I started asking him questions. We are not supposed to. I asked him how long it had taken him to get here. I asked him how he was. I asked him if he knew anyone from here but… still to my surprise he said nothing. He just continued to stare into nothing. I was extremely uncomfortable by then so I thought okay, maybe he is not well, maybe terrible things have happened to him so I should not bother him. I felt bad being there, so I turned to leave him in peace." Omar swallowed some more tea.

"But then just as I was leaving, my back already turned to him, he suddenly asked me to tell him the name of the person that I knew from his city, so I turned back. Now he was looking at me straight in the eyes. I cannot explain it but there was something about the way he was looking at me, it was strange. Not friendly... I did not feel at ease with him. I can't explain it. But now I had a problem because I had already told him and now, he was asking me for the name. But I was thinking now ... well, what if he is a bad person and I go and I give him your name? I didn't know what to do. But he asked me again, this time he was more insistent.

Ria realised she had been holding her breath and spluttered.

"Ria, drink some tea. Omar, hurry up, my love for such a short story you are taking forever!" Shabana said gently.

Ria did not even look her way. Her eyes were fixed on Omar's mouth. Even now he looked uneasy.

"Of course, I tried to avoid his question. But then I saw his hand, one of his fingers was missing, it looked fairly recent, but not bandaged or anything. Anyway, I think I must have stared at it...I don't know. But I did and he caught me. Then he did a very strange thing, he laughed. A real laugh. Strange, yes? I was about to apologise and leave but then he said something like now that you have seen something about me, you must tell me, who is it that is here from my town?"

Ria was getting impatient and anxious. Was this the moment she found out something really bad about her family?

"I felt sorry for him, but I could see he was a proud man. A young man, maybe only a couple of years older than you Ria. He stared at me, and I knew there was no way out of it, so I told him your family name, only that, not your first name, not saying that it was a man or a woman. Nothing more. As soon as I told him your family name, I saw his reaction. He tried to cover it, but I saw it, it was a flash of something, I don't know what, like satisfaction more than surprise. Then he shook his head and said that he didn't know that family. He thanked me and went back to staring into space. I just wanted to get out of there, so I left." Omar finished.

"Omar, so what? That is nothing!" Ria cried and started to feel disappointed and relieved at the same time. There was no good news but also there was no bad news about her family. She looked at the food. It looked better now.

"Ria, Omar has not finished. Be patient." Shabana said. "We wouldn't bring you here knowing you had to be with Fatima for just that."

"Later on, we had to distribute the food packs for the night and the next morning, so I had to see him again. Anyway, he was still on my mind. When I go there, he was still sitting there on his bed as if he hadn't moved since. As I handed him the food bag, it somehow fell and some of the tins fell out of the bag. We both went to pick them up and then as we were both crouched down on the floor he said in a low voice. 'I know that family name. Please, tell me, what is the first name of the person?'"

"I was shocked. I hadn't even been expecting him to speak. I said I could not say. I said that things were complicated here and that was not information I could give out. I told him that in these places people tried to forget the past and it could be dangerous to find someone from the same place....I tried to explain to him about the rules we have to keep people safe, especially coming from wars or persecution but then he grabbed my arm and said that I was the one who had come there to tell him. He hadn't asked me. Then he started telling me that he had lost his finger fighting with the son of a family with that same name. Then he said this and Ria, I remember it word for word." Omar paused. He said to me. 'If the person you know is from the same family as Jamil the Young Fighter, then I must meet them because maybe it is his family and Jamil is looking for them."

Ria's pulse quickened. *Jamil.*

Omar stopped. "Well after he said that I just didn't know what to say. Then he stood up. He is a very big man, strong you know. I just finished picking the food up and without saying anything I left quickly to finish the deliveries to the rest of the men. I am sorry Ria, but I was afraid. You know. He said he had been fighting so that got me worried."

"Ria are you okay, you have gone completely white! What's wrong? Do you know someone called Jamil?" Shabana asked.

Ria could not speak. She could not even breathe.

188

22

Ria stood up quickly knocking over her glass of tea as she did so, she couldn't quite get enough air into her lungs, but she felt excited at this turn of events.

"Omar, you must take me to this man. Now." Ria said hearing her voice tremble.

"What? No, Ria, I can't do that, you know that women are not allowed there. I can't just bring in 'visitors'… especially women to other migrants! You know that. You can only go there if you are registered there, or if you work there like me, or you are a medic… or a lawyer or… a social worker. That is not possible. I wish I had not told you. It is probably nothing anyway."

"Well, I must speak to him before they move him. They could move him any time, to another city and then I won't know where he is. I must see him. Omar, my brother's name is Jamil. I must see him today. He will have news of my family!" Ria said.

"Ria, you don't even know if it is true what this man said. It could be another Jamil. You don't even know." Shabana said. "Or he could be lying. When people are desperate, they will try anything, say anything. I have seen it many times" Omar tried to reason with Ria.

"Omar, I have to see him. If it is true...if it is true that he knows us, that he knows Jamil, I have to speak to him. He will know things. He has just arrived you said. He might have the information that I don't have."

"Yes, that is what he said, but I don't know how long he has been travelling on the migrant routes. People can take weeks, months or sometimes even years! You might have got here faster than him! It is at the intake stage that they get all the details. I just take the name and place of origin, set him up in the pavilion cubicle and distribute the food kit."

"Omar, Jamil is my brother's name. I don't know what he means when he says, *'Jamil the Young Fighter'*, my brother was not a fighter, but who knows, maybe now he fights in the war. I remember he would sometimes talk about that, but I thought it was just talk. ...but now with the situation like it is at home..." Ria felt her words stop dead as if her mind had arrived at a red traffic light. Her mouth was open, but the sentence remained unfinished as a memory showed itself, brief but there.

"Ria, you cannot be serious. It is too dangerous for you to go and see some strange man you don't even know. And if Omar is involved, he could lose his job! That would be terrible for us. I am sorry for you, but it is selfish of you to even ask this of him, knowing what could happen to him, or to you if they catch you with this man. Ria, has it occurred to you that this man could even be part of a terrorist group. We don't know anything about him." Shabana's voice was louder now, tense with the potential consequences of Ria's request.

Her voice brought Ria back.

"Shabana!" Ria's tone was raised now too as frustration and excitement collided. "If this man was a terrorist, why would he come here? Well, yes, he could I suppose to recruit. That is not a good question. But I know my brother is no terrorist, that is impossible." Ria said.

Ria heard those words echoing in her head. She felt dizzy. The words sounded oddly familiar.

"My son is no terrorist." Ria said out loud staring down at the table.

"What?" Shabana looked at Omar who shook his head and sat down. "Ria, come and sit down and I'll bring us some more tea. You need to get something in your stomach. We haven't even had lunch yet. I am sure you are excited by the possibility of someone being here who might know your family. It is normal but you cannot go to see this man. We should not have told you, but we decided we had to because as you say Omar thought he might have news. But that was before the man acted as he did. Those are not the actions of a normal man!"

"My son is no terrorist." Ria repeated.

Then she said it again. She heard Shabana's words, but she was not listening to them. That sentence, she knew it

191

was a memory, she could hear the voice. It was her mother's voice who was saying the words.

"Maybe, you should call one of Ria's friends, Shabana." Omar said to Shabana, looking worried.

"Ria!" Shabana took Ria's hand and pressed her thumb deeply into the middle of Ria's palm.
Ria whipped her hand away at the sudden pain and looked at Shabana.

"You were not here Ria" Shabana said gently. "Did you remember something? What happened?"

"No, nothing, I was just excited about the possibility that this man might know something." Ria lied.

"Are you sure? Look, sit down Ria. Let me get some fresh tea and we can talk some more while we eat, but calmly." Shabana warned and left for the kitchen.

Ria still feeling agitated turned to Omar. "What did he look like? Tell me everything about him. Maybe I know him."

"Ria, I don't know anything more than I said. He was young, maybe a few years older than you, maybe twenty-two, twenty-three, it's hard to tell. I don't know. He looked very dirty, but not smelly. He had a short beard, dark eyes, and was tanned from the sun. As I said already, he is a big man, strong, not fat. I can't tell you any more than that... He spoke very good English. The thing I most remember was his hand and the missing finger, and his staring into space. I know that sounds terrible. Look, I was afraid. That way he just kept staring into space, it's a bad kind of stare, you know? I have seen that kind of stare so often from people coming from wars. But the way he grabbed me, that wasn't normal. No Ria. He said your brother was a fighter. You know what that means. You cannot go and see him. He could be very dangerous. Fighters come often pretending to be refugees for many reasons Ria. We know that, but we ask no questions. It is not *our* job."

"Omar, I don't care if he is strange, or dangerous. I must ask him about my brother. I need to know where he is so that I can contact him. If he knows my brother, he will know about my mother and my sister! I have to speak to him! Do you not understand? Imagine you were in my shoes, Omar." Ria pleaded.

"But how do you know it's your brother?" Omar asked gently. "You can't know. This man could be anyone."

"I don't know if it is my brother. But what if it is and I let this chance pass? Omar, what if all you have to do is pass him a note when you pass out the food? Then, it is up to him to decide whether to act or not, not you. You will be protected. You don't even have to know what is written on the note. I promise. I will put it in an envelope. You won't even see it. Will you do it, Omar, please?" Ria had lowered her pleading voice to a whisper.

Omar stared at her for a while, looked towards the kitchen and said in a low voice. "Write the note, but make sure I cannot see what you write. Then meet me on the bridge before I go back to work later to give it to me. I'll come to the bridge an hour or so after we finish eating, so leave soon. You can't write it here. If he is still there when we hand out the food later and no-one is with me to see, I'll give it to him. No guarantees Ria. I will not take any risks.

You must not tell Shabana please, she would not like this. You must promise me you will not ask me to do anything more than this. Do you promise?"

"I promise. Thanks so much, Omar!" Ria smiled and touched his hand, impatient now to finish and leave, but knowing she would have to go through the motions of eating.

Shabana came out of the kitchen bearing more glasses of fresh tea.

"Look at you Ria, the colour is back in your face. Now please, try to eat a little." Shabana said, looking at Ria from time to time.

Ria noticed and said "Thank you, Shabana, I am so sorry for before. I feel better now. I just got too excited. Thank you for telling me, Omar. I won't stay long, as you know Shabana, I said I would be with Fatima when they come for the baby."

Ria forced herself to eat some of the food on her plate. They chatted a little. No-one mentioned the man again. Ria finished quickly but not too quickly, then again, citing her need to be with Fatima and get news of Naira, she got up to leave.

Ria hugged Shabana briefly, and kissed Omar on the cheek. She thanked them both, pulled on her jacket, grabbed her rucksack, and left the flat towards the town centre going as fast as she could.

It had stopped raining for a change, but it was very cold. She walked along a street lined with shops until she found one that looked like it sold what she was looking for. She chose a pen and found a small pack of small envelopes and a small notebook. She added up the prices in her head but didn't have enough money to pay for it all, so she sacrificed the notebook. She needed the envelopes more.

She approached the cashier who looked at Ria with barely concealed distaste and spoke to Ria as if she had a nasty taste in her mouth. Ria avoided eye contact, paid, and left.

She checked the time and walked quickly towards the centre. She wanted to be there when they came to take Naira's baby. It was the least she could do but all she could think about was the note. If she went back to the centre now, she would miss Omar and that wasn't an option.

Just near the bridge, she stopped at a Café she often went to run by three Turkish brothers and asked one of them if he could give her something to write on. He handed her a couple of pages ripped from a food order notebook and she sat down at a table, took out her pen and the pack of envelopes and wrote the note as quickly as possible. Omar would soon be on the bridge, and she knew he wouldn't wait. She wrote the note.

Hello.

My name is Ria. I have a brother called Jamil. My friend told me he met you today. You say you know someone called Jamil and my family name. If it is the same Jamil, then we must speak. It is urgent. It is easy to get out of the centre you are in now even though you are not allowed to leave even during the day. It is not well guarded at night. It is more difficult for me. Please, try to meet me this evening. I will wait for you between nine and ten tonight. They might move you stop another centre soon, so it is better that we meet tonight. Otherwise, it could be too late. I cannot leave the detention centre at night, but I will try to get out tonight. I will wait for you at the café around the corner from the pavilion you are in. It's called Black Coffee. Please, come.'

She thrust the note hurriedly into one of the envelopes, sealed it, and left the café, walking quickly towards the bridge, still hoping to make it back to the centre in time for Fatima.

23

Ria made it back to the centre after meeting Omar on the bridge just in time to hear the disparaging mutterings of Karine as she noted down Ria's entry time, shaking her head in disapproval. It was only late afternoon, so there was no reason for her to complain. Ria felt shivery inside, not the kind of feeling she got from the cold but a different kind, more like the one that had lingered since she had been in Shabana's flat.

What had been so strange for Ria was that on the way back from the bridge, those words *"my son is no terrorist"* kept repeating in her head. She was sure that she was hearing the words in her mother's voice. Her mother had a very distinctive voice. *Has*. She corrected herself.

Out of breath from rushing to get back to the centre in time she made her way down the corridor to her room. Ria felt her usual irritation at all the noise, but she was more preoccupied with the unpleasant, trembling way she was feeling.

She had given the note to Omar, but now how was she supposed to get out of the centre past curfew to go and meet the man in case he did come? She hadn't thought that part through. The man might come tonight, or not. She had no way of knowing. It was such short notice. She had written the note without thinking, in a rush. There was no way for her to get out after curfew. No way that she knew of at least and if she left before curfew and didn't come back, Karine would notice.

She opened the door to her room and stopped dead in her tracks. The women were seated in their usual circle, talking quietly, but Ria was shocked to see Naira lying on the bottom bunk. How could she be back? Shabana had said they would probably take her to a special centre. Yet here she was curled up like a ball, her back turned away from the women.

Ria's thoughts about the man were forgotten as she rushed over to the bunk.

"Naira?" Ria said softly.

Ria looked over at Fatima, who shook her head. Ria sat down slowly next to Naira, not touching, just sitting. There was no baby in the room.

"Naira?" Ria said again and touched Naira's shoulder gently.

Naira immediately flinched and moved further away.

"It's me, Ria, Naira. You don't have to speak. I just want to tell you that I am here if you need me." Ria said.

Naira said nothing but seemed to unfurl her body ever so slightly. One of the women came over and handed Ria a cup of hot tea. It warmed her cold hands.

"Naira, here, look, have a little tea. It's that tea you love. Fatima made it, so you know it will have a lot of sugar!" Ria said trying to inject a smile into her voice but failing.

No reaction. Ria took a sip of the tea. It felt so good after the cold out on the bridge. Ria got up and put the tea on top of the fragile set of drawers at the end of Naira's bunk. Standard issue cupboards, unsteady and battered. From there she could see a bit more of Naira's face despite the shadow cast on it by the bunk above her. Ria was shocked by what she saw. Naira's face looked so drawn and pale. Her eyes were open and fixed on the wall. Ria searched for her wrists, but Naira's arms were crossed over her chest and her raised knees blocked Ria from seeing them. Where was Naira's son? Surely, they had not taken him now that Naira had been released.

Ria looked at Fatima, who again shook her head. Ria could see that Fatima had been crying. What had happened? She had to speak to Fatima.

How could she even think about leaving the centre that night with all this going on? She couldn't leave Naira when she most needed her. But she had to get out of there tonight in case the man came. She could not miss him. If she did, then that was it. If he came to the meeting place and she wasn't there, she would never see him again and she might never know about her family. She had to go. But how?

She walked over to Fatima and sat next to her.

"When did they bring her?" Ria asked whispering. "I heard she was going somewhere else for a while."

"I don't know. We were surprised too. They brought her in here just after lunch. They came earlier than expected and they had already taken Khal before they brought her. Ria. I think she already knew, and I think it was planned that he wouldn't be here when they brought her back because she didn't ask about him when she arrived. She didn't even look for him. She hasn't said a word since they brought her. She has thick bandages that go from both her wrists right up to her elbows. They just left her here on the bunk, she turned to the wall and since then she has said nothing. The nurse who came with her said she would be back to check on her. We tried to talk to her…. give her tea…. food. Yet, she says nothing. She does not even move. Not even for the bathroom, Ria!" Fatima lowered her voice to a whisper. "But she hasn't even asked us about Khal."

"Well, she is not well yet. Maybe they have put her on medication. After what happened it is probable. Perhaps they told her at the hospital that they were taking him. I am sure they will bring him back when she is feeling better. I am sure she is medicated, maybe for the pain. But what I don't understand is why they brought her today. It's strange to let her out so soon." Ria said. Fatima looked so sad.

"Ria, I miss him so much already, we all do. But you know as we do that Khal is too much for her. She cannot manage him. It's understandable that she cannot." Fatima said. "But we can help her with him, and in time she will get better. I don't understand why she is not looking for him."

"Look, it has not even been two days so, she is probably still not feeling well. You know. But I'll ask anyway, and Fatima, she will ask about Khal, just give her time." Ria said.
They sat in silence for a while, both watching Naira's still body. Ria was trying to think.

"Fatima, I need a favour, a big one," Ria said urgently breaking the silence.

"What is it, Ria? What favour could I possibly help you with from this place!" Fatima said with a laugh.

"I need to get back out after curfew," Ria said quickly.

"Back out where? What are you talking about?"

"Out of the centre, tonight," Ria replied. "No questions asked."

"Then you should not have come back, Ria. It is easier that way. Once you are in and they have closed for the night, it is very hard to go out again. You know that. You could still go out and just not come back, you have fifteen minutes."

"I didn't think of that and anyway I wanted to come back in time for when they came for Khal, to be here with you. I can't go back out and not come back in time, it's Karine on the desk tonight so if I go back out and don't come back, she'll notice and say something. She hates me. Also, I'd like to stay here with Naira for a while. Is there any way of getting out at night? I have to be somewhere at eight." Ria looked at Fatima, who said nothing.

"Look Fatima, I can't explain why, and anyway it's better if you don't know why, but believe me it's very important, if not, I would not ask you and I would never even think of going out at night. I know you know people who can do things. I have been here long enough to hear the rumours. Please, Fatima, if you could just help me with this."

"Get you out at night? Ria, that is a lot to ask. No one can leave after curfew, you know that. What rumours, I know of no rumours. What is going on? What are you

201

doing? I am not even going to consider anything until you tell me. You know it is a very big risk for any of us to be out there at night. Where would you stay until the centre opens again in the morning? Have you got a boyfriend out there, is that it?" she nudged her playfully.

"No, it's not that Fatima" Ria said impatiently. "I need to meet someone, someone who came in from the routes yesterday. He says he's from my town. He says he knows my brother."

Fatima's eyes widened.

"I sent him a note to meet tonight. He is in the processing centre for men on the other side of the city. I have to see him. If it is true that he knows my brother, he can tell me where he is. And maybe he knows about the rest of my family too. Fatima, you know there are so many things that I can't remember. Fatima, please. There may never be a chance like this again. It is worth the risk, is it not?" Ria said pleading with her eyes.

Fatima sighed. "I don't know Ria, maybe for you. But meeting a man you don't know out there by yourself, now that could be dangerous. Anyway, how do you even know he will come?" She asked.

"I don't know, but if I don't go, I'll never know," Ria said.

Fatima looked long and hard at Ria, but eventually she sighed, got up and left the room. Ria paced a little, now more nervous. She went and sat next to Naira again. Then she got up again and paced a little more. Then she sat down again. She looked down at her legs, fingers tapping hard on her thigh

After a very long time, Fatima returned. Ria stood up. The window to leave before curfew had already passed.

"Well? Ria asked.

"At exactly eight o'clock, go to room 12 in Block D. If someone sees you, tell them you are going to borrow a period pad from your friend. Anyway, there's never anyone around. You know they don't check on us once they know we are all inside!" Fatima said.

"But, then what?" Ria was worried now.

"Then, do as you are told. After you get out go and do whatever it is you have to do. That is your business. Keep it to yourself. Just do as I say. Stay with Naira until then, and then go. But Ria, know this, you will have a debt to repay to the women who will help you get out tonight. I don't know when or what that payment will be. They will let you know. It is not my business."

"Thank you so much, Fatima. Pay? Okay, but I have no money." Ria was speaking fast now, thoughts racing.

"It won't be money. Whether the man you want to see comes or not is out of your control. You can only go but you cannot control what he does. But if you do go in the end, please be careful. Once you are out of this centre, the risk is yours to manage. You will be told at what time and where to meet for the return. Ask no questions, Ria. You are young and you do not have much experience, so be very careful, things are always very different at night. I will watch Naira, so don't worry about that." Fatima said.

Ria nodded and touched Fatima on the shoulder.

"Thanks so much, Fatima. I'm sorry about Khal, I know you'll miss him, but I'm sure he'll be back soon." she said quietly and went over to sit on Naira's bunk deep in thought.

Then, when it was time, she slipped out of the room into the dimly lit corridor and headed quietly over towards Block D, heart pound

24

As Ria entered Block D, she caught sight of a dark shape hovering in the dimly lit doorway of one of the rooms. She walked towards it. There was still no moon, so it was hard to make out the shape's face. As she got nearer, she saw three women standing there. They were all quite small in stature and their faces were covered, revealing only their eyes. Each of them was dressed in black from head to toe. Ria felt uneasy at only being able to see their eyes, it meant she had no facial expressions to scan, and the blackness of the corridor accentuated her feeling of uneasiness.

One of the women held out a hood to Ria. Ria took it but hesitated.

"Put it over your head. You put it on, or you do not come," she said.

Ria pulled the hood on over her head and the sensation of blackness and panic was total. She ripped off the hood and threw it away from her onto the floor.

"I'm sorry," Ria said, embarrassed, as she looked for the hood one the floor somewhere in the dark.

A woman handed it to her. She took a deep breath and put it back on trying unsuccessfully to suppress the intense feeling of panic she felt. Someone grabbed her by the arm and guided her with a strong arm. Ria could not see a thing.

After a while they stopped.

"Get down on your knees" one of the women whispered in her ear.

Putting her weight on the woman's arm Ria slowly lowered herself onto her knees.

"Now crawl forward." The woman said.

After crawling what seemed like a very short distance, Ria felt a blast of cold air through the hood and her jacket.

"Get up, slowly now" The woman whispered.

She helped her up onto her feet and then they made their way forward again walking slowly. It wasn't far but Ria stumbled a couple of times on the uneven terrain, but the woman never once let her fall. Ria could feel such strength in the woman's arms. The longer she wore the hood the surer she was that she was going to be sick, she was surprised too at how terrified she was in the hood. She thought too about the fact that soon she would be left out there alone at night and began to regret her stupid, desperate plan. What if she got caught? She had never been out past six in the evening. What if the man was a liar or worse still, as Omar thought, dangerous? What if he didn't come? She would be out late at night, on her own, a young, foreign woman, who could not speak the language and had no right to be out there.

"Stop" one of the women said, still quiet but no longer whispering.

Ria stopped. The hood was pulled off much to Ria's relief, but the tight feeling in her chest remained. She looked around and saw they were standing in a poorly lit narrow street. There was no-one else around. As Ria's eyes adjusted, one of the women said "Be back here by three am, not a minute later or we will go back inside without you. Understood?"

Before Ria could ask them anything or even answer, the three women had slipped quickly away, already shadowy figures in the distance. She watched as they split and went off in different directions. Ria stood disoriented in the alleyway. She checked her phone, it was not that long before nine, she had better get to the meeting place in case he did come. Where the hell was she? She marked the location on her phone so she could get back and moved off quickly.

She headed out of the alleyway and onto the main street. Not recognising the area, she looked around for something familiar and in the misty distance she saw the crest of the bridge. Aware of the time, she walked quickly. As she got closer to the town centre, there were more people around, some sitting in restaurants, others just strolling, and people of all ages were entering and leaving crowded bars. She pushed on faster now, slightly out of breath, up the hill towards the Black Café.

She got there with still some time to spare before nine. She looked for a spot opposite the Black Café from where she would be able to see both approaches on the wide street. She didn't want to wait inside the place on her own. She pressed herself against a small monument and hoped no-one would see her. It was a strange thing to be doing. On her way up, she had passed by the café, making sure that her jacket hood was pulled up and down over her face as she had glanced in. He didn't know what she looked like, and she didn't know what he looked like. So how would she recognise him? There were only two or three tables occupied by couples or friends. The Black Café had a huge front window and bright lighting, so it was easy to see inside, that is why she had chosen it. Also, not many white people went there. She knew the owner and he knew her, so it was a safer place to meet this man. If he came.

  It was cold but at least there was no wind, and for once it wasn't raining. However, the moonless night made everything darker and after her experience with the hood she felt very nervous standing there. She could feel the film of sweat she had worked up from her quick walk turn icy cold against her skin. Her eyes scanned up and down the street, checking doorways, peering into the café, but she did not see any man sitting there alone. After a while, she heard footsteps coming down the street towards her and tensed. Her heartbeat accelerated. She looked up, but no it was just a couple of young men. They went into the café. She sighed and looked the other way, shivering. What was she going to do out here until three am? The Black Café shut in a few hours, and she couldn't sit in there all night. A young woman all alone just sitting there for hours at that time of the night. No that was not an option.

  "So, you say you are Jamil's sister?"

Ria, startled by the voice, whipped around. A tall, bearded man was standing just a couple of meters away, enshrouded by the shadows of the wall, almost completely out of sight. She wondered how long he had been standing there. She shuddered at the thought that he might have been watching her. She could only see the outline of his body, not his face, just the beard. He fit Omar's description, and his accent was the familiar accent of her region.

"If it is the same man, then yes." Ria answered proudly, as she took a step back, wary now. "But who are you?" Ria asked, hearing the slight tremble in her voice.

"Do you need to know my name? You can call me Malik. It has not been easy for me to get to this country, and it is dangerous for me to be out here like this. It was easy to get out of that centre, especially for someone like me, but I don't know how this country works, so I am vulnerable out here. I cannot be caught." He said.

"Where is Jamil? How do you know him? Is he okay?" Ria asked, she had to make sure he did know her brother.

"I don't know. It has been a while since I've seen him. I've been busy travelling for a couple of weeks. Surviving." He said dryly.

"Why did you come here?" Ria asked, her tone a little bolder now. His tone irritated her, but she did not know why.

"Here to this place? Or here to meet you?" He asked.

"Both." She replied.

"I came tonight because Jamil is the leader of my unit and a good friend. If his family is here, then it is my duty to him to meet them and to be of service if necessary. Jamil and I are bound by our common cause. But, let me ask *you* a question first. How do I know you are really Jamil's sister?"

Ria laughed, surprised and taken aback by this unexpected challenge.

"Do you think I would risk getting caught outside the detention centre to meet with a total stranger at night if I wasn't? I have taken more much risk than you in the hope that you were talking to my friend today about Jamil *my* brother. There are many people called Jamil where we come from. It is a very common name. You were the one who said you knew my family. How do I know you are not lying?" she said.

The man stepped forward towards Ria, he moved like a cat she thought. She instinctively stepped back.

"The Jamil I know was involved in the protests at the university in your town. He had two sisters and a mother. His father had been killed years ago by the regime. They murdered his father when you were still a young child. Jamil told me his older sister - you - helped him with the protests. He told me what happened at the campus protest that day. He told me you were there too and that was the last time he had seen you. He has been looking for you since that day." He looked at her, eyebrows raised. "So, is it the same man?" he smirked.

Ria stared past him. Her body had gone rigid. She wanted to speak but couldn't get her mouth to form any words. She was surely going to faint.

"What is wrong with you?" He asked sharply, stepping closer.

Her light-headedness increased, and she wavered on her feet. He got to her just in time to stop her from falling and held her upright by her arm, his grip strong on her arm.

"Let's go and get some tea. You look pale" he said, and without waiting for an answer he ushered her over to the Black Café. "Pull yourself together or someone will notice you looking like this and think I have done something to you. You will have chosen a café where you would be safe, I imagine." he stated.

She felt as if she was floating in a dream. He stopped and shook her arm hard. She looked at him, confused.

"I'm sorry. I had to do that. You are acting strangely, and this is dangerous for both of us. Pull yourself together. If not, people will notice us. Notice you. Notice me. We are going to enter the café and act as if we are friends. Do you understand?" He was speaking in a low voice, but she could feel his tension.

She shook herself and looked at him, pulling her arm from his grip.

"Don't ever do that again." She said to him and strode into the café.

She forced a smile and nodded at Boubacar, who was busy making food, one eye on some sport on the TV as usual. He barely registered her. She went straight into the bathroom. She leaned on the sink and stared at herself in the mirror.

She looked paler than ever, she tried to breathe more deeply. What was it that he had said? The campus? What was he talking about? She felt as if she knew something about the campus but didn't know what. It was as if there were things she knew but they remained just out of reach. This man knew things, and he could tell her what, fill in a lot of her memory gaps. But did she really want to know? She was afraid of him too, he was an imposing figure and he felt dangerous, just as Omar had said. Yet she felt more afraid that he would tell her something bad about her family, something he would assume she already knew but didn't. Or what if he told her something important but because of her missing memory she would have no way of telling the difference between a truth and a lie.

She splashed cold water onto her face, dried herself with some paper towels, pinched some colour back into her cheeks and left the bathroom jittery but a little more composed. The Black Café had filled up more and was quite noisy.

He was sitting at the table furthest away from the big window facing the main entrance. There were two glasses of steaming tea in front of him. She could see him clearly now. His hair was jet black and longish, his beard dark too. He looked so young, just like Jamil. She sat down opposite him and took one of the glasses of tea in her hand. She avoided his stare.

She understood what Omar had meant. There was something strange about him. Now though she saw it wasn't menacing as Omar had said, but not pleasant either. It was his eyes she thought. Something about his eyes. He looked on guard, tense, distant.

They sipped on their tea in silence eying each other warily.

"What are you doing here?" he asked her.

She searched for words. "I don't know. They will not let me leave."

"What do you mean?" he asked.

"I woke up injured in a hospital here a few months ago. They won't tell me how I got here, who brought me here or why. They won't let me go back home either. They will not explain why." She said.

He looked at her, his stare like a truth scan.

"How can you explain that?" he said.

"I cannot" she answered. "I wish I could."

"Tell me about my brother. What were you saying about the campus," Ria said changing the subject by going into murkier territory.

She felt a knot tighten in her stomach. She had a bad feeling about this.

The man sipped his tea. "You look just like him you know." He stared at her, looking suspicious. "Everyone knows about the campus incident. Everyone at home that is! You were there! Why are you asking me about something you saw happen with your own eyes, I was not there."

He looked at her frowning, now even more guarded than before. His right hand by the glass of tea shook slightly, his other hand was out of sight. She saw the distrust in his eyes.

"You are right to ask that. If I was there, why would I ask you? The truth is I do not remember anything about the campus or anything else for that matter. Nothing. As I said I don't know how I got here. I don't know where my mother and sister are. I don't know where Jamil is. I don't know what happened to me or my family." Ria was talking fast now, but tears began to run slowly down her cheeks. "I don't remember anything. They say it is because of the head injury, that is why I was in hospital. But they won't answer any of my questions about why I am here or why I cannot return…"

The man sipped his tea again, studying her carefully while intermittently scanning the café and the street outside. He seemed to decide.

"Drink your tea and let's go. I will tell you what I know. But not here." He said and got up before she could disagree.

25

Ria followed him out of the Black Café. It was bitterly cold, and an unpleasant damp mist hung in the air, giving everything a sinister feeling. As Ria shivered, the man pulled up the collar of his thick jacket and looked back at her.

"Let's walk, that way we will be warmer. I can't stay out here for too long. They might notice that I'm not there and you know what that means. Questions." He said.

"Yes, I am aware," Ria said irritated. She was the one who had to stay out in the freezing cold until three in the morning before she could get back into the centre with those women, but she wasn't going to tell him that.

"How long have you been here?" he asked her.

"Not that long. Almost three months. I woke up in hospital with that bad head injury, they said I had been unconscious. I had to stay there for a few more weeks. Then I was placed in the detention centre about two months ago. The neurologist said that the memory problems are because of what happened to my head."

"Is that what you believe? He asked.

"What do you mean?" she asked sharply. "What other reason could there be?"

"I don't know. All I know is that you should never trust these people. I have seen some very strange things happen to people at home since the war started." He said.

"I have a huge scar on my head." Ria retorted. "And I was in hospital for weeks. I don't trust the people here, but the head injury is real. Anyway, we are not here to talk about me, or even you. We are here to talk about my brother, my family and what you were saying about what happened at the campus. So, talk."

He laughed but wasn't a warm laugh. It sounded more sarcastic Ria knew he was laughing at her.

"I met your brother through a friend about five or six months before the campus incident. I could see as he did that things had to go beyond just protesting. Jamil was already very committed to the revolution, as I was, and we still are. We are more or less the same age too. But he inspired me to act, so I began training with his unit. That and spending time with Alana and your brother changed the way I saw our country and how things were. I understood what needed to be done to change things for the better. Jamil is charismatic and very persuasive too."

215

He laughed, a genuine laugh of affection.

"He led different fighter units at the same time. It was a great honour for him to lead so many groups at his age, but Jamil is a natural leader and a brave fighter. He is also very good tactically. There were ten of us in my unit, men and women too. We were all so young and naive at the beginning with dreams of a successful revolution that would be quick like in had been in other countries and would get rid of our rotten regime and give everyone a better life and future. We might have been very naïve and idealistic, but we were all very motivated."

He seemed animated now as he talked.

"We understood that the student protests would not achieve much because we did not live in a democracy. We understood also that no-one lives in a democracy, not even in the West. Jamil would say that those democracies were false, just illusions, or delusions as he used to say. Now that I am here, I can see that he was right. We knew that the only way forward was to fight violence with violence, not with words. Words had done nothing to change anything all these years. The time for words would come he would always say. But most of us lacked experience in real combat and the realities of war. But we saw what was happening around us, how desperate the regime was to preserve itself. Every day we would see more and more terrible things and hear of terrible things happening to students elsewhere in the country. More and more people were disappearing, or being murdered outright, not a few here and there like before, now it was happening on a much larger scale. Anybody who dared to say anything was gone the next day without a trace."

He paused and lent against a wall, out of the light of the streetlamp. "Then the incident at your campus happened."
Ria noticed she was hanging on to every word as if she were on the verge of finding the key to a long-lost treasure.

"It was the incident that changed everything for all of us. It was the last straw, a turning point. We all understood that. As you know, Jamil was there with one of the main leaders of our group, Alana. Jamil told me she stayed the night before the protest at your house. She had started her activism work a long time before Jamil, but as I am sure you know, Jamil and Alana were more than just friends. She was supposed to speak at that protest at your university. Surely you remember, you were there! Jamil said you helped him to organise it." he stopped and looked at her, waiting for her answer.

"No. I don't know. I don't remember. Please go on." Ria replied. "What happened at this protest?"

"The army came with a huge squadron of armoured vehicles with mounted machine guns, and they just started firing into the crowd of students. More than two hundred students were massacred that day. Many died from their injuries because no one went inside the campus to help after the military left. Out of fear. Some survived but no one knows how many or who they were, or if it is even true that people did survive. The state-controlled news did not report anything about it of course, but news of it spread through whispers and online groups - from people like the market people in the town who had heard it happen, maybe even seen it begin and of course from Jamil and Alana. So as news of the massacre got around the country students were even more angry. Jamil managed to escape with you and Alana, then he said he left you to get Alana out of the town. We think the military massacred all of those students as a warning to all the other student groups in the country who were beginning to protest, thinking the massacre would stop others. But after a few days it was obvious that it had had the opposite effect, it had made young people so angry that they lost their fear and even more rallied, protested and called for an end to the regime. More young people joined the revolution. Our group grew a lot in just a few days."

Ria stopped. "I don't understand. You say this happened at my university? Not reported … well that explains… my god… that is so terrible. My friends would have been there. Many of the people at the protests were my friends." She felt a tinge of emotion, but it dissipated as quickly as it appeared. The story felt unreal, not her story. Perhaps he was lying. If she had been there, it was hardly something she would have forgotten, head injury or not! But she would have been at a protest at her university.

The man continued to observe her closely as he spoke "Jamil always said it was a miracle that you were not harmed. He said that you were right there on the steps below him and Alana. He found you just standing there, bodies all around you, unharmed, he couldn't believe it. Jamil never believed for one second that it was luck that he and Alana were not killed. He was sure the military let her live thinking that she would feel responsible. That what had happened would undermine her and cause the movement to lose its momentum. Military intelligence would have known about Jamil's activity but Alana being there was for sure the reason they did what they did. She had been organising brigades, training, preparing, and carrying out attacks months before the massacre, with Jamil." The man paused.

"They were both so devastated after the massacre. It was a terrible thing to witness, but I think they both carry guilt for having survived it. After that, they became more driven, even more determined to fight, and win. So, we wanted to attack a bigger target than usual that night and then attack them more often. The idea was that it would inspire others to fight and send the regime a message. The attack that we carried out that night was a retaliation and a call to action." He said.

Ria's eyes widened at all this information about Jamil being a fighter, not just a fighter a Unit leader and Alana! It all sounded so surreal.

The man was studying her closely.

"Do you believe what I am saying?" he asked, an intense look about him.

"I don't know." She said. "That is the truth. If I told you I did, I would be lying. It is hard to see my brother in this way, or even Alana. I remember organising the protests, helping him, I remember Alana at our house but nothing about them being involved in any armed group. That doesn't sound like my brother."

"That doesn't sound like your brother?" the man laughed. "There is only one thing Jamil thinks about, and that is armed insurrection."

He looked at her.

"There is more. You will believe what I am saying in the end because somewhere inside you will recognise the truth when you hear it." he said. "Let's walk some more, it's so cold in this place."

He shivered and started to walk. She quickened her step to catch up, caught off guard.

He waited and then continued to speak.

"I admit I didn't think we would succeed in attacking a bigger military base, but it was easier than I imagined. They were not expecting anyone to attack them back then and we used several units to carry out the attack. it wasn't like it is now. There were quite a few soldiers there that night, but they were caught off guard." He said and frowned as if looking back in time.

Ria could not comprehend this information about her brother or the massacre or now this attack on a military base. Was this man delusional perhaps? She couldn't even imagine Jamil holding a gun, let alone use one!

The man continued. "We lost two people in that attack but after some initial difficulties we managed to take control of the base. I was helping to gather up all the weapons and equipment in the base ready to load when Jamil shouted for me to come over to where he was. When I got there Jamil was standing over the body of a soldier. He was a foreign soldier, that was obvious from his looks, but also from his uniform. But when Jamil had looked for the country insignia on his uniform jacket but there was none. Jamil told me that this meant that the man was a mercenary and that if there were mercenaries here already that was bad..."

The man stopped and looked at Ria.

"Then Jamil looked at me and said that we would pay for this attack. After that we left quickly before they sent reinforcements. Jamil looked very worried and went straight to tell Alana."

Ria stood rooted to the spot. The talk of military bases and the mention of dead mercenaries sounded oddly familiar to her. Why? She had seen a lot of things about her country on the news, perhaps that was it. Maybe she was just mixing things up. It was frustrating to remember nothing about this massacre he talked of. Was it even true?

"Then what?" she asked curious to see what he would come up with next.

"It is important first to go back a bit to the evening of the campus incident, hours before our attack was planned." The man paused and looked at her.

"Because that is when Jamil got the news about you."

221

26

Those words stopped Ria dead in her tracks, but the man kept on walking. He didn't even look back at her. She stared in confusion at his tall frame moving steadily forward.

She hesitated. Doubt flooded her mind about this man. She didn't know who he was. She had never seen him in her life. Jamil had never said anything about these things. She had no memory against which to check his story. She had to test him somehow before hearing another word of this far-fetched story. She couldn't just trust him blindly. She was a woman out here in the middle of the night with someone she didn't know, someone who could be dangerous or even mentally disturbed. If it was true that he had fought back home, he must be dangerous. She thought it was strange that he would just be talking about these things to a total stranger.

What he had said about Jamil could have been anyone. A story from the TV or someone he had heard of. After all their country was at war, everyone was involved. But now he was talking about months before the war had really started and saying that her brother had already started fighting. Even if what he had said about the campus was true, anyone could know that. He could have heard it from someone else. If she had been there, she knew it was not something she could have forgotten. She was sure of that and how could just three people survive when hundreds had been supposedly killed? He was obviously lying. But why? Why would he risk coming out of the migrant processing centre just to tell her a pack of lies? What did he want with her? It made no sense. Unless he wanted to hurt her or there was something wrong with him. He could be anyone and might be mentally unstable as a result of the war. A shiver went down her spine as she remembered what Omar had said about his hand.

But then what if it was all true, what if he did know Jamil? He knew Alana's name too. What if something bad had happened between them all and now he wanted revenge? It was all a bit too much of a coincidence him being in the same place as her. That thought scared her. She looked around her, there was nobody else around. It had got later with all the talking and much colder. She had taken no notice of where they had been walking. She looked around to get her bearings and saw that they were now in a more isolated part of the town, a part she did not recognise. It looked more industrial. Gone were the shops, bars and cafés. She felt afraid now. Vulnerable and alone.

She considered running back in the opposite direction before he noticed, he was quite far ahead of her, but not far enough. His back was still turned to her as he continued to walk on. But she had noticed in the café that he looked fit and strong. If he had come here along one of the migrant routes as Omar had said, she knew from hearing other stories that he must be tough. She was not. She was not allowed to exercise, and she had not felt fit and well since they had brought her here. She did some light stretches every day, but running was not allowed or anything else for that matter so her muscles were weak. There was no way she could outrun him and anyway she had nowhere to run to. She checked her phone. It was not far off midnight. Still too many hours to go before meeting the women to get back inside. She had nowhere to go. She felt lost and trapped. She hated every single moment she had spent in the centre, but now she longed to be back there, it was safer.

"Hey! Hey, wait, stop." She shouted out to him. He ignored her and just kept on walking. She felt annoyed and began to quicken her pace to catch up. "Hey, wait!"
He did not. So, she sped up a little more to reach him.

"Did you not hear me asking you to wait?" she said, out of breath by the time she had caught up with him. He stopped. He looked annoyed.

"I heard you." He said. "But it was you who stopped all of a sudden, with no explanation. Why should I stop?"

Ria stared at him infuriated. "Look! I don't know who you are. I don't know if you are a liar or not. I don't even know if you really know my brother" Her finger was punching the air at him.

"So, it is proof that *you* want from *me* then, is it?" He said with heavy sarcasm. "I am the one who has come to meet a stranger in a country I have never been to in the middle of the night. I am the one who has risked *maybe* meeting someone from Jamil's family. What other reason do you think there could be? Some sinister plan involving you?" He laughed in scorn. "It is disappointing that a family member of Jamil's acts in this way. You are just a young girl who ran away from her country. A girl who knows nothing of the way things are now there and who obviously doesn't care either. Sitting here watching the war from a safe distance. I have wasted my time telling you these things. I have taken a risk for nothing! "He said angrily.

"What was Jamil's favourite music group?" Ria asked suddenly.

He laughed. "You test me with such a trivial thing after everything I have told you?"

"If you knew Jamil as well as you say, if you are truly his friend, then you would know the answer," Ria said.

"We did not have the luxury of time to sit around and talk of music for hours. But it is funny you ask this question because it is such an easy one to answer. It is of course *Khebez Dawle*! [1] He listened to them a lot. I like them too. We both liked rock." He smiled.

Ria was surprised by this answer because it was Jamil's favourite band. She felt uncomfortable and embarrassed. She had made a fool of herself and disrespected him.

"Look. I'm sorry if I offended you. Please understand. This is all a lot for me. I don't know you. We are both out here where we shouldn't be in the middle of the night in a country we don't know. You have to believe me when I say that I remember nothing of how I got here. I am grateful for you telling me these things. I never knew Jamil had started to fight. You are right, I was naïve." Ria paused.

Then she continued.

---

[1] Syrian Rock Group

"I am not lying to you. I know it sounds like I am, but I really can't remember. You can believe me or not. It is your choice, but I can tell you that it is a terrible thing to wake up one day in a foreign country and remember nothing. Well, not nothing, I remember my family and my life before but nothing recent. When you can't remember, how can you trust anyone? It is only since I cannot remember that I have realised how important memories are for knowing who you are, and for judging people and situations as safe or dangerous." Ria said looking at him, searching for some understanding in his face. She saw none.

"You must lose this poor young girl you cling to. Memory or not, it does not matter. You have seen the TV and read the newspapers. Our country is at war. It is a disaster. Things will never be the same for any of us ever again. We have all been through so much already and it is still just the beginning. Thousands are dead, even more injured. Children are killed every day, our elderly too. No one knows when they go to bed if they will wake up the next day or not. All of the countries involved are bombing children and hospitals like such a thing is normal and acceptable. The state is murdering doctors! None of them care about human beings. There are no more rules. If you can't remember the campus massacre, then that is a blessing. Be grateful. I remember everything I've seen, heard and done and I wish I didn't. You are lucky". He said.

"Lucky? Go to hell!" Ria snapped.

"Hell? Don't worry Ria. I'm already there. Now, do you want to face reality or skip off back to the safety of your detention centre? It's your choice. I don't care. But, if you do not believe me, then I will say no more. It would only be a waste of my words and my time. But I don't think that is what Jamil would want. I think he would want you to hear the rest. Especially, now with this memory thing you say you have."

He had stopped talking now, and they stood now facing each other about a metre apart. She realised she had been holding her breath. She let it out slowly now and breathed in again. She felt her anger cool a little and unclenched her fists.

"I am not a child. I'm nineteen. Tell me what you want to tell me. I am not afraid. But I am not walking any further with you." Ria said and stood her ground.

He looked around and pointed at some concrete steps that led up towards some higher level. She nodded and they made their way over to the steps and sat down. Ria sat one step above him.

The man sighed heavily. "After the massacre, as soon as Jamil got out of your town, he tried to call you and your mother many times, but your phones were off. He was worried all afternoon, and he was still affected by what had happened. He knew the town was sealed off by the military so there was nothing he could do, just keep waiting for you to call." He paused.

Ria no longer felt the cold.

"A few hours later, maybe early evening, he received a voicemail from your mother's phone, it was your mother saying that you had all been taken by the military and that he should come, Jamil could hear men with her, the military he assumed. Jamil was in a terrible state. He didn't know what to do. I called my mother to see what was happening there and she said the place was full of soldiers and no one could go out. She told me not to call again because it would put them in danger, so we stopped calling people. We knew nothing, we had no information. Jamil was so scared. I had never seen him like that. He wanted to go, turn himself into the military, but Alana talked him out of it. She made him understand that they wouldn't release you even if he went. Also, Jamil knew too much about the group to just turn himself in. He knew Alana was right when she said turning himself in would change nothing but still..."

"Then, later on, it was night by then and not long before we were about to leave to carry out an attack, Jamil got another message on his phone. It was from an unknown number this time. I was with him when he got it. It was another message telling him to turn himself in or he would never see any of you again, it wasn't your mother's voice his time, it was one of the military commanders. But this time they had sent a photo and a recording. Jamil played the recording, and he showed us the photo. We were all in shock. I will never forget that recording, it is in my head for the rest of my life, and I know it is even worse for Jamil." He stopped.

Ria felt a slight stir. Something about what he was saying sounded familiar to her. She was afraid to ask the obvious questions.

The man remained in silence, waiting for the obvious questions to be asked.

"Tell me," Ria said, terrified. This was surely the moment she found out something terrible.

"This may be hard to hear but the recording was of your sister. She was screaming, terrible screams. Really terrible and there were terrible photos too of what they had done to her. Jamil, well he was changed by all that." he stopped. "I'm sorry Ria. This must be terrible."

Ria chest was tight. Hana's screams. "I don't know. Please, go on." Ria said, feeling numb.

He looked at her and hesitated but then he continued. "After the attack I already told you about, the next day he received another photo. I am sorry to tell you Ria, but that one was of you. You were very badly beaten and now in the message from the military, they were calling Jamil a terrorist. When Jamil saw your photo, it sent him into a rage. He destroyed his phone and had to be calmed down by Alana and myself before he took his weapon and went to do something stupid."

Ria felt like the wind had been knocked out of her. A photo of her beaten up, Hana beaten too, Hana screaming. How could it be? She would not have forgotten that. But he had been right, it did feel true inside. Jamil a terrorist? That word again.

"I'm sorry." He said. "It must be difficult to hear that."

"It can't be right. Surely, I would remember all of that." Ria said shaking her head, her hands trembling.

230

"Maybe not. Anyway, Jamil kept saying that it was all his fault for not going home with you. He was almost crying, saying if he had been there none of that would have happened. Saying that he was a bad son and brother who hadn't protected his family. He just kept saying that he should never have left you alone. He was in a terrible state. He felt so responsible. And he had so much rage in him. But he was sad too. He knows what they do to people, to women, and he had seen and heard what they had already done to you and your sister. He was terrified of what they might have done to your mother too."

He paused to clear his throat and then took a half-crushed pack of cigarettes from his pocket, lit one and inhaled the smoke.

"Jamil wanted to find out where they were keeping you and attack the place that same night. But, they have so many bases, it would be like looking for a needle in a haystack. That is what we all thought, but he didn't care. No one could talk to him."

Ria inched a little closer.

"After he got the photo of you, our unit met. He told us that a few of us would go to observe a military base that night. He had an idea that it was there they were holding you. We weren't going to do anything he said, just go and see. It was a base near the border, the nearest to your town."

He stretched out one of his legs, rubbing it as if it were bothering him. It was then Ria caught a glimpse of his hand. She stared. Omar was right. One finger was missing, his index finger. As she looked at it, suddenly a different image flashed into her mind, of a different hand, a dirty hand with missing fingers. She felt disgusted and confused by this intrusive, disturbing image and shook herself.

"Then what happened," Ria asked needing to get that image out of her mind.

"We prepared our equipment and left soon after." He said.

27

She looked at the man more closely now as he paused to light another cigarette. He looked tired and worn and seemed more reluctant to continue. She was unsure whether or not she wanted him to, but this was the only time they would meet. She was silent for a while mulling over her options before deciding whether to press him for more. How much more was there to tell? She was afraid to hear any more, but she had to get to the end. Then she could decide if she believed his story or not.

"Then what happened?" Ria asked.

"We were doing all our pre-checks with our network sources to make sure everything was okay in the general area of the base when word came in that something was going on there. There was more military activity than usual going on at the base near the border. There was even talk of foreign soldiers there. Jamil had been worried about the foreign fighters and mercenaries as I told you before."

Ria realised she had caught her breath. She knew somehow that now she teetered on the brink of finding out something terrible but still she felt compelled to know it, no matter what it was. She tensed.

"Can I have a cigarette?" She asked.

He picked up the crumpled pack of cigarettes with his good hand and passed her one. She took one and he lit it, noticing her much her hand was trembling as she held the cigarette. She was not a smoker. She had tried it before and hated it but now she needed something to hold on to as she waited for what was coming.

"There were just four of us from my unit, and then Jamil and Alana. We were armed so we had to be careful as it was still daytime, sometime in the afternoon. We left the truck hidden in the trees a few kilometres away from your old house. We walked from there. Your house had been burned down. Jamil said nothing."

Ria felt something stir again. Burned ruins of their house near trees? Her house was near fields of olives. She could feel something pull free in her mind. She saw an image of smoke in the sky in her mind but nothing more. Her heartbeat accelerated slightly, moving up a gear.

The man continued. "We walked for a long time through some olive groves until we came to a group of hills from, we walked quite a while until we found a position from where we could observe the base without being seen. We had to be careful, there are always a lot of patrols near the border and the soldiers are better trained in those border bases. Jamil said he didn't know the base, but he did know some people in the town who worked there, you know cooks, cleaners, and people like that who were employed by the military, but not military."

Ria inhaled deeply on the cigarette, spluttering as she did. In her mind's eye, a brightly lit building in the middle of darkness flitted across her mind. Hills. She flinched.

He must have heard her splutter. "What is it?" he asked. "Maybe this is too much for you, or too quick? Maybe it is dangerous for you to remember too fast? If it is true, that you have no memory that is…" He said.

"Don't worry about me" she snapped. "I am fine, just cold." She felt very irritable. "Maybe it would be too much if it was true."

He looked at her with contempt and stubbed out his cigarette vigorously on her step. "If you aren't going to believe it, why bother listening?"

"What I don't understand about your story." Ria started.

"Story?" he said, "This is not a story."

Ria ignored him and continued. "Jamil is not a terrorist so why would the military say that about him? You said we were being held by the military, that there were photos of my sister and of me beaten up. Do you not think I would remember if that had happened?"

Ria heard herself speaking loudly and too quickly. Ria felt sick. The screaming. She somehow knew that something about that was all true. How she knew she could not tell, she just did.

234

"You are right. Jamil is not a terrorist. He's a revolutionary, like all of us. We were not working with any of the terrorist groups except for information sharing, but Jamil didn't care what they were saying about him. All he cared about was what they were doing with you. He felt responsible." the man said.

"Why don't you let me continue Ria? Soon you will understand. As I said, from our position on the hills we could see the military base below. Jamil was distracted or affected. Jamil is usually very calm during operations but up there on the hills we could all see he was very agitated. We watched for a while but there was not much to see, just a military base in the middle of nowhere."

Something stirred again in her.

"Jamil wanted to go back to your house. He wanted to speak to someone he knew. It was dangerous but he convinced Alana to let him go so he took me with while she stayed with the others. She gave us an hour. It was dangerous for them to stay on the hill and dangerous for us to go back to where he lived. She wasn't happy but I think she just understood that he had to get answers."

"Jamil and I walked back to your neighbourhood. Then we went up to a nearby house. He knocked on the back door. He didn't tell me anything. It was early evening by now, and no one answers their doors anymore. We went round to the back door. It was locked so Jamil took out his knife and broke the lash on the window and we went in through the window. There were two men just standing there, one older man and a younger one about our age looking very frightened." The man said looking straight at Ria.

Ria said nothing. Her brother breaking into their neighbour's houses with knives. What the hell? She did not know this version of her brother.

"Jamil greeted the man. He called him 'Abu'. When they saw it was Jamil they relaxed and seemed happy to see him, though they looked worried about him being there."

"Abu you say?" Ria echoed.

She knew Abu, their neighbour and his son. She knew too that Jamil knew him. She saw their faces clearly. Their mother was very close to Abu's family. Maybe this was not a story this man was making up after all.

"Jamil told this Abu about the messages the military had been sending him about you all, and that he had seen what they had done to the house. The man put his arms around Jamil's shoulders and said told him that as he knew well it was the military who had done that soon after the massacre. He said these words more or less. *'Your mother is sharper than anyone. She knew they would come looking for you, so she took your sisters, and they ran for the border. She called me before they left to tell me in case you came looking. But the military arrived at the house more quickly than she expected and burnt the house down straight away.'* Then he told Jamil that your mother probably didn't have enough time to get away. The younger man was Abu's son and he said he had heard talk that one of the patrols had caught your mother and you and your sister in the hills. He knows a few people who work at the base, and one had told him that they had heard some of the soldiers talking about you, that the military had caught you and had you there. Jamil was devastated." Malik stopped and turned to look at her, watching her expression closely.

Ria suddenly felt as if there was a fist clenched around her throat. She no longer saw the man sitting on the step below her. All she could hear was a loud noise in her ears, like a deep throbbing, and then a blanket of blackness surrounded her, and she felt as if she was falling away into blackness.

28

Ria felt a sudden hard weight smack into her. She tried to stand up and to push against whatever it was but almost fell.

"I was just trying to stop you from falling. You looked as if you were about to faint!" He snapped, his hand firmly gripping her arm, indignant.

"Shut up!" She screamed at him. "Don't you ever touch me again!"

"Keep quiet!" He said. "People will notice us. Do you want the police here?" she could see he was indignant and angry. "You said you wanted the truth!"

"I don't care! I don't want to listen to any more of these, these *lies*! Why would you lie about things like this?" Something had become unhinged in Ria, and she felt as if she was about to lose control.

"I wish they were lies, believe me. It is the truth. I think you know it is." He said. "If not, you would not act in this way."

"Go to hell!" Ria said and with that turned and stormed up the steps.

She had to get away from him. The steps were very steep though and she didn't have enough air in her lungs so after a few she was forced to slow down. She slowed to take the steps one at a time, rage propelling her upwards and further away from him. She glanced back over her shoulder to see if he was following her, almost too scared to look, but was surprised to see that he was still sitting there on the step, smoking. His legs stretched out in front of him, facing forward, unperturbed by her flight.

She stopped and sat down on a step, relieved he hadn't moved because she was too dizzy to continue running. But she wanted to stay too. As she had come up the steps, she had noticed that there was a narrow street with a dimly lit wooded park next to it. She felt safer being up there, further away from him, ready to run again if necessary. She needed time, time to think, time to get her breath back. How could she, her mother, and Hana have been in some military base, locked in a cell and not have any memory of that now? Yet, though she didn't want to admit it, there was just too much about the story that resonated with her and rang true. Malik could not have known about Abu, her mother's friend and neighbour. He seemed to know a lot about Jamil's personality too. How could he know these things if he was lying? What would even be the point of making up such a story? There was no point.

"I will stay up here. Please, continue your story, I want to hear it all, but quickly, soon we must go. I do not have much time." she lied. "We are both far now from our centres and it is very late"
She saw him nod.

"You *must* hear what I have to say. You will see that when I come to the end of my 'story' as you call it, it will mark the beginning of yours" he said looking up at her

She shook her head in exasperation. "Stop talking in riddles. I am not a child."
He smirked. She baulked.

"After hearing what that man Abu said, Jamil now knew for sure that you were in the base Alana and the men were still watching. Jamil asked the son if he had heard anything else, but he hadn't. Jamil was very upset. Anyway, we made our way back to the hills where Alana and the others were."

Ria sat there listening. When he talked of this Jamil it sounded like her brother. Ria felt a connection to this Jamil he talked about, this sad, upset, angry Jamil, not to the fighter. She checked her watch it was almost one thirty, there wasn't that long to go before she had to meet the women. She did not know how long it would take to get back to the meeting point from where she was now, and she could risk missing them.

The man had stopped talking but She had caught a slight difference in his voice before he stopped. Maybe, something terrible had happened next, to Jamil, or to him? His hand maybe.

"Then, what happened?" She asked more gently now, feeling calmer and less panicked, now more focused on getting back to the women in time. She tried to feel more compassionate towards him but found it difficult.

"Jamil went to speak to Alana, I assume he told her what the old man and his son had told him. I saw her hug him. Then, he came back to where I was. Jamil led one group off to one side, and Alana led the other in the opposite direction, I was with Alana's group. There were no instructions. We just stayed there, watching. There was no plan." He said

Ria felt the familiar feeling of terror rising in her chest again. She had an urgent need to urinate. There was no time, and she could hardly interrupt him for that. Anyway, where would she go? It was the cold step perhaps. She stood up and pressed her thighs harder together, one eye on the time on her phone. She glanced at the map as well to check how far away she was. She walked down a couple of steps. He stood up to face her, barring her way.

He lit yet another cigarette and continued. "I did not like us being up there. We were extremely exposed on that hill, too near the base and it was still late afternoon. We had no cover at all. I thought it was reckless. If we stayed there much longer, we were sure to be spotted by a patrol. Then what? But with Alana, you did not question orders, you did as you were told." He paused. "I am no coward, but I was afraid. Alana and Jamil were watching the base from two different hills, and the rest of us were just double checking each other's equipment and weapons in case a patrol did find us."

"I have to go soon Malik. Please." Ria said impatient for him to get to the end as he called it, and an eye on the time.

He ignored her. "Then, suddenly out of nowhere we heard a very loud sound. It was coming from the air. It was an incredible sound to hear. Planes, loud planes. I can't even describe the sound. It was like nothing I had ever experienced. Those planes were so loud that we had to cover our ears. I looked up and at first, I couldn't see anything, then some indistinct flashes. Then it happened, I couldn't believe it. As we watched from those hills the

241

whole military base below us blew up and turned into a mass of black and orange flames and smoke. It took a while for us to realise that those planes had blown up the base. Alana told us to run back to the truck as fast as we could. This airstrike would bring more soldiers. So, we ran like hell to get away from there. It was a terrible thing to witness for all of us, but it was to be the first of many such airstrikes. But can you imagine what it must have been like for Jamil knowing you were all down there?"

Malik stopped speaking as if seeing it all in his head again. Then he looked up at her, a dark expression on his face.

"So, Ria, how can you explain that you are here? Alive, and apparently well?"

Ria felt him become larger at the bottom of the steps.

Ria turned quickly and started running back up the steps again and this time she didn't stop, she kept on going, and she didn't look back either. She just ran down the street next to the park and kept on running.

29

Ria's breath was ragged, and her underwear felt bulky from having wet herself and was chafing against her skin as she ran. There had been neither time nor place to stop for anything. She ran on, along the dimly lit streets and kept heading straight until she saw the more brightly lit part of the city up ahead. She stopped and bent over hands on her thighs, trying to regain her breath while keeping a watchful eye on her surroundings. She looked behind her and was relieved to see no sign of him. There were very few people around, the ones there were loud, young people milling outside bars or nightclubs. An ambulance siren screeched by causing her to start.

Ria felt relieved to be rid of the man, she took out her phone to check the time and saw there was only half an hour to until the meeting time with the women. She stood up and looked around to get her bearings and caught sight of *her* landmark, the bridge. It was always there when she needed it. She started to walk towards it, stopping now and again to make sure he was nowhere in sight. He was not, or at least not that she could see. She hesitated. She was early.

As always, she felt that strange draw to the bridge and to the river below it. After what she had been listening to for the last few hours, all she wanted to do was to go to it. But going there now would be stupid. Not only would she be much more exposed on the bridge if the man came looking for her, but also any miscalculation in her judgement of the distance might make her late for the women. On the other hand, she couldn't just stand alone in a dark alleyway that had only one way in and one way out for thirty minutes either. She would be trapped if he did find her. If she waited on the street, she would stand out to any patrolling police car, which would surely stop and question her. She would have neither explanation nor papers and they could arrest her, then she would have to explain how she got out and that would involve others. She didn't know what to do. She felt out of any good options. She looked around again, this time more slowly and more carefully.

There were a few people outside some sort of bar. That looked like a better place to wait. From there she could see the entrance to the alleyway and there were other people around, the kind of people who were with their friends and having a good time. They would pay no attention to her. They looked pretty drunk anyway and she would blend in better with people. She almost laughed out loud at that thought. How could she possibly blend in here?

She started to cross the road in the direction of the bar where a couple of groups of people were hanging around outside. As she got closer, many of them melted away and there was now only one group of four young men remaining. She hesitated a little as she saw them. She swore under her breath and kept her head down. They were smoking and laughing but then she saw one of them notice her, she watched him say something to the others as he nodded in her direction. They all turned round to look, no longer laughing, all silent now. Ria thought she saw anger in their expressions. She felt the hairs on the back of her neck stand on end and a chill run down her back. She could see now as she was closer that they were the wrong group of people for someone like her to be near and alone. But it was too late to turn back. They had seen her.

"Hey, jihadi." one of them shouted to her in English. "Did you piss yourself?" he said, and they all laughed. Then there was more laughing as more comments were made in their language, no doubt at her expense. She was grateful she didn't understand them. But she had understood the significance of the greeting 'Jihadi'. She stopped, wary now.

They were standing on the pavement about three or four metres away. She could not outrun them and anyway, she had no more run left in her. She glanced at her phone. Still twenty minutes to go. Too long. She cursed her decision not to go to the bridge.

The group, led by the man who had called her 'Jihadi', edged nearer.

"What are you doing out here so late, Jihadi, eh? All by yourself. That's strange, isn't it?" He said speaking English now. "Are all you jihadi women not supposed to be always with your man? What are you doing out here so late? I bet you are planning to attack this bar here. That's what you people do. Well, we cannot let you do that now, can we boys?"

Ria took a step back, but he continued to insult her, and the group now surged forward as one towards her.

"Who will protect us from you people, if not us? The police? Fuck them! All they do is protect you parasites! Our government gives you beds, food, and clothes all paid for with *our* hard-earned money and all you do is blow us up and attack us in the streets! Our government is as stupid as you people. You dirty Jihadi bitch!"

He was shouting at her now, his face contorted by anger. She was afraid. The others were jostling next to him, but all of Ria's senses were focused on a small, muscular-looking blond man who had taken a bigger step forward, the leader of the pack, she thought. His fists were clenched into a ball, and he stood like a boxer. Ria registered his barely contained rage. He took another step towards her, then another, and then he sprung forward, the others moving swiftly behind him. She glanced around, there was no-one else. No one to stop this. She braced herself for the blow that she knew was coming. They had gone so quiet, so deadly quiet. She was powerless.

The first blow hurt a lot. He hit her right in the stomach with his fist. She had expected to be struck on her face, so she was not prepared for that. But it was the second blow that hurt the most. As she instinctively doubled over at the sudden pain in her stomach region, she received a hard knee strike up into her jaw, executed with such force it caused her head to snap backwards, and she crashed backwards onto the hard ground. The impact of her jaw against the knee had caused her to bite down hard on her tongue. She felt the intense pain of the whiplash-like feeling in her neck, the hard road hitting her head and the intense pain of her tongue, she tasted the blood that was quickly filling her mouth. Horrified, she lay on her back on the side of the street, helpless as they began kicking her all over her body. She managed to turn onto her side defensively and tried to protect her damaged jaw and head with her arms. She would not make it out of this alive. The kicks just get on coming.

"Stop!" She heard a woman's voice ring out.
Was that her voice? Was she dying? But then she heard it again, very clearly.

"Hey, nazi boys! I said Stop! Either you stop doing that now or …. look what we have for you." The woman's voice shouted again.

The kicking suddenly stopped. Then, words were shouted in the men's language, and Ria heard them running away shouting back insults as they did.

"Ria! Ria, are you okay? It's us from the centre. It's okay to look, they have gone. Look at me." The woman said, it was the same voice she had heard shouting at the men to stop.

Ria uncovered her face and looked up. All she could feel was pain. The woman's face was still covered as it had been before. She crouched down beside Ria, her hand gently touching Ria's forehead.

"It is okay, we are here now. We will get you back. Come help me lift her." she said to legs beside her.

Ria felt herself being lifted like a feather. Once in the alleyway, the women put her sitting down with her back against the wall.

"Let me look at her" she heard the same woman say.

She began touching different parts of Ria, starting with her jaw, then she lifted her sweater and gently pressed her stomach and sides. It hurt like hell.

"Ria, I need you to open your mouth now very slowly okay."

Ria shook her head.

"I know it will hurt, but I really must see inside, okay? Open your mouth. I will help you. Hold her shoulders back a little, gently now Ria, open."

Ria could not stand the pain. Blood flowed out as she opened her mouth wider.

"Ria, I am going to put my finger inside, okay? Even if it hurts a lot, you cannot close your mouth, or you will bite me or your tongue and that is dangerous for us both. Do you understand?"

Ria nodded reluctantly and felt the woman's cold finger pressing up against her tongue. It was agony. She flinched but managed to keep her mouth open, resisting the urge to close it.

The woman explored her mouth for a few seconds and then withdrew her finger.

"Ria, you have a very deep cut on your tongue from what I can see, but I can't see it properly without a torch. It might need stitches, and some of your teeth look cracked. I am not sure about that, it's hard to see out here. At least two or three of your ribs are badly bruised or cracked and your jaw is badly bruised, but it might not be as bad as it looks. Does it hurt anywhere else Ria? We must get you back to the centre, I can do more there."

"My neck" Ria mumbled. "My neck."

The woman felt her neck and shoulder muscles. "It is probably the muscles, like whiplash, Ria."

"This is going to complicate things." Ria heard another woman say.

"Give me the hood." The woman who had examined her said.

Ria tried to speak but it was as if there was some enormous balloon in her mouth. She pointed to the hood with great difficulty and shook her head. Shaking her head caused her great pain so she stopped.

"She was afraid of the hood coming out. Now, we cannot make her put it on, not after this." The woman said.

"We cannot trust her. She will see." A different woman replied.

"Ria, we understand about the hood, but we cannot let you see. I am sorry. Will you let us blindfold your eyes only?" The woman asked her.

Ria nodded. Anything, she would do anything if it meant she didn't have to wear that hood. Ria heard a sharp tearing of cloth and then the woman wrapped a piece of dark cloth gently over her eyes. The blackness she experienced was terrifying again, but it was better than the hood. The woman took her hands in hers. The touch felt calming to Ria and kind. Slowly the other women helped her up.

"Ready?" The woman asked. Ria nodded. "Let's go, it will take us longer. We can't be late."

The women carried Ria effortlessly for quite a while. She was in a lot of pain, and it only got worse with all the moving.

Eventually, they removed the blindfold. They were back inside the centre. She was with two women now, one had gone. She recognised her corridor, her block, her door. One of the women knocked very softly on the door. It was Fatima who opened it, and Ria heard her gasp.

"What happened? Ria! Quick bring her in. I told her this was a bad idea. She should never have gone!"

Fatima took one side of her, and with the other women, they brought her in and closed the door behind them.

"It was not her fault. Some racist pigs got to her just before we arrived. They would have killed her. She is very badly injured. We do not have much time before the morning activity starts. They cannot see her like this."

They laid Ria down on one of the lower bunks. Any movement hurt so much.

"Now Ria, take these two pills. One is for the pain and the other one will relax you a little so I can look at the damage better. Shine the torch into her mouth, but not into her eyes." the woman who had examined her said.

After a while, Ria felt a very pleasant foggy sensation and surrendered herself willingly to it.

30

Ria felt herself being shaken gently, but still hard enough for it to hurt.

"Ria, wake up. You're screaming."

The voice sounded ghost-like to Ria.

"Ria, Ria" the ghost kept on calling to her.

She must be dead.

Ria strained to open her eyes but closed them quickly again, her eyelids felt so very heavy. She had to keep them closed but she didn't want to stay in here with the ghost.

"Ria!" The voice said, sharper, louder now, less ghostly.

"What?" She tried to say, eyes still tightly closed.

She heard her slurring voice, incomprehensible even to her, jolts of pain shot through every inch of her mouth as she moved it to form that short word.

"What did she give her?" Ria heard someone ask.

"I don't know. Something for the pain." Another voice replied.

There was something about that second voice. Ria forced her eyes open, dazzled as the light hurt her eyes. She squinted.

"Naira? Is that you?" Ria formed the words clearly in her head, but they came out all garbled and it was so painful to speak.

She stopped, forcing her eyes open. She could see now that it was Naira.

"Ria. How are you feeling?" Naira said.

Naira was here. They must both be dead. She felt sad for Naira, and for her son.

"Ria, listen to me. I am here with Fatima and the others. One of the women who brought you back last night is coming soon to check on you. She will help us decide what to do. Ria. Ria! Can you hear me?"

Ria heard her and saw her, but her mind was still floating so it was hard for her to understand what Naira was saying. She tried to nod. There were shooting pains in her neck and shoulders, and her head. She closed her eyes and stilled every muscle. Much better.

"Naira, maybe we should sit her up, if not she will fall asleep again and start that awful screaming. Then they'll hear her and come in. We can't let them see her, not yet. We have no story, no plan yet."

Naira's voice again. "Ria, you must sit up, I know it's hard, but you must try. I know you just want to sleep, but you can't, not yet."

Her voice was firm but gentle.

Ria felt arms pull her up and lean her back against something cold, more hands on her, then the weight of a blanket. She opened her eyes again, now a little more awake, but barely. What was going on?

"Screaming? See me? What?" Ria muttered in a low voice, but again it came out as garbled nonsense.

Ria felt herself being lifted by her underarms as someone else moved her legs. Then she was lying up against something nice and soft.

"Ria, try not to speak. Your mouth is injured and so is your jaw. Speaking will make the pain worse." Fatima said. "And we can't understand you anyway."

"Ria, come on, open your eyes. We are all in danger, you have to stay awake!" Naira's voice was louder now.
Ria's eyes snapped open.

"Here, drink this, careful now, it's only a little warm because of your tongue but it will help, Fatima has put some of her special herbs in it." Naira said as she leaned forward towards Ria with a small glass.

"Here Ria, let me help you."
Ria opened her mouth instinctively to sip but there was no response from her mouth. She tried to bring her hand to touch her mouth to investigate but was immediately stopped by a searing pain that shot from her side right up her forearm. She winced.

"It's okay, Ria, I know it all hurts. Your lips and the inside of your mouth are badly hurt, especially your tongue and jaw. So are your arms and ribs so don't move. You must drink this to hydrate, the woman said you are dehydrated, but do it carefully, a little at a time." Naira said and tried to give Ria some of the liquid, but it just spilled down Ria's neck.

It was nice and warm, comforting even.

"Fatima, bring me Khal's drinking cup. We can use that."
Fatima rinsed out the baby cup and handed it to Naira, who transferred what remained of the warm tea into the baby cup with a spout. Ria was able to take slow sips, but the liquid stung her tongue like a knife, and it was

extremely hard to swallow. The pain was making her feel less drowsy.

"Naira. So good...." Ria attempted to smile but stopped as her whole jaw protested. "......to see you."

"Ria don't worry about me. I'm fine. I'm sorry about what happened. But we can talk about that another time. Do you remember what happened last night?" Naira asked Ria in their language.

Ria tried to respond. "Naira, so many terrible dreams. Terrible things. I do not know what is real and what is not. I thought I was dead. I remember the men...beating me, the women carrying me, and then nothing more. It seems like a long time ago. Like a dream but I can feel the pain, so I suppose it was real. But then other things too. Terrible things."

"What is she saying?" Fatima asked Naira. Naira translated.

"Yes, Ria, it was last night." Naira switched back to English. "The women found you while those men were attacking you and stopped them before they could finish you off. But we cannot explain what really happened to the staff because you were outside of the centre past curfew, which is not permitted, and they will want to know how you got out and back in. That would not only be dangerous for you, but also for the women who helped you. So, we have to decide on a story that they will believe and that explains... well...that explains why you look like you do. It is not something we can hide, the injuries look very bad, some might look worse than they are, but they are impossible to hide. You look like you were beaten up. Also, you cannot speak properly. If they see you, they will ask questions and we have no explanation. Do you understand?"

Ria nodded very slightly wary of incurring more pain than she was already in. She gave up on speaking.

"One of the women who was with you last night is a doctor. She's coming back soon to see how you are, and to help us plan. The women are discussing that now. They want to make sure they are protected. You owe them that. But don't worry, everything will be ok, I promise. But Ria, you can't sleep now. I know you want to, that you need to, and I am so sorry Ria that this has happened to you. But you cannot." Naira said.

She took one of Ria's hands gently in hers, and gently stroked Ria's hair with her other hand. Ria felt a couple of tears slide down her cheek, but she could not cry, it would hurt too much so she shoved the lump in her throat back down.

Ria nodded. She flinched as she remembered the blows to her body, heard the sounds of the men shouting insults at her, then the silence only broken by the thuds and cracks of the boots on her body. Short microfilms playing over and over in her head. What had she been doing out of the centre? The man. Yes. Malik. She saw him clearly now, she saw herself running, and running. Why had she been running away from him? She wasn't supposed to be running. The neurologist had said that.

What drug had that woman given her? Those dreams had been so terrible. She was grateful for the sleep she had had, even though it had been filled with images of terrible

255

things. It had been so very long since she had last slept. The pain was getting worse. The worst of the pain was coming from inside her mouth and from her jaw. Her tongue felt gigantic, so big she found it impossible to swallow so she began to panic, eyes wide and trying to move.

"Ria, what's wrong?" Naira asked a worried look on her face. "Is it the pain?"

Ria shook her head. Naira seemed to understand that it was something more than just the pain. Naira took her hands in hers and smiled at Ria. Ria saw the bandages on Naira's wrists scuffed by the dirt of the centre. Ria stared at them, then looked at Naira.

"It's okay now. You don't have to worry about me." Naira said. "I'm okay, and I'm okay about Khal."

Before Naira could say anything else, the door opened, and two women came in. As they bent down to look at her in the bunk, she saw that their faces were still completely covered. Just eyes looking out at her.

The smaller one came nearer. "How is she?" She asked Fatima.

"We just woke her up because she was screaming badly in her sleep. We had to. We were afraid they would come in about the screaming and see her like that. She is in a lot of pain. She can't speak with her tongue and jaw, and she can't move."

The smaller woman looked at Ria. All Ria could see was her eyes, she had kind eyes.

"Ria, I need you to open your mouth again." The woman said to Ria. "I'm going to shine a torch in, okay? Don't close your mouth. Promise?"

Ria shook her head and closed her mouth as much as she was able. Her heartbeat accelerated and she felt lightheaded. No way was she opening her mouth. The pain with her mouth shut was already too much.

"Ria, I know it hurts a lot to open your mouth. But I must see the cut better and examine the jaw in a better light. Outside there was no time, no light. I need to check for any breaks, or any infection starting in the cut on your tongue. I will be quick I promise. Just open it a little at a time. Be brave, okay? Then I promise I will give you something more for the pain." the woman said.

Ria hesitated but the promise of something for the pain was enough, so she opened her mouth very slowly. Tears streamed down her face with the pain, soundless tears. Oh, the shame with everyone looking on at her crying. How could she be so weak in front of these strong, brave women? How could she have been so stupid last night as to put them all at risk? She was so stupid.

"Okay, you can close it now. You will have to get on antibiotics as soon as possible. I don't think the cut is deep enough on the tongue to need stitches as I thought before so that is good news. It will take time to heal though. You are brave Ria. I know that hurt a lot. Now, let me check the rest of you. Fatima, bring me some scissors" the woman doctor said.

Ria watched as the woman cut her sweater up along the arms and cut her jeans along the sides of her legs. She was gentle. She watched the faceless woman examine every part of her. She felt embarrassed. She could smell her own rancid body odour and the faint smell of dried urine. The doctor moved her body parts back and forth and pressed and pushed. Ria felt a cold sweat form on her brow.

The woman was quick, yet she did not rush. She must be a very good doctor Ria thought. Better than she had ever had at least.

The woman finished and sat down on the bunk looking at Ria with the other women looking on.

"Ria, there are some very bad cuts which need better antiseptic cleaning and cleaner dressings. I would say you also need an X-ray on your left wrist, it could be fractured. Your ribs are very bruised, and I cannot tell if any are cracked, it's impossible to know. Either way, it is binding them and then resting for a few weeks. The rest of your body is badly bruised all over, deep bruises, they must have been wearing heavy boots. You have cuts all over your body too, some quite deep that might need some stitches. You will have to be seen by an 'official doctor' for all of that, and as soon as possible. The cuts on your tongue, in your mouth and all the other cuts must not become infected, and as I said, we need to get that wrist checked. So, we need a plan and fast. It's almost morning." The doctor said, looking at the other women expectantly.

"You say they saw her come in yesterday evening?" The woman asked looking at Fatima.

"Yes, the woman who was at reception control last night hates Ria, well, she hates all of us, but Ria in particular, so she always notices her and tries to provoke her. If it had been someone else who had been there, perhaps something could be done but not with this woman. Anyway, it doesn't matter, Ria signed in… so…" Fatima said.

One of the other women spoke. "Discussing options, we came up with this plan. We have to get Ria outside again without them seeing her like this, then we will need her to have an 'accident' happen somewhere outside of the centre. That way, she will get the medical attention she needs, and no questions will be asked about what really happened and no-one will need to know that she was outside last night, or who with. The injuries are still fresh enough if we do not delay."

"But she can't even walk!" Fatima said indignantly. "How is she going to leave here? And look at her face? She will be seen for sure by one of the staff. How will that plan work?"

"Look, we have been trying to think what to do since we got back and we can see no other way, she has to leave while the injuries are still very fresh. She needs medical attention now, so the accident has to happen outside the centre, and as soon as it opens. There is no other way because it cannot have happened in here. There is no fall or fight that can explain all these injuries that does not get someone innocent in here in trouble. This way is the only way." The taller woman of the two said.

"I will take her. Most of the staff, except that woman Karine, confuse Ria and me. You know what they are like when you are not white. We all look the same to them — just Arabs — we are almost the same age too.

Fatima, you can help me with her. Today is very cold and wet so we can cover her head and face with scarves and winter clothes and walk supporting her one of us on each side. Ria will just have to keep her head down, especially away from the camera at the entrance. I will cover up too in a similar way, similar colours." Naira said.

"But what about signing out? How can she do that without them seeing her face? Or her hand? She can't even move her arms let alone walk up to the reception desk alone and sign a sheet." Fatima said.

"I can do it," Ria said with difficulty.
No more tears. She so wanted to be brave. She didn't want to be a problem for anyone, especially not these women who had saved her life.

"Look, what if we send someone to reception before you go down with Ria, our person will help distract the person in reception control while Naira signs out for Ria. You said they can't tell the difference between you on a normal day so with headscarves and hoods, they won't notice. We checked who was on reception control today and it's that big man who is always on his phone, watching videos, playing games and those things. We will make sure he is looking at something else and talking to the person we send when you all get to reception control. When it is Ria's turn to sign, Naira signs for her. We will send someone down who we know he likes a lot. You know. Young, pretty, and of course, white." The taller woman said wryly.

Ria saw the doubt cross Fatima's face. Naira looked determined. Ria knew it was the only way. It was a good plan, but she didn't want to put Fatima or anyone at risk.

"Fatima, this is the *only* way. Now let's all get moving and get it done!" The taller woman said in a tone that was not to be ignored.

"Okay, but then what? What do we do when we get outside?" Fatima asked.

"Once you get outside, you find a place very near here. She cannot go far in that state even with your help so find somewhere with not many people, but close by. Then, lay her down half on the pavement, half on the road and call the emergency number for an ambulance. Say she was hit by a cyclist who was going too fast, and Ria didn't look before stepping off the pavement. They won't ask many questions. The police will not come for something like that, and if they do, well, just repeat the story."

"A cyclist?" Fatima exclaimed. "They won't believe that. Look at her! Why not tell the truth and say she was attacked by those little racist pigs?"

"Fatima, no. If we do that, the police will be called, they will ask too many questions, which will require too many lies. Also, they won't care if Ria was attacked, believe me. We must not get the police involved, just the ambulance people and the hospital. Keep it simple. No police. It doesn't matter what the ambulance people or medical staff believe, they will know the injuries are more than what would happen with a cyclist, but they won't do anything. They won't want the police complicating their day either. All you have to do is keep telling the same story. You were about to cross the road, you were talking, Ria didn't see the cyclist, who came very fast along the road, and she stepped into his path. He crashed into her, got up and rode away. He didn't stop to help. You are indignant, angry even. You don't remember what he looks like, you were attending to Ria. That is it. Nothing more. Now get her ready. There is no time to waste."

31

The women left. Fatima and Naira exchanged worried looks, or at least that is how it looked to Ria in her foggy state. Ria did not want to move. She knew just how much it was going to hurt, not to mention the risk, but there was no other way. She was not going to be the one who exposed the same women who had come to her rescue when she was in trouble. No way.

"Mirror," Ria mumbled.

Fatima looked at Naira who nodded. Fatima took her small make-up mirror over to Ria so that she could see herself. She looked, but nothing could have prepared her for what she saw. She gasped and recoiled at the reflection in the mirror. Who was that? It didn't even look like her. She stared at herself, wanting to look away but was unable to, transfixed by the grotesque ugliness of the person looking back at her. She looked up at Fatima, tears in her eyes and saw tears in Fatima's too. Pain was so familiar to them all Ria thought.

Ria nodded, braced, and tried to pull herself together both mentally and physically. Fatima put the mirror away and the two women got to work on dressing Ria. They were gentle but it was agony for Ria. She could feel the tears rolling down her cheeks. She bled into the clean clothes, and blood ran down her forehead from the gash on her head.

"Let's get you up onto your feet now Ria. The women said to be in the reception control area in twenty minutes, so we don't have much time." Fatima said.

They hauled her up slowly, supporting her carefully, until she stood with help. Ria immediately felt much worse, and very anxious. She shook her head very slowly back and forth. No. No way. She could not do this. They would have to find another way.

Naira stood in front of her, standing tall, one arm still supporting Ria. Ria caught Naira wince as Ria's weight on Naira's bandaged wrists must have hurt her.

"Ria, I know this is hard and it is a risk. I know it is going to hurt a lot for a long time. But we have no choice. If this plan works, you will be treated by hospital staff and feel better. You must do it for yourself and for all of us involved. There is no other way. Use your anger. Use your anger against those racist pigs. You will not be their victim. Use your anger. Now come on." Naira's rousing words were delivered in their language.

Fatima looked on impatiently.

As Naira spoke Ria felt the anger Naira was summoning rise quickly and with force. It felt very raw. She thought of the unfairness of everything, and let herself feel self-pity, but mostly she felt angry. Very angry, angry enough to forget her fear of the pain for a while. Angry that Naira had to hurt herself to do this for Ria.

"That's it Ria, keep the rage! Now, just keep thinking of all the things they have done to you, here and back home. Just stay focused on that. We will get through this. We will get you out. Remember they will be

265

distracting the man at reception so he will not pay any attention to us. And our faces will be covered. But you cannot make any sounds of pain or give any sign that something is wrong no matter how much it hurts. All you have to do is lean on both of us, without it being obvious. Ria, just do the best you can. Then I will sign twice. He won't even notice. Don't worry. Come on. Time to go. Ria, keep your head down, especially in reception and away from the camera." Naira continued.

Ria with new-found motivational rage, felt stronger. She would not let them down. She knew where the camera was. Fatima and Naira put a long, thick coat on Ria and then covered her head with a large hat, her face covered by a scarf right up to her nose and then a thick winter scarf wound over that. They put on large snow gloves to cover the bruising on her hands. Then they covered themselves in the same way and helped Ria to lean on Fatima mostly, she was the strongest and Naira had to sign twice.

"Are you ready?" Fatima asked gently.

Ria nodded. She was cold sweating in the coat, but she kept focused on staying angry. She called up the images of the faces of the men who had beaten her to keep her mind off her pain and channel more anger. It was easy to feel angry at the men who had attacked her, and at Malik too and at all the faceless people who had brought her here and were now keeping her from her family. To her surprise, she felt very angry at her brother, Jamil. Why she felt that way she did not know but of all the people she directed her anger at, it was her brother who angered her the most.

By the time they were shuffling out into the brightly lit corridor, Ria had managed to bring frustration into the mix. She could barely move but pushed herself to walk as normally as possible. It was slow going, but at least she could manage more than a shuffle. They could not afford to attract anyone's attention on the way to reception.

She kept her eyes down. There were cameras in the corridors as well. As they moved closer to the reception control area, she heard people laughing.

They exchanged looks but kept moving forward. As they entered the reception area Ria saw a white woman, with very long dark hair, draped over the reception counter. She was pretty Ria thought, but she kept her head down. The man behind the counter was standing and she seemed to be showing him something on her phone. They were both laughing at whatever it was. The woman was wearing a very low-cut t-shirt, and the man paid no attention to the three women as they walked towards the exit. Fatima moved Ria near the exit and stood there while Naira went to sign out for the first time.

Ria could not see much, but she could hear everything. That annoying laughter, the booming voice of the man. In seconds Naira was back at her side, she took Ria's arm to support it and Fatima went to sign out. As soon as Fatima came back, Naira went back to sign out as Ria. Ria could hear Fatima catch her breath and Ria dared not breathe.

As Naira was walking towards the counter, the dark-haired woman shrieked in laughter and the man said something to her and they both laughed again. Naira came back quickly and took Ria's other arm, and all three of them went out of the main exit and outside, the sound of the woman's laughter still echoing in Ria's ears. In the end, it had been easy. Ria could hardly believe it.

Once outside they kept moving, they were almost lifting her off her feet now to move faster, which was causing more pressure and pain in her ribs. No-one looked back.

"They are good, those women," Naira said.

Ria wanted to know more about who they were. They had saved her life. But as she could not speak that would have to wait. They seemed very secretive so she didn't think she would get much information about them. Maybe she could join them in whatever it was they were doing. It seemed exciting. They probably wouldn't let her. They were probably not very impressed with her.

"I know a place. It is right around there. Never any people around. Especially now with this rain. Come on Ria, just a couple more steps and you will soon be taken care of." Fatima said breathless now with the effort of carrying most of Ria's weight.

Ria nodded and put up with the pain in her ribs and mouth as if her life depended on it. Let it never be said she was weak! Soon they came to a small park area with swings and slides and a small green space. There was a man there walking a dog, but he soon moved off in the opposite direction. It was raining heavily.

"Here. This is a good place. Fatima, you should call the ambulance, not me. You know, with all this." Naira said and raised up one of her wrists. "They will be less suspicious if they talk to you. We should remove the face coverings now. Ria, we are going to put you down on the pavement, okay? You need to be wetter and look more fallen. Fatima, here grab her arm, and let's position her half on, half off the pavement."

Ria felt as if she was dying. The agony of being laid down on a wet, cold surface in that position was a living nightmare. The rain was cold, and the large ice-cold drops hit her damaged mouth and face like sharp knives.

"Fatima, call, do it now. She can't stay like this for long, the pain will be too much and maybe they will take their time to get here. Say it is urgent." Naira said.

Ria saw Fatima cast an irritated glance at Naira, Fatima perhaps did not want to call either, but she did it, and very well too.

It wasn't that long before they heard an ambulance siren and soon an ambulance pulled up near where Ria lay, lights flashing. It had come quickly Ria thought with relief, but she was worried too. She did not trust these people, and she knew all too well that they did not trust people like her.

Two men and a woman jumped down from the ambulance, all dressed in red and white uniforms, the woman had a large bag with her and seemed to be in charge.

"What happened to her?" She asked as she knelt next to Ria, looking over her wounds.

"We were out walking, and she stepped out to cross the road. She didn't see the cyclist coming on a bicycle. He was going very quickly, and he crashed into her knocking her down. She must have hit her head on the side of the pavement."

"Where is the cyclist?" One of the men asked with a frown.

"He insulted us! As if it was Ria's fault! Then he picked up his bike, got back on it and rushed off. He was angry and you know, and we did not want any trouble with him." Fatima said indignantly.

The man raised an eyebrow but didn't ask any more questions.

"Bring the stretcher, she needs to get in out of this rain." The woman said.

The two men moved her carefully onto a stretcher, Ria protested at the pain and soon she was inside the ambulance with the doors wide open. It was cold but at least it was dry.

Ria could not see Fatima or Naira.

"What is her name?" The woman shouted out to the women.

"Ria" Her name is Ria." Ria heard Fatima answer.

"Ria, I need you to open your mouth." The woman said to Ria. Her voice was firm but gentle.

Ria did as she was told. Pain was just pain, and it could be endured she told herself. The woman had a little pen torchlight. She was gentle but as soon as she touched Ria's tongue, Ria pulled away in pain, clamping her mouth shut. The woman pulled out her latex-covered fingers just in time.

"Let's take her to the emergency ward. She will need to get some X-rays on her jaw, rib cage and maybe her wrist. I don't like the look of that cut on her tongue, it will need to be looked at better with local anaesthetic. We'll have to check for fractures all over. Get one of the friends to come with her, they will need her details at the hospital, and she can't speak. It seems a lot for a cycling injury." the paramedic said.

The woman looked at Ria. Ria looked away.

Ria saw Fatima's face come into view as she stepped up into the ambulance. She was disappointed, she wished it was Naira who was coming. But she was grateful to Fatima and understood why Naira would not want to go to a hospital again so soon, or even get into an ambulance.

"Ria, I am going to inject you with a very mild painkiller, okay? I cannot give you anything stronger until they have seen you at the hospital. But it will help a little for now at least and make the journey less painful" The woman said and smiled.

Ria nodded. She felt the prick of a needle, then a warm blanket was placed over her. It all felt so comforting she felt herself about to cry again. Stop! Fatima sat next to her, hand on her shoulder, looking nervously around her.

The doors slammed shut and Ria closed her eyes, exhausted and tense. She jumped as the siren came on, and off they went.

32

A few days had passed since Ria had been picked up by the ambulance. The hospital doctor had told her that she had been lucky. Lucky? He said that her mouth would heal with time and there would likely be no infection because of the antibiotics they had given her. For the cuts and bruises they couldn't do much either. Some of the deeper gashes had been stitched and the previous wound on her head re-examined. She had had a head scan just to make sure all that was okay. Her ribs were very badly bruised, but again, in time they would heal. She had been dispatched after a few hours from the emergency ward clasping a bag of antibiotics and painkillers and 'something to help her sleep'. Those she would not take. She was treated with polite indifference and the occasional sterile smile. Even though Ria was beginning to get used to that polite indifference, it still affected her deeply and the hurt she felt each time nurtured her anger.

Ria was supposed to remain on a liquid diet for a couple of weeks, which had been a battle for Fatima to get the centre to comply with, but in the end, the doctor's report had carried more weight than their reluctance and she had eventually received her daily liquid diet. Naira and Fatima had been helping her move to and from the bathroom for several days now. She was still in great pain all over her body, but Ria was surprised at how much comfort she found in the minute-to-minute experiencing of agonising physical pain. This type of pain was real, tangible and it had a known cause. The pain she had felt before the beating had been a different kind of pain. Pain was perhaps not quite the right word, but she could find no other word that fit the sensation well enough. But now, if her mouth hurt, she knew it was her mouth, if her ribs hurt, she knew it was her ribs. The pain in each place was different but distinguishable.

Months ago, when she had first woken up in the hospital with no idea of how she had come to be there, the headache she had experienced had been terrible, but what had been so much worse was the other type of pain that she never managed to shake off and could not find any reason for its presence. It was worse than anything she had ever felt before, and it had lingered in her body, a constant companion, since then. She was pleased that now this physical pain in her body distracted from that other pain. She knew it was still there, that it would resurface so to delay its return she made sure to only take half the quantity of pain medication she was supposed to take, flushing the rest down the toilet. She wanted the real pain to last as long as possible.

Ria also found herself with far too much time to think, confined to bunk and bathroom as she was. She still couldn't speak because of her mouth. She didn't care about that, she actually preferred it that way, it was a blessing in disguise. She hated all Fatima and Naira's fussing around her, and hated even more that she needed them. But the time gave her a much-needed opportunity to reflect on everything that man Malik had told her that night. There was so much for her to remember, examine, and analyse so that she could answer the most important question of all - was any of it true? She regretted running away from him. It was because she had detected a hint of an accusation in his question about how it was possible that she had survived that plane bombing. Why had she run when he had asked her that? It was a logical question to ask especially if he had really seen the base blow up. All she had needed to do was answer his question with the truth. She had nothing to hide, or did she?

If she had stayed with him a bit longer the beating would not have happened, but she did not know what would have happened either if she had stayed. Because she had run away, she still didn't know if Jamil was alive. But she remembered that Malik had referred to him in the present tense, so, he must be. But she knew nothing of her mother or sister. Had they died in that bombed military base as his story implied? If they had, why had she survived? From the way he had described that bombing, it didn't sound like something you just walked away from, popping up later in a hospital thousands of kilometres away. But maybe they were never there, in that base. That would explain her being alive but not her being here.

She believed most of his story, she had eventually decided, not because she remembered anything but because it sounded true, and he seemed sincere. She believed the parts he had told her about Jamil and the fighting and all of that even though she had had difficulty accepting all that about her brother. She really had no choice but to accept that he was fighting. She had more difficulty with the story of her, her mother and sister being held in that military base, but certain things he had said, had sounded oddly familiar to her even though they triggered no memory. Then there was the house burning down. If that was true, where had they gone? She mulled over that, willing herself to remember, yet nothing came back.

She also thought about the faceless women she had left the centre with. Who were they and what were they doing out there at night? And how had they managed to stop that group of men from killing her? What had made the men run away so fast? She really wanted to know more about these women. When she recovered, she would find them, speak to them, and ask if she could join them. She would figure out a way to get back in touch with them, to thank them too, and show that she could be useful to them. She knew Fatima knew more about them than she let on. Ria suspected that she was one of them. Ria would find out.

"How are you feeling Ria?" Naira came over and stood next to the bunk.

Ria gave her a thumbs up.

Naira smiled and sat down carefully next to Ria, knowing that the slightest move of the mattress would cause her pain.

"I'm sorry about what I did Ria. I'm sorry I worried you, and Fatima." Naira paused briefly showing Ria her bandaged wrists and then averting her eyes from Ria's.

"I cannot explain it. I felt so empty inside and felt no hope for the future, only despair. I was in too much pain, not physical pain, it's hard to explain. You must think I'm a terrible person, having a child and then doing that to myself, abandoning him. But, Ria, you have to believe me, I thought he would be better off without me. I knew he would be." Naira said.

Ria moved her arm with care and took Naira's hand in hers. Naira looked back at Ria, and Ria saw that Naira was dry-eyed. Neither had any tears left. Perhaps the more pain you experienced, the fewer tears you got. Ria did not know, but that seemed to be the way things worked.

Ria tried to smile at her, but her mouth hurt too much so she just nodded. Naira smiled back, but her smile did not meet her eyes. Then, suddenly Ria noticed her body change, she was no longer hunched into herself with her shoulders slumped, now she sat up with her shoulders back, back straight and chin out. To Ria she looked determined to mask any vulnerability.

Naira began to speak. Her voice sounded unsure at first.

"When they picked me up… you know… back home, there were about eight or nine of us. They took us and then separated the men and the women. I was very frightened, we all were, we had all heard the stories of what they do to you in those places, specially to young people. Everyone had a friend who had suddenly disappeared never to be seen again or seen but no longer be themselves. I know you don't know my town, but it is a brave town. We are a proud people, a people who have resisted the regime for decades despite the consequences. My father had always told us the truth of things, you know, the reality. He told us stories from when he was younger and the stories that his own father had told him. My mother told us stories too. They were all stories of resistance and tragedy. They did not hide from us what the state was, there was no pretence. Our parents had always taught my brothers and me to stand strong, to stand up to injustice no matter the consequence. You know, things like that. So, my brothers and I... I was the only girl, well, we had been little activists all of our of lives really. The whole region was like that. Of course, we had to learn how to pretend, which was well almost impossible, but all our lives our parents had been preparing us to fight back."

Ria listened with great interest watching Naira's every facial expression.

"When they came to take our father, we were having dinner. They just came in and took him. What shocked me the most was the speed of it all. My mother screamed at them. I was only fifteen at the time. One of them hit her in the face with his gun, but she didn't seem to care, she just kept running after them screaming and crying, blood running down her face. I think she knew that it would be the last time she would ever see him. We watched while one of the soldiers beat her repeatedly with his fists and kicked her with his boots until she was unconscious on the ground and bleeding, like you were before the ambulance. We didn't know what to do. I think we all just froze. I know I did. Talk is easy but when violence happens, it is never like you imagined it. I was crying and afraid. When the soldiers left, my brothers rushed to bring my mother inside, one of them ran for help, but I could not move. It was the first time I understood the reality of our country. It was the first time I understood how paralysing violence is and what it felt like to have no power to do anything to stop it." Naira stopped talking and just kept on staring, looking off to the side lost in the past perhaps.

Ria gripped Naira's hand tighter. Did something like this happen to her own father Ria wondered? Was Naira's description of what had happened similar to Ria's family history? Was it just that Ria had been shielded from it by her mother and not been curious enough to ask the right questions?

"My mother Ria, she looked so much like you did the other night after they beat her. Not as young as you obviously, but you know what I mean. The beating, the injuries. What happened to you reminded me so much of a time I have tried so hard to forget. But seeing you like that... well, I suppose it brought it all back. Then I realised that I had to remember! All this time trying to forget, wanting to die, no, that is not my path. That is not my family's way! Seeing you like that Ria, and remembering who I am was the best thing that could have happened to me. I know that sounds very strange but the whole thing has given me back an identity which I thought I had lost for good. But it's still there, it was just that I had got lost in my despair and forgotten who I was and what I was meant to do." Naira smiled.

"Ria, you know, the face of the oppressor changes all the time. The colour of their skin might change, the way they oppress might be different, but oppressors, they are everywhere, in every country, town and village everywhere in the whole world. It will always be like that. In countries like ours, they do not even bother to hide. In countries like this one, they hide behind masks of respectability, and their false discourse of democracy. I am glad that I did not succeed in killing myself this time either. That would have brought shame on my family name and on me too. My family don't just give up. It was wrong what I did. Like you, I want to go home. I must fight again alongside my brothers and my people. I will not stay here, just doing nothing. That is not helping anyone." Naira said and looked at Ria.

Ria nodded. She understood Naira all too well.

Naira continued to speak. "I don't know why you left the centre the other night. You must not trust me enough to tell me. I understand that. After all I had just tried to kill myself for the second time. I wouldn't have trusted me either. But I do not know why you of all people would take such a risk. You have always been so... " Naira seemed to be searching for the right word. ".... absent, docile, a loner.... You always seem so... afraid. So, it is even more shocking to me that you would do something so dangerous. What are you afraid of Ria and why did you leave that night? It was a great risk to take. It must have been very important to you."

Ria shook her head. She didn't want Naira to see her as afraid. Naira was so strong.

Naira continued. She knew Ria could not answer her. "I think something happened to you back home. I mean more than your head injury. I saw the strangest things happen when I was in prison. The mind has a lot of survival tricks. I have seen things happen with other women in the prison I was in and experienced some of the mind's tricks myself. Sometimes the mind works against us, or that's what it feels like, but somehow, I think it is trying to protect us. I saw many women lose their minds in the prison, women I had come to know well, strong women who I thought would not break in a million years. I have seen others lose themselves, watched as they retreated so far inside themselves to escape the terrible things the soldiers would do to them and never come back out again. They were alive but gone, and so was I."

Naira paused and put her other hand over Ria's. "I think that something like that happened to you Ria. I will help you to remember, help you to find your way back like you have helped me. You must remember everything and make your peace with it. Only then can you decide what your path is. If not, you will exist, but you will never feel alive and that is no way to live."

Ria nodded feeling certain that Naira was right. She let her mind flit back, for just a second, to one of the terrible nightmares she'd had when the woman doctor had given her that drug the night of the beating.

What if those had not been nightmares, but instead her memories. Ria shuddered and Naira got up to get her a blanket.

33

Ria felt as if she had slept for days even though she had actually slept very little. She knew the worst of the pain was over, and that like a visiting friend, it would inevitably leave her alone with that other pain soon. Everything still hurt but she could now move without having to suppress a cry of pain. She could chew a little if the food was soft enough and she had received two visits from the centre dentist. Both had been a nightmare for her tongue, but at least now the cut on it was not getting even more irritated from rubbing up against the jagged cracks on her bottom teeth. She was grateful for the imposed silence of not speaking. She did not feel much like talking and just focused on pushing down her anger until she could actually do something with it. As she lay on her bunk with the centre coming to life, she decided that she had had enough recovery time. She had thought a lot about what Naira had said to her that evening. Ria was going to change. She wanted to get some fresh air, so she sat up, put her feet on the floor and slowly stood up.

"I want to get some fresh air. I need it. I've been stuck in here long enough." Ria said to Naira and Fatima, who were there in the room, alerted by her independent movement and looking at her in disapproval.

"Ria, you cannot go out. You are not ready. Look at you, you are so thin and pale, the police will think you are an illegal immigrant if they see you and drop you off at social services!" Fatima said in disbelief, hands planted on her hips.

"I'm fine, Fatima, thanks. Don't worry about me. I can speak, I can walk, I am okay." Ria replied, smiling a little.

"You can speak then, can you? Move too?" Fatima said laughing. "Khal was more understandable than you are, and you move like a 90-year-old. My mother could run ten kilometres before you could even get outside."

Naira laughed. "It's fine Fatima! I'll go with her. She does need some fresh air. It will be good for her. We won't stay long."

Naira cast Fatima a meaningful glance, Fatima shrugged and turned back to her book mumbling in her own language and shaking her head.

"She's not wrong, Ria. Are you sure you are ready?" Naira asked.

"I don't know but I need to get out of here. I feel... I feel very claustrophobic, so many days stuck in here doing nothing. If I don't get out I swear I will go crazy Naira. I need to call my case worker too, I have questions, and I missed an appointment because of this. What if there is news of my petition?" Ria said and frowned. "Maybe he doesn't know."

"Know what?" Naira asked.

"About the beating and why I didn't turn up at my appointment." She replied.

Ria was also thinking about Shabana, who she hadn't texted or called either despite Shabana calling and texting her several times, texts that reflected her increasing worry. But Ria hadn't been able to talk or type. If she was honest, even when she could have, she didn't want to. She was at a loss of what to say and she knew Shabana would come if Ria told her what had happened, and Ria didn't want her coming to the centre.

It hurt her to speak but it was nowhere as bad as Fatima said, Naira seemed to understand her.

"Let's go to the park behind, then you can call him from the bench. It is not such a nice day but at least it is dry for once." Naira said. "I need to get some things so you can make your calls while I go to the supermarket."

Naira helped Ria on with her coat and then supported her arm as they left the building. They made their way slowly to the park. The cold breeze that hit Ria's injured face was painful, but she welcomed it, feeling more alive out here.

Naira helped her to a bench a little way away from the playground.

"Do you want me to get you anything?" Naira asked.

"Maybe a bar of soap?" Ria said and opened her rucksack to look for money.

"Please, don't worry. I can get you a bar of soap!" Naira laughed. "Some chocolate too maybe?"

Ria smiled and nodded. Naira walked off leaving Ria sitting there. Ria felt content just sitting there watching the trees swaying in the breeze. She watched a few mothers supervising their kids as they swung back and forth on swings. She thought of her own mother. Was she dead? Surely, she would *feel* it if she were, but she felt no sadness or any emotion at all when she thought about that possibility. She had no confirmed information, so she could choose to believe that her mother was alive, that all her family were alive. She herself was alive so why not her mother and sister too? Why should she trust this Malik. She would not dwell on that. She had other matters to attend to now. This new, stronger, braver version of herself had to be built up from nothing.

She took out her phone to call her case worker's office and made an appointment. Then, reluctantly, she called Shabana.

"Shabana?" Ria said when she answered.

"Ria! Thank God. I was so worried, and Omar has not slept well since we last saw you. Are you okay? Why have you not come here every morning as usual, it has been two weeks!" Shabana said sounding very worried.

"It has not been two weeks. I'm sorry I didn't respond to your messages, I really am. But I was in an accident, so I haven't been able to move or talk, but I'm better now." Ria said.

"Yes, I can hear you are talking strangely. What kind of accident? Are you okay now?" Shabana asked.

"It was stupid, you know how distracted I get, I stepped out onto the road without looking and was hit by a cyclist who was going very fast. I was lucky, I was with friends at the time, and they called an ambulance. My jaw and mouth are still damaged, and a few ribs. It's hard to talk." Ria said.

"Let me come and pick you up and bring you here. You will be more comfortable here during the day, then Omar can drop you back in the evenings." Shabana suggested.

"That is so kind of you Shabana and I *will* come, soon, I promise, but for now I am not allowed to leave the centre for long. I have many medical check-ups and Fatima and Naira are taking very good care of me. I will come next week, I promise. Are you and Omar okay?" Ria asked.

"Yes, yes, we are fine. Omar, you know what he's like. He was so worried about that man he told you about. I don't know why. You never met him, did you?" Shabana asked.

"How would I Shabana? I don't even know him." Ria said feeling bad at the lie. A lie Shabana would detect if Omar had already told her about the note, and knowing Omar, he probably had. Especially when they hadn't heard from her for so long. But if she admitted that she had met him, she would get a lot of questions. Questions she did not want to answer.

"Okay, Ria. If you say so. But you will come here next week, yes? We would like to see you. Omar will be happy that you are okay, I will call him at work and let him know." Shabana said.

They said their goodbyes and Ria put the phone away and just sat there enjoying the different sensations of being outdoors. What was she going to do to change her situation? How would she build this new Ria who was not afraid to resist like Naira, like Jamil? She needed to speak to Omar again and to Naira. If Naira was going to go home, perhaps she could go with her. Why was she sitting here waiting for permission from a foreign country to go back to her own country? To hell with that.

It took a while for Naira to return. When she did, she looked a bit irritated.

"Sorry Ria, such queues I have not seen there in a while. Are you okay? Did you get an appointment? She asked as she handed Ria a bar of chocolate and sat down and opened one herself.

"Yes, for tomorrow," Ria replied, wrestling with the wrapper.

"Here, let me help you," Naira said.

"Naira, are you going to go back home?" Ria asked.

"Yes, Ria. I am. I am not going to stay here. My family needs me, my town needs me. Staying here serves no purpose for me, for anyone. I have to try to save some money and prepare myself physically, but I think I will go as soon as it is springtime. It won't be as cold on the routes as now."

Ria did not know how to ask.

"Will you go alone?" Ria asked.

"Alone? No, there are always groups going back. Did you not know? There are networks" Naira said looking at her.

"No, I suppose there is not much really that I do know," Ria answered sadly. "Will you teach me?" She asked Naira, looking at the ground.

"Teach you what?" Naira asked.

"Everything Naira. Everything you know. I am like a girl who knows nothing about our world or their world. Like you said, I am afraid of everything. It is time for me to become an adult, an adult like you and help my people resist... I would like to go with you." Ria said reddening as she said it and not knowing why.

Naira said nothing but Ria could feel her eyes on her.

"You always talk about going back, are you sure this is the way you want to do it? It is a dangerous route Ria, and you did not come here that way like the rest of us. You came a different way. You don't know what it is like to have to travel that route. Terrible things happen Ria. You are injured too, not just from what happened with those Nazis but before that, your head. You know they will take better care of you here than at home, especially with the way things are. They are bombing all of the hospitals!"

"I know. I don't care about my head. I want to go with you. I don't want to stay here alone. And as you say, stay to do what when our people are suffering at home?" Ria said.

"What about your memory? Naira asked. "Don't you want the doctors here to help you get it back?"

"I can get it back from others faster I think," Ria said.

"Why were you out there that night Ria?" Naira asked. "What happened?"

"Now that Naira is a story for another day. So, can I go with you or not?" Ria asked shyly.

"Let's see how you recover these next few weeks okay?" Naira said and smiled at her.
Ria nodded, happy at Naira's answer and ate her chocolate bar.

34

Ria was preparing for her appointment with her case worker. She had to go downtown to his office.

"Do you want me to come with you, Ria?" Fatima asked.

"It's okay Fatima, I'll go with her. I have some things to do in town. I'll drop her off and pick her up when she is finished." Naira said. "Anyway, you know they never see you at the appointment time. We could be there a long time." Naira said rolling her eyes at Fatima and Ria.

Naira was like a different person since they had taken her child. It was a strange thing to see, like seeing a doll come to life. When Ria arrived at the centre, Naira had already been there for a few months and so had Fatima. Naira had moved around in slow motion. She rarely talked to anyone, and she was constantly leaving her child with Fatima and disappearing for hours. Ria had helped Fatima with Khal sometimes, but it was mostly Fatima who cared for Khal. Naira never spoke about where she would go, and Ria never asked. It was as if Naira was in some sort of trance when she was in the centre. Her baby, Khal, cried constantly, and Naira would get irritable, shout at him, then leave. Ria had been surprised when Naira talked about how she thought Ria was like that too - distant and not present. Ria had not seen herself like that until Naira had pointed it out, but she could see it now that she had had time to think about it. The centre was full of women who were alive, but not living. Why should she be any different?

They left the building walking slowly for Ria's sake. Ria always felt better outside of the centre. They waited at the bus stop. There were a few other women from the centre there too. There weren't many houses in the area of the centre, and it was the last stop on the bus route. One of the women looked over at Ria and nodded. Ria did not know her, but there was something familiar about her, so she nodded back. Maybe it was one of the women? She wanted to look at her more carefully but stopped herself. The bus pulled up and they all got on. Naira helped Ria up. The bus was pretty empty, so they sat in seats the front of the bus, just in front of the woman who had just nodded to Ria. She looked young, only a little older than Ria or Naira, more Fatima's age.

When it came to their stop, Naira helped her down. The woman also got off at the same stop. She must have an appointment too Ria thought, but then she moved off quickly in the opposite direction. Naira and Ria made their way slowly up the street towards the State Centre for Refugee Affairs.

"Naira, those women the other night. Who are they?" Ria asked.

"Ria, remember I told you not to ask about them." Naira's answer was final.

Ria left it alone, for now.

The building that managed refugee and migrant affairs was a cold-looking grey building. It was always felt cold inside too despite the eternally full waiting room. As they walked in, Ria pulled her scarf up over her nose at the familiar scent of too many human bodies packed together for too long. She longed for the outside breeze again. She took her ticket from the machine and looked around for somewhere to sit. As usual, there were no free seats. Ria could not stand for long with her injuries, but a lot of people were already standing so it was unlikely she would get one. She sighed, leaned up against the wall and waited. But Naira walked over to a young man, said something to him and he offered his seat up for Ria. Ria embarrassed sat down, shooting Naira a look. But she was grateful, she could not have stood for much longer.

Two very long hours went by before her number was called. Her whole body was very sore by that time, so it took her a long time to walk down the long corridor to the office. By the time she got there, they had already called the following number and she'd ended up having to argue with a quite aggressive man who had tried to take her place. She even had to show the receptionist her bruised side to explain her delay in getting down there. Damn, this place!

Ria was fuming and in pain when she entered the case worker's office. Her case worker did not look up, he was busy shuffling through papers and looked as flustered as usual. Ria did not envy his job eyeing the stacks of files everywhere. Ria sat in the only other chair and waited.

Sasha, her case worker looked up. "My god Ria. Your face. I didn't realise it was that bad from what you said on the phone. I am so sorry. That cyclist bastard. They are always flying around this city at ridiculous speeds as if the rest of us were invisible. So, how are you now?"

"I'm much better thanks, Sasha. You? You seem to have a lot of work!" Ria said politely.

"Yes, always!" Sasha laughed, but then as he looked down at the open file on his desk his expression changed.

"Look Ria, the last time you were here, there was still no news about your petition to return to your country. As I told you these things don't usually take very long because as you know they are always happy for people to leave. It's just that the bureaucracy is very slow. I wasn't expecting a quick response, even to this type of petition, as I told you the last time. But something strange has happened, the response to your petition came yesterday afternoon. I know two months does not seem quick to but believe me it is very quick. So much quicker than normal." Sasha hesitated and frowned.

Ria felt very happy. "Fantastic! That is great news, Sasha!" Ria said. "So, I can go home?"

"Well, Ria, that's the thing. It has been quick, but it is not the answer I expected." Sasha said. "It is not good news Ria."

Ria felt a knot in her stomach. What now? Could nothing go right? Sasha had said this would be the easiest petition, hardly anyone ever wanted to go home.

"Your petition to return home has been permanently denied," Sasha said and looked at Ria sympathetically

"What?" Ria said, feeling tears hovering. "What do you mean? No! How is that even possible? What do you mean permanently denied? There must be a mistake. How can *this* country stop me from returning to *my own country?* I don't understand. You said it would be easy, just that it would take some time." Ria said noting the slight accusatory tone that had crept in. There was only her case worker to direct her frustration at.

Sasha looked uncomfortable. "I know, and I have to admit it is very unusual. This is the first time it has ever happened to one of my cases. But, Ria, I'm afraid there is something else. What is worse is the reason given in the document. It is a small sentence but not a good one." He paused, seeming unsure of how to tell her.

Ria waited, holding her breath.

Sasha paused and took a deep breath.

"... well, I do not really know how to tell you this, but the paper says your petition has been denied because of your alleged links to terrorism prior to your arrival in this country." Sasha said and looked down at the paper file frowning.

Ria could not speak. She could not even process. Eventually, though she found her voice.

"Terrorism? What the hell are you talking about Sasha? I have *never* been involved in terrorism, never! I wouldn't even know how! And remember I did not even 'come here'! I was brought here. How and why I still do not know." Ria said. "What links? To what? They can't just say that and not say why. People here, they are always accusing us of this terrorist thing, it is like an obsession! We are not all terrorists! What the hell is wrong with you people? We are people, just people." Ria was shouting, and loudly.

She was very angry. Angry at the unfairness of the decision, but even more angry about the reason given 'alleged links to terrorism'! Her? Now this was the last straw!

"Ria. I understand your anger., but there is nothing else in the document about why they are saying this. I did some checking with some of my colleagues, but they too say it very unusual. When it comes to anything to do with counterterrorism, it goes beyond refugee matters and political asylum. It becomes more of a police thing and from them, we can never find out anything about anyone." Sasha said. "All of this means too Ria, that as of today I can no longer be your case officer. I am so sorry Ria. But this does explain in a way why you were brought here, rather than came of your own accord." He added.

Ria was so stunned that she could not think of one question to ask.

Eventually, she spoke. "What does this mean Sasha?"

"Well, according to the document, you will soon be transferred to a prison to await trial. I have put in a stay order because of your injuries but they will probably ignore that so you could be transferred whenever they want." Sasha said, looking at her and frowning.

"What? Prison! I haven't done anything! How can they do that?" Ria said, raising her voice again.

"Because they say that these alleged links to terrorism had something to do with this country. That is all it says, they are not obliged to give any more reasons, and they have your passport so you cannot leave, and anyway they would stop you." Sasha warned. "Also, Ria, one of my contacts mentioned that perhaps they have had you under surveillance."

"Surveillance? What? For what!" Ria could feel she was about to cry.

"Look I don't know, it's just speculation." Sasha said, "Maybe you're not.".

"How can they put me in prison, and have a trial without explaining what I am supposed to have done? What the hell Sasha? Trial for what? There has to be a mistake. There must be. They have got the wrong person, there's no other explanation! You have to tell them it's a mistake Sasha!" Ria shouted moving forward in her seat.

"Ria, I wish it was that simple! This is a serious document - alleged links to terrorism coming from counterterrorism is not a small thing. Especially nowadays, especially when it concerns your country or others in that region. It is not like I can speak to counterterrorism. I cannot. What this paper is saying is that counterterrorism believes you had links to a terrorist organisation back in your country and they want you to face charges for something that was done to this country's interests over there. Because there is no embassy here for your country, there is no recourse, and you can't just contact your government either. There is unfortunately nothing I can do. When it comes to anything to do with terrorism, everything changes." Sasha said. He looked grim.

Ria started to cry. So much for strong Ria. It was just all too much. She gave up and let it all out. Her sobbing was long and loud, and the cascade of tears was plentiful. Her body shook so much it hurt her ribs, but it was the frustration and anger that stabbed the most.

Sasha came out from behind his desk and touched her shoulder.

"Ria, look, I am sorry, but in these circumstances, there is nothing I can do. I wish I could have given you happy news." he said.

Ria thought Sasha sounded as if he believed the accusations and she felt ashamed and small.

Sasha held out a small white card.

"Take this. It is the number of a good lawyer friend of mine who works on cases like these. He is very good, but expensive. I have told him you might call. Try to see him before they transfer you, if not it will be hard to do anything. He will not even know where you are." Sasha said.

Ria took the card, terrified at these last words, and stared down at the card, terror spilling into every pore.

Sasha shook Ria's limp hand and then he helped her out of her seat, and she shuffled out of his office. Sasha had many more people like her to see. Well, not like her.

35

Ria could not stop trembling as she walked slowly back to the seating area. Naira was nowhere in sight. Ria fished around in her rucksack for her phone as she made her way out of the building to get some fresh air. Anything to help her breathe. It had started raining. But before she could call Naira, her phone rang. It was Shabana.

"Ria, how are you? Just checking up on how you're feeling and to see if you need anything?" Shabana said.

"Shabana!" Ria said quietly and started sobbing.

"Ria, what's wrong? Where are you?" Shabana sounded alarmed. "Tell me where you are, and Omar will come for you and bring you here. Is it your health?"

"No" Ria managed to say, the lump in her throat now huge.

"That's a relief! Just send me your location and he'll come by taxi. You can't walk here upset like that in this weather, and with all your injuries."

"I have just received terrible news from the case worker Shabana. I am in big trouble." Ria tried to stop crying but could not. It was all flowing out, unstoppable now.

"Hang up the phone and send me your location. We can talk when you get here. Don't worry, Ria. Whatever it is, I'm sure it is not so bad." Shabana said.

"I came with Naira, so I have to wait for her to come back. Let me find her first then I will call you back.

Please don't send Omar yet, okay? Not until I call you back" Ria said, and hung up, still crying.

She needed to see Naira first. Naira would know what to do. But would she? Shabana had more knowledge of the law, the system, and how things worked here from working in human rights. Shabana would know more than Naira. She called Naira. No answer. Where the hell was she? The rain was coming down hard, so she decided to go back to look for Naira inside, or if she wasn't there, call her again.

Drenched already she walked back into the building, dripping water all over the floor. There was no sign of Naira in the waiting room. She checked her phone, no messages from her either. She waited, taking time to gather her thoughts. Terrorism. Now that was a shock. She had never done more than print a few flyers about a few student protests. Was this about Jamil? It had to be. She was 'linked' to Jamil, and from what Malik had told her and from what she had read in the newspapers, the distinction between revolution, fighter, civilian and terrorist seemed to be a bit blurry nowadays. Shabana spoke about this a lot.

Ria believed Malik about Jamil being a fighter. She could understand how her own government would use the word terrorist for anyone fighting against them, anyone not aligned with their agenda. But here in Europe Ria had the feeling that many people saw anyone from her region as a potential terrorist anyway. They were already judged. She had seen all the racism, but she had never imagined that something like this could ever happen to someone like her. She was a nobody who had done nothing. She was the furthest thing from a being a terrorist anyone could be. But Sasha was probably right about this being the reasons she had been brought here from her home and why there were never any answers to her questions. Could it have something to do with Jamil? There was no other logical explanation. But why would they wait so long? She had done nothing, but she knew that wouldn't matter. She had no proof! Did they have any proof? Did they even need any? They could make up anything. No one would believe her. They could show that they had caught another terrorist, and that now everyone could now feel safer! But she was damned if she was going to go on trial in this country for a lie. This was how 'strong Ria' would be created. Yes! Anger and fight took over from her desolation and shock, and she stood up taller.

"Ria, what's wrong?" Naira was standing in front of her frowning. "You've been crying. Was there still no news about your petition?" She asked.

"Not here, come, I'll tell you outside," Ria said, her voice strong again and they left.

When they were outside, they stood under the awning for shelter, Ria stopped and looked around. There was no one near.

"Naira, my case worker just informed me that I am going to be detained and taken to a prison to await trial for links to terrorism. It is going to happen very soon. The only reason it hasn't happened already he said is because of my injuries. He said I might have been under surveillance. He says they will come soon and then I will be imprisoned while I wait for trial. Imprisoned for 'alleged links to terrorism' Naira, I mean… can you believe it?" Ria said and forced her tears back, she would never cry again.

"What!" Naira exploded into a stream of swear words. "No, this cannot be! What the hell! Are you sure?" Naira said

"Am I sure?" Ria snapped back. "Sorry. Yes, I am sure Naira. There is a document. My petition for return to my country has been permanently denied and the document gave the reason I just told you." Ria said, feeling her rage surface again as she talked about it.

"But you never even fought back home. How could they possibly do that to you here?" Naira looked stunned still. Yet, not stuck for words. "Did you know any?"

"Any what?" Ria said

"Any … you know… anyone from one of the terrorist groups," Naira asked warily.

"For god's sake Naira, look at me? Do I look as if I would be taking tea with terrorists?" Ria said. "You know perfectly well that here we are all terrorists to them. You have said it many times yourself." Ria said.

"I know, but one thing is seeing us like that or even treating us like that. You know moving away from us whenever they see us in the street, or in a café and another thing is the state system imprisoning you for links to terrorism. That means they have to have a reason, Ria. If not, how can you explain it?" Naira said looking very worried.

Ria did not respond. She didn't want to talk to Naira just yet about what Malik had told her, about Jamil and all the

301

rest. She didn't even think she could repeat Malik's words out loud. Not even to herself.

"I don't know," Ria said eventually. "I need a coffee. Please Naira."

"I'm sorry Ria for my reaction, I'm just... you know...shocked. I don't understand it." Naira said shaking her head.

They crossed the road and entered a café.

Ria sat down at a free table while Naira got up to get their coffees. She came back with some water as well.

"Thanks" Ria said and sipped the hot coffee gratefully. She needed to clear her head. She looked at Naira who looked a bit agitated.

"Can you believe the thing about the surveillance?" Ria said shaking her head in disbelief.

"For how long?" Naira asked. "Did he say?"

"Well, he said it more as a possibility than a fact. It might not be true." Ria said. "I am just guessing, but I suppose it would be logical for them to watch me I suppose. Well now this all explains why I am here, doesn't it?"

"So" Naira seemed to be thinking. "So that means anyone you are with is watched too, maybe even heard." Her mouth opened in shock as realisation set in.

"I know Naira and I am so sorry, but how could I have known? It also means that maybe they know about all the other things... you know with the women and the beating and all that. But I don't know. Maybe not. The case officer didn't say... well I didn't ask much about the surveillance, the rest was such a shock. I doubt he would know anyway. But isn't it easy nowadays with phones?

Who knows what they can do with phones, probably a lot. There are a lot of cameras in the centre too! But don't worry, you haven't committed any crimes, Naira." Ria said reassuringly. "Or have you?" Ria struggled to joke.

"Turn it off." Naira mouthed to Ria.

Ria looked at her confused. Naira picked up her own phone and turned it off, disabling the location and microphone and putting something over the camera.

Ria nodded and did the same.

Naira forced a smile.

"Not lately anyway." She said. "Damn them, Ria. Now what? We will have to leave sooner than the spring - money or not, injuries or not! I know some people. We could even leave tomorrow!"

Naira's rebellious side was flowing now.

"Naira, thank you, but you know I can barely walk and then you would have committed a crime too. Just by helping me. I can't do that to you. Look, I have to go and see someone who knows more about these things soon - you know, my friend Shabana, remember her? The human rights activist. She will have contacts. I will see what she says, hear what she advises, then we can talk later on okay? But Naira, don't worry about me, and please put any thoughts of putting yourself into my mess out of your head, and Naira," Ria warned, "you cannot tell anyone about any of this, not even Fatima. Please." Ria reached across the table and clasped her hand. "And Naira, thank you, you have already done so much for me."

"That sounds like a goodbye Ria. No. We will not give in to this nonsense. When you get back, we will talk some more, while you're at your friend's place, I'll make some calls to people I know." Naira said. "Go to your friend now, it's important to get some advice, but you know once it becomes about the terrorist thing… everything changes. We don't know when they will come for you so go now. I'll wait for you back at the centre. Come on, let's go. They could come at any time and with no warning, I've heard about it happening from others in other centres, but it's usually men they take." Naira said and came around the table to help Ria up and outside.

36

Once Naira had left, Ria sent Shabana her location details but hesitated in calling her back. She didn't want to have her phone on for long. What if they were listening? She shuddered at the thought of having been watched and not having known. She could barely think straight. She had understood what Sasha had told her, but it hadn't fully sunk in yet. What was she going to say to Shabana? Omar would suspect that she had met the man and that was the reason for all this. He would think that Malik was the terrorist she had 'links' to. Ria was convinced that when they had heard nothing from Ria after the beating, Omar would have told Shabana about passing the note to the man. Malik didn't matter now anyway. This new situation was the important thing now. Malik was irrelevant, her beating was irrelevant, and her wanting to go back home was irrelevant now too. If it was Omar who came to get her, she would have time to speak to him alone in the taxi before seeing Shabana. But she would say nothing to Shabana or Omar about Malik or her brother. She didn't want to get them into any trouble. It was better they knew as little as possible.

She decided to turn on her phone to call Shabana, who again answered straight away.

"Ria, you took so long I was worried! Omar is waiting for the taxi right now. Are you okay?" Shabana asked in such a kind way that Ria felt like crying all over again, but no, the time for crying was over.

"I'm okay Shabana, sorry for the delay in calling," Ria said, her voice sounded strained but at least she was not crying.

"Omar's saying that the taxi will be here in ten minutes so he should be there in about twenty minutes, depending on the traffic." Shabana said. "Are you out of the rain?"

"Yes," Ria said. "I'm outside a café."

"Now, tell me what happened!" Shabana said

"Shabana, I know you are worried, but I will explain it all when I get there. It's better that way. It's about my petition, I've just seen my case worker. !'ll explain when I get there, okay? See you in a while." Ria hung up before Shabana could press her for details, details she did not want to give over the phone.

She turned her phone off. Her thoughts raced. Was Naira, right? Should she run? Would that even be possible? She could barely move without pain. But the alternative was to stay and face a trial that would not be fair, she could not defend herself with no memory intact and what if all this had to do with Jamil? She needed to talk to someone who knew the law here. How could it be possible to put someone with no memory to trial? Maybe the case worker was wrong. But what if they intended to keep her in prison until her memory returned? Prison, just the word sent her into despair. She had heard rumours in the centre about people who had come here for safety but had instead ended up in prison but those had mostly been about men, not women.

"Ria!" lost in thought she jumped at her name being said, but then she saw Omar standing in front of her with an umbrella. "Come, the taxi is over there." He said and seeing she couldn't move quickly he offered his arm out to support her.

He looked at her in concern and then put his arm around her waist and started to pull her towards his body to half-carry her. She cried out in pain as her ribs crushed against his body. He flinched and detached himself from her.

"I'm sorry Omar, I didn't mean to frighten you. It's just that my ribs are hurt. Sorry," Ria said.

"It's okay, I'm sorry I hurt you." He said and helped her over to the waiting taxi.

"Thank you for waiting." Omar said to the taxi driver, who scowled as they got in and said, "Now where?"

"Back to the same place where you picked me up," Omar said and turned to Ria.

"Ria, what the hell? Did that man do this to you? Look at your mouth, your face! I knew that meeting him was a bad idea. I should never have passed him that note." Omar said.

"It was not him, Omar. It was some men from here." Ria said. "Omar, did you tell Shabana about the note and what it said?"

Omar looked away from Ria and nodded. "I am sorry, Ria, but you were not answering our calls, and I was worried. We were both worried. You know what Shabana is like when she gets something into her mind, and then the timing of it. We had just told you about the man. She threw questions at me every second of the day! I tried to avoid answering, but after so many days passed and there was still no word from you, I was so worried that I broke, and I told her about the note. I only said that you gave me a note for the man, nothing more. Anyway, I did not know anything more. I didn't read the note, and she already knew from when you were here that you wanted to meet this man." Omar said. "She was not surprised. She was just relieved you were okay. So was I. Don't worry about that now."

Ria looked out of the car window at the passing buildings and then turned to look at Omar keeping her voice low.

"Omar, it's okay. I didn't want you to lie to Shabana for me." she said.

Omar looked miserable but Ria squeezed his arm and smiled at him.

"It's me who is sorry for putting you in that situation Omar. Please, forgive me." Ria said, and Omar smiled at her.

After a while the taxi pulled up at Omar's building, Omar paid and jumped out, his umbrella opening as he came around to Ria's side to help her out.

Once inside, Omar pressed the button for the lift and looked at Ria. "I know you don't go in lifts, but now in your state. It's too much to take the stairs." He said.

She nodded. Omar looked as if he wanted to say something.

"Okay. Omar, what is it?" Ria asked as the lift pinged open.

"I have something for you. I think it is from him, from that man. An envelope was passed to me last night by someone else. The man left the centre many days before, but he wasn't moved I checked. It's an envelope with your name on it." Omar said helping her into the lift. "Ria, I have to say I am worried about all these things that have been happening to you since this man appeared. This envelope can only be from him."

"Where is it? This envelope." Ria asked feeling dread. She couldn't take any more.

"It's up in the flat. I'll give it to you when we get there. Shabana knows." Omar looked worried and tense, but there seemed to be something else he wanted to say.

"The envelope Ria, I didn't open it of course, but I did feel it. I think there's a photo inside. It feels like a photo." Omar said and looked at her.

A photo! Never before had the thought of a photograph filled her with such terror. Now, the recent terrible news from her case worker faded a little and fear of what this photograph might reveal took over. She knew it wouldn't be good if it was from that man. Malik had told her that Jamil had received a photo of her from the military, a photo in which she was supposedly beaten, and one of Hana. What if Malik was sending her those photos? She could not deal with seeing something like that, not now. It would mean having to accept everything he had told her as true.

The lift arrived on their floor and Omar helped her out. He rang the doorbell and Shabana was there in an instant, hugging Ria tightly.

"Shabana, stop that, she is hurt," Omar warned and helped Ria inside. "You'll hurt her with all your hugging" Omar scolded.

Shabana pulled away. "I'm sorry Ria, I'm just so relieved to see you," Shabana said and took a step back to look over Ria more carefully.

Ria saw tears in Shabana's eyes, but neither said anything.

"Come and sit. Let me make you some nice strong tea, I've made some food too. Then, you can tell us what has happened today to make you so upset. Okay?" Shabana smiled reassuringly and Ria felt better just by being with them again.

Ria nodded, and let Omar help her into the living room where he helped her take off her drenched coat and soaking shoes and socks and put a blanket over her.

This envelope Omar had told her about had thrown her off even more. Her thoughts went back to the prospect of prison, which made her break out in a cold sweat. It wasn't possible that whatever photo was in that envelope was worse than that!

Ria sat back on the sofa unable to shake her feelings of dread about prison and the photo. She wanted to get it over with and see what it was, but she knew she would have to wait. She was in pain and there were going to be a lot of questions from Shabana. Shabana would have to be content with short answers as it was still hard for Ria to talk for long with her tongue.

37

Omar and Shabana listened in silence as Ria told them what the case worker had told her. She told them about the beating but left out her night escape from the centre after curfew with three faceless women, and she did not mention her meeting with Malik. As she spoke, Ria watched their expressions reflect back the drama that had enfolded since they had last met. Exhausted and in pain, she stopped and took the tea in her hand. Her hand trembled and she spilt some tea. Shabana wiped it up. Ria's tea was now lukewarm but still comforting. She sipped at it and looked at Shabana.

"Ria, you poor thing! I cannot believe this happened to you. You should have called us. We would have helped you after they beat you. You could have stayed here! You would have been better looked after and you know we have a lot of contacts. What did the police do? You must have been terrified." Shabana said and moved to sit next to Ria on the sofa. She gently put her arm around Ria's shoulders and kissed her forehead gently.

Ria felt her tears surface again. It was kindness that upset Ria the most.

"No police," Ria said and Shabana nodded.
Ria knew she understood.

"Ria, you said your case worker said you might be under surveillance." Shabana said.

"Yes, I remember it clearly. It scares me so much to think that.... you know that someone might have been watching me all this time." Ria answered.

"Where is your phone?" Shabana asked.

"My phone? It's in my bag. Don't worry it's off and everything else is turned off too - location, and camera." Ria said. "Do you really think they would have been in my phone?"

"Yes," Shabana said. "They do it all the time, especially when it comes to terrorism. It is as easy as getting your nails done, well, maybe even easier. People forget how easy it is, or they don't even know. We are a world under surveillance."

"What should I do?" Ria said.

"First things first Ria, you've barely eaten anything. Let's get some food into you before you waste away." Shabana said. "Let me make a call. I will be discreet.

"Don't worry. We will get you a different kind of phone. I'll take you somewhere later. Keep only the important numbers and memorise them. We will erase everything in your phone and then dump it." Omar said.

Ria nodded. They will have heard her conversation with Malik if they had been listening in on her phone.

They will have it translated. What if he was the terrorist link they were talking about and not Jamil? That sounded more real as it had happened here, but Sasha had said it was to do with before she had come here so it had to be Jamil. Also, it didn't explain how she came to *be* here in the first place, so it couldn't be Malik. But they will have heard what he said, everything he said about Jamil. Her heart raced now with the possibilities of what they would happen now with that evidence.

"Ria what's wrong, you have gone completely white!" Omar asked. "It's okay, you can tell us.
"Omar, what should I do? I swear to you I have done nothing! I have no links to terrorism. Can you even imagine it?" Ria said.

"Let's just wait for Shabana to make her call. Drink and eat Ria," Omar said kindly.
Soon after, Shabana reappeared at the table.

"Ria, think carefully, I know you can't remember, but before you came here, did you meet anyone who, well, you know might have been in the wrong kind of group?" she asked directly.

"No! How could you think that!" Ria said indignantly.

"Ria, it doesn't matter what I think. What matters is what *they* think. Is there anything you have done here that could look suspicious?" Shabana met her with a hard stare. "I know about the note Ria. Maybe this man has links. Tell me what happened, if not, I can't help you and I will not trust you."

Ria felt ashamed. She looked ahead at nothing, feeling so exhausted by it all.

"It can't have anything to do with that man, they brought me here before he even appeared," Ria said adamantly.

Ria broke. She sighed and told them everything. As she could remember nothing about before she came here, she told them what Malik had told her that night she had met him. There was a tense silence when she finished her recounting and she had seen a lot of concerned looks exchanged between Shabana and Omar. As she told them what he had told her, she felt more and more ashamed and stupid. She sounded really stupid. No intelligent person would have gone to meet such a man. Jamil sounded more and more like a terrorist even to her as she repeated Malik's words. She braced for a harsh response.

"Ria, you must have been very frightened. I'm so sorry." Shabana hugged her gently. She looked over at Omar, his kind eyes were still kind, and he reached over and touched her on the hand.

"Ria, do you think that this man could be the reason for this sudden order to move you and talk of trials?" Shabana asked.

"That possibility only occurred to me when Omar told me about this envelope. But I don't think so. Remember, I was brought here by someone, I didn't come here like the others, so I don't think so. It must be from before. That's what the case worker said as well. But you have to believe me, I have no links to terrorists. I don't know if that man is a terrorist, I don't know what my

314

brother is these days, I haven't seen him in months, but he was not of a terrorist leaning when I knew him. But I know from the short time I've been in the centre, from the things people say, that war changes people in unexpected ways, so I don't know what has become of my brother or what my brother may have become." Ria said, tears threatening.

All she wanted was to be believed, but at the same time she knew she had no real facts about anything. Nothing for them to believe in.

"From what the man said about their group, it was not that kind of group," Ria added.

"The envelope. Omar, get the envelope." Shabana asked Omar.

"This man, Ria, it all sounds too much of a coincidence. You say he knew your name. He was suspicious of you, you say. Is that why you ran away from him?" Shabana asked as Omar left his seat.

"I don't know why I ran. It was just the look on his face and all the things he was telling me, it was just too much to take in. Such horrible things. Saying I had been taken and held in a military base with my mother and sister. I do not remember that, so I believed he had to be lying. But now I don't think he was. He seems to know my brother well and he mentioned some other people who I know too. I did not know what to think. I just got scared and I ran. Now, I wish I hadn't. He was suspicious about my memory loss though. I could see that. Just being out there in the middle of the night with him… it suddenly felt dangerous, so, I started running. It was stupid. But you

315

are right, it does sound a bit too much of a coincidence him being here in the same town and now this happens. I didn't think of it like that before." Ria said and held her head in her hands.

"It's okay Ria. You have been through a lot." Shabana said and drew her closer. "Try to eat something. That's enough for the moment. Give me the card your case worker gave you. It's probably a legal aid lawyer. Let me see who it is. I'll try my friend again." Shabana said and walked over to a desk.

Ria stared down at the food. She had no appetite, but she knew she had to eat something. Omar had come back and sat down, envelope in his hands, holding it as if it were a grenade.

Ria stared at it. Such a thing that a mere envelope could stir so much fear in her.

"Let's eat first." Ria mumbled looking at Omar, and put some food on her plate, trying to act strong. "Let's wait for Shabana to come back first before I open it." She couldn't wait to open it, but she didn't want to disrespect them after all they were doing for her.

Omar nodded. "I'm not so hungry, but we must eat, you are right."

Inside Ria felt agitated and terrified. She did not think she could take any more shocks, but she had to know what was inside. She wanted to see it and at the same time she didn't want to see it.

Shabana walked back over to the table and sat down. She put some food on her plate. She didn't look very happy.

"Ria. I have spoken to a friend of mine. She is a human rights lawyer for asylum seekers and refugees who are at risk of being returned to their countries against their will. I explained your case briefly, no names, don't worry. She says that the only cases she has heard of like yours are when, as your caseworker told you, there is evidence of links to a terrorist organisation in the county of origin or the country of reception, or that the person has done something illegal in the country they are currently in. She told me that the terrorist laws here are extremely expansive and are becoming more and more so every day. A person can be held indefinitely on suspicion of terrorism for as long as they want without the authorities having to prove anything, but they can only charge you and take you to trial if they have evidence. She said that trials related to terrorism are very different. I asked her if she knew anyone specialised in such matters who could take your case, and she said that it depends…" Shabana paused.

"Depends on what?" Ria asked sharply, shocked at the whole thing all over again.
Evidence? What evidence could they have?

"It depends on what evidence they have and what you were involved in back in your country," Shabana said. "What she means is, if they have evidence, it is no longer a human rights matter, but a counter-terrorism matter and you would need a lawyer specialised in that, but until they charge you, and she thinks they will, they can seal all the evidence."

"I am no terrorist Shabana, how could you think that?" Ria said, hurt now.

"Ria, I'm just telling you what she said, not what I think. The problem is that we don't know what evidence they have against you or why you were brought here in the first place. They can keep it from you until the trial with no need to share it with any defence lawyer. All this is not helped by your memory loss, is it? I mean, you cannot be sure of anything, can you? I believe that you believe that you are not linked to anything like that, but the reality is that you do not remember what you were doing before you came here, or who you were hanging around with. A lot could have happened that you can't remember. Then, there is the problem of this man and the story of you in that military base back home. Why did you go to meet him? Why is he sending you an envelope? It all looks bad, and they will know it all Ria if it is true that they have had you under surveillance since you arrived. Do you understand how escaping from the detention centre in the middle of the night to go and meet this man who was involved in fighting in your country will look to them? Especially if they already had you in their sights before they put you in the centre!"

Ria did not answer. She was sweating and feeling more nauseous with each additional nail in her coffin that Shabana pronounced. She was trying to process Shabana's words, but she was too scared. She knew everything Shabana had said was true about how it would all look. Calm down she told herself. Brave Ria, come on.

"Yes. I know how it all looks." Ria said eventually and sighed. "I was just trying to get news of my family, that is no crime, is it? But I do understand it will not look like that to them, no matter what I say." Ria said.

Shabana continued "The words your case worker used weren't 'suspicion of terrorist activity', he used the words 'links to terrorism' so it seems they do not think you *are* a terrorist, but that you are involved *by association*. They could be just waiting to gather more evidence. Who knows? These counter-terrorism laws are very broad, and the suspect never has any rights. The biggest problems I see is first, you don't know who that man is, and second is the problem of your lack of memory about what happened before you got here. That man could easily be from any one of the many terrorist organisations proliferating in your country and beyond. We don't know. Maybe your brother is involved, or he joined a group later on. You don't know. You can't remember anything to defend yourself with! He said you, your mother and your sister were in a military prison, what if that *is* true? Why would you all be in a military prison, Ria?" Shabana sounded as if she were suspicious.

Omar muttered some calming words to his partner.

Ria sat bolt upright on her chair opposite them feeling like she was already on trial.

"I don't know Shabana!" she said in a loud voice, she was speaking fast now, tumbling over her words with the need to defend herself. "What I *do* know is that I am not a terrorist. I helped with the protests. I helped my brother, and his friends organise them. They were just student protests, nothing more. It was fun, it was exciting. It was just making posters and pamphlets. I read stuff about revolution, of course, who didn't? But back then it hadn't even started! Not when I was there. The revolution, the war, and what is happening in my country now only started after I had already gone. Do I know what my brother was doing every damn minute of the day? NO! If the man was telling the truth about Jamil, then it is obvious that I did not know my brother as well as I thought. I had no idea about what he was doing if what that man says is true. But maybe the man is lying. Am I to be accused of being a terrorist in this country because of my brother Jamil?" Ria paused, seeing the looks on the faces of her friends.

She felt her face and neck redden.

She took a deep breath. "Look, all I know and remember is that I organised protests and nothing more. I don't know what Jamil was doing. I don't remember anything about being in the prison this man from home talks of to answer your question Shabana! In my country, they can put you in prison for just saying the wrong thing to the wrong person. If anyone should understand all that surely, it is you!" Ria noticed her very raised tone now. Who was she trying to convince?

"Ria, calm down, we are not accusing you of anything. I didn't mean to at least. I'm just telling you what my friend just said, and how it looks, and pointing out the problems. ..." Shabana said.

Ria had to make great efforts to swallow the food. Each time she was about to swallow, she felt her panic rise and again that feeling that she would vomit if she swallowed. Her forehead felt clammy again. Who was she? What had she done? Maybe she had done something bad to deserve everything that was happening. What about those terrible things she had seen during her drugged nightmares after the beating? What if… no, she could not be. Ria shook her head.

"Omar, I would like to see the envelope now please," Ria said looking straight at him.

She felt a new sense of determination. Omar looked at Shabana who nodded.

"Are you sure that now is a good time?" Omar asked Ria.

"No, I am not. But I have to see what it is, Omar." Ria said.

Omar handed her the envelope and as she took it, her hand trembled visibly. Shabana moved her chair over to be nearer to Ria and placed her hand on Ria's shoulder.

"Ria, we are here to support you, you are not alone in this, no matter what is in the envelope." Shabana said.

Ria stared at the envelope, feeling the light weight of it, feeling her panic grow stronger. It was as Omar had said, it felt like a photo, not a letter and not a card either. It was too flimsy.

"Do you want me to open it for you Ria?" Shabana asked.

Ria shook her head unable to take her eyes off it. A terrible sense of foreboding had taken hold of her. She breathed in deeply and opened the envelope slowly. She could see it was a photo with writing on the back. She took it out with the writing facing towards her, wanting to delay seeing the image.

321

It said.

I have found her. Remember now? You should not have run. Meet me here on the 17th at 17h.

Below the scrawled writing was an address of a place she did not know and had never heard of.

"What does it mean?" Shabana asked. "Translate."

But Ria was not listening, she braced herself and turned the photo around to look at it and gasped. Instinctively, she hurled the photo away from her as if it had burned her hand. She stood up and rushed across the room, feeling no pain now, to the large windows that looked out onto the park far below. She pressed her hands and forehead up against the cold panes. She was sweating profusely now, and her head was spinning.

"Ria, what is wrong? Who is that in the photo?" Shabana at her said. Ria could barely breathe. "Do you know her?"

"Shabana, I can't breathe, I can't breathe."

38

Ria immediately felt Shabana's gentle arm curl around her. Ria pressing her head up against the cold pane of the window even harder, somehow it curbed the impulse to run. She felt dizzy and incapable of producing a single, coherent thought or word. An image of the bridge rose dark in her mind, the dark, white-specked river that snaked its way underneath, enticing her.

"Ria, come back and sit down. We'll have some more tea. You've barely eaten. You don't have to talk about the photo unless you want to. Ria, take a few deep breaths, and feel your head on the glass and your feet strong on the floor as well. Stay there for a while and try to take some deep breaths as you feel yourself. Try, Ria!"

"No! Leave me alone!" Ria was shocked at her outburst.

"I'm sorry Shabana. Please. Just leave me here for a while. Please, Shabana." Ria said, pleading.

Shabana did not move for a while, then Ria felt her finally leave her side. Ria kept her eyes closed and pushed her sweaty palms against the glass of the window with even more force wishing she could just push the glass out of its frame and be done with it.

The woman in the photograph was wearing a uniform, she had cold unsmiling blue eyes and blond hair. She wasn't from Ria's country, that was obvious. But Ria knew that she knew this woman. What she could not explain was her reaction. What the hell? And why had

Malik sent her this photo, and with that message. It must mean something. It had to.

'I have found her.' He had written in his message on the back of the photo. *'Do you remember now?'* he asked her. So, there was a connection between the woman and her. He had said nothing of this that night on the steps, but he might have had she not run away. Why was he asking her if she remembered this person, it sounded more like a question that he already knew the answer to. He must know she would remember, or he would not have sent it. He still didn't believe her about her missing memory. But he was half right. She did know the woman, but she didn't know how.

But was her recognition of this woman from her memory or from her nightmares? She had seen this same woman often in her nightmares, especially after the beating by the men. What was so frightening to Ria now was seeing that the woman from those terrible nightmares was real. That meant that the other things she had seen in her nightmares – such terrible things – could also be real. It meant that they could be memories, not nightmares. She stayed there at the window for a long time trying, but failing, to get a hold of herself. She was embarrassed at her behaviour here in Omar and Shabana's flat where she was a guest. She could still barely manage a single breath. Her chest was so tight. So, finally heeding Shabana she forced herself to inhale a little more deeply, then a little more. What a hard task.

Ria tried to divert her focus to what was going on outside the window and get away from what was inside her head. She watched cars go by, children jump into puddles in their little coloured raincoats, and the sea of black umbrellas that battled the howling wind and thick rain. In the background, Shabana and Omar were whispering. What must they be thinking of her now! If Shabana had any doubts about whether she was a terrorist before opening the envelope, then Ria was sure that after her reaction to a photo of a woman in a uniform Shabana would be more suspicious. Shabana was no fool, and neither was Omar. They were people who knew life as it was for people like them. She felt herself become a little less jittery, and as she forced herself to take deep breaths, she heard Shabana get up and then the familiar sounds of tea being prepared calmed Ria a little more. It reminded her of home. Now was not the time to lose her mind.

She turned around slowly, dropping her hands down by her side, the pain returning now to her body. Omar stood up, looking anxious. She searched for the photo. It lay face down on the table, which had now been cleared of food. The photo was in the middle, the focal point.

"Come and sit Ria. Shabana is bringing some fresh tea." Omar said. "Do you feel any better?"
Ria nodded to him and made her way over to the table. She felt sick. She could not find a way to explain her reaction because she didn't understand it herself, or the message.

"What time is it, Omar?" Ria asked, her voice sounding wooden.

"It is almost six. Have some tea, we can talk a little if you like, then I will get a taxi to take you back to the centre in time, and we can go and do the phone thing" Omar said, then hesitated. "Ria, you know that if you do not go back, they will look for you, and of course, the first place they will come, will be here. You know that is not an option for us now Ria. You know..." Omar looked embarrassed.

Ria felt ashamed of the predicament she had placed them in. She felt bad for Omar and Shabana and knew she had to leave them alone for their own safety. Omar knew it too. They had a lot to lose.

"I know. I have to go. It is not safe for you to be with me. Shabana can call me when her friend calls with news. What if they are looking for me to take me already!" Ria said remembering the old worry, which for a moment had been erased with the shock of the photograph.

The photograph, the man Malik, those were not her biggest problems! The prospect of prison had even begun to feel safer. She could feel the terror inside her and knew it for what it was. Her fear of the woman in the photo was so visceral, but it felt like more than just fear. The photo of this woman had caused a new feeling to form inside her that she could not identify.

"It is possible. But they are not here yet, are they?" Omar said. "It will not take long to have some tea and to prepare yourself better for your return."

Ria sat, the pain from her injuries replaced now by fear, raw fear. This fear was not new, it felt familiar, but she had not been so aware of it before. She sat on the edge of her chair, leg tapping to the rhythm of her distress.

Shabana entered with a tray of small glasses filled with green tea and a plate full of fresh mint. Ria loved the smell of fresh mint. It reminded her even more of her home, of her mother and of better times. Her dry mouth now craved the liquid she had shunned only minutes before.

Ria stared at the overturned photo on the table, thinking about Malik's message about the meeting. She looked now more carefully at the place, time and date. The date he had written to meet him was not far off. Who did this man think he was? Did he really think that by sending her this photo she would simply take off and go and meet him in some city she didn't know? He must be mad or delusional. He made her so angry. She was grateful for the anger now. Anger was better than fear.

But then, there was that taunting question too *Do you remember now?* She could not get it out of her head. Who was this woman and what had it to do with her and this man? Better to leave it alone and focus on her bigger problem. Imminent prison.

She would focus on that problem and put Malik and his mysterious message out of her head. There was no way she was going anywhere near that man. Still, an insistent voice inside her questioned whether focusing on being tried a terrorist a better option. She thought not. She would be convicted at nineteen, imprisoned, branded something she was not. The shame! *Was* she a terrorist? No. Was Jamil a terrorist? She didn't think so. Did he know some people who were? Probably. She certainly did not feel like a terrorist, but how would she know what being a terrorist feels like! Stupid girl. So many unanswered questions and there was only one person who seemed to know the answers. Malik. She had to speak to Naira.

"Here Ria, drink this," Shabana said and handed her a steaming glass of tea with a lot of mint. It was hot, so Shabana had put a napkin around it.

They all sat in silence keeping their eyes off the photo and each other.

"Who is she, Ria?" Shabana asked eventually. "What is she to you?"

After a long silence. Ria moved forward and turned over the photo. She recoiled again but this time she was a little bit more prepared, but still, her reaction just built on her previous one. She forced herself to look at the woman.

"I know her, but I do not know how. That is the truth. Omar, what is the uniform she is wearing? Do you recognise it?" Ria asked and looked at him.

"Those are mercenary uniforms, Ria, that is why there is no country insignia on it. You know. They use mercenaries in all of our countries. Especially in yours now. They do the dirty work. That way there is no consequences for those meddling in our affairs with accusations of war crimes or extrajudicial killings. All the countries use them all over the world to meddle in other countries. Even though they call themselves soldiers, they are not, most were kicked out of the army. These people follow the orders of whoever pays them. They are nastier than real soldier, they are usually ugly people inside you know, not right in the head. They only live for the high of the violence and the money, but especially the violence. Do you know what I mean?" Omar looked at her, his eyebrows raised.

Ria nodded. She did.

"Do you remember anything about her, do you think you met her here or back home?" Shabana asked again, more insistently it seemed to Ria now.

Ria stared at the woman's face as if in a trance. Inside her head, she seemed to know the woman was speaking English. Who was she speaking to? She couldn't hear any of the words, but she could see that the woman was in the same dark place as during her nightmares. Was this the prison Malik had spoken about? Ria looked away from the photo quickly.

"I don't know where or how. I just know I have seen her before," Ria responded.

"If you want Ria. I can go and see a friend tomorrow. I can take that photo. He was a mercenary himself for years, so he knows many of them. You know it's like anything, each special world is a small place. He keeps files because he is always saying that one day he will write a book about his life and all that world. Maybe she is in his files, or he knows someone who might know her. He would tell no one and you could not tell anyone either, do you understand Ria" Omar said.

"That is too dangerous Omar, what are you thinking!" Shabana scolded him. Shabana looked worried.

"Omar, they are watching Ria, us too, probably. If you meet him, you will also be putting him at risk, not just yourself!"

"She's right Omar. It's okay, I am grateful for your offer, but I have brought you both enough problems as it is. I think it's time for me to go back to the centre and well, accept my fate, and forget all about this photo. I have bigger things to worry about now than the photo of this woman or the man who sent it!" Ria said.

"Are you sure?" Omar said, not looking at Shabana.

"Yes, Omar, it is not worth putting you or your friend at risk for nothing. This man is crazy, we do not know what games he is playing. Let's just forget him and this woman. I have to focus on this terrorist thing now. I had better be getting back. Omar, can you call me a taxi?" Ria said, feeling calmer now.

"Okay, if that is what you want. I will come with you. You must get a new phone. I'll take you." Omar said and got up to make the call. Ria looked at Shabana who looked relieved.

"Yes, get rid of your phone, make it known that you lost it. Give the new number to no one but Omar. Omar knows these things very well. He will show you. Will you be okay?" Shabana said.

"Shabana, thank you so much. Both of you. I am so sorry about everything. You have been so good to me. I wish I could tell you more, but I swear I don't remember anything." Ria said, almost on the verge of tears again.

"I am sorry this is happening to you Ria. If they come to take you, you'll let us know, won't you? In the meantime, I will continue to see about getting a lawyer to help." Shabana said.

331

"Twenty minutes the taxi people say. Why is it always twenty minutes no matter when you call?" He joked as he put away his phone.

Omar nodded. "I will take you first to Josef's, we will get you two phones. Okay? You always need a spare." Ria nodded.

"When you get them, Ria, only turn on one, keep the other one without its card in it and turned off. Do not give the numbers to anyone else. I'll take both numbers. Then, as I said before, memorise the really necessary numbers and we'll dump your other phone. Make sure as many people as possible know you have lost it and that you are pissed off about it. Wait for my text. We will communicate on that one only. Understood?" Omar smiled at Ria.

It all felt very spy-like, but Ria felt reassured. There was a plan. They were not abandoning her. Shabana would find her help from a lawyer if she could. Ria had her doubts whether Shabana would help her if it turned out the state had strong evidence against her, or... against Jamil. But Ria knew that even though people here were always associating people from her country with terrorism, Ria knew that in her country, they knew the difference. She was convinced that neither she nor Jamil could ever do what a terrorist does. She felt pride surge again. She would not succumb like a lamb to the slaughter. She remembered what Naira had said about her own family. She thought now about her own father, the man she had never known.

"The taxi is here, let me help you, Ria," Omar said from the window and moved to her side.

Ria hugged Shabana goodbye as best she could, sensing that perhaps she would never see her again. She let Omar help her put on her coat, and her now slightly drier shoes, and together they shuffled out of the flat and down to the waiting taxi. First, they went to do the business with the phones, then they dumped her old phone in a litter bin and Omar dropped her off at the centre.

As soon as Ria walked into the reception control area, she knew something was wrong.

39

A police officer was standing behind the reception control counter when Ria entered. He gestured for her to approach the control desk as soon as he saw her come in.

"What is your name?" he asked.

She told him and saw his expression change.

"Where have you been?" he asked.

She hesitated. "I had a case officer visit downtown, then, you know, just looking around the shops. "Nowhere really." She lied, flushing slightly.

He frowned and wrote something down. He looked up at her.

"I have to notify you there is a transfer order for you tomorrow at noon. I am sure that your case worker has informed you of your situation if you have just come from there. If not, you will receive a call soon. You have until tomorrow morning to get ready and prepare yourself. Here is a copy of the order." he stated. "You will be picked up at eleven tomorrow morning. ."

She felt frozen to the spot at this news and just stood there. The police officer held out a piece of paper.

"Take your copy." he said.

She took the paper. It was all happening so quickly. So soon. She couldn't speak. Maybe her case worker had tried to phone, but her phone had been off, and now it lay deep inside some rubbish bin in another part of the town.

"Do you understand what this means?" he asked, looking at her.

Ria didn't answer. She understood all too well.

"What this means is that effective immediately you cannot leave this centre. You are instructed to wait here until you are transferred tomorrow to await preliminary proceedings. Do you understand? You are no longer free to leave this centre." he said dismissing her with a gesture.

Ria muted by this news said nothing and moved away from the desk with some difficulty as her legs again seemed too stiff to move. Ria walked down the corridor in a daze, everything that had happened to her in the last few weeks was too much. It all felt so surreal. Since she had woken up int hat hospital it had all been a relentless, living nightmare.

All the doors she passed on the way down to her room were shut. The only sound she could hear was the sound of the odd police radio crackling, a sound that felt oddly familiar to Ria. The place had never been as quiet as it was now, but it was an unnatural quiet. She saw a couple of police officers moving down the corridor in another block across the way. Were they here because of her? Here to watch her until tomorrow morning?

As she opened the door to her room, she saw Naira and Fatima sitting on the floor deep in conversation. Naira jumped up when she saw Ria enter.

"Ria, damn you! Where did you go? I was so worried, you just disappeared and then hung up the phone! You can barely walk. Where have you been all this time? Are you okay?" Naira's questions were fired off rapidly, but she came over to Ria looking genuinely concerned.

"It's okay Naira, I'm fine. I was with Shabana. What's going on here with the police? I have been informed of my transfer time. They will come for me tomorrow morning at 11, so it's very real now. I saw two police officers in the other block too." Ria said.

"What do you mean Ria? Who is coming for you tomorrow? To take you where and why?" Fatima said, frowning suspiciously.

"It's nothing Fatima," Ria said.

"Those police are here asking questions about something else. It's not about you, I don't think." Naira said.

"What do you mean?" Ria asked.

"We think it's about the women." Naira looked at her.

"The women? What happened?" Ria asked.

It was Fatima who answered

"One of the women got arrested last night past curfew. It was just bad luck. She was in the wrong place at the wrong time. She wasn't doing anything except for being outside the detention centre so late. The other women who had gone out with her saw it happen. She was spotted by a patrol car and well, you know, at that time of night....They asked her what she was doing out there, she made an excuse, but they did obviously did not believe her, so they took her to the police station. The other women know she won't tell them anything, but they are worried about her because she has not come back yet. They can't arrest her for breaking curfew, so it is unusual that she has not returned. Then the police arrived here about an hour ago.

337

They have been going around asking people questions about different things and about what goes on in here. There is one at reception, as you saw, and two more walking around, going into peoples' rooms. Who knows what they are doing here. They have already been in here asking questions, they were very interested in where you were. We told them nothing." Fatima said proudly. "But why such interest in you?" Fatima asked slyly and stared at Ria.

Ria saw the accusation in her eyes.

"I have no idea why they would be interested in me." Ria said and took off her coat.

"Really? You just said they were coming to take you tomorrow. And you do a lot of disappearing Ria, every morning as soon as the centre opens, off you go! You don't even have any breakfast and you never shower here. Where do you go?" Fatima said, pressing now. "Maybe you have said the wrong thing to the wrong person about what happened to you the other night."

"No, Fatima. I would never speak to anyone about that or say anything about the women. My comings and goings are none of your business. They are taking me tomorrow for reasons I do not understand. I have nothing to hide." she lied. She had plenty to hide.

Then it occurred to her. "Will they come back in here to question me?" Ria asked worried now because she didn't think she could lie well enough if they did. One thing was lying to Fatima, and another was lying to the police.

She felt so exhausted by everything, and her ribs were killing her. It was slowly sinking in that tomorrow she would leave this place to go to a much worse one. She would be in a real prison, with real criminals, cut off from the few people she knew. Completely alone. Even in a million years, she would never have imagined that she would end up in a foreign prison accused of terrorism. Prison! She felt her fear of it grow much stronger now that it was a reality, and she had a time appointed for the moment she would be taken away - eleven tomorrow morning. So little time left and what little freedom she did have was now being taken from her. The prisons here must be better than in her country, not that she had ever seen one in her country, but she had heard the rumours. Here, surely, she had rights. But Shabana had seemed to imply that with terrorism it was difference. Not the same rights. She longed to run, but now that she was confined until the next day, that was not even a possibility. Since the police officer had her, she could not leave, her urge to flee grew stronger. The last thing she needed now was to be questioned by the police about the goings on of the women. She was such a terrible liar.

"Why did they say they were taking you, Ria?" Fatima asked her, not giving up her line of questioning.

"Here come and sit down and tell us." Fatima coaxed still eyeing Ria suspiciously.

She passed Ria a mug of tea, and Ria sat down on Naira's bunk. Fatima sat on the floor as she usually did. Ria shivered. She was cold despite the stale heat of the room. She had nothing to lose now by telling Fatima and no energy to keep lying.

Ria kept her voice low. "When I went to see my case worker this morning, he told me he had received an answer from the state to my petition to return home. He told me that my petition had been denied 'permanently'. Ria began but was interrupted by Fatima's expressions of shock and her swearing.

"Wait! That is not all." Ria said. "The reason for that and why they are taking me away tomorrow is that I am to be held in a prison to await trial."

Ria stopped there. She could not bring herself to utter the words of why.

"What!" cried Fatima and was immediately told to lower her voice by Naira. "That can't be right! Why would *you* be going on trial? I don't understand. Why? Ria, what have you done?" Fatima asked frowning and looking visibly distressed.

Ria said nothing. She couldn't. It had been hard enough telling Naira, Shabana and Omar, but now, here, with the police and everything. What would Fatima, who had been so kind to her in this damn place, think of her now?

"Ria, you have to tell me. What have you done for this to happen?" Fatima asked, calm and controlled, but now she did not even bother to mask her suspicion "Is it about what you did the night you left here in such a hurry after curfew? Was it you who told them about the women? Is that why the police are here?"

"Shut up Fatima!" Naira snapped. "Ria would never do a thing like that and what happened to her that night wasn't her fault. Wait and hear the reason before you judge her!"

Ria looked at Naira gratefully but shook her head. "It's okay Fatima, I wish it was that, but to be honest it's much worse," Ria said.

"Worse? What could be worse than that?" Fatima asked frowning.

"Terrorism, Fatima, terrorism," Ria said. There, she had got it out. It wasn't something that exactly rolled off the tongue she thought. "They have accused me of having links to terrorism back home, before I came here. But Fatima, it is not true. I swear to you."

There was an uncomfortable silence in the room. Fatima's eyes were practically bulging in their sockets in disbelief. Naira looked at Ria in sympathy.

"They will come for me tomorrow morning at eleven and I am not allowed to leave here in the meantime. My case worker said that it was possible that I have been under surveillance since I woke up three months ago in that hospital. I don't know if that is true or not but if it is, I had no idea. I'm so sorry" Ria said and swallowed in shame.

"Naira, you knew about this already, didn't you? And you never said a thing." Fatima said to Naira, looking disappointed.

"It was not my thing to tell, Fatima," Naira said calmly.

"A terrorist? You? No, they are crazy!" Fatima said, her focus swiftly back on Ria. "I know they think all you people are terrorists, but this is too much. I don't understand. Is it not usually the men they go for? Do you know why they are focusing on you?" she asked.

341

"It's not for being a terrorist Fatima, they said 'links' to terrorism, from before I even came here. That's all I know. Shabana told me it means that they think I associated with some terrorist group or someone who was a terrorist when I was back home. I don't know, I don't understand, I am as shocked as you are Fatima. More shocked because this is all happening to me! I have never done anything in my life, I have not even fought. I could not believe it when my case worker told me, and I still can't believe it. I can't believe that they can just do that without ever even having spoken to me. It is not that different here to home after all, is it Naira?" Ria said, looking down at the floor, feeling ashamed again.

"Maybe they are not so crazy, maybe you did do something back in your country and you have just been pretending all this time about having memory problems!" Fatima said and Ria felt Fatima's dark eyes on her, seeking the truth in Ria's eyes.

"Fatima do not say such things. We all know how things work here for people like us, and anyway, who the hell are you to judge anyone?" Naira said to Fatima.

"What is that supposed to mean Naira?" Fatima sniped back. "You are certainly no angel, are you? Perhaps both of you have been up to something like that. It's on the news all the time about terrorists acting here in Europe. Or maybe, you are just inventing this story Ria to cover up that you have told the police about the women!" Fatima said turning back to Ria.

"Stop it both of you!" Ria said and began to cry. "Fatima, I am telling you the truth, and everything I know.

I have never even been questioned. How could I give up the women? I don't know who they are even." She paused. She had to say it. "The only problem is that because I might be under surveillance, they could have tracked me that night, I don't know. But they would only have tracked me, not the women. I do not know what level of surveillance they might have on me or even if it is true. I am hardly an important person for them, if I was, they would have taken me to prison sooner. I am sure that they have more important things to do than follow a nineteen-year-old around twenty-four hours a day judging from what's on the news! I have said nothing to anyone, and I will never tell anyone anything about the women, never! I have no reason to. I admire them and they saved my *life!*" Ria said, finding strength and indignation despite her shame.

"Naira, you must prepare yourself in case they heard anything we talked about. I don't remember what or when or anything...but it is important that you think because I cannot!" Ria said.

"See! You have been doing things!" Fatima said.
Naira glared at Fatima and came to sit next to Ria.

"Ria don't worry about me, I have dealt with worse, and so has Fatima. We will be fine. We have done nothing wrong. It is you who needs help now. Did your friend get you a lawyer or anything?" Naira asked.

"A lawyer?" Fatima said, scorn in her voice. "They don't give terrorists lawyers here! They don't give people like us things like that Naira! Have you learned nothing yet about white people? You young people!"

"Fatima! Stop talking like an old woman! You are only twenty-four! Either be of help or just shut up! This is stressful enough for Ria without you accusing her of things she hasn't done!" Naira spat back.

Fatima turned her head away to study the door. She looked angry.

Ria looked at them. "Look, both of you. I know this is a shock to you. I understand your reaction Fatima, I do, but I have to rest for a while. If they come to question me, so be it, but I must rest now, it has been a very difficult day, and I am in pain. We can talk some more later." Ria said and got up onto her bunk and just lay there on her back.

Ria did not want to rest. Rest was not an option or even possible, but she did need the mental space to think, she had very little time left and was trapped in here with the police roaming round. She could leave the room but not the centre. She needed to text Shabana to tell her it was already happening, but she didn't want to risk it now with the police around. She would have to get rid of them tomorrow somehow before the police came. They were the type of thing that would make her look very suspicious. She would leave them with Naira.

Ria felt she had a choice to make. Either she let them do with her what they wanted, or she made a run for it and went to meet Malik. At least he seemed to know how to handle himself, even in this country. But even if she did choose to run, how? The police were here. Perhaps they would leave soon, perhaps not. It was very bad luck that the woman had got arrested now of all times! If not, the women could have helped her leave the centre tonight. But then what? How would she even get out of the town, injured as she still was, in the freezing night, with only enough cash for a couple of coffees? No, there was no way. She didn't have a choice to make really. She would be taken and spend who knew how long in prison, branded a terrorist. That would be her life now. Innocent but proven guilty. But was she innocent though? She didn't think she was somehow. It was an odd feeling to have but she had felt that way since the case worker had told her, as if somehow, she deserved to be punished.

40

Ria lay on her bunk going over and over her situation. She was trapped. She didn't know how much time had passed, but Fatima and Naira had gone to bed without bothering her and the lights in the room were off. She had to decide herself. She could not let the decision be made for her. She was young, too young to go to prison and for something she hadn't even done. Something that was more likely to do with Jamil or Alana. She hated it here. She wanted to run so what was stopping her?

Her mind sifted through all the rumours she had heard about people like her. People said that the police often invented evidence about people being terrorists and put them in prisons, just because of where they were from. Preventive measures. She had no chance of winning any trial, she couldn't remember anything. Shabana's lawyer friend had already said she wasn't optimistic. Anyway, it would be too late, she'd already be in prison tomorrow. No. She had to get out of here before they came. She had decided. She felt a slight weight lift and a flutter of excitement in her heart as she sat up on her elbows on the bunk, her mind racing. She would make a run for it, let them catch her. At least she would have tried instead of just giving up. She just had to figure out how to get out of the centre before the morning.

The only way out of here was with the help of the same women who had got her out before. But they were now possibly being watched by the police, they wouldn't risk helping her. But there was no other way out. She had to try.

She got down from her bunk as quietly as possible and padded silently over to Naira's bunk.

"I'm awake, Ria. How could I be asleep?" Naira whispered sitting up. She was still in her clothes.

"Be quiet"! They'll hear you!" Fatima hissed from above Naira.

It would be impossible to discuss this without involving Fatima, who seemed to have turned against her with all this terrorism thing. She may not believe Ria was innocent, but she would not turn her in. Fatima must be involved with the women somehow. She had known who to go to that night Ria needed to get out. Ria needed Fatima.

"Fatima, get up, I need to speak to both of you, please, I'll be quiet," Ria whispered up to Fatima.

"Ria, you are just going to get us into trouble. This is your problem. Not ours!" Fatima said.

"I know Fatima. That's true. But if the situation was reversed, I would do anything I could to help you. I am not going to let them be judge and jury over me and not even be able to defend myself because I cannot remember anything. It is not fair. You come from a country at war too, you know what it is like. Nothing is black and white. These people, as you say all the time, are not to be trusted." Ria said.

"She's right Fatima. If it were you, Ria and I would both be searching for solutions now, not turning our backs on you! There is no real truth in any war, or even anything Fatima, you know that." Naira whispered.

Silence. Then, eventually, there was a soft rustling of sheets and Ria saw Fatima's bare legs dangle down from the top bunk. Then effortlessly and without making a sound, she jumped down from her bunk and was now standing facing Ria.

"What do you want me to do Ria? There is not much time. The police may have gone but still, more people are watching you now. More people are watching us." Fatima said.

"I'm leaving. Let them catch me but I am going to at least try to get away. I am not going to let them come here tomorrow and take me like this. They haven't even had the decency to speak to me." Ria said, feeling more determined now.

Her statement was met with silence from both Fatima and Naira.

"Leaving? How?" Naira said, and Ria thought she caught a hint of excitement in her voice.

"I don't know, that's why I need both of you to help me to think of a way. There is not much time." Ria said. "All I know is that I have done nothing to deserve spending years of my life in one of their prisons branded a terrorist. So much talk of democracy! First, they bring me here against my will, with no explanation, and now this! Not to mention possibly following me around without my knowledge like I am some sort of criminal, it's unacceptable! It's almost worse than the state we are fighting back home! I will not let them do this to me. I will run. I'd rather do that than go tomorrow like a quiet little lamb just because that is what *they* have decided. I have rights! And in our family, we do not just submit. We fight back!" Ria said, feeling proud of herself for once.

"Fatima, I know you know them. I'm talking about the women who got me out the last time. I have to speak to them. They got me out before, they can do it again. All you have to do is tell me how to contact them. I won't put you or anyone else at risk, I swear it, all they have to do is just show me how they get out and let me go! They don't have to take me themselves." Ria pleaded.

"Keep your voice down, you stupid girl," Fatima said in a low but commanding voice.
Naira got up from her bunk and the three of them stood there between the two sets of bunks.

Fatima sighed. "Ria, I told you already, the woman they arrested last night will not say a word, no matter what the police threaten her with. They will not find the other women either, but to do what you ask is too risky for them now. Especially tonight, and especially with someone like you. We will be fine. We will just wait it out. Our sister will return and that will be it. She has done nothing illegal so they cannot deport her. But you Ria, you must be careful. You are not like us. You have no experience and not much wisdom. You are too young. Even if you did get out of here, then what? You can barely walk with all your injuries, and you have no money. You are far from your home and your people. What we have is a web, Ria. You have no such web." Fatima said, not unkindly.

"You are right about everything Fatima. I lack wisdom and I am not resourceful. It is true too that I do not have the means or the experience to get away from them, but I refuse to let this be my life. I would rather die than spend my life in their prison, at least there is honour in that." Ria said.

"Honour? What would you know about honour?" Fatima said.

"Perhaps it is time she learned Fatima." Naira said. "I will come with you, Ria. There is nothing for me here and I do have the experience, after all, I came here by myself with a baby. I know what it is like. I can help you. I want to go home too. I am tired of being here doing nothing while our people are killed every minute of the day, and no one cares!" Naira said. "But Fatima, you are wrong about one thing. Ria might not know about a web, but we do have one."

Fatima looked at Naira in surprise, but she also seemed sad to Ria. Naira and Fatima had shared a lot. Ria was delighted but worried.

"If it is both of you, it is even more of a risk to get you out," Fatima said. "But perhaps there is a way to make this work for us too. High risk, high price, yes?" Fatima said, eyebrows raised.

"Name your price!" Ria said and looked at Fatima boldly.

"Wait here." Fatima went back up to her bunk, then dropped back again. "I'm going to the bathroom." She opened the door and slipped out of the room.

Ria looked at Naira.

"Naira, what do you mean you will come with me! It is too dangerous. You planned to go much later, in the spring. Now, it is still winter. Also, I haven't been able to tell you yet because of Fatima but earlier Malik sent me a photo of a foreign soldier – a woman – I know her, but I don't know her... I mean... I can't remember who she is, but her face is familiar. He sent me a message too and a meeting place, it's in another town, and a date to meet. I want to go there to meet him. He has answers and he will take me back home to my brother. You don't have to come. You will be doing a dangerous thing for nothing." Ria said.

"A photo of a soldier? And you know her?" Naira asked.

"Omar says she is a mercenary. I recognise her but I cannot remember anything about her, but he wrote me a message on the back of the photo. He knows something. If I have to choose between going to prison and being called a terrorist, which I am not, and meeting Malik to find out more about what happened to my family and me, then I choose to meet Malik. What is the worst thing he can do to me? If he is my brother's friend, as he claims, he will not harm me. He will help me." Ria said.

"He could kill you, Ria. You don't know him. You don't know anything about him. He could easily be lying about your brother, or maybe something went wrong between them. Sending you this photo and asking you to meet somewhere else, not even here. Why? It all sounds very strange." Naira said.

"I know. But it is better than the alternative, isn't it? And there is the chance that he is not lying. I know that woman, my nightmares are filled with images of her Naira. I have to find out who she is and how I know her and why she is in my nightmares. You should stay here. He will not harm me" Ria said.

"There is a third option, Ria. We just go home, and you forget about that man Malik. He sounds like trouble. I can sense it and I don't even know him. We get out of here and we go home. It will be colder on the routes, yes, but we will manage, we can steal some thick jackets and blankets!" Naira joked a little.

Ria did not smile. It was not the time for joking.

"And as I said I have the network to get us back." Naira said.

"I can't Naira. If I don't speak to him again. I may never know who she is."

"Who cares who she is! Once you are back home, it won't matter. Your brother can tell you." Naira said, impatient now.

"No. I can't explain why Naira, but I have to meet him. The town he wants to meet in is about two hundred kilometres away, I checked the address he gave me on the phone map. He must have left here already. We could go there, meet him, then we could go home, it is just a few hours. We talk to him and then we leave." Ria said.

"Ria don't be naïve. This man is playing games. Who sends someone a mysterious photo and tells them to come to a city they've never been to that is two hundred kilometres away? No one normal. You can't do this, it's too dangerous, and for what? Just over a photo of someone you have dreamt about! I speak from experience when I say this Ria, the faces in our nightmares can never be anything good. When you saw the photo, did you feel anything?" Naira asked.

Wrong-footed here now by a more experienced Naira, Ria was unsure of how much to tell her, so she just nodded and grimaced.

Naira opened her mouth to say something when the door opened, and Fatima returned.

"I've left word. We'll know in a while. Now, let's think. There will be a price, Ria. Are you sure you are willing to pay it? Naira, I don't think you should go with her. It's a bad idea. She's wanted by the police for terrorism, and they will just let her go easily. They will hunt her down. If you go with her, you will be guilty too, just like her, another terrorist on the run or you'll be in trouble for helping her and risk prison yourself! Is that what you are prepared to risk Naira? Two people are easier to catch than one. Especially two women who look like you two do. It's not like you blend in! Even if you do make it out of this centre, or even this town, how will you get out of the country? You say you have a web Naira, but do you really? It's a crazy idea Naira, and your baby son is here. That matter is not resolved. You have unfinished business with that, many papers to sign, a process to go through. You know that. You can't just abandon him in the middle of it!"

"He will be better off with a proper family, a family from here. A rich family. They can offer him more. I can offer him nothing." Naira snapped, defensively.

"I know, but you haven't finished the paperwork, if you leave it will delay everything." Fatima said.

"You are still his *mother!* A mother is a mother no matter what!" Fatima said. "Naira, you have tried to end your life too often in here. You have a baby boy who needs you. We do not kill ourselves when things get hard. We fight. We put our strength together and we fight together. We don't give up. But you people, you always run!" Fatima said visibly agitated.

Ria said nothing but looked at Naira whose frame seemed to become smaller with each harsh word Fatima uttered. Ria tried to catch her eye, but Naira was looking down at the floor. Ria did not know what to do. Fatima was being difficult, but Ria knew that Naira already felt bad and didn't want to say the wrong thing and end up hurting her even more or aggravating Fatima. Ria needed them both for her plan to work.

"You are right Fatima about everything. But I cannot stay here. I'm sorry. I cannot be his mother, not even during the process of giving him up. We've talked about this. I have to go home. Things there will get much worse before they get better. I cannot stay here just for him. He's being looked after. I have signed the consent. That's the most important thing. The rest will happen with or without me. I know he will have a better life here. He is too young to remember me. He won't even know I ever existed. He will have a good life here with a good family." Naira said not moving her eyes from the floor, talking down to it.

Fatima sighed and walked over to hug Naira. Ria felt relief. Fatima could be tough, but she had a huge heart.

354

"Then, if you must go, I will help you, my sister. I am helping you Naira, not this one." Fatima said looking at Ria, her tone dispatching undisguised scorn in Ria's direction. Fatima loved Naira. Ria could see that. Ria did not defend herself. The stakes were too high for pride.

Naira looked up, her dark eyes filling with tears, and she hugged Fatima back.

"Thank you, Fatima, for everything you have done for me, and especially for Khal. Will you watch over him? Will you and the others make sure to let me know when he gets placed with a family? And tell me what they are like? I just want to know he is okay and not with some fascists, you know." Naira joked through her tears.

Fatima laughed. "Don't worry, we will check on him from time to time and if he is with anyone we don't like, we will get him back and... well, you know, make sure he gets a better family. You don't need to worry about that. You can trust us, you know that."

"I know," Naira said and looked over at Ria. She smiled at her. "So, my friend, it looks as if we are going home together! On a big adventure!"

"Naira, are you sure? It is a lot, and it's dangerous. Fatima is right about that. I have no web, no money and I am still injured." Ria said.

She had to make sure. She was so happy she did not have to go alone but she didn't want to feel responsible for Naira if something went wrong.

"Ria, I have a network of contacts. How do you think I got here with a baby? What we don't have is money. Look, this is an opportunity for me. I know the risks and I am okay with them. We will make it together! Now, Fatima, what can we do? Ria, get as many clothes on you as you can. It will be cold on the run, and a wear a good pair of boots."

Ria started. That sounded familiar. From where?

"Naira, are you sure about leaving Khal here? Never seeing him again?" Ria asked.

"You haven't told her?" Fatima said looking at Naira.

Ria looked at Naira, who seemed to avert her eyes, embarrassed.

"No," she said curtly.

"What haven't you told me?" Ria asked Naira.

"It's not important now." Naira said, shutting down any further questions.

"What is the price, Fatima?" Ria asked, eyes still on Naira. What would Naira tell Fatima, but not her?

"I don't know if they will agree yet. Wait here," Fatima said and slipped out of the room again.

Ria looked at Naira to see if she would say something, but Naira turned and started to pack so Ria did the same. The whole thing felt unimaginable. How could it possibly work? Her heart was pounding, she was terrified but also excited at the thought of escape and the possible reprieve from prison. But more than anything she was relieved that Naira was coming with her, that she didn't have to be out there on her own. The whole thing felt more possible with Naira by her side.

Fatima returned alone.

"Soon two women will come in here. They will be covered like the last time. One of them is very tall. She is the one who will decide whether to get you out or not. She does not say much, but her questions are important. She watches and she listens, so Ria be careful not only of your words but of the story your face and body tell. Get ready to go but leave your bags out of sight under the bunks." Fatima said, seeming in awe of whoever this tall woman was.

About ten minutes later, the door opened, and two women slipped in. One was tall and the other one shorter, just as Fatima had said. The faces of both were covered. Fatima was practically bowing as the women walked in. They must be important to her. The small room now felt crowded with so many people. Fatima gestured for them to sit on the floor. They all sat cross-legged except for Ria who sat on the bunk. Ria felt tense as she looked down at this tiny circle on which her immediate future depended.
Silence. The tall one kept her gaze on her.

"The last time we took you out was a disaster. You could have got us all caught. We were lucky there were no police around" The smaller of the two began. "Now, with your new complications and this unfortunate incident with our sister, it is not a good time."
Ria didn't think she was finished and there was no question, so she decided to say as little as possible.

"Fatima has told us about the order to transfer you to a prison, for terrorism. What is it you have done? We do not help terrorists!" The smaller one asked looking directly at Ria. Ria felt the eyes of the taller woman burn into her. She avoided them and focused on the smaller woman.

"I do not know what this accusation is about. I am not a terrorist. I can only give you my word. I have done nothing like that. I would never hurt anyone." Ria replied looking up at the tall woman with what Ria hoped was a very heartfelt response.

The tall woman stared at her for a while expressionless.

"It is just your word. Why should we believe it? We don't know you." she said eventually.

"If we do not have our word, then we have nothing. We already have so little here in this place. Fatima will have told you that there is much I do not know about my past. So much that I do not remember. But I believe that I still know who I am and who I am not. I may not remember what happened to me before I came here, but I do remember who I was before I came here, and I was not a terrorist! I was just a student. I understand this is a very bad time to ask you to take this risk for us, well, for me. I will do whatever you ask of me, but I must leave this place before the morning. The only way I can do that is with your help. I wish there were another way, believe me." Ria said, feeling herself sit up taller now, feeling surer of herself and more sincere.

"You will have to take a package for us. Well, more than one. We will not be able to leave here for a while in case they are watching us and these packages need to be delivered urgently. They cannot wait. They are to be delivered to different addresses in another town. You must promise to deliver them on the exact dates marked on each package. Not before that date and not after it." the taller woman paused. "If not... there will be consequences."

"Consequences?" Ria asked. "What do you mean?"

"Consequences for Fatima. She has offered and she has agreed to the terms. It is the only reason we have agreed to this madness. Now, be ready in twenty minutes, when you hear the knock on the door, leave and follow the person. Once outside the centre, she will give you the bag with the packages. Let us hope you are not a lying terrorist! If you are, it will be Fatima who will pay for your deception." The taller woman said and then stood up with ease and grace.

They all stood up.

"Thank you so much. Please know that your packages will be delivered. I give you my word. I would never put Fatima in a bad situation, or you for that matter. Please know that I am very grateful for everything you have done and for saving my life that last time. I am heavily in your debt."

"I hope your words are true. But time will tell, will it not?" said the woman, her eyes darkening as she looked one last time at Ria and then as quickly as they had entered, they left.

41

Once the women had left, there was an uncomfortable silence created by the imbalance of Fatima's pledge that rested on their commitment to follow through.

"Fatima, thank you. Don't worry we will not let you down!" Naira said. "They don't mean that they would hurt you, do they? Surely not. You are one of them, are you not?" Naira asked slyly.

"There are rules, Naira, so do not fail. They are very serious, and I am not an elder in the group. She will make me pay in a way that hurts me if that is what she says she will do. There are many ways to hurt someone, not just by harming the body. She has no time for mistakes of judgment. Our work is more important than one woman." Fatima said proudly. "We are not like you people!" She said looking at Ria.

Ria turned to Fatima, face reddening and in an instant, she felt something snap inside her. Ria caught Naira wince at Fatima's words. Ria stepped towards Fatima feeling so tall compared to the woman's short, strong body. Ria raised her hand and like a flash lashed out to strike Fatima, anger and frustration driving her hand with such force only to feel it effortlessly blocked mid-way by Fatima's hand. Her arm went dead, locked in Fatima's grip. Fatima had barely moved. She stared at Ria, a slight frown on her face.

Ria stared at her in shock.

"Who are you?" Ria asked.

"Who are *you*? Fatima replied. "Is that not the real question? I offer myself up to save your skin and you try to strike me? Ria, you have no idea of who, or even what we are. You cannot even imagine. How dare you even attempt to hit me!"

Naira stood looking on speechless.

Ria said "I'm sorry. I don't know. I truly do not know who I am anymore. You can think we are all terrorists in our country if you want, but we are not. We are also victims of white colonialisation, just as you were, and still are. We are ruled by a tyrant the West has tolerated for decades, as they have tolerated all the other leaders who harm their own people and steal their futures from them. I am just a nobody born in a terrible place... I am sorry I went to strike you. I am just so tired of being called a terrorist, but it feels even worse coming from you." Ria said, feeling ashamed as she pulled out of her anger and plunged into shame.

Fatima released her vice grip on Ria's raised arm and Ria rubbed the part that hurt.

"Please do not judge me, Fatima. You know nothing about me, and I know nothing about you. But you are a part of these mysterious women, women who creep out at night and spend all night out. But I know they are women of honour and that means you are too. You helped saved my life once, and now you will help save it again. You have staked yourself on our ability to deliver those packages. I am ashamed of my reaction, please accept my apology." Ria said looking at Fatima.

Fatima nodded and Ria went back to making sure she had everything she needed and was wrapped up well. She heard Naira thanking Fatima for all of her help with Khal and for their friendship. Ria felt her eyes prick with tears as she watched them.

Ria jumped at the soft knock on the door. It was time. She looked at Naira and time stood still for a moment, she saw no doubt on Naira's face, not even fear. Ria cast a glance at Fatima who nodded. Naira hugged Fatima and moved towards the door.

"Remember Ria, I am in your hands now. Please do as the tall woman asks. Naira, remember I am the one you asked to look over Khal from a distance, make sure I can do that. Make no mistakes with those packages. The dates on them are very important and not flexible. You miss just one date, and I will pay." Fatima said, her face reflecting her concern.

Ria nodded at her and slipped out after Naira into the dimly lit corridor. There was just one woman, there, her face covered. She had a bag on her back which didn't look heavy. She gestured for them to follow her, and they walked quietly down the empty corridor. At the end, they stood outside a door marked 'No Entry' and she passed them two hoods. Naira put her hood on, but Ria hesitated.

"Put it on or stay here. Your choice." The woman whispered.

"Ria, put it on," Naira whispered sharply. "Hurry up."

Ria pulled the hood over her head and again felt the panic instantly. She felt a hand grab onto her arm. Naira! She was always there when she needed her the most.

Clasped together the trio shuffled along slowly, then crawled for a while in the pitch dark for what felt like forever to Ria, who, like the last time, felt very panicked in the darkness of the hood. It was not long before she felt herself being pulled up by someone strong and felt the familiar blast of cold air hit her face. They shuffled along for another while in the hoods and then stopped.

"You can take off your hoods now." The woman said.

Once her eyes adjusted Ria saw they were not far from the centre, but not in the same alleyway as the last time. They were behind a large, dark building, which looked like an abandoned garage. It was cold and dark and there was no one around.

The woman took their hoods and handed Ria the bag she had been carrying.

"Here. Take this. You know what you must do. There is a date marked on each package. Do not miss any of the dates, not even one. There is no margin for error. You know what will happen if you do." the woman said.

The woman turned and was gone before Ria could say anything. She looked at Naira in surprise.

"Well, they said there was a price. We must respect it, Ria. For Fatima's sake." Naira said.

"I know." Ria said. "I would never let those women down. They saved my life, and now this risk they have taken for me tonight. The packages are my priority, don't worry."

"We have to get as far away as possible from this town before daylight. Well before they realise you are not there." Naira said.

Ria nodded "We need to check the addresses and the dates on the packages Naira, we can't just go racing off without knowing where to. We have a responsibility now to Fatima."

"You're right. We won't put Fatima in any danger, but we can't get caught either. But, okay, let's look quickly to see where it is we have to go and what the dates are. I'll shine the torch from the phone, and you look at the places on each package." Naira said.

"How many are there?" Naira asked anxiously.

"Wait, let me see. Shine more down here." Ria gestured and opened the bag wider on the ground as they both knelt beside it. There were three packages inside, all about the size of a large smartphone. Ria picked them up, they were very light. They were all wrapped in the same brown paper and covered with tightly wrapped plastic. The packages were well sealed. There was an address written in blue marker on each one and a delivery date written in smaller writing on the back.

Ria said. "I don't know this city. Do you?" Ria asked Naira who was peering into the bag.

"Let me see one." Naira juggled the torch function and the map function of her phone and checked each one.

"They are all in the same city. It's about two hundred and fifty kilometres from here, north. The dates?" Naira asked.

"Three consecutive days, starting the day after tomorrow! That only gives us tomorrow to get there." Ria said.

"And your meeting with the man? Where is it?" Naira asked.

Ria took her bag and opened a flap, reached in for the envelope Omar had given her, and not looking at the photo on the other side read the name of the town out to Naira. Naira looked down at her phone again.

"Okay! The two towns are only one hundred and seventy kilometres apart. Your town is slightly more north of the other place, to the west. But, Ria, you know what?"

"What? said Ria looking around her anxiously. They needed to start moving.

"Both cities are near the northern route," Naira said.

"What route, Naira? We have to move." Ria said in exasperation, stressed now.

"Our route Ria. It's one of the migrant routes we can use to get home. It is not the one used most, especially in winter, because of the cold, and the snow. It is not the way I came but I know of it. Your mystery man must also know the same routes. That is good!" Naira smiled.

Ria stared at her. "Good? How will we do all these distances, deliver packages and get to the other place the day after we have to deliver the last package! And all

366

without getting seen or caught! I fear truly for Fatima! It is impossible!"

"Ria, you are such a worrier, all the time the glass is empty. We can do it. Don't worry, there are more of us out here than you think!"
Ria nodded.

"Naira, what did Fatima mean when she asked you if you had told me? What she said back there just now?" Ria asked gently.

"I promise I will tell you Ria, but now is not the right time or place, and we have to get moving. Okay? Let's get out of this town first. Then we can plan the journey so we can make it to the other city in time, it's very manageable in a day. It will be tight, but we are lucky it is at five in the afternoon. The last package must be delivered the day before, so we have almost a full day to get there. It is possible. Difficult, but possible. The good thing is that we have a long time to get out of here before they realise you have gone." Naira said. "We can get a good head start."

Ria nodded, gathered up the two bags and stood up. They kept close to the buildings and quickly left the detention centre behind them.

42

As they walked Ria finally had time to think. How had she managed to get into this situation? After her initial excitement, now out here in the dark, silent streets, reality hit her. What they were doing felt so desperate and impossible. How had she thought that anything good could come of this escape, as she was calling it in her head? The added complications of having to deliver packages and the possible consequences for Fatima if they failed weighed heavily on her. Surely the women wouldn't harm Fatima. Still, Ria could not risk messing up the package deliveries even if it did seem a bit drastic what the tall woman had said about Fatima. Once out of the centre anything could happen, they could get caught or not manage to get there in time. A thousand things could go wrong that had nothing to do with their commitment to fulfil their side of the bargain and Ria was certain the tall woman knew that. Still, she would do as the woman had asked.

As for the two of them managing to get away from this country and get back home safely, Ria had serious doubts about that. Home seemed so far away. But if she didn't expect to make it back, what *did* she think was going to happen to them? She turned her thoughts to Khal. Her heart bled for Naira and her baby, and for everyone in the centre who was in one way or another damaged. Ria could understand Naira not wanting her son to be brought up in a place like the detention centre, but still, it seemed strange to give him up so easily, barely shedding a tear.

There was something she didn't know, and she felt sure that the exchange between Fatima and Naira had to do with what she didn't know. Fatima knew something about Naira that Ria didn't. It didn't bother her, they rarely talked about their pasts in the centre. She had learned that unwritten rule fast and welcomed it.

And what about Shabana and Omar? What would they think of her just disappearing like this without a word or even a call after all they had done for her? She hoped they would understand that she could not contact them. Given her situation, she was sure they would be relieved to not hear from her again. She had seen the look of fear in their eyes when she had told them about the terrorism charge. She had seen their worried expressions as they witnessed her strange reaction to the photo and heard all the things she had told them about Malik. Still, even though she was sad that she would never see them again, what hurt her more was knowing that on some level they believed the accusation against her. That they would surely take her sudden escape from the centre as an admission of her guilt stung. She could not stand anyone believing she was in any way connected to terrorism. She hoped they wouldn't get into trouble because of their relationship with her. They did not deserve that.

Ria had another problem. She had no passport. Naira had hers but Ria had been brought here without any documents. She had asked how they had known her name, but her case worker Sasha had just shrugged and said that the authorities must have withheld her passport or got hold of it somehow. She probably didn't need a passport

anymore. For what? Ria smirked as she remembered her young naïve self who had thought that getting her passport at eighteen had held the promise of freedom and travel. She had learned since she had been in the centre that passports from certain places were a curse, a liability, even a weapon that could be used against you. She had come to understand that a passport was not a key to freedom, but something used to control people and their movements. She had not realised any of that before. She had not realised how deep prejudice ran in people, herself included, until she had left her own country.
Naira who was walking just ahead of her had stopped.

"Where are we going Naira?" Ria asked frowning.
Naira had been leading the way but to where? What was the plan?

"There is a contact here from the network. It is very late, and he is probably sleeping, but I'm going to try to call him. He could help us get out of this town and on our way to where we need to deliver the packages." Naira said.

"You don't sound very convinced. Do you trust him?" Ria asked.

"Trust? I don't trust anyone any more Ria." Naira said. "But if not what? How will we get there? It's not like we can just catch a train. You have no ID, no papers, and anyway, that's the first place they will check."

"Why do you need ID to catch a train?" Ria asked in surprise.

"I don't know to be honest. I've never caught one, but it would be too obvious for us to do that and anyway there won't be any trains until the morning and by that time, they'll know you're gone," Naira said. "The safest way always is in trucks."

"You mean know *we're* gone." Ria corrected.

Naira glanced at her. "They won't care about me, Ria."

"This contact is used to moving people around a lot, that is what he does. He is not a particularly good person, but what he does, he does it well. He is our best chance." Naira said.

"Will he not want something in return?" Ria asked worried.

"I don't know. I hope not. We have nothing to give." Naira said. "What do you think?"

"Is he dangerous?" Ria asked.

"Define dangerous?" Naira replied. "Let me text him, see if he is awake. I don't want to annoy him."
Before she could discuss it further, Naira had already typed and sent the message. Almost straight away a reply pinged back. Naira looked at Ria.

"He must not sleep much," Naira said, texted back and waited.
After a few minutes of texting, Naira turned to Ria looking relieved. "

He said he will meet us in half an hour and no problem. He said he can get us all the way. Let me check how far away the place he said to meet is." Naira checked on her phone again. "Okay come on, we have to hurry, it's about twenty minutes from here. It's near a small park."

"A park?" Ria said frowning.

She didn't want to meet a dangerous man in a park at this time of the night.

"It will be fine Ria. We don't have any choice. He's our best option. Our only option. Come on!" Naira said already moving off. It was already decided.

Ria picked up her bag and followed Naira, who was walking more quickly now, as best she could, her heart heavy and that familiar trembling sensation coursing through her veins.

After a while, they came to the top of some steps. Ria stopped to catch her breath as they looked around. There was something familiar about where she was.

"This is the place," Naira said looking around, not looking as sure of herself as twenty minutes ago.

There was no sign of anyone. They walked over to a wall with a wooded area just beyond it. Ria and Naira leaned against it, waiting, and watching from under the hoods of their coats. What if he had gotten there first? Where were they? She couldn't shake the feeling that she knew this place. They could not risk waiting like this for long, out in the open. Two young foreign women standing like this would be spotted straight away by any police patrolling. Then it hit her, the steps, the park. This is where she had run from Malik! This could not be a coincidence.

"Naira!" Ria whispered.

Naira turned to look at her but just as Ria was about to tell her, she saw a dark, hooded figure approach. It was not Malik, that much she could see. Had she really expected Naira's contact to be Malik! This person was smaller. She felt Naira tense beside her. The figure looked menacing as he approached them. Then he pulled down his hood and smiled broadly at Naira.

"Long time!" he said.

"Yes. Thanks for coming. How have you been?" Naira responded.

"Good. Busy. Who is this? You didn't mention her in your text." The man eyed Ria suspiciously.

"Don't worry, she's one of us," Naira said.

One of us? What the hell did that mean Ria wondered. She studied the man. He was about the same age as Jamil, but he looked very tired. He had the same regional accent as Naira.

"So, you're not staying in the end?" He asked, attention back to Naira again.

"No." She responded. "I'm going back but there are things we have to do first," Naira said.

"Things are bad at home. You know that, yes? Where's the baby?" he asked.

Ria looked at him in surprise.

"With someone who will take better care of him" she said.

The man nodded.

"I know things are bad. That's why I have to go back." Naira said

"We can't pay. We have no money." Naira said.

He looked at her. "No problem, we don't charge fighters going back. You are badly needed. So many are leaving."

Naira looked at him with pride. He smiled.

373

"Let's go then." He said.

Naira immediately went to go with him, but Ria hesitated. Naira looked back at her, gesturing. Ria understood, no choice. She followed them across the dark park. It began to rain heavily. They all pulled their hoods down harder over their face as the night turned even darker. She could feel her nervousness growing. She had entered a different world now.

43

Ria trailed a little behind them. She could hear them chatting amicably but couldn't make out what they were saying. The words were lost to the wind. She had trouble keeping up. Had Naira forgotten she was injured? They were walking much too fast for her. Not once did Naira turn around to check on her. She could have disappeared, and they would be none the wiser. Damn Naira for ignoring her for this man! How did she know him anyway?

As Ria half trotted, half walked, her ribs aching, her mind sifted through what she knew about Naira. It did not take long. She knew her name, knew a little about her baby and the two attempted suicides. She knew what Naira had told her about her family after the beating. She didn't know much she concluded, but it was more important what she did know. She knew Naira was a kind person. At least she had been kind to Ria, kind to Fatima, and she had seen her be kind to many others in the detention centre.

But she knew nothing else. She knew only what Naira had told her about her family and where she was from. How was that possible? Was Ria forever talking about herself and her problems and never asking about others? No, it was not that. It had more to do with that same unspoken code amongst the women in the centre. Never ask people questions about their past. Everyone had a past they did not want to be reminded of, so she had quickly learned to ask no questions and to answer none either. But with Naira, it was different, they had spent more time together so now she was surprised to realise how little she knew about her. Naira had not been well for a long time and had been away from the centre a lot and so had Ria, but Ria had always considered Naira her friend, more so since the beating.

It was different for them. Apart from sharing a room, they were also the same age more or less and from the same country, so they spoke the same language. They also shared similar views about their country and the war, though Naira knew so much more than Ria. Yet, despite all that, Ria knew nothing about her life. Naira knew more about Ria's. Naira had told Fatima things that she had not told Ria. It was true that Naira and Fatima had been sharing a room for much longer than Ria, and Fatima had helped her so much with the baby but still, surely Ria should know more about who she was embarking on this escape with! But as soon as that thought crossed her mind Ria saw the irony of her silly concern. She was the suspected terrorist, not Naira! What the hell was wrong with her, would she ever grow up?

They turned a corner and went up a long flight of concrete steps. Naira and the man took each step effortlessly, they were fit, but she fell even further behind. She was tired by now, and her ribs were hurting so much she had to take it slower. When they got to the top, Naira finally turned around to check on her. Ria saw her nudge the man's arm with her elbow and say something, they now waited for her. As she walked up the steps feeling embarrassed as she walked up them like an old woman, she had time to look at him. He had a longish, dark beard which stood out against his very pale skin. As she neared the top, Naira smiled at her encouragingly and asked if she was okay, Ria nodded and they turned again and walked away at a slightly slower pace now, but still too quick for Ria. Damn them!

After a while, the man stopped and looked around. He waited for Ria to catch up and then quickly opened a door into what looked more like a garage entrance than a house. They went inside. The place inside was dimly lit and as Ria's eyes adjusted, she saw it was sparsely furnished. There was a long line of thin mattresses laid out on an unfinished concrete floor. It was very cold and smelled damp and stale. Ria noticed the smell of stale urine and scrunched up her nose.

"Wait here." The man said. "Rest for a while, you will leave in an hour. I'll be back then, and you'll leave. You can make tea over there" he said pointing to an electric kettle propped up on a makeshift counter and sink. "I'm sorry it's not warmer." He said to Naira who shook her head and thanked him.

After the man left, they just stood there. Ria had so many questions but did not know where to start.

"Well, at least we will be safe here," Naira said. "We were lucky about the money. That could have been a problem. He has agreed to get us to the city where we have to deliver the packages, but he has no way to get us back up to the other place in time for your meeting. But after we have finished there, he will get us home. That is fantastic news, and he won't charge for that either. So, the only part we have to do on our own is get from the package city to the city where you are meeting that man. But still, that is great news, isn't it Ria? See I told Fatima we had a web too! We will get there in time to deliver the packages and he has given us a place like this where we can stay hidden. He said it's better than this. I'll have to deliver the packages Ria, you know that. You can't. They won't be looking for me, not there anyway."

"It is fantastic news Naira, thank you so much. But Naira, who is this man and how do you know him?" Ria asked.

"Does it matter Ria? It's a type of network, that is all you need to know." Naira answered, suddenly defensive. "In just an hour we'll already be on our way to where we have to go, and with a place to stay, and a way home. That should be all that concerns you. You should be grateful."

"I am. Very" Ria said and smiled. "It's just that it almost seems too easy, that's all."

"You worry too much. In this life, worrying is of no use." Naira said, smiling now. "Come now, let's get some tea and warm up. It's colder in here than outside!"

Ria sighed and walked over to the counter to fill the kettle. She leaned back against the sink and closed her eyes for a second. There was no way she was lying down on one of those smelly mattresses. She looked around, there were a couple of folding chairs lying against the back wall.

"Naira, chairs." Ria pointed and grimaced at the pain in her ribs. Naira nodded and walked off energetically. She brought the chairs up and unfolded

379

them, swatting the dust away with her hands. There was no table.

Ria poured two mugs of tea and they sat down. Time to get to know Naira better. There was nothing else to do or say for the hour they had to wait.

"Naira, about what Fatima said. Can I ask?" Ria said after a few minutes of silence.

Naira looked up at her.

"Now? Seriously! Now you want to hear about that?" Naira said in surprised.

"I do," Ria said. "Unless you don't want to talk about it."

"I don't. But I will tell you. That way, you will understand better what I have done with Khal and why I am going back. We don't know each other that well really, do we?" Naira said.

Ria laughed. "I was just thinking the same."

"A story for a story Ria, deal?" Naira said.

"Deal!" Ria replied wondering what story she could tell Naira that she didn't already know.

Naira took another sip of her tea. She swallowed it with difficulty. Ria thought she didn't seem to know how to start.

"I was raped Ria. Khal is a child of rape. I was raped in prison many times, by so many different men that I do not even know who his father is. After a few months, I realised I was pregnant. It happened to most of us there at some point. Some of the women tried to help me to lose the child, you know with whatever was at hand in there, not much as you can imagine. There was a prison doctor, but he was only used for fixing people for the torturers to continue. He wasn't there for our health, so we had to make do. But something went wrong, and well, I almost died, it was an infection or something, but unfortunately, I didn't manage to lose the baby. Anyway, they found out that I was pregnant and that I had tried to abort so they put me in solitary isolation for the remaining months until Khal was born. The only person I saw all those months was a male doctor who came and checked on the baby from time to time. I don't know why they were so interested in the baby's health. Maybe some patriotic stupidity, you know what they are like." Naira paused.

Ria was shocked and tried to touch Naira's hand, but Naira moved her hand away.

"I'm so sorry Naira. How many months were you locked up alone?" Ria asked

"Six," Naira said.

Ria felt her sadness, but also noticed she was becoming anxious.

"During all those months, they brought me barely enough food for a growing baby inside. I had no human contact apart from those doctor visits, which were few, and very short. He would do some checking and then ask questions about the baby. That was all he came for. I saw no-one else. I lost myself in there Ria. I really did. The only measure of time passing that I had was the growth of my belly with a child inside it who I already hated. When the time came, they took the baby out of my belly with a knife. They used no anaesthetic and stitched me back up. Look." Naira opened her coat and lifted up her clothes, there was a large, red jagged, scar right across her belly and several smaller ones.

Ria gasped but didn't know what to say.

To her surprise, Naira laughed.

"Terrible, isn't it? I could have sown it up better myself. I passed out with the pain. After that, they put me back with the other women, but now, I had this baby I hated. It was the other women who named him Khal, not me. He was a distraction for some of them from their own pain. But I had no interest in him. I had gone inside my head in solitary, and I had not come back out. I had no milk, and I was very sick, the cuts they had made getting him out became badly infected. But the women helped me. You know in that prison there were doctors, nurses, and every kind of profession you can imagine. I am alive today because of them and Khal is alive because of them. No thanks to me. I could not have cared less if he had died, or if I had died. They saved our lives, and I wished they hadn't. All I wanted was for us both to die in there." Naira said and stared straight into Ria's sad eyes.

"But that was not to be. With all of the women caring for me, slowly I got better physically, and mentally too though my mind was still not right, I was not like before. I could not bear to look at Khal. Can you imagine Ria? He was a constant reminder of what they had done to me. Countless rapes and beatings. I could never love Khal even though I know none of it is his fault. When I see him, he reminds me of what happened, he reminds me of how he came to be, so abandoning him is the best thing I can do for both of us. He will never know that he is a child of rape, a child created from violence, and he won't grow up with a mother who hates him. He will grow up only knowing love, as he deserves. Fatima and the women will make sure of that." Naira paused.

Ria could not speak. An enormous lump had formed in her throat and her mouth had gone dry. Her heart was pounding in her chest. Rape. She felt very distressed at Naira's story.

Naira continued. "Two months after that, they let me go. I don't know why they did that. Just one day, they came, and I was thrown back onto the streets with Khal. Ashamed, I decided to leave the country as soon as I could get the money. Some other fighters I knew lent me some money, enough to come here. But I never went home. My family does not even know that I am alive. So, I got myself and Khal over here so that I could leave him here to a better life and then go back. I never intended to stay for long but once I got here, I realised that things were not going to be easy or fast. I didn't know that until I arrived. When they put me in that detention centre, it felt like I was back in that prison, and I couldn't take it. If I had known that was what happened here, I would not have come. I got stuck in a tiny room again with the child. It was not his fault the poor thing, but I could not stand it. Every day in that tiny room with him was hell for me. Things are never black and white. Not love, not hate, not anything. I just had to get away from him and out of that place. I couldn't bear to be imprisoned again, so that is why I did what I did. Twice." Naira said raising one of her wrists, now with just small, taped dressings.

She took her mug of tea, wrapped her fingers tightly around it for the warmth and looked at Ria looking so pale, and so very sad.

"I don't know what to say Naira. That is such a horrible thing to happen to you. I am so sorry. You have suffered so much, and here am I complaining about my situation. I have been so selfish all these months!" Ria said quietly.

But Ria did not feel quiet at all. It was as if a switch had been flipped inside her. Why was her heart pounding like that? She felt a wave of nausea. She could not let Naira see her like this, she could not let her down and make this moment about her!

Naira smiled sadly, "Sometimes Ria, there is nothing to say. This same thing has happened to so many of us, even to our mothers! But it is never spoken about Ria. Not ever. Everyone knows what happens in those places, but you cannot truly understand what it is really like until you are in there and it is happening to you. No-one says anything about what they go through even in there. Outside, as you know there are always rumours, but unless you've been in there, you always wonder if all those rumours are true or not. Then you see that the rumours are not as bad as what it is really like in those places. After being in a place like that, if you are ever released, and it is unusual to be released, you can try to get on with your life as it was before, you can pretend to *be* like you were before, but you know that nobody trusts you anymore, so you can't even fight with your group anymore. The only other option is to give up. We are all trying to do one or all of those things Ria and sometimes all at the same time."

As Naira was telling her about the rapes, Ria was shocked that she had visualised the rapes in a disturbingly vivid manner, but the face in those images she saw was not Naira's. Her body too had reacted strangely. Ria felt detached from the room they were sitting in, even from Naira herself, and could no longer feel the compassion she so desperately wanted to give her friend. Her mind seemed to be away somewhere else, searching for something.

"Your turn, Ria" Naira said. "Ria? We had a deal." Naira said it again a little louder. "Ria, are you okay? "

"Sorry, Naira, I was just, you know, thinking about what you just told me. You are very brave to have done what you did. To bring Khal here by yourself so that he could have a good life, that is so brave... and generous, Naira."

Ria got up slowly from her chair and bent to hug Naira. Naira met Ria's hug stiff as a board.

"Let me make us some more tea. I wonder if there is a toilet here!" Naira said, changing the subject.

"From the smell of those mattresses, I would say that the answer is no." Ria joked to break the awkwardness of her attempted hug, and her own strange reaction to Naira's story and went to put the kettle on again.

Why could she not feel compassion for what Naira had been through? What was wrong with her?

Naira sat there quietly as Ria made more tea. She must be remembering terrible things Ria thought. She shouldn't have asked Naira to tell her. Maybe Ria was lucky to not remember anything. She felt ashamed of all her complaining about her memory loss. Some people would give anything for that luxury. Ria looked at Naira. That irony again, all Ria wanted to do was to remember, and all Naira wanted to do was forget. But Ria was no longer so sure she wanted to remember. Not after the images she had seen in her mind since meeting Malik, not after the way her body had just reacted to Naira's story and certainly not after the photo Malik had sent. The photo of the face that haunted every second of her days and nights.

"What is this place, Naira? Who are those mattresses for?" Ria asked.

"Ria, you must learn that it is not always a good thing to ask questions. Is it not enough that you are out of that centre and *not* on your way to a prison?" Naira said without looking at her.

Ria heeded the warning and kept quiet.

"Let us enjoy our first taste of freedom, Ria," said Naira smiling as she raised her mug of tea as if at a wedding toast.

Ria reluctantly raised hers not feeling at all free and sipped the tea. It felt warming to her freezing body, but it did not taste of freedom.

Ria felt Naira studying her and looked up to meet her stare.

"Look Ria, I know you have a lot of questions. About me. About the women. About Fatima. And of course, especially about what happened to you before they brought you here and why they have accused you the way they have. It's a lot to not know, I understand. But, believe me, Ria, now is not the time to look for answers. The more you know about me, about those women, and about this man that is helping us now, the more dangerous it becomes for all of them. Do you understand?"

Ria nodded. She did finally understand.

"We must continue to do as we did at the centre. We ask no questions of each other, and we give no information. But now, we have escaped, and we are not just two refugees who slipped out of a detention centre. No, you are more than that to them and they will want you back. So, it is even more important what I say. No one we meet must know who you are. They must not hear your name and you must not ask theirs. Give no information about yourself, not even where you are from, and ask no one anything. In this world we are in now, it is as if we were back home where having information about others is a burden. You must learn not to tell your story, even when you finally find out what it is. This is about survival for you, and for me, and for all of the others Ria. Okay?"

Ria nodded. "Okay. I understand. Please forgive me for asking about you. But it helps to know. "

Naira stared at her. "Does it?"

Ria felt her face redden. She looked away. Change the subject.

"So, what happens in an hour?" Ria asked.

Naira smiled. "Again, with the questions Ria! We will get in the back of a truck that will take us there. Then, we will stay in a place like this just on the outside part of the city where we have to deliver the packages. That is it. That is all we need to think about for the time being. One thing at a time."

"Why did you not leave before if you had all these contacts Naira?" Ria asked. Her look was determined.

"That is my last question, I swear.!" Ria smiled.
Naira laughed but then her expression shifted to one of sadness.

"It's not so easy to explain. I think like I said before, we can love and hate in equal measure. I am talking about Khal now. I barely looked after him and that made me feel ashamed, guilty. He was just a baby. I could not see myself reflected anywhere in him, so I let Fatima care for him. That was bad of me, but she needed to do that for other reasons I can't explain. It is not my story. I had tried as you know to take my life before you arrived at the centre because putting him up for adoption was impossible while I had no status granted." Naira hesitated before continuing.

"You know the second time I cut my wrists, Fatima spoke to me about giving Khal up to a better home in a different way, a way that they would arrange. You know what I mean. So, we started that. I could have left him with Fatima, but I could not leave alone, I was not strong enough, in my mind. Then, after you left the centre that night and got beaten so badly and then all this terrorist thing happened, well, I felt I could leave with you. As I told you that night on your bed. Seeing you like that helped me remember who I was, and I changed. I would have waited to go with you later on because even though Khal had already been taken, as Fatima said, the matter was still not over. There were more parts to complete, but Fatima and the others will do that. So, when you decided to run for it, I couldn't just stay there. I badly needed to put distance between myself and Khal. I need to go home and show my face once again, show my family I am alive and help my people. So, your situation I suppose just accelerated things" Naira said looking at Ria. "So, thanks!" She joked again.

"You're welcome!" Ria said sarcastically and took another sip of tea.

She kept quiet now, thinking and trying to take it all in. It was a lot. She leaned back wearily against the hard wooden frame of the chair and stopped trying, taking small comfort in the fact that she would not be going to prison. Not yet at least.

44

They sat there drinking tea. The time passed slowly.

Naira eventually spoke and said. "Ria, we had a deal, a story for a story. Why do you want to risk spending more time than necessary in this country by going to see this man. Do you not think it is better to leave it be? We need to get out of here as fast as possible. They will be looking for you, the longer we spend here, the higher the risk. Once we cross the border, we will be in another country where no one will be looking for you. This journey is long and dangerous enough at the best of times but if they are looking for you, and rest assured they will be, it's a long time to stay here when we could just leave straight away after delivering the packages. You don't even know if this man will turn up. Why don't you reconsider going there? That way we will have a better chance of leaving sooner and less risk." Naira said.

Ria sighed, Naira was right, and it was tempting to just leave.

"Believe me Naira, I have gone over and over the same thing myself. I know it's selfish of me to want to go and meet this man. I know it's a risk. But I can't get that photo out of my head. I just have a very strong feeling that the face in it is an important part of my past. But it's not just that." Ria paused, heartbeat reacting as she spoke about the photo out loud.

"It's not just that I recognise the woman in the photo from my nightmares. It's not even the fact that

Malik knows that I know her and has a photo of her which is strange in itself. You and I agreed to exchange one story. You have told me yours and I am grateful, but I do not remember mine. The only thing I can tell you is that when I have nightmares - well they are more like waking dreams, that woman is in all of them. So, when I saw the photo... well you can imagine, I reacted very badly."
Ria could see that Naira was interested now.

Ria continued. "I don't know why that woman appears in my head all the time, but her face terrifies me so much that I start sweating and as you saw when I was on the medication, if I sleep, I scream. When Malik sent me that photo, I knew she was real because I had already seen her in my head. His message confirmed that there was a connection. She is a memory. His message said. *'I have found her. Do you remember now?'*. I just can't put those words out of my mind so I can't leave without knowing what he means by that, or finding out who she is to me." Ria looked at Naira willing her to understand.

"After your beating, that day in the park, you said that the reason you had gone out that night was a story for another day. Why did you go out? Was it to meet this man? What happened when you met him?" Naira asked.
"He told me a lot about my brother, things I didn't know, and he said that my mother, my sister, and I had been taken prisoner and kept in a military base that had been blown up with us in it. He told me that he and my brother had witnessed the air strike. They saw the planes bomb the place. He knew my name and asked me how it was possible that I had survived that bombing. He was

suspicious. I told him about my memory, but I didn't think he believed me, so I got scared and I ran. Then...well, you know the rest. Then almost two weeks later he sent the photo of the woman with the message and meeting details" Ria said.

"And you believe him?" Naira asked gently.

"I don't know. I think a part of me does because the things he said sounded true. And he talked about people that I know, apart from my brother. But at the same time, it all seems so disconnected from me, from my life. I have no memory of being in a prison, let alone one that was blown up! But then, when he sent the photo and I saw the woman, I believed his story more." Ria said, voice shaking a bit. "I believe it."

Naira looked thoughtful. "I understand why you would want to meet him. I probably would too." She said.

Ria nodded "If any of what he told me that night is true, and I think it is, I have to know the rest. I can't shake the feeling that this woman from the photo, the one in my nightmares, is the key to everything. I know that this woman is not a good person. I need him to tell me who she is, and how we are connected. There is a reason he has come here and there is a reason he sent me this photo. I do not believe it is a coincidence. I could be wrong, but I believe it is my brother who has sent him here. He says they fought together and that they were close, and I believe him. Him coming here must have something to do with this woman."

Naira just sat there, frowning, taking it all in.

"So, Naira, I have to go, but you don't have to come with me. I know it makes it more dangerous for you, and it is not your problem. I just can't leave it alone even though I agree it means more risk of getting caught. Whatever this is about, I know in my heart that it is something bad. I think it has to do with what happened to me and my family and I can't shake the feeling that meeting him will not end well. Malik feels dangerous to me. I have no experience of life. My life at home was not like yours. My life was small, sheltered, and protected. But something about him tells me he is not only a man who has fought but a man who is still fighting. He is no refugee or asylum seeker. Whatever this is about, it concerns my family, I just know it." Ria said.

Ria had spoken more words than she was accustomed to, so she stopped suddenly as she heard the intensity of her emotions. She looked down at the floor. Hearing her say those words out loud had affected her deeply.

"Ria" Naira said softly. "I will come with you to see this man. I would never let you go there alone. I understand, I would go too if it were me. Remember once I told you about some of the women in the prisons back home who could not remember things fully, only in dreams, and then only fragments, after terrible things had been done to them. It made them crazy. I know I said that you are lucky not to remember, to be able to forget terrible things. I said that because I remember every single detail of what they did to me, and to others in that prison." Naira paused. "But I should not have said that. There is a pain in only remembering fragments or in nightmares. It is terrible to see things but not be able to connect with the image long enough to figure out what they mean. Many women could not remember enough to explain in words, but they would remember in other ways - in their reactions, in their bodies. I saw it and it was like that for me as well, and I see the same types of reactions in you. I see your body reacting even if your mind cannot recall why."

Ria felt afraid now.

Naira continued "Most of the women in the centre have suffered terrible things, things that remain unspoken about. There are things that are done to people that are unspeakable. If you took all of the suffering from each woman and child in all of the centres, camps and prisons in the world and put it all in one place I believe that is what hell would be like."

Ria felt her eyes fill with tears as what Naira was saying resonated somewhere deep inside her.

"I have no desire to do anything else in my short life than exact some form of retribution from those twisted people who work in the prisons like I was in. It is the only thing that keeps me going. Those prisons are filled with so many men and women who have done nothing wrong. Nothing. I will never hurt anyone who is innocent, but I will fight those who do these things to us until the day I die. There is no other path possible for me now. I cannot forget what they did to me, to others. Maybe you don't understand this yet, but you will, of that, I am sure. This man, Malik, will be the one who fills the gaps in your memory, and it will be painful Ria. It will be very painful for you to remember. I am sure of it. If this man has been sent all this way by your brother to find you, your brother, like me, may be seeking some form of retribution and that might involve you somehow. You should prepare yourself for that possibility and prepare yourself for what he will tell you."

Ria nodded. Naira was so much wiser than she was despite being the same age, but Ria was coming to realise that age and wisdom had little connection.

"If this man is a friend of your brother's, as he says he is, and a fighter, then my fight is the same as his, do you see that? Our purpose is the same. So, I'm coming with you, not just for you. I am coming to fight by your side because I know that is what you are going to do." Naira said, stopped and drained the rest of her tea.

Ria was stunned by Naira's words, but she said nothing, taking in the implications of it all, weighing it all up in her head. Fight? Her? No, she would not.

"Thank you, Naira. I mean it. Do you think we will get there in time?" Ria asked.

"We will make we will!" Naira said and smiled.

Ria smiled too, relieved she would not be going alone to meet the man she feared so much, to find out about this woman who terrified her. She was relieved to have an ally and felt better than she had felt in a long time.

45

Ria felt the heavy truck start to move and gradually gather up speed. She looked over at Naira, seated with her back against a huge wooden crate on some dirty blankets that had been left there for them. It was freezing cold, and the truck had taken a long time to get going. They had not seen the driver and now he was sitting blocked off from them in his truck cabin. It had been well before daylight when the man had come back and put them on the trailer. It would be dawn in a few hours, but they would not see it. The journey wasn't that far really the man had told Naira but the truck had a few stops to make along the way so they wouldn't get there late in the afternoon when it would be dark. It was better that way. It got dark so early here in winter.

"Let's try to get some sleep Ria. We're going to need it. Even if these blankets stink, it's better than the floor!" Naira said.

"Yes, good idea." Ria said.

She welcomed the idea of being alone with her thoughts, she could rest her body, she felt exhausted even though she knew she would not sleep. It was almost completely pitch black in the trailer, but they had a small torch the man had given them which cast enough light to see each other. She closed her eyes and then felt someone shaking her awake.

"Ria, wake up. We're here. You were snoring!" Naira was saying.

Ria was drowsy and felt a little bruised, her neck was painfully stiff. She turned up her nose at the dank odour of the blankets on her clothes.

"I slept?" She said to Naira. "I can't believe it!"

"Slept? I had to check you weren't dead a few times!" Naira said.

"Did you sleep?" Ria asked as she sat up, slapping her hand gently on her cheeks to get rid of the drowsy feeling. She couldn't believe she had slept.

"A bit. I'm fine. Now, get ready, the driver has been stopped for quite a while and it's around the time we should be arriving, so I am sure he'll open up the trailer soon. We need to be ready." Naira said.

Sure enough they heard the heavy trailer bolt slide back and the door opened just enough for a man to push his head through.

"You go, now. I stopped in front of the place so no-one can see you go in. Come. Be quick, I must go." He said, looking around to check.

Naira went first and Ria followed. It was quite a jump down, so Naira and the man helped her down. She hated being so weak and wished her injuries would heal faster. She was a burden for Naira, slowing everything down.

Once on the ground, the man gestured to a door that was slightly ajar. Ria followed Naira in. It was a large industrial-looking building. Ria closed the door to the building and looked around. The place was dimly lit inside and there was no-one to be seen. There was only one door, so Naira went up to it. She looked back at Ria and opened it, and they walked in. It was certainly better than the last place. There were mattresses stacked up against the wall, but the room was nice and dry, it didn't stink, and it was much warmer. There was a small cooker, electric kettle, and a pile of blankets that looked in better condition than the ones in the trailer.

"It's okay isn't it, Ria? Just a few days and we'll be gone." Naira said. "He gave me the key to the main door."

"Yes, but why is this man doing all of this for us?" Ria asked.

"I told you Ria, he is one of us, this is what he does. Remember, no questions. We all help each other. Fatima thinks they are the only ones with a network. She's wrong. Ours is large too." Naira said.

Ria nodded and sat down on one of the chairs at a small round plastic table.

"Are you hungry?" Naira asked.

Ria had not thought about food in a very long time. The last time she had eaten must have been at Shabana's. It hurt her to think of that day. She felt no pangs of hunger but knew she had to eat.

"I could eat something light. You?" Ria asked.

"I could eat a flock of sheep!" Naira said. "Let's check where we are. We don't want to get anything near here and be noticed. I'll have to go to a busy place, further away like a supermarket." Naira studied her phone and grimaced. "We are far from the town centre. Very far. And the shopping centres are on the other side of the city.

Ria got up and walked around. She opened cupboards and drawers under the sink and found two plastic shopping bags there.

"Look! There is food here." Ria said, glad to be of some use.

"Great!" Naira said, rummaging through the bag, they probably don't want us going out and risking this place. Makes sense. Noodles?"

"Noodles sound great." Ria said and put on a pot of boiling water and Ria took off her coat.

As Naira occupied herself with the noodles, Ria picked up the bag with the packages they had to deliver. She took out the packages and laid them on the table. She could study them better now in the light of the room. The first package was for tomorrow. She wondered what was in them.

"Don't" Naira said looking at her. "Forget what might be in them. We have one job and that is it."

"How will they know if we have delivered them or not?" Ria said, worried still about Fatima.

"They'll know Ria, don't worry about that. Put them away. After we eat, I'll turn location on again briefly to check where the first package must go, then I will deliver it after midnight."

"I think it is better you do it during the day, you know, really early in the morning when there are people around. A young woman like you out at midnight on her own in the middle of nowhere? No, Naira, that is not a good idea. Remember what happened to me!" Ria frowned, concerned at Naira's thinking.

Naira said nothing at first then she said. "Yes, you are right, I was thinking more about the police, but it is better for me to merge with others, not stand out. By now, they will have come to take you and found you missing. When I am out, I will check the papers for your face, but I don't think they will go that far. If you were such a big deal terrorist, you wouldn't have been kept in the centre."

They were going to have a lot of time to kill, especially Ria, who could not go out, and could have no phone to keep her occupied. Nothing but her own mind. She could think of nothing worse.

The noodles came and went and were surprisingly good. Ria found herself with an appetite after all. She got up to wash the plates. Naira let her.

"I've got a surprise for you Ria." Ria turned around and laughed.

Naira was waving a pack of cards. "You always need to bring a pack of cards whenever you escape from somewhere!" Naira joked.

"I wish I had brought a book as well, but thankfully you brought those!" Ria said. "Naira, I know you have to take all the risk with the packages, and I'm sorry about that."

"Don't be sorry, it's much worse having to stay in here on your own bored to death." Naira laughed.

"That is true, there are a limited amount of hours I can amuse myself with your cards!" Ria laughed back. "So, what are we playing?"

"We are playing Naira beats Ria at every single card game known!" Naira said.

It wasn't too long before Naira felt too sleepy to play anymore. She had probably not slept at all in the trailer, so they set up two of the mattresses, and laid down under blankets. She heard Naira's deep breathing before long. Ria had already slept so didn't feel tired enough to quell the activity in her mind. She lay on her back, eyes wide open until Naira woke up a couple of hours before dawn.

Ria made her some tea and a sandwich, and they ate their breakfast in nervous silence. Naira was nervous, Ria could tell, her jaw looked tense. She hurried her breakfast. She wanted to get going.

"How are we going to communicate if anything goes wrong?" Ria asked, feeling nervous herself.

"Nothing will go wrong Ria. I will get to the place, deliver the package, and come back. According to the phone map, the whole thing should take no more than two or three hours. Okay? But if I am not back in two hours, don't worry, you know how things are with phone distances and stuff, then I might get lost. Nothing will go wrong. No-one is looking for me. They are looking for you, or at worst, two girls. I will not speak to anyone. I'll go straight there and straight back, and I'll take extra care coming back this way. Don't worry. Okay? It's better you don't have a phone. I have mine off all of the time, only on to see the map steps which I will now memorise, then I'll turn it off." Naira said.

"I had two special phones that Omar got me, but I left them there. I was too afraid to bring them, but I should have." Ria said.

"Better that way." Naira said.

"Yes, but I still think we need to be able to communicate these days, just in case something does go wrong. I wouldn't know what to do if you didn't come back. Why don't you get a couple of those phones I had when you are downtown. They sell them, you know in those internet and phone places."

"We don't have much money, but I agree it would be better. Perhaps they will take a trade of this phone. It would be better not to keep it, but I have contacts on it that I need and who know my number. I will try, but not today. Okay?" Naira said. "Now let me memorise these steps. I want to leave before it gets light."

It was not long before Naira left, and Ria felt alone and afraid, nervous in this place all by herself. The next few hours would feel like an age. How the hell would she get through them? She was terrified something would happen and Naira wouldn't come back and that she would never know what had happened. Or that someone would come in and find her there.

She decided to wash herself. She was filthy and disgusting, so she boiled the kettle and washed herself at the sink with washing up liquid and a cloth. That took up all of fifteen minutes, but she felt much better now that she was cleaner. She wished she had brought more clothes. She pulled out a change of underwear from her bag and a fresh t-shirt. She hadn't brought any spare jeans, too bulky for her bag. She sniffed her jeans. They still stank of those foul blankets from the trailer. She decided to wash them, they would be dry before they would leave to meet Malik. With her dripping jeans hanging off one of the chairs, she sat down at the table with a blanket over her legs, laid out the cards in solitaire formation and sighed long and hard.

46

Ria discovered that was a limit to how long you can play solitaire when you're panicking so she decided after a while that moving would be better. She would try to get fitter. She started to do some stretching and light exercising. The least she could do for Naira, and for herself, was to get fitter and stronger. Enthused by her idea of how to kill time she pushed herself even though the slightest stretch would hurt like hell. She dug deep and exercised for an hour or so, feeling satisfied. She would do some more later. She would be much fitter by the time they left here and less of a burden. She started to pace, but it was too cold to walk around in underwear after her exercise warmth had worn off, so she was forced to take to the mattress and the warmth of the blankets. She listened to see if she could hear anything, but she could hear nothing close.

    Ria kept looking at the door, willing Naira to come through it. There was a key in the lock she noticed, so she got up and locked it, just in case. She didn't want anyone wandering in and finding a young, half-clothed woman lying on a mattress. She tensed at that thought.

    Finally, she heard a sound that seemed nearer, in the building itself. Naira? She watched as the handle was pushed down from the outside, then a soft knock as the person realised it was locked. Ria got up and ran to the door.

    "Naira? Is that you?" Ria asked.

"Yes, let me in." Ria felt a flood of relief and hand shaking slightly she fumbled for the key to open the door. Naira was drenched and dripping and looked frozen. Ria rushed over to get one of the blankets and a towel.

"Quick take off your clothes and put this around you." Ria said, seeing Naira's teeth actually chattering.

"It's terrible out here, wind, rain, it's freezing, it even looks like it could snow!" said Naira as she got out of her dripping wet clothes.

Ria rushed back over to the sink to put the kettle on. She could not remember a time she had felt so relieved to see another human being.

"How did it go, apart from the weather?" Ria asked her as Naira hauled the blanket over her.

"Fine. It's a long way on foot though. It took longer than I thought. I saw that there was a bus, but I was afraid to take it. But maybe, tomorrow I will. It's faster and drier, it goes into the centre about two kilometres from here, but it didn't seem to be very frequent. Also, I don't want to stand there under the bus shelter, exposed, or have the driver notice me, so maybe it's better not to take it." Naira said.

"Yes, better not to, I think. Did you speak to anyone at the package address?" Ria asked.

"No, it was just a sort of post box inside a larger building, the door was open, so it was no problem, I just put it in there, and left. The less I know the better." Naira said.

"Here, some tea. You must be starving. Do you want a sandwich?" Ria asked.

"No, not yet, just the tea. I have to admit, I was nervous." Naira said.

"Me too, but for you." Ria said. "Thank you. You know, for doing this."

"I checked for you on the front of the newspapers. No sign. I don't know about inside the paper. I didn't want to carry a paper in this rain, but at least you are not front-page news!" Naira said, warming up a little now, though her hair was dripping.

Ria passed her a towel and Naira wrapped it around her long, dark hair.

"I see you have been busy." Naira said glancing at Ria's dripping jeans.

"Yes, we both have dripping jeans now." Ria laughed. "Let me wash yours, those blankets in the truck were disgusting. But I don't know if they will be dry for tomorrow. It's not that hot in here."

"I brought a tracksuit. I'll wear that." Naira said. "I would like to wash the jeans. They stink."

Ria nodded and turned back to the sink to give Naira some privacy.

They spent the rest of the day killing time. Naira told her a little bit about the town she had seen, then they went to bed after playing some more cards, and Naira left again the next morning at the same time. She had not bought the phones because of the weather. She would get them tomorrow if she could she said.

But she never did, and Ria didn't insist. But what was just two days now felt like twenty days to Ria but in the end all three packages were delivered safely without incident.

They celebrated with the last of the noodles. Ria felt a weight lift, Fatima at least would be fine. They had done it. Well, Naira had.

Ria raised her tea after the noodles in a toast. "To Fatima and to Part Two of our escape."
Naira smiled, looking slightly sad at the mention of Fatima perhaps, and toasted with Ria.

"It was never about Fatima. It was Khal." Naira said.
Ria opened her mouth to question and remembered Naira's warning about that. Naira smiled and nodded gratefully.
Now, they were free of obligations. Well, Naira wasn't. She still had to go with Ria to see Malik instead of just going onwards with the long journey home.

"Now we need to see how to get to out of here and to your city. I checked on the map, it's mostly highway and bits of main road. Our best bet is to try to get a truck to give us a lift but that means we will have to walk to the petrol and rest area here, see it?" Naira pointed to the phone map. "Then ask some truck drivers for a lift. To avoid being seen we should go very early tomorrow morning well before dawn, walk there, and then wait there until we see if someone will take us in their trailer."

"Is that not risky? Ria asked. "Should we not get a bus or a train?"

"No, Ria, we can't do that. Too dangerous." Naira said. "Let's stick to trucks, they can't check them."

"Yes, but who will be looking for us here, in this town? It is not like we have been on the television!" Ria replied. "Or in the newspapers."

"Just because we are not in the newspaper does not mean we can travel on public transport! It's too dangerous. Trucks are always a better option, even though there is no one here from the network, most will take money." Naira said.

"Money? I only have twenty euro, you?" Ria said.

"I have a hundred. That's why I didn't get the phones, and I still need my phone to communicate with my contact for the route after we meet your man, Malik. For fifty euros, someone will take us the mover said. It's easy money for them and it's not far. They won't know who we are. They'll think we're just another couple of migrants travelling in." Naira said.

Ria marvelled at her knowledge of all this. She would be lost on her own.

"I am not looking forward to meeting Malik." Ria said to change the subject.

"You talk about him with such fear Ria, yet you have come all this way, taken all this risk just to see him. And he too has risked himself to see you. Perhaps you like him a little more than you let on." Naira teased.

Ria snorted in disgust. "No way! I have taken this risk to get away from going to prison. He is just a stop along the way." Ria said. "Come on, let's get to bed, we only have a few hours to rest."

They got up at three am, Ria hadn't slept a wink. She pulled her woollen hat down over her head and made sure the flaps of her rucksack were closed tight.

"We will have to be careful, now we will stand out more, two women walking in places not so normal to walk, at a time not so normal to go walking. We will be less exposed once we get to the highway petrol station area. Have you got the torch?" Naira asked.

Ria checked her jacket pocket and nodded. Naira put on her jacket, her hat, and covered her face with her scarf like Ria. Then she pulled on her gloves.

"Okay, let's go." Naira said, and with that she strode towards the door, Ria following.

Even though Ria was nervous about all of this next part, she was relieved to be leaving this room and getting some fresh air despite the danger. As they stepped outside however, she was shocked at just how much colder it had got since they had arrived three days ago.

"Keep your head down, they have cameras everywhere in this place," Naira said.

Ria nodded and they walked on, Naira checked occasionally on the phone's GPS that they were going in the right direction, then turned the phone off. It was about a seven-kilometre walk and they walked fast, heads down from the cold and cameras towards the road that would eventually meet the highway and fuel and café stop. Ria could feel her body gradually warming up now with the vigorous walking and was feeling the benefits of all the exercising and stretching she had been doing. She felt stronger and was in less pain. She felt slightly exhilarated. She was anxious to get there safely but at the same time she couldn't get rid of a sick feeling in the pit of her stomach at the thought of what Malik was going to tell her about the woman and the past. Naira would hear whatever he had to say too. What if it was something bad about her?

She wished she could prepare herself for whatever it was. She was feeling stronger, but she was still very jittery inside. Everything would change once she met this man again, she just knew it.

"I hope he turns up," Naira said after they had been trudging through muddy fields a few metres from the side of the road that led to the highway, hidden behind hedges.

"Don't say that!" Ria stopped dead in her tracks. "Do you think he would do that?" Ria asked, throwing another worry onto the pile.

"Who knows? You don't know him, and anything could have happened since he sent you the photo. Also, you don't know why he is doing all this. We won't know until we get there, will we? So, we have to try. I just don't want you to be disappointed, because, with these things, and these kinds of people, you never know. You must never trust anyone Ria. I am sure he will come, if not, why go to all the trouble to send the photo? He's probably more worried that *you* won't come." Naira said, nudging her forward and they both strode on, Ria now picking up the pace.

Ria kept on walking, head down, ruminating on this possibility.

The woman's face floated into her mind. The image as clear as the photo itself. Her mind was running its own photo show now, flashing her images of the woman's face with different facial expressions. Occasionally, her mother's face appeared too. She had that familiar hard expression on her face when she was angry about something. There were never any images of her sister Hana. Ria felt her chest tighten again as the images flashed. She tried to concentrate on where she was putting her feet, it was very muddy and the last thing they needed now was a sprained ankle or worse. It was hard to see in the dark.

"Are you afraid Ria?" Naira asked suddenly.

"I am, very. I am afraid of Malik and of the woman, and of all the things I don't know."

Naira put her arm across Ria's shoulders as they walked, a little slower now.

"Ria, terrible things happen in our country every day, you have seen them on the news with your own eyes, and we see only a small part of what is happening. Isn't it strange that fear can paralyse us so totally? There are more of us than them, but they use our fear to control us." Naira said.

"Sometimes I met people who had disappeared and then came back. We knew they had been taken. This was before I was taken prisoner. They never spoke of the things that happened in there, but you could see it in their eyes, they had a different look about them, a dead kind of look. I thought there was something wrong with them, you know, in the head. I didn't realise why they looked like that until I saw it in myself once I was in prison. I had that look then. Everyone in there had it. You know you are alive. You know that your body is alive, but you know too that something important has died inside you. I think that what dies is your soul, and that is what is missing in our eyes afterwards." Naira said quietly.

"I think the prisons are for that, not so they can kill us off, but to murder our souls, murder our identities, make us betray the ones we love, and above all make us betray ourselves. Then, with our soul no longer intact, they release you so that everyone else can see that you are no longer you, and that makes people afraid. Do you understand?" Naira asked.

Ria was trembling but just grunted. She didn't want Naira to see her. Naira continued. She had removed her arm from around Ria's shoulders and was now walking quickly as she spoke.

"No-one will ask you after what has happened to you in there, and anyway you could not explain it. You know no one trusts you anymore. They begin to avoid you because they do not know what you said to the torturer about them. That is what torture does Ria. It breaks down trust in our society." Naira said.

Naira stopped and turned to Ria.

"Ria, you might not want to hear this, but I am sure that whatever happened to you is like that. I can see it in your eyes too, or what I mean is that I can see what is not there. You never sleep, you are easily startled and irritable. Ria, whatever you learn about your past from this man, or whatever you might remember that happened, especially if it is bad, you must know and believe me when I tell you this. No matter what happens in those places it is never your fault. You must understand that because it might be true that you were also in one of their prisons." Naira paused.

Ria's chest tightened even more, and she could not swallow. She wanted Naira to stop talking about all of this. But Naira continued.

"They try to make us think that we *deserve* the depraved things they do to us in those prisons or make us do. But nothing we are forced to do in there is our fault, Ria. Never. Do you understand what I am saying?" Naira said.

Ria caught the intense emotion in her voice. Ria could not see her face well as the torch was pointed down in front of their feet, but she could sense she was upset, but to Ria it felt more like she was trying to convince herself.

What surprised Ria was how well she understood what Naira was saying, how it connected with her on a deeper level. She had also noticed something about herself that didn't feel right. She was aware that she always avoided looking at herself in the mirror. She had noticed that look, a look she hadn't had before coming to this country. She looked the same, but different, just like Naira had said. She had also buried the feeling that she was guilty of having done something bad in her past. It was just a feeling, but it was a strong one. She had strung together some meaning from the snippets in her mind combined with what Malik had told her, and the way he spoke to her and looked at her. She had seen that suspicion, that distrust, that distaste in his eyes. She had felt guilty before, but it wasn't really until now, as she listened to Naira that she felt the sheer weight of it. She thought back to her many visits to the bridge back in the town where the centre had been, and that urge to just let herself fall and disappear.

She snapped out of her thinking and realised she hadn't answered the question.

"Yes, I think so, Naira. Thank you. I am so sorry about what happened to you, truly. I just don't think something like that happened to me. Perhaps Malik will tell a different story. At the end of this, I hope I will know what happened. No matter how terrible the truth is, I want to know it. Only then will I be able to deal with the consequences." Ria said and kept her eyes firmly down at the grassy, mucky ground, feeling determined as her tears fell.

"Be careful about seeking the truth Ria. I have not lived any longer than you, but I have lived hard and amongst a lot of women much older and wiser than myself. I thought I knew what the truth was. I thought I knew who was good and who was bad. Everything I did was for the good cause, then, I realised, there are no good causes. Look at what is happening in our country now. Look at how many of us have been slaughtered, women, children, and so many young men. Look at us now living amongst the rubble, or in shitty camps and detention centres or worse still, maimed or dead. Generations ruined for generations to come. Children who will never live, never play. Children who will never live any sort of normal lives. There is no more revolution, we are just small pieces in a bigger game played in our country by the bigger powers. We are no more than a convenient battle ground for them. They don't care about us, or our country. We call ourselves revolutionaries, others call themselves martyrs, but deep down we are all so afraid. Those prisons are full of people like you and people like me. No one cares. No one cares Ria. Our lives have been measured and deemed to be worth less than theirs. Ordinary people's lives are worth nothing to those in power, not just in our country, but everywhere on this planet." Naira said, her sharp words contrasting with her quietly spoken tone.

"I see who you are now Naira. I see it. You are brave, courageous, and generous. And you are mature and wise." Ria said. "I hope to be like you one day, strong and fearless."

"You do not want to be like me Ria. I can assure you." Naira said. "Now come on, enough talk, let's move, it's hard walking through these fields and it won't be long before dawn."

Ria understood and remained silent, walking as quickly as she could despite the terrain. She mulled over what Naira had said. Naira had been through a lot. Ria felt disconnected from her country's current situation because she could not remember it like that. It was like she was viewing a film on TV about somewhere else, somewhere that had nothing to do with *her* home. It didn't feel real. It was a reality she didn't know, this war, these prisons. The terrible reality that Naira knew so well, Ria knew so little.

Lights appeared in the distance and their tedious, muddy march was coming to an end. It was time to be more careful. There was no sun, but the night had turned to day without any need for the sun. Ria tensed with the knowledge that she would soon be exposed, out in the open for the first time since she had left the centre. But who would know them here? Police patrols would.

They stopped under a tree just a few hundred metres from the large garage and highway stop. They had to be careful not to be seen approaching from the fields as that would be very strange and out of the ordinary.

"We're covered in mud, that will look strange." Ria said. "No-one goes hiking along a highway in the dark."

"Yes, we've got to try and get as much mud off as possible now and then move to the road for the last bit. Look, use stones to scrap it off your boots, and the wet grass for the legs of your jeans." Naira said.

Ria bent down and started the whole cleaning process, able to see better now as the grey light became slightly brighter. Thankfully it was not raining, but a sharp northerly wind bit into her thin body.

"That looks much better. Now, we just look like we are into the normal hiking that these people are all so into." Ria joked.

Naira smiled and shivered. Maybe she was trying to shake off her dark mood from earlier. She looked more alert. Ria looked down at her boots and jeans to check once more and they strode off, climbed over a gate and walked on the inside of the crash barrier. It was much faster this way. There was some traffic but not much. Ria tensed each time she heard the sound of a car. It could all go wrong if a police car happened to pass. Thankfully, one didn't.

Relieved, they walked into the well-lit area.

"Look confident, Ria, like you belong. Not wary." Naira instructed.

"I could really do with a hot coffee." Ria said.

"Me too." said Naira. "Let's go to the bathrooms, clean ourselves up a bit more, then I'll get us some coffee, but you'll have to wait here in the bathroom okay. There will be cameras here. We can't risk it."

"Okay, let's go." Ria nodded.

They made their way to the bathrooms, hats, hoods, and scarves covering their faces, like everyone else in the place. Ria entered an empty stall and Naira left to get coffee. She was back quite quickly. They freshened up, grateful for the heat of the bathroom. There was hardly anyone there. They decided to leave one by one and meet in the car park before checking out what was happening with the trucks. They took their coffees and stood out of the wind near the truck section observing the activity there, it seemed that many trucks had spent the night there, and a lot of drivers were eating their breakfast in their cabin or checking their vehicle. Now was a good time to find a willing truck driver.

47

Naira broke the silence

"Wait here. Stay out of sight. Look, there is a Turkish truck over there, see the registration plate?" Naira said.

Before she could say anything, Naira was striding across the large tarmac area and walking up to a large black and red truck. Hunched at the back of the restaurant building, next to the big industrial-sized bins, Ria looked on. The large man with a beard looked at her in surprise when he saw her. Not usually a place for women as far as Ria could observe. Was this not dangerous, going in a strange man's truck? They seemed to be arguing now from what Ria could see, then Naira was walking back. Ria could see her face, she looked furious.

"What's wrong? What happened?" Ria asked frowning.

"Men! They are so disgusting. That is what is wrong. I could not even repeat to you the disgusting things he said and what he wanted in return." Naira said.

Ria tried to look empathetic but instead got a fit of giggles and could not stop herself laughing. She laughed so hard that her ribs hurt terribly. Tears streamed down her face.

Naira just stared at her, fuming, and incomprehension all over her face. Her expression made Ria laugh even more until finally Naira cracked and joined her in the laughter.

"Ok, I'm sorry, Ria said, but your face! You look so indignant. I mean Naira what did you expect?" Ria asked, shaking her head, and smiling widely. "He probably hasn't been able to speak to a young woman like you in decades!" Ria joked and they both started laughing again.

For the first time, Ria felt like herself, like a normal girl having fun with a friend. No drama, just for a few minutes.

Naira swore and looked back towards the trucks. "We can't stay here long. But I can't go through that again." she said

"Maybe, but we look kind of desperate too. For a ride, I mean." Ria said, causing another burst of laughter from the two of them.

"What about cars?" Ria asked. "Maybe we could wait and see a friendly-looking, safe elderly kind of couple and ask them if they will take us."

Naira sniggered. "That would be ideal but look at us. Who's going to give us a ride in this country? We look suspicious!"

"Let's wait over there." Ria said pointing to some benches further away from the main entrance and near the cars. "From there we'll be able to see the people who are coming and going better, and maybe we'll see people of our own age, maybe, you know, who look a bit more like us. They might agree to take us if we choose well and ask nice and normal." Ria said trying to lure Naira away from the truck-driver plan.

"Okay, let's try. But there won't be many people travelling at this time of the year, it's not like summer, but maybe you're right. It could be safer. Perhaps we could ask a woman? Just pray you are not circulating in some news piece. Truck drivers are better for looking the other way, you know, but, as you say not without risk if they are not a contact. There are no contacts here, such a shame, but we have got to move. It's only two or three hours from here so surely someone will be going there, or past there." Naira said, sounding worried.

"It's a long shot, looking like us, and so dirty, but what else can we do?" Ria said, and began to move over to the other side, to the picnic tables nearer to where the cars parked. Naira followed her.

It was early in the morning, so a lot of people were stopping off for coffee or breakfast Ria supposed. She was amazed at all the different types of people. All kinds of people from everywhere under the sun. After a freezing half hour of just observing, Ria nudged Naira. She had seen two girls around their age pull up. They got out of their car. They were dressed casually in jeans and hiking jackets, much like Ria and Naira except cleaner. Only one of them was white, the other looked like she might be of Moroccan or Algerian origin or somewhere like that.

Naira nodded. "When they come out, we'll ask them. Nothing to lose."

After a while the two girls came out with coffee cups and two paper bags. Naira and Ria had positioned themselves nearer their car, but far enough away so as not to look as if they were following them.

As the girls approached, Naira stepped a little into their path and said "Hi there" in English.

The two girls looked at each other and stopped, looking taken aback. Naira told them that they were trying to get to the city. She said that they were supposed to go with a friend, but at the last minute, their friend had become too sick to travel. Naira asked them if they would mind giving them a lift if they were going that way.

The girls looked very uncomfortable, but the northern African looking one nodded and said okay, that it was on their way, and that they would drop them at the nearest highway stop to the town.

Naira thanked them and they followed the girls to their car. One of the girls held the door open for them, and they piled in the back. They looked at each other in satisfaction. Not so hard after all.

Once in the car, the girls paid them no attention, and they drove in silence listening to the radio. Naira and Ria remained silent too just looking out of the car window, hats still on and scarves still covering part of their faces. Just in case. After a few hours, one of the girls turned to them.

"We're going to drop you off up here, okay? It's the nearest petrol station to the town. The town is still a few kilometres away but maybe you can find a lift here to get the rest of the way."

Naira nodded and said, "Thank you so much!"

They dropped them off and the car pulled away leaving them in an almost identical petrol and restaurant area.

Naira checked her phone quickly and said. "It's still six kilometres away. But it's still early. If we walk along the main road at this time, we risk being seen by the police." Naira said.

"Yes, but if we go through the fields, people will see us too." Ria said. "That will look even stranger." Ria looked towards the truck area. "Let's try a truck driver again." Ria said.

"I'll just go from one truck to the next and see if anyone is actually entering the town." Naira said and walked off before Ria could say anything.

Ria watched Naira change direction as she caught sight of a group of men drinking together at a picnic table. They all looked like truck drivers to Ria, though what made a truck driver look like one, she could not say.

From what Ria could see the conversation was going better this time. Naira was smiling and chatting. Then, one of the men, pointed to a large, white van that was just over at one of the fuelling pumps. A young man was standing there fiddling with the petrol cap.

Naira came jogging back. "That man is a messenger, you know the people that deliver all the packages. He is going into town apparently, and they said he's a good guy. Come on, let's go."

"You go and ask him, there are cameras over there. Keep your face covered. If he says yes, then we can get in when he is finished fuelling." Ria said.

"That will look strange Ria. He will think we are on the run or something." Naira said.

Ria looked at her and laughed, they risked getting giddy again.

Naira said "Stop! We can't! He'll be leaving once he has paid. We can't walk to the town, and we can't stay here. He's our best chance. Come on, you just stay here. Let me go and ask him. But keep watch and be ready in case he agrees."

Ria nodded and Naira sped off. Ria watched as she approached him as he was coming out of the petrol station shop, he looked surprised, but then Naira pointed over at the men at the picnic table and he smiled and waved at them. Then, she pointed over at Ria. At first, she saw him look confused, but then a car started shooting for him to move and free up the pump, so he got into the van to move for the car, gesturing to Naira to get in too. Naira hesitated, but then got in.

Ria's heart thumped. He could leave her there. But the van pulled off to one side and the passenger door opened. Naira beckoned for Ria to come. Relief flooded over her, and she sprinted as fast as she could over to the van keeping her head down.

"I am not allowed to take passengers when I am delivering so I'll just drop you in the centre of town, okay?" the young man said.

"Thank you." Naira said, and flashed a triumphant look at Ria who smiled, and off they went.

As they drew closer to the town, Ria could feel herself become more and more anxious. It would not be long now before she would meet Malik again. If he came. Part of her hoped he would not be there, but part of her too was terrified he would not.

48

They jumped down from the van onto a busy side street and looked around. Now what? There was no sign of any police, but they would have to get out of the streets somehow.

"Look there's a café over there with a very small window and lots of people inside, let's go in there and see what it's like. It's only a few hours before we have to meet Malik." Ria suggested pointing to a very busy little café.

"Okay, let's go, better to get off the streets and think for a while. We have been very lucky so far, let's not get caught now after all that!" Naira said wryly as they walked across to the café.

As they walked in Ria was struck by the scent of coffee and the warmth. There were a lot of people milling around. It would be hard to get a table, but the more people in the place the better for them.

"Wait here" Naira said and pushed her way through the people queuing to see if there was a table anywhere free. There wasn't. Ria saw her shake her head as she came back.

"Let's just get some coffee and wait until one becomes free" Ria said, Naira nodded, and they joined the queue.

Ria noticed that a lot of the men in the queue had long beards. She found it ironic and said so to Naira in a very low voice.

"Yes, I thought the same when I first saw them. It is so funny that they have those beards in this country for fashion. It's like they don't even realise who they look like! Whoever made that a fashion doesn't read much." Naira laughed.

"Or watch TV" Ria said and laughed too, and they stood there shaking silently before pulling themselves together.

There was something about this next step of their journey that was making them very giddy in a strange way, it must be nerves Ria thought. As they stood in the slow queue of bearded, ear-pierced, tattooed men and women, Ria could think of nothing else but the meeting that was fast approaching. Her stomach was in knots, and she was afraid. Naira seemed more relaxed now that they were here. The stakes were not so high for her, Ria thought, almost enviously, but then she quickly reminded herself of everything Naira had already been through, not to mention the whole thing with Khal. She was so grateful that Naira was with her, if not, she would undoubtedly be in prison by now. Caught.

Eventually, they got their coffees and stood around watching table movements like hawks. They wanted one well away from the window and off to the back, but not near the bathrooms. They had a lot of demands for a busy café. But they also knew from experience that people in this country were always busy and that eventually one just like they wanted would free up. When it did, they had already finished their coffees. They couldn't just sit at a table with nothing, so Ria stayed at the recently vacated table covered with empty coffee cups and cake crumbs while Naira went to order some tea and something to eat. At least they hadn't had to pay a truck driver.

Naira came back after a long time in the queue.

"Can you believe the prices in here!" she said in disbelief. "For tea!"

"Just tea, I know, basically it's water. They don't even know how to make a good green tea." Ria said. "Such a simple thing, yet…" She shook her head.

"Why don't we stay here until it is time to go, no one will notice us unless they stop being so busy and that looks unlikely from what I can see. Whatever makes this place so popular, I am not getting it. But it doesn't seem like the sort of place the police would stop for a coffee. Too busy, too young." Ria said.

"I agree. It's nice and warm in here too. Better than risking the streets. Plus, the music is good!" Naira said and smiled.

"Yes, and loud too! No-one will be able to hear us." Ria agreed.

"What?" Naira said jokingly.

They laughed and sipped their teas. Naira took out her phone.

"Give me the place he said to meet at again. I'll turn on the phone quickly. Lucky I was able to charge it at that last place. I'll check how far it is from here. He will probably have picked an isolated place. He won't know about your situation." Naira said. "But he will be careful if he is what he says he is. He won't choose somewhere exposed."

Reluctantly Ria pulled the photo out of her bag and pushed it across the table face down with the location details showing.

Naira looked at it, and then at Ria.

"Can I look at it?" Naira asked.

Ria hesitated. She didn't mind Naira looking at the woman, but she did not want to see her. Each time she had seen the photo, it had caused bad feelings inside her and she was already feeling very on edge.

"Do it while I look away, I know it sounds silly, but I don't want to see it. Not today." Ria replied.

Naira looked a bit longer at her, but Ria looked away. She heard Naira pick up the photo. She didn't say anything after seeing it, just put it back on the table face down and began entering the address into the map app on her phone. Ria looked back, picked up the photo and put it back into her bag. Neither said anything for a while.

"Okay, I've found it, it's a little far, but there's a park there. It's not in the centre and from the map there seems to be more houses and cafés than shops. It's about a thirty-minute walk. We should get there before him."

"Why?" Ria asked.

"That way we can know the area better, you know, in case anything happens. We need a plan to get away just in case. You always need to have a Plan B and good knowledge of the place when you are going to meet someone like this. It is dangerous to go blind." Naira said.

Ria was impressed with Naira's knowledge of all things covert and realised she needed to learn more from Naira if

429

she was to be an asset and not a burden on their long journey home after meeting Malik.

"Tell me more about this man we are going to meet Ria. I need to be prepared. To make you come all of the way here on the basis of just one photograph, he must be pretty convinced it would work. He must have known how you would react, so he may not as you say believe you don't remember anything. You could very well not have remembered this woman and just ignored his message." Naira said looking at Ria.

Ria tensed. "He said he was a fighter, led by my brother. He said my brother and his unit, that is what he called it, attacked military bases and stole weapons, and I suppose fought the state. Revolutionaries he said, not terrorists. He told me that when my brother found out that we were being held in a big military base near the border, he went crazy and went out there straight away to watch the base with this man and some more of the group. That was how they saw the planes fly over it and bomb the base to bits. I don't know any more than that. I just ran away from him after he said that. But his question about how I could be alive after all the bombs terrified me because I couldn't answer it." Ria said.

Ria looked up at Naira, tears in her eyes, but feeling embarrassed too about admitting her cowardice in running away.

"I just felt that he had become more dangerous somehow as he asked that question, call it instinct, I don't know, it was just like a voice inside telling me to run, so I did." Ria added.

"How could you not? It was in the middle of the night! You were alone out there with a stranger! Who wouldn't have run, Ria, who? You were so brave to even go and meet him like that." Naira exclaimed.

"Really, you believe that?" Ria asked, surprised.

"Yes. He sounds strange and dangerous. There are a lot of reasons why you could be alive even if it is true what he says that you were in that bombed military base. Not everyone dies in a bombing. There are always more injured than dead. Always. When they talk about the bombings on the news, you'll always see that yes many are killed, but there are always so many more who are injured." Naira said.

Ria's thoughts raced with this new information. If that was true, then maybe Hana and mother were both alive too. Hope coursed through her. The way the man had described the bombing, it had not occurred to her, or to him it seemed, that anyone could have survived such a thing, that is why she couldn't believe she had ever been there. But now…

"So that means, if it is even true that we were kept there….that my mother and my sister could also have survived. Like me. Or maybe they still have them, in some prison somewhere." Ria said.

Ria shuddered at the thought after what Naira had told her about the prisons.

"Of course it's possible. Anything is possible. But look, don't get your hopes up. In war, it's better not to hope. War is an unpredictable beast. Who lives, and who dies, well, it's a lottery, you know. War leaves no one and nothing untouched. I don't know. I know this is a terrible thing to say, but if your mother and sister did die in that air strike, from what I've seen, it would be better for them than if they were still in one of those prisons. They have continued to bomb prisons, bases and hospitals, all sides have. I am not trying to make you sad Ria." Naira said.

But what Naira was saying wasn't making Ria sad, she was feeling something else, that same feeling that came any time she spoke of her mother or her sister. Like her flesh was crawling.

"I know." Ria said. "Thank you. You want to know more about Malik. I don't think that is his real name. I can't tell you much. He is very large, not fat, but tall, and strong. He won't be expecting you, so we need to plan for that in case he reacts badly and tries to separate us. We cannot let that happen. What if he takes me? What if that is his plan?"

Ria heard the panic in her voice now. Naira reached across the table to grasp her arm.

"Keep your voice down Ria. I won't let that happen. That is why we must get there first. We cannot shout for help or anything like that because of your situation, well, not just yours, mine too, so we must make sure that we know the place well and have an escape route planned." Naira said.

Ria nodded. "It's at five so it will be dark. Hopefully, the place has good street lighting."

They continued to talk about all the different things that could happen and what they would do if they did, and the time passed by quickly. They left the relative comfort of the café and ventured out into the streets. It was still light, though it was getting darker by the minute. They made their way to the meeting place. They had decided to get there at least an hour before five so they could check out the area and then wait near out of sight until the meeting time so they could see him arrive. Ria suspected Malik would do the same. Naira agreed but said that there was nothing they could do about what he did, they could only control what they did.

Standing up to leave, Ria had felt her legs shake, she was very nervous. Now Naira looked more nervous than Ria had ever seen her. Perhaps she understood that this could be one of the most dangerous parts of their journey home. Or, maybe she just knew, like Ria did, that they were simply no match for this man.

49

Ria leaned against the wall behind the bus shelter and looked around. They were near the place he had indicated for them to meet forty-five minutes before the meeting time. They had looked around a bit already. There was quite a lot of traffic, schools, and shops but it had more of a residential feel than the other part of the town they'd just been in. It was certainly not a place in which poor people lived. Ria noticed how big and well-kept the houses were with their immaculate lawns. She noticed too the expensive-looking cars parked in the large driveways. Why would he arrange a meeting in such a place?

"This is a rich area." Ria said to Naira. "Strange place to meet, is it not?"

Naira nodded. "Yes. He must have a reason."

"The meeting place is over there, in the park. There are a lot of trees and picnic benches. There are a lot of parents and children there now, at the swings and people walking their dogs, but as it gets dark, they'll go." Naira said as she pointed.

"Maybe instead of going to the exact place, we should stay near the playground, it is more open, we'll see him coming." Ria said.

"Yes, that's a good idea." Naira said nodding as she looked over towards the playground. "Stay here while I go over and take a closer look. It's better you stay here. He doesn't know me."

Ria nodded. Naira was over there by the playground for a few minutes walking around, and then she turned to come back over to Ria.

As Ria watched Naira cross the street on her way back, she saw her stop dead in the middle of the road. Ria stood up straighter now, alert, concerned, her eyes on Naira. What the hell was she doing? She would get knocked down by a car. Then, she felt a heavy hand on her shoulder, and she whipped around.

"Hello Ria, I see you brought a friend with you this time."
It was Malik. Naira must have seen him approach Ria but didn't have time to warn her. He was standing very close to her. Ria could not get her mouth to work. She had been right. He had come before, just like the last time.

"Don't look so surprised Ria, I have been watching you for over half an hour. Introduce us please" he said gesturing to Naira, who was rushing over to them, looking very concerned.
Ria still could not speak. She watched him standing there in front of them looking expectantly at Naira.

"So, who are you and what brings you here? He asked, his voice calm, his tone conversational.

"Hello, I'm a friend of Ria's from the detention centre. Nice to meet you." Naira said calmly.
She had been thrown off guard, but she had recovered more quickly than Ria. Naira did not answer his second question.

"I see. I had hoped to meet Ria on her own. Would you mind leaving us for a while?" Malik replied.

Naira looked at Ria. Ria took a step closer to stand right next to Naira.

"That won't be possible. She stays, or I go." Ria said.

"Are you still afraid of me Ria?" Malik taunted. "I told you, we are practically family, there is nothing to fear. Well, except the truth."

He smiled at Ria, but his smile did not meet his eyes. His expression remained hooded and dark. He was dressed in black jeans and a black jacket with a hood. He looked more menacing when he tried to smile than when he didn't bother.

"I am not afraid of you." Ria lied. "I am not afraid of the truth either. I don't even know if what you told me before is the truth. My friend stays because we are together, and that is it. Whatever you have to say, you can say it to her. I have told her everything."

"Everything?" Are you sure Ria? I thought you had lost your memory, yet you come here just because I sent you one photograph. You *do* remember her, don't you? If not, you would not have risked coming here." He said.

Ria said nothing.

Malik nodded. "Okay then, have it your way, your friend can stay. Now let's get off this street and go and sit on one of those benches over there. We can't stay there for long or people will notice us. This is not the kind of place people like us would live." He said.

He looked around him, subtly but carefully and started to walk across the same street Naira had just crossed. He didn't even look behind to check they were following. Ria looked over at Naira, who nodded in his direction, and they walked tentatively behind him towards what Ria hoped would be the truth.

Malik led them to the picnic bench that was the furthest away from the street. Naira glanced at Ria in concern. This was not their plan, she knew that, but what could they do? He was in control, not them. There was no-one around at all. Malik stared at Naira and gestured for them to sit down at the table as if they were in a restaurant, with a slight sardonic bow. Ria avoided eye contact with him once seated and stared down at the wood grain of the table. Naira was silent too. Ria dared not look at her.

"So, you came Ria. All this way. I have to say I am surprised. Leaving your safe little detention centre even though you are so afraid of me. Why did you run off like a scared cat that night? Why did you come here today? What changed? Why did you bring this woman here too?" The man said turning to stare at Ria.

"Do not refer to her like that!" Ria said wanting to show him that she was not afraid of him.

But despite her tone Ria felt the weight of her fear settle in the pit of her stomach and she was having trouble swallowing her saliva again. She felt Naira fidgeting beside her. He waited for her to answer his questions.

"Look, I know I shouldn't have run away that night. I'm sorry. I was frightened by those things you were saying, and you didn't seem to believe me about my memory. I was afraid, all those things you told me that I don't remember. I ran. But... well...when you sent the photo, it was different. I knew immediately that I knew the face. I have no idea how. I don't know who she is or how I know her. But I want to know everything that I can't remember, no matter how bad it might be. I thought you might be lying, but then, when you sent that photo, it was kind of a strange proof. I believe you when you say you know my brother. Also, I have had some other problems back there. But I have come to find out what you know about my family, and about me and this woman and her connection to me." Ria said and was surprised at how calm her voice sounded.

She could see Naira looking at her out of the corner of her eye, but Ria stared straight back at Malik, determined to not let him see her fear of him.

He said nothing. He seemed to be weighing up the truth of what she said. Why did he care why she had come? She had come, hadn't she.

"What about her? Why is she here?" He asked, staring at Naira.

Ria ignored his question.

Malik looked back at Ria.

"I don't believe you when you say that you don't remember the campus massacre. How is that even possible?" he said, "We have all seen terrible things, but unfortunately, we remember them. Sometimes much too well."

"You can believe what you like, but it's true, I don't remember." Ria said.

"It is more common that you think." Naira said.

Malik silenced Naira with a withering look but she held his stare.

He turned his attention back to Ria.

"If you hadn't run, I would have explained. The plan was for you to come with me." Malik said.

"Plan?" Ria said, frowning.

"Yes." Malik said.

"I don't understand." Ria said.

"The last time we met, before you ran, I told you about the airstrike and asked you how it was that you had survived that." Malik said. "Why did that make you run away? It is a logical question to ask, is it not?" he said narrowing his eyes.

"I don't know. It was too much. You sounded as if you didn't believe that I didn't remember. I was afraid." Ria said, more sadly now. "What do you mean about a plan?"

"I will explain that later." Malik said. "After witnessing the air strike and believing you, your mother and your sister were down there, your brother, Jamil, well, let's just say he was devastated. He blamed himself for everything. At first, he was convinced you were all dead. We were too as it didn't look as if anyone could possibly have survived such a strike. But we were new to airstrikes and bombs back then."

Ria looked at Naira, who was hanging onto every word he was saying. Ria saw Malik look at her.

"Where are you from?" he asked. "You don't have to give me your name, we all know the burden of information, but you can tell me where you are from, can you not?" He said to Naira suddenly, catching her off guard and Ria too.

439

Naira told him and also, she told him the name of the group she had fought with. He smiled, a real smile, not one of those half-smiles he used with Ria.

"Your people fight well. You have had a very hard time against the regime since the beginning, not to mention your resistance all these years which has been punished harshly. I am sorry for that. We have good contacts from there in our network. You must be proud, as anyone from your region would be. What are you doing here?" He asked her, kindness in his voice now.

"I got caught back home and taken to prison. You know how that is. Then they let me go, so you understand what happens and what you have to do." Naira said.

He nodded. "I do. I am sorry that happened to you. They captured a great fighter no doubt. I don't know what it means to be in one of those prisons, but we have heard many things and someone close to me... well." he paused. "You are brave to do your duty and leave. You are brave to come with Ria to meet a strange man like me."
He smiled broadly and his whole face transformed in the dim light of the dark evening and Ria stared at him in wonder. How could she ever have been afraid of him? He looked so young, just like Jamil. A young man, barely out of his teenage years. He was just like them.

Naira looked pleased, but uncomfortable. "Thank you." She said nothing more.
Ria was glad that Malik had accepted Naira so well.
Malik turned back to Ria, smile now vanished.

"Now, Ria, I will ask you the same question again and I want an answer. How did you survive that airstrike?

You admit you know the woman in the photo so this story about your memory… it is hard for us to believe it…" Malik said.

"Who is 'us'?" Ria asked quickly. "Did my brother send you here?"

He ignored her and waited. Ria said nothing, she just sat there. If he didn't believe her, she had no answers for him, she had come here for answers, but it seemed that so had he.

"It is true about her memory." Naira said. "She doesn't know how she got here or anything before that. I have been with her for about two months. I would know if she was lying after all this time. I have also seen her medical reports and accompanied her to her doctor's visits. There are reports about her head injury and memory loss written by specialist doctors. She was in hospital for a whole month before they sent her to the detention centre where we shared a room. It is also very possible that if she was in that place during the airstrike that she injured her head there and suffered the memory loss. Ria's head injury was very bad so why do you not believe her?" Naira asked him, looking him straight in the eye.

He looked at Ria, his sceptical expression now replaced by curiosity it seemed to Ria. Naira was her salvation.

Ria wanted to take back some control of the conversation, so she looked at him and said. "If I knew things, as you seem to think I do, why would I risk coming all this way here? I came here so that you could tell *me*, not the other way around. If you don't know anything about my family, or this woman, or anything about what happened, then I will leave because you are of no use to me, and I will have come here for nothing!" Ria spoke sharply now.

He said nothing, but she saw anger flash in his eyes.

Ria continued. "They brought me here. Remember that. I did not come here myself. I saw that woman in the photo before but only in terrible nightmares. I have seen images of my mother and some other strange things but only as... well......fragments. There is no story to them. There is no making sense of them. I promise you. At least nothing that I can understand. I have come here so that you can help me make sense of all those fragments I see." Ria paused on the verge of tears.

She composed herself and continued. "Has something terrible happened to my mother, Hana, or Jamil? You must tell me. Did my brother send you here?" Ria said.

Malik stared at her and sighed. He reached into his bag and took out a few papers. From them he took a photo and placed it down on the table in front of Ria and Naira, keeping his thumb firmly on it to stop the wind from blowing it away. The girls leaned forward to get a better look, it was dark already but there were enough streetlamps dotted around the park to see. It was a photo of Jamil and Malik, arms around each other's shoulders, both smiling into the camera. They looked so happy. Ria started to cry as soon as she saw her brother again. Malik put the photo back and held out another one. This time it was a photo of Jamil, Alana, and himself. In this photo they were wearing some sort of bandana around their foreheads. Jamil looked a little older now, wearier. They were all holding up the victory sign. Ria took the photo from him and stared at her brother. All three of them were in some kind of uniform, they looked dishevelled but happy. Jamil was kissing Alana's cheek in the photo. Ria just sat there and cried. There was something she badly needed to ask but could not find the words.

"He's still alive Ria, and so is Alana. And yes, he did send me to find you" Malik said.

Ria gave the photo back to him. "Why did you not come sooner?" she asked.

He laughed. "We didn't know where you were. We only found out that you were alive by chance. Someone in our network said they had seen you in one of the hospitals just across the border from the base that blew up. They said you were moved here but then moved again. We didn't understand why. Then things started getting more serious at home, with the uprising and all that. They were confusing times Ria for everyone. We had a lot to do."
"But Jamil never stopped looking and kept the networks aware. Eventually we got word about where they had moved you to. By then you were in that detention centre but all of that took a lot of time and a lot of contacts. Then, it took time for Jamil to figure out what to do. He was busy with what was happening at home too as you can imagine. A few weeks ago, he asked me if I would come here to find you because he couldn't because of his responsibility as a leader. He trusted me. I told him the truth, that I didn't want to come here, that I wanted to stay and fight, that

going off to look for you was not a priority for me. He understood, but in the end, I agreed to come for a short time. It was not difficult for me to pretend to arrive as a refugee. It's a small world for us outside of our own country." Malik said.

Relief flooded over Ria that her brother was alive, but then she felt angry.

"Have you come to take me back?" Ria demanded in between her tears.

"Take you back? Yes, of course. It's just a bit different now that you can't remember what happened.
I don't know, we didn't know about that." Malik said.

"What does it matter?" Ria asked.

Malik placed another photo on the table. It was a different photo of the woman. It was taken from a different angle, and she was with other soldiers in similar uniforms, a whole group of them. The photo seemed to have been taken without their knowledge. They were not posing, but were moving up a dusty street in formation, heavily armed and heavily equipped, all looking very alert. They were at work Ria realised. She felt her heart sink.

"Do you want to know who she is?" Malik asked staring at Ria.

"Of course, I want to know who she is! But first I want to know about my mother and sister… are they… are they alive too?" Ria said loudly agitated now at seeing the woman again.

There was something about the men in the picture with her as well, some of them looked familiar.

"Ria, quiet! Someone could hear you!" said Naira putting a hand on Ria's arm. "Stay calm. It will be okay."

Malik ignored her question about her mother and her sister. "This woman, Ria, is Veronica Furner, she is a well-known mercenary used by whoever pays her. These are the men she usually works with and leads. She calls herself a captain, but that is not a real rank. Mercenaries have no rank. They just invent them to make themselves sound like soldiers. She was in the military for this country a long time ago, but she was dismissed. I don't know why, but for nothing good, I am sure. This is a photo taken of her unit not too far from your town. These mercenaries do the dirty work for the countries who don't want to get their hands dirty or don't want too many body bags returning home of their soldier boys. This woman is a self-proclaimed counter-terrorism expert and a vicious interrogator with a reputation for terrible cruelty. It's what she enjoys apparently. She is well known in our country already and in other countries too. All our networks in other countries know her well. She is referred to as 'the Black Snake'. She hunts us all, terrorist or not. She worked in Iraq for years, and Afghanistan too." He paused.

"How do you know all of this?" Ria asked.

Malik continued "We found out that she and some of her men were in the same military base as you just before the planes dropped the bombs. We did not find that out until after. Apparently, there was an incident involving some of her men. At first, we thought that she must have been killed in the bombing but sadly It turns out that like you, she is fine. If she was even injured, it can't have been anything serious because she was seen back in action soon after in our region. All of this came through from bigger group's information. They have better sources." Malik paused, checking around him before continuing.

"After the airstrike, we heard that there was a lot of military activity out in that area. It was a no-go zone. It was not a good look for the regime that one of their military bases so close to the border had been bombed."

Ria fidgeted, worrying about how this story was going to end.

He continued. "But of course, the regime had to have its blood. They knew none of the local armed groups had any air power, so they knew very well it was a foreign power, probably the Americans. The military in our country needed to send a message to groups like ours. The day after the airstrike, they sent their soldiers to your town. They pulled thirty-six young men out from their houses in the early morning and shot them in front of their families, they just left the bodies lying in the street. They also took thirty-six young women with them. We believe they were taken to different prisons. Nothing has been heard of them since, except the usual rumours. This was another warning to the town, to the armed groups in the region. It was like the massacre at the campus. A warning. Retaliation." Malik paused watching Ria's face like a hawk.

"Why thirty-six?" Ria asked.

"What?" said Malik, looking confused.

"Why thirty-six men and thirty-six women?" Ria repeated.

"We think that was how many of their soldiers died in that airstrike, but we don't know for sure." Malik said.

Ria nodded and averted her eyes. She had seen the deep sadness and anger in Malik's eyes. It was too much to bear. Malik was silent for a while, remembering perhaps. Then, he seemed to gather himself together, took a deep breath and continued.

"Soon after, everything started up, the revolution, then the war and it all evolved into what is happening today. When Jamil got the information about you, he also got the information that the woman, the Black Snake was back in action. All the groups share intelligence like that. Her group are very dangerous. As the fighting intensified, Jamil had more and more contact with other groups in the same region. One day he was at a meeting with some of the black flag group leaders and some other regional leaders. He was chatting afterwards with a friend of his, one of the black flag leaders who told Jamil to be careful. They had heard that the Black Snake was looking for Jamil and she wouldn't stop until she found him. Then, he told Jamil everything they had heard had happened at the military base before the airstrike. These groups always have the most information because they have people everywhere. Even in the military. He told Jamil that Veronica Furner - the Black Snake was there with you, your mother and your sister, with her men."

Ria felt as if turned to stone by his words. "What do you mean that she was there with us? Looking for Jamil? Why would she be looking for Jamil?" Ria was now really terrified.

"We know Ria. We know what you did. Jamil knows too." Malik said and grabbed her hands in a tight clasp across the table.

50

Time stood still for Ria. There was a shrill ringing in her ears. She sat unmoving on the bench, silent but for the rapid beating of her heart. She felt no rise and fall of breath. His sentence had put her whole system on hold. Each word repeating itself in slow motion in her head. She lowered her gaze down to her hands, hands that were covered by his in a very tight grip. Then she snapped out of it and tried to pull her hands away from him, but he was too strong and she too weak.

"No, Ria, you are not running this time. No more running." Malik said quietly. "It is time to face it. I have a letter for you, from Jamil."

Ria raised her eyes to look at him, not even bothering to hide her fear. She so desperately wanted to hear from her brother, but this was not the atmosphere of happy times.

"Please. No. I cannot." Ria cried.

Naira by her side, laid a hand on her arm.

"You have to Ria. This is what Jamil wants. It is the only way you will believe it is true." Malik said.

He removed one of his hands from hers and picked up one of the papers from the pile and placed it on the table facing her so she could read it while he kept one hand firmly on her arm, his other hand on the letter. His grip felt stronger now, he was hurting her. She could feel his stare on her as she looked down at the piece of paper. She looked at the writing and immediately recognised the familiar scrawl of her brother's handwriting. Her heart beat faster. She felt sweat form beads on her forehead despite the cold breeze. What was she so afraid of? It was just a letter from her brother who she loved and who loved her. There was no need to fear her own brother. What the hell was wrong with her?

"Read it Ria. You are wasting valuable time. We have to move soon." Malik snapped.

Ria began to read as slowly as possible having trouble making sense of the words because her mind was sluggish.

Ria my dear sister,

If you are reading these words, then my friend has found you. I could not come myself. There is too much to do here. I am so sorry I left you all alone after what happened in the campus. If I could change the past, I would, and I would run back with you to our house. That might have changed everything, or nothing but at least we would have been together.

But instead, I thought about revenge before making sure my family was safe. I was so angry that day, at how they had slaughtered all those poor students like dogs at the campus. Our friends. You, Alana, and I lived and maybe a few others, no one knows, but no one was ever okay after that ever again. Malik will have told you that I had already been fighting. I didn't tell you. I didn't think you would understand, and it was as much for your protection as ours. But our mother knew.

Alana and I both feel the weight of responsibility for what happened at the campus. But I also bear the blame for what happened to my own family after that. I will bear it all my life. Thankfully, I know my life will be a short one.

Ria stopped reading. It was too much. Scenes from that day at the campus now erupted into her mind, she tried to rid herself of them but couldn't. She could not see herself, but she saw the blood covered sand strewn with dead bodies with open eyes, blood all over them. She saw a fleeting image of the line of army vehicles and their massive guns. She stifled the scream that rose inside her. Then, still in her mind's eye she saw Jamil crouched down at her side shouting at her, but she couldn't hear what he was saying. Then sounds of running. She remembered being in a dark passageway, all alone. Where was her brother? Her chest was getting tighter and tighter. She tried to pull her hands away from Malik's grip but could not.

"Ria, what is it? What is wrong?" Naira's concerned voice seemed to float into her mind from far outside of her. Naira gripped her arm and shook her, and Ria started and whipped her head around to face Naira.

"Naira, do not touch me." Ria snapped pulling her arm away as best she could despite the man's vice-like grip.

Ria saw the hurt on Naira's face but ignored it and turned to face the man.

Malik said sharply "Read the rest, Ria. Now!" She could see his eyes harden and his grip tighten.

"Can't you see her. She's gone white. Stop it's too much for her!" Naira said to Malik.

Ria looked back down at the page, feeling lightheaded, the writing blurry and indistinct now. She tried to control her breathing and to fight her panic. She felt compelled to run, but he was stopping her. She looked at him. He was right. He nodded. It was time to face it. She tried to take a breath but there was no air. She continued to read her brother's letter.

I was at a meeting as Malik will have told you, of local commanders. After, I was smoking outside and one of the black flag leaders who I know well. He had asked to talk to me. He told me about the foreign woman – the one they call 'the Black Snake'. He told me that she had been looking for me because she thought it was me who had killed her men during two of our attacks. It is true that in one attack we found a mercenary. He told me to be careful, that she had survived the airstrike and was back. I already knew about you by then, they had told me that as well. But now he had more information about what happened at that base. He thought I should know what had happened there, so he told me what his sources in the military had told them.

He told me that you, our mother, and Hana had been found by a night patrol and once you were identified as my family, this 'Black Snake' had insisted on taking over the interrogation. He said she just went there with a few men and took over. No questions asked.

Ria read faster, she knew what was coming now, she could not see it all yet, but she could *feel* the horror of it. She wanted to finish the damn thing. The terror she felt, the sickness in her stomach was no longer of consequence to her. All that mattered now was getting to the end of her brother's words.

He told me what the Black Snake had done to Hana and to you. I had already seen the photos the military had sent and heard the recording but what he told me then was even worse. He told me that she forced you to choose to take the life of either our mother or our sister, and if not, she would have her men rape and kill you all. He said you chose Hana and killed her. He told me that you shot our sister.

It was too much. Ria turned to the side and vomited onto the grass. The man loosened his grip.

"Keep reading." He said.

"Ria, you don't have to, what is this he is making you read!" Naira said in a loud voice. "You have to stop this! It can be dangerous for her to remember certain things too quickly!"

"No, she has to read." He replied. "Read Ria."

Nauseous, Ria turned back. Hana. No. No. NO! It could not be true. She would not have done such a thing. There must be a mistake. But Ria knew instantly it was true. She knew she had murdered her own sister. She had seen it in her nightmares when she had been drugged, she had felt it. But she had refused to believe it.

"Read Ria!" he shouted.

Ria jumped. She turned back and looked down at the paper, feeling now somewhat detached, panic replaced by something else, something quiet and dead.

I know you Ria and I cannot imagine the situation. My friend told me about this 'Black Snake' and some of the things she is known for, and she is well known for this kind of torture. I was not there. I can only hope that you did the right thing, and you chose Hana humanely because of what they did to her.

Perhaps I would have done the same and rest assured if there had been no airstrike, she would have made you kill our mother too, and then she would have killed you. Since then, I have studied this woman carefully. It was a shock to me as you can imagine when he told me. At first, I was very angry at you, but then my friend explained how she works. I have been studying her now for months, the hunted studies the hunter.

My friend told me to be careful, that she was still hunting me. She never gives up he told me. It is the hunt and the slow kill that she enjoys the most. We are nothing to her Ria, no better than cockroaches, people who have no value, people to be played with, then stepped on and crushed in the cruellest ways possible.

I have no doubt that you carry as much guilt as I do, if not more, for what you had to do. I know you well sister and you are no murderer. I know how much you loved Hana and how much she loved you.

There is no end to the horror in our country.

At the beginning of all this, I thought the violence of the fighting would be the worst thing, but now I know that it is the other things that happen, all the torture, all the executions, all the bombing of little children, and all the horrific things that are happening here that have so little to do with my ideals of revolution and fighting for something noble. This is a terrible place now. Ria, my beautiful sister, no one is the same as they were before. We are all changed so terribly.

Ria began to cry, long wailing sounds that emerged from some deep, unknown place inside her. She knew that everything he said was true. She wailed in pain and as she did, she no longer saw fragments that made no sense. Now she saw all the images that her mind had been keeping from her and understood what they were, she was able to piece them all together. She saw her sister's face explode. She saw men clawing at her sister one after another as they raped her in front of her mother and herself. She felt the heavy body in the pitch-black cell on her as she herself was raped. She remembered the fists on her face as they beat her. She heard the woman's laughter ring out in her head, saw her cold blue eyes as they looked straight into her. She saw her mother's face nodding to her, her mother's voice shouting at her desperately. Her memory dumped all that into her mind all at once.
Naira put her arm around Ria's shoulders and pulled her towards her. Ria let her and felt the man's grip relax a little more. Ria pushed the letter towards Naira so that she could read it.

Naira read it and sighed. "I'm so sorry Ria. This is so terrible. I cannot imagine...But, he's right Ria. It is not your fault Ria."

Malik interrupted. "Ria, we know what they do. We know this woman very well now as Jamil says in the letter.

The regime has been doing things like this for many years, but this is a different kind of torture that this woman does. You must not give this so-called Black Snake the satisfaction of breaking you. If you do, you let her win. In there, you had no choice. I understand now how you could not let yourself remember such a thing. To shoot your own sister in front of own your mother is not something anyone would remember easily, especially in the state you must have already been in. No one blames you." Malik's voice had changed, it was softer now.

Ria felt Naira's body tense in reaction to Malik's words in her body. Now Naira knew what she had done but she did not pull away from Ria despite knowing she had murdered her younger sister. Ria could not bring herself to look at either of them. The shame and the pain were too much. She just wanted to go away, leave them, and disappear. Not run, disappear. A more definitive option.

"Ria, I know it feels terrible, but you must understand, as I told you as we walked through those fields earlier today, it is NOT your fault. Malik is right and I am sure your brother, more than anyone, understands that perfectly well." Naira said.

Ria struggled to speak but couldn't. There was too much in her mind. She felt so overwhelmed by all those terrible images in her head and emptied by the deep pain of her wailing. She tried to gather herself but when she spoke it was as if she was speaking to Jamil himself.

"It was all so fast, I swear I thought Hana was begging me to do it, you know after what they had done to her, it was so terrible what they had done to her... she

456

begged me to do it…. I don't know…that is what I thought. She begged me…. my mother wanted it to be her… she was pleading…Hana too…but because of what Hana had suffered… they had already taken two of her fingers… You didn't see what they did to her… how she was….it was too much ….But I should not have done it, I should have refused. But I saw what they had done to Hana, and I knew what they would do it to us all… so I don't know, I panicked, and I just pulled the trigger… the woman was shouting at me… my mother… everyone was shouting at me. it was all so confusing. Our mother had told me before to protect Hana, but I did the opposite! I murdered my own sister." Ria started sobbing again. It became darker as night fell. The man was no longer keeping her hands prisoner, he was holding her hands, warming them, no longer restraining her but comforting her.

She felt a terrible relief wash over her as she began finally to face the horrific deed she had carried out in that terrible place. She was also forced to face all the other things that had happened there too, to Hana especially. She understood now, why she had always felt such shame, so dead inside. She drew unexpected comfort from Naira and this stranger sent to her by her brother. She let herself feel her pain deeply, pain that she knew she would not be able to live with for long now that she knew its origin. Jamil said he understood what she had done, and he blamed himself for so much. But she was the one who had pulled the trigger, and she knew she would never understand why she had done that, or ever forgive herself.

She looked down at the letter, there was still another paragraph there unread. Malik turned on the phone torch so she could read it, as she braced herself for news of her mother.

51

Ria felt Naira brace beside her as the cutting breeze turned into a stronger wind. She heard the rustling of leaves from the nearby tree too as she looked down at the vigorously flapping page of Jamil's letter which would have taken flight if not held in place by Malik's hand.

"You have to finish it Ria, then, we have to get moving!" Malik said, looking around him all the time. She barely heard him. She no longer cared about getting caught. It would at least serve as some form of the punishment she deserved for what she had done to her sister. Ria Ignored Malik and went back to Jamil's last paragraph.

There is no news of our mother as I write. It is not likely she survived, even if she survived the airstrike, the information we have is that all prisoners were shot. I hope that she is not in some prison somewhere, she would not want that. I still check, as I did for you, with all the networks just in case but so far there is nothing. It is all very difficult Ria. I feel responsible for all of this. The last time I saw our mother, we argued and that is not easy for me to live with.
We don't know how you got to where you are now. We think it was a rescue team or aid workers and then somehow you got transferred to where you are now, but we don't know how or why. It is also possible the Black Snake had something to do with it once she realised you were alive, or she may have been with you after the bombing. We can't

know but as Malik will explain to you, there are too many coincidences. What the war has taught us all is that there is no such thing as a coincidence.
There is something you must do before you come home Ria. Malik will bring you here safely. We can be together again although our hometown is now nothing like it was before. Malik will explain it all to you. Trust him with your life. I trust him with mine and I trust very few people. He is my brother, so he is yours too. Do as I ask Ria. We owe it to all the dead, not just our own family. Think of nothing else, think of all the students you saw the military slaughter that day at the campus, the massacre we survived. Think about what they did to Hana and our mother, and what they had done to you. You and I survived that massacre against the odds, but we have to honour those who didn't by fighting back. Let nothing and no one stop you. Do not be afraid Ria, this is the time for courage, not fear. When you come back you will join us, and we will fight side by side.
Your brother,
Jamil.

Ria released her breath, she read the letter again from start to finish, taking care now to read each sentence more slowly, to make sure she had understood it correctly. As she read, she searched for any nuance, any possible ambiguity in his meaning that would prove to her how much he hated her for what she had done. She found none. She tried to picture her brother as he wrote these words, not the Jamil she had thought she knew, but as he was now, a fighter, a leader, just like in the photos Malik had showed her. She could feel the pain in his words. She felt no relief that she found no hatred hidden there. She needed it from him.

Her mother. She felt sad and she felt ashamed when she thought of her. Pain at what they might have done to her after the bombing and like her brother she prayed that she was not still in some prison. Ria could not bear to imagine what it must have been like for her mother to see her own daughter murder Hana. There would be no forgiveness there, she knew that. She watched yet again the silent image of Hana's face exploding before her in her mind as the woman with the cold blue eyes smiled. She couldn't hear it in her mind, but she remembered how her mother had screamed at her. She was relieved she could not remember what she had said. Now she knew what she had done, she realised her body had always known as she now welcomed the familiar pain and the shame she had felt since waking in that hospital. She would willingly carry that pain and use it, as Jamil had said, to fight back as her brother was doing. She welcomed the thought of fighting by his side, but Ria wondered if he would be able to look at her and not be reminded each time of what she had done to their sister.

It hurt her to think of Jamil shouldering all the blame for what had happened. It was not his fault. But had she not blamed him too when she had been holding the gun back in that military base?

Ria looked up at Malik, would he tell her now what it was that she had to do before going home?

"Ria. Are you okay?" Naira asked with concern. "That is a lot to find out all at once, you know. I think we should go somewhere warm and talk."

Ria turned to look at Naira, who was visibly cold and uncomfortable. Naira nodded and gave Ria a quick hug before standing up and starting to jog on the spot. It was bitterly cold. Malik quickly gathered up the photos and the letter and put them back in his bag.

"Malik, please, let me keep the letter and this photo of Jamil. Please. The letter is for me." Ria said firmly.

Malik hesitated. "I will give you the letter, of course. You are right, it is yours to have, but not yet. Now we must leave. It's already dark. It's time to go, we have things to do." He finished closing up his rucksack and then stood up and looked at Ria. "Will you do as Jamil asks Ria? Will you trust me as he does even though you do not know me? Will you trust me like a brother?"

Ria looked at him. She saw his face more clearly now. He looked tired and unkempt but there was a restless energy about him and a certain sadness.

"If my brother tells me to trust you, then I will. You have my word. It would be disrespectful to Jamil, and to you, to do otherwise. Especially after all you've done. You came here to find me and take me back. I will go with you and do whatever Jamil wants. But, what about Naira? She has no reason to trust you or even me, especially now that she knows what I've done. Naira, what do you want to do?" Ria said.

Malik nodded and looked at Naira too.

Naira stopped jogging. "Malik knows about the people in my region, Ria. He also knows my group and we know his. That means he and I have the same purpose. I know that I can trust him as much as I trust you, Ria. Malik and I are fighters. We understand the harsh realities of war. And so do you, Ria. You've always known somehow but it is not until now that it has all come back into your consciousness. At least now you know what you have been carrying all this time. You are no longer that young, confused, transplanted, frustrated young girl. You are a woman in pain, burdened down like so many of us now who have witnessed the depths of human cruelty and the love of violence that so many have. Don't worry about me Ria, nothing in your brother's letter has changed how I feel about you. Nothing, I have been in those places with those kinds of people. It is not your fault. As for you Malik I will do anything to continue our struggle and honour our fallen brothers and sisters. I will stay with you both if you will let me and I will give you the same trust that Ria's brother gives you."

Malik nodded and smiled in Naira's direction. "That is settled then. You are welcome, Naira. Now, let's move. I have a place where we will be safe that's about fifteen minutes from here. I'll lead the way on the other side of the street, you follow behind on the other side. Keep the same pace as me and cover your faces well. There are cameras everywhere."

Ria and Naira nodded. Ria stood up; her legs were weak. She covered herself up more. She stood next to Naira who gently hooked her arm in Ria's. Ria knew Naira was trying to comfort her, but Ria didn't want contact.

Ria stared ahead at Malik. "Why here Malik? We could have met in the town we were in before, why here?" Ria asked frowning.

"There is a reason, but this is not the time or place to explain that now Ria. I will explain when we get to the flat and you will understand why." Malik said.

"There is something you should know before we leave here Malik." Ria said hesitant now. "We didn't leave the detention centre only to come here. We left so suddenly because they were about to arrest me for links to terrorism. That is why we left. Don't ask me any more about that because I don't know anything else. I was due to be taken to prison the morning we left."

Malik frowned. "Well, that explains why you ended up here then. That Black Snake woman must have had something to do with all that. She probably passed on information linking you to Jamil, saying falsely that Jamil is a terrorist. He is not. We are not. We'll have to be even more careful then, you know how seriously they take terrorism here."

"We know!" Naira said. "They wouldn't bother about two refugees leaving a detention centre, it happens all the time, but with Ria's terrorism link accusation, it's a different matter. We have been very careful, and so far, we haven't seen any pictures of her in the papers."

"They won't panic people by doing that." Malik said. "Or admit that you got away."

"I am sure they have more important people to worry about." Ria said mutely.

Malik cast her a sharp glance. "Ria, you may not think you are important to them and that they will not bother about you. It would be a big mistake to think like that Ria. If they are convinced that you have something to do with a terrorist or a terrorist group, they will do anything to catch you. Catching anyone they think is involved with terrorism, true or not, is important to them. It stops the panic that all that stuff on the news is creating. The governments in the West want people to think they are doing their jobs to keep their people safe. The truth does not matter to them. The goal is to keep us out, but if we are in their countries, they make sure we are all watched. So, in their thinking Ria you are a suspected terrorist who has escaped, and your escape proves to them that you are guilty and dangerous. They will take finding you very seriously. They will hunt you down, do not doubt it. Quietly, for sure, but with determination." Malik finished and Naira nodded.

Ria shivered as his words sank in. What he said hardly fit what she was, she was not a terrorist on the run! It was ridiculous, but she knew he was right. They would see things differently like he said. She was guilty, just not of what they thought.

"I understand." She replied. "Just tell me why we are here. Please."

Malik hesitated. "Ria! You are as stubborn as your brother!"

"Malik, please." Ria's voice had gone very quiet.

Malik hesitated, looked around him and then looked back at Ria.

"We are here Ria because *she* is here. The Black Snake is here in this city. That's why. Now, no more talking, let's go." Malik said, turn and walked across the park.

Ria's legs had turned to cardboard once again as she stood there unable to move. It was Naira who pulled her forward after Malik.

52

As they walked behind Malik who was on the other side of the street, Ria felt as if she was just part of an ongoing nightmare, one that had no end. She wanted to run, no, more than wanted, she had to somehow get away from Malik. Her heartbeat had taken off, accelerating to new speeds, she felt lightheaded, and her thoughts were all jumbled up. She was unable to think about anything but the one command her mind was issuing. Run! Ria could not be in the same place as that woman again. She looked around her, warily, checking the faces of all the women that passed. She was relieved that Naira was there. But just the thought that the woman from her nightmares was here in this city was too much to absorb. She felt very panicked. She had to get away. She would not occupy the same space and time again as that woman.

"Ria, stop looking at everyone. It looks strange, just look ahead. Someone will notice you!" Naira's voice startled her.

But she could not stop.

She could turn and run now, just leave Malik and Naira and get back home by herself. She had to get out of this city. This was no coincidence. The woman being here must have something to do with her brother's request. He must have some plan. She was prepared to do anything her brother asked of her, anything because of her guilt and her shame, but not if that plan involved that woman. She felt herself trembling. What if she passed her here in the street? What if the woman saw her?

Ria's mother came into her mind. She was sure that if her mother was alive, she would never speak to Ria again, she would never even look at her again. She remembered how her mother had rejected her in the military base. All she had seemed to care about was Hana, not her. Once again, just as she had in that military base, Ria yearned for the strength and comfort of her mother now. She would have done anything to have her mother look at her and forgive her and tell her that it was okay what she had done, that she understood why Ria had done it. She would do anything to hear her mother tell her that she would have done the same. She wanted her mother to say that she too had heard Hana plead with Ria to shoot her.

But much as Ria needed that from her mother, she also knew that if her mother were alive, it was not what her mother would say. She knew that her mother would never have done what Ria had done. No. Her mother was stronger than that. Ria had shot beautiful, innocent Hana right in the face, as if it were nothing to her, she had just pulled the trigger and blown off Hana's face. She was sure that Hana had pleaded with her to do it, but Ria realised that Hana could not have been in her right mind after everything they had done to her. What about herself? Had she been in her right mind? Clearly not.

As she walked it all came flooding back. She remembered the feel of the soldier's strong grip on her arm and the weight of the gun in her hand. She remembered how cold and stiff the trigger had felt as if it was now. She could see the woman standing there smiling at Ria, her gun pointing at Ria's head. She had to explain to Jamil how it had happened. He had to understand that because of the soldier she could not have pointed the gun at the woman. She remembered that now too. She couldn't have turned the gun on herself either. Jamil had to understand these details about the situation. But it didn't matter which moment of the scene her memory took her to, there was no escaping the fact that in the end she *had* chosen. She had pulled that trigger herself. No one else had pulled it. She had shot Hana in the face. She had done that, and it was time to face it. No excuses. Even if Jamil did know more about Hana's death from Ria, it would only hurt him more and it would change nothing.

If she ran now Jamil would never forgive her. Malik would not let her get away. He watched her every move. She had nowhere to run to even if she did manage to get away from Malik. She had no money, no documents, no experience, nothing, and the police would still be looking for her. Nowhere to hide and nowhere to run. She was trapped, again. She did not have Naira's contacts, or network, as Naira and Malik called it. Exhausted now, she felt something shift inside her. Despite the enormous weight of what she had done bearing down on her, the immense pain of it and the paralysing shame, her feelings suddenly dissipated and were replaced by a sense of nothingness. She was not numb because she could feel it, but she had uncoupled herself somehow from some of her pain.

She could always turn herself in.
Naira tightened her grip on Ria's arm, Ria had been going more slowly.

"Keep up Ria, we should be there soon, he said fifteen minutes. Not long to go." Naira said in a low voice.

Ria nodded absently, and quickened her step slightly, but even though she heard Naira, she was in her own head. She waited for more images. She stared at the woman's cold smile and let her mind roam free now. Her numbness allowing her to see everything her mind had retained and kept hidden from her until now. The more she saw, the more intense the rage and shame she felt. After a while the rage she felt at herself, at the woman, at her brother and at all the bad things that had happened since grew large enough to push away the fear that had paralysed her since she had stood there at the campus and witnessed the gunning down of innocent students. She held herself more upright, she felt new strength in her legs as she let the energy of all her rage spread throughout her body. She took a deep breath of cold air and walked more independently of Naira. She felt the tension in her jaw, still tender after the beating, as her teeth clamped down.

She felt better, stronger, and even older. If Jamil had sent Malik all this way just for her, she could not fail him. It was not something her brother would do if it was not important. She doubted he could spare Malik. As she thought about this, she was reminded of her mother again. She remembered now what her mother had been saying to the woman before Ria shot Hana. Ria could hear her mother's word's now in her head. Her mother's promise that her family would hunt the woman down. Yes! She remembered that now. She had to tell Jamil. Or maybe that was what Jamil had planned anyway and she was the one who would carry out her mother's promise to that woman. She could still do something her mother would be proud of.

But why did Jamil need her if it was that? Malik was much more experienced and trained than she was. Maybe, it was her brother letting her avenge their sister and their mother. That must be it. She would do as her mother had promised that woman, that Black Snake. Ria strode on, her resolve growing stronger with each step. She could finally do something right. She caught Naira flash her a look as Ria increased her speed. Ria could not care more about her fear of this woman than what her mother would want done, what had to be done. It had to be her because of what she had done. It wasn't that Jamil was allowing her to do this, he was making her do it as punishment, to take responsibility for what she had done to his sister. She smiled slightly and stared calmly into the cold blue eyes of the woman in her mind, fighting back the terror she felt every time she saw her. She forced herself to look at her face over and over, preparing herself for the day that she would come face to face with the Black Snake outside of her mind.

Malik had stopped and was standing outside a building. Ria looked around her. No police.

"It's here." Malik said. She and Naira waited while he opened the door, and they followed him into the foyer.

Ria welcomed the warmth of the building. There was a lift, but thankfully Malik chose the stairs. Up and up, they went until they reached the last floor. Ria could hardly breathe with the effort and her legs still felt like lead. Naira went up faster but waited for her on the landing. A door was slightly ajar where Malik had already gone in.

They went inside.

Ria looked around her. It was a spacious, cosy looking room, with a few doors leading off the main area.

"You can have a shower if you want, and I bought some clean clothes for you." Malik nodded in the direction of one of the doors. "Forgive me Naira, I was not expecting you, but you are about the same size as Ria so there are enough clothes for you both. You will have to share the bedroom."

Ria went to open the bedroom door. It was basic, but clean, comfortable and warm. She saw a couple of tracksuits, a few t-shirts of different colours and some black jeans and black sweatshirts laid out on top of the bed and a large folded blue towel. There were a couple of pairs of hiking boots too, she looked, there was a few different sizes. Jamil would not have known her shoe size. She smiled. The bed was a double one and it looked comfortable and inviting after their long journey. She felt her weariness, but it was just her body, her mind was sharp and alert. It was time for a shower, she felt disgusting, bed would come later. She needed to find out what her brother had planned for her.

Ria undressed and stepped into the shower relishing the initial pain of the hot water against her cold skin. She confronted the woman's face in her mind again. It would take time and practice to face the woman in her mind without feeling the paralysing terror, but she knew that the more she did it, the less terrified she would feel. Or at least that is what she hoped because she was nowhere near that happening yet.

She stopped soaping herself and stared at the woman in her mind.

"I'm coming for you." She said out loud as she rubbed the shampoo into her filthy hair.

53

Saying those words gave her a strange feeling of courage, for a moment at least. But why had she pulled the trigger? Had it really been to save Hana or was some part of her ashamed of what had been done to her sister. But how could she possibly feel ashamed of Hana? She had seen with her own eyes how those animals had mauled Hana like she was meat on a table and beaten her beyond belief. What would Ria have done if she had been the one on that table and not Hana? What had Ria done in the cell? Nothing. Hana had shown courage and fought back. Ria had done nothing. She hadn't even said anything when that faceless man had violated her in that pitch dark cell. She shuddered at the memory.

What had been done to Hana defied comprehension. Ria wished she could say with truth in her heart that she would willingly have taken her sister's place on that table, but that would be a lie. She knew her mother would have done so immediately though. Ria was a coward. In that cell when the man came in, she had just laid there, in silence, and taken it, she had not even screamed. She had not even struggled under the weight of him. Hana had struggled hard and screamed.

She rinsed herself off realising she was using a lot of hot water and stepped out of the shower. As she dried herself, she caught her reflection in the mirror. It was the first time in a long time that she had seen herself. She rarely looked at herself. Now as she looked at her reflection, she realised she did not know that person anymore. It wasn't just that she felt different inside, she looked different outside. Naira was right. That was someone else in the mirror - the murderer. She felt a wave of nausea and without warning vomited into the sink.

Scrambling now in self-disgust, she opened bathroom drawers to look for a cloth to clean the sink and the spatters of vomit on the mirror. She found one, grabbed it and made sure that no sign remained of her distress, she sprayed some air freshener she found to get rid of the smell. She reached for clean clothes. These feelings of self-hatred would be hard to bear. They were flourishing, thriving and spreading through her like a disease. She would not be able to withstand the sheer scale of her self-hatred, her body wasn't big enough.

She realised that it wasn't the woman who was the problem. The murderer was standing right here, in this bathroom, safe and sound while her sister's body lay rotting somewhere. Ria was ashamed of the relief she felt at the probability of her mother's death too. While just a while ago she had yearned for her mother's comfort, Ria knew that even if her mother was alive, she would never give Ria anything, let alone comfort. With her mother dead, at least Ria would never have to face her. Jamil wanted revenge. He did not know that he was seeking revenge from the wrong person, or maybe in a way he did. The woman must pay for what she had done, but Ria too would have to pay. One thing at a time. Welcome all this pain that you deserve it, she told herself.

Ria sat down on the toilet seat trying to gather herself before going back out to face Malik and Naira. She could not let them see her like this. It was time to pretend she could function.

When she emerged from the bathroom, Malik and Naira were chatting by the cooker, they seemed at ease with each other. Ria smelt the familiar scent of cooking from home but instead of feeling nostalgic or hungry, the smell of food only made her feel more nauseous.

Naira turned to look at her as she heard Ria come out of the bathroom. "Ria, look, we've made a dish from home!" she said.

Naira's smile turned to a frown. "Ria, what is it? You don't look well. Come and sit. You need to eat, and then get some rest. Let me shower quickly and then we can eat." Naira moved off to where Ria had come from, gently touching Ria's shoulder as she passed her.

"The clothes are in the bedroom Naira." Ria said. Naira veered off into the bedroom and then into the bathroom. She took much less time than Ria and was soon back out. Her hair was wet, and she was wearing a grey tracksuit bottom and a red t-shirt. She smiled. She looked relaxed.

Malik put some dishes on the small wooden table and then placed a large steaming pot in the middle. Ria hesitated. She could not sit with them now and act as if everything was fine. She would not even be able to eat. But she had to. She drew in a deep breath and watched as Malik and Naira sat down.

"Ria, sit down," Malik said. Ria sat down next to Naira.

Ria glanced at Naira. She was again struck by how much Naira had changed since she had given up Khal and how much she had changed since her last suicide attempt. Naira bore no resemblance to the person Ria had known before Ria's beating. Not even two weeks ago Naira had been in hospital, her wrists cut open, almost dying, but not quite. Two weeks! It felt like months had gone by. Time was indeed a strange thing.

Malik served the food. It did smell really good but as Ria looked down at her plate, she felt her mouth go dry.

"Are you not going to eat what we have prepared for you Ria? I'm offended" Malik said eyebrows raised in mock disapproval.

Ria smiled faintly at him. Naira laughed. She picked up her spoon and plunged it delicately into the stew, loaded it with as little as possible and sipped it slowly off the spoon into her mouth. As she tried to swallow, she felt her panic resurface and she was sure she was about to vomit again. She tried to think of something else and forced the food down. She had to eat.

"It is very good, thank you for making it." Ria said with a smile.

Naira beamed and thanked him too.

"It's nice to have real food again!" Naira joked. "And a warm place, and to feel less disgusting. That was the best shower I have had in a very long time!" she said, a little sadly.

Ria nodded and smiled too, genuinely this time.

"Yes, it was" she said, understanding why Naira had said what she had said about the shower.

They chatted easily about home before the war for the rest of the meal. Ria realised that Malik wasn't at all dangerous. He was warm and funny although at times she saw sadness in him. Ria found herself relaxing with their happy banter and was actually able to suspend reality for a while.

Naira got up and started clearing the plates away.

"Naira, leave the plates, I'll do them later. We have to talk now." Malik said.

"Do you want me to wait in the bedroom while you and Ria talk?" Naira offered.

"That's up to Ria." He replied looking at Ria.

Ria hesitated then shook her head, gesturing for Naira to stay. She did not want to be alone with Malik not knowing what he was going to tell her. Naira sat down, looking a little uncomfortable. She looked at Ria and then sat waiting for Malik to speak. Ria's body was tight with tension, and she noticed she was clenching and unclenching her fists under the table as she waited for the next bomb to drop.

"As I told you in the park, the Black Snake, the woman who interrogated and tortured you and your family, is here in this city now. She is staying with her sister. That is how we found her. Otherwise, we would not have. Mercenaries live secret lives, and they cover their tracks well. The mercenary world is a small one. We managed to find out that sometimes when she is not away, she comes here to her sister's house. I imagine she comes

478

to see the children. Her sister has two young children. They can't be more than 6 years old. I have been watching the house since I got here after I left your city. It was easy to find the sister, if you have money, you can find anyone nowadays." Malik stared at Ria and Ria felt herself fade under his gaze.

Malik continued "It was easier to find the sister than to find you. I did not want to be the one to come here, I am a revolutionary, not a spy and I would rather be back fighting at home where I am more useful, but your brother asked me so I could not refuse. But understand this Ria, I do not want to stay here a minute longer than necessary, and Jamil does not want our return delayed either. Are we clear, Ria?"

Ria just nodded. "Why did Jamil not come himself?"

"It just wasn't possible. Leave it at that. The less…"

Ria interrupted him. "I know, information is a burden."

He turned to Naira. "Naira, this is not your problem, you did not know what you were getting involved in by coming here with Ria, you can stay here in this flat, and when we have finished, you can come home with us. I will make the call tonight to the mover. Or you can leave by yourself and go your own way back, it's up to you."

Naira said nothing but looked thoughtful.

"Thank you." She said simply and waited.

Then she seemed to change her mind and said. "Look, I don't know what you are planning to do but I pledged my help to Ria. Malik. I don't judge her for what happened in that base with this woman snake. I know what those places are for, and I have seen what people like that woman do. I want to help if I can, it will help me to help you if you get what I mean. I will not go home without Ria, I promised. I have experience and training so I can be useful to you."

He nodded, seeming pleased. "Great, you are welcome, I'll call the mover after we talk."

"So, Malik, what are we doing here? I imagine my brother would not send you here for something of no importance, especially given the city we are in!" Ria said wearily.

"You are right, Ria. You know your brother well." Malik said.

Ria tensed further and she kept her hands under the table where he would not see them trembling.

"Naira, thank you for your offer to help, and you can help, perhaps, but it is Ria who must do what is to be done and she must do it alone. My presence here is only to make sure she does it, and to help her do it." He looked back at Ria who averted her eyes.

Naira looked at Ria, but Ria could not meet her eyes. Ria's stomach lurched. She looked at him but kept her eyes averted so that he wouldn't see the fear in them.

"What is it I must do?" Ria asked without looking at him.

Malik hesitated, but then spoke. "Jamil wants you to take the sister's life. Just as she took your sister's, and indirectly your mother's too. You have to do it tomorrow morning, first thing, because after that we leave. There is no more time to waste. I have to get back and Jamil wants us back. Now too, with your complications with the police, the sooner we go the better. The arrangements are already made for our journey." He paused. "I have been watching the sister for a few days now. It will not be difficult, even with the woman here. The woman will not be there when you do it. But she will know it was you." Malik said.

Ria pushed back her seat and stood up. She was revolted. Jabbing her finger at Malik she said in a loud voice "No, you cannot ask me to do that. You said we were here because of the woman, the Black Snake, that evil woman, not her sister. Her sister is not the one who did all of those things to us. I cannot take an innocent life. I will not do the same thing she did, I will NOT be like that woman in any way. I will gladly kill the Black Snake! It will be my pleasure. But my brother cannot ask me to take the life of an innocent person. How could he even ask such a thing! It is not like him." Ria said raising her voice even more.

"Ria, sit back down and stop shouting." Malik said loudly. The room went quiet, the atmosphere tense. Ria stood there with her whole body trembling.

"Your brother is not asking, and you *will* do it." Malik said.

"I will *not* do it! Not for Jamil. Not for you. Not for anyone." Ria said. "It is wrong!"

"Not even for Hana, Ria?" Malik said softly.
The blood drained from Ria's face. She sat back down onto the chair, her hands limp by her side.
Her head hung down towards the floor, eyes wide as she stared into nothing, feeling the intense trembling

sensation inside her. She could also feel his tension and his anger flow out from him. She let herself feel her anger again, her only energy source now seemed to be her rage. She kept it close, at the ready, a red-hot heaving mass swirling inside her chest, waiting to be finally unleashed, but now was not the time.

54

What the hell was wrong with Jamil? This was not like the brother she had known. Had he become so broken by the horrors of the war, and by what had happened to them in that base that he had become just like them? She could understand his hatred of the woman who had captured and tortured them, and she could understand his thirst for revenge. She too wanted revenge, not for herself but because her mother had promised the woman herself that they would find her and kill her. But Jamil had chosen the wrong person. Murdering an innocent woman, a mother of two young children, to hurt someone else, someone who had nothing to do with all this senseless violence was not right. It was not their family's way. It would not be her mother's way. Or maybe it would, she did not really know her mother. But to Ria it felt like a sick plan, something exactly like what that cold, evil woman would do.

Ria knew that her resistance was not only because she felt it was wrong, but also because it would not let her redeem herself somehow for her dead mother and sister. She had no issue with the woman's sister. She needed to face the woman who had made her life a living hell, despite her terror of her, and she would consider no alternative. Her mother would have wanted her to do this. She didn't know about Hana, but after what the woman had done to her, she was sure Hana would want it too. She knew Hana would not want an innocent person killed on her behalf, that much she was sure of. That woman who had tortured them was a cruel, twisted mercenary who would kill for money, and, as Ria had seen with her own eyes, she enjoyed human suffering. Ria was no better after what she had done to her own sister, but at least the world would be a slightly better place without this evil woman, But the woman's sister? No. That would serve no purpose or end and had nothing to do with the greater good. She had to reason with her brother. She had been there, he had not. He needed to hear about his mother's promise to the woman.

Jamil knew Ria very well. They were only separated by three years, and he had always looked out for her at school, and at home too on occasions when her mother was being particularly harsh on her. He would defend her and charm his mother into giving Ria what she wanted. Jamil could do no wrong in her mother's eyes until he had started with the protest movements. Ria thought now about how strong her mother was, having to bring up three young children on her own after her father had been killed. They had all been so small. As Ria thought about her mother now, she remembered how fierce and protective her mother had always been when it came to her family. Ria had always admired her but there had always been an unexplained distance between them, their relationship had never been warm as it was with Jamil. Her mother had never been an affectionate woman, and feelings were never spoken of. The first time she had seen her mother show any emotion was in that military base for Hana. She remembered how tenderly she had spoken to Hana as she lay unmoving on the table.

Ria sighed and looked up to face Malik again. He had not moved a muscle. He seemed to be giving her time, knowing perhaps what she was thinking.

"Ria, you will do it. You have no choice. Jamil has decided that is what is to happen so that is it." He said in a matter-of-fact tone. "We will leave before dawn. That is when the sister will be alone."

"Jamil may be your leader, but he is not mine Malik! I will not be commanded like some soldier. He does not know things that he should know. I need to speak to him." Ria said. "There is something important he must know."

Ria pushed her chair back again wincing as the legs scraped harshly against the floor. She stood up again and went towards the bedroom door. She sat down on the bed, her head in her hands. She hadn't even turned on the light. She needed to be in the dark. After a while, she heard a soft knock. She ignored it. The door opened, she looked up, it was Naira. Ria looked away. Naira stood there for a moment in front of Ria and then sat down next to her on bed.

"I don't want to talk Naira. I just want to be left alone." Ria said. "There is nothing to say, I will not do what my brother wants. I would prefer to die."

Naira sighed. "Ria, I can't imagine how you must feel. After all that you have been through today, not to mention what has happened to you before. I experienced terrible things in prison, as I told you, but I was not forced to do what you what were forced to do. I know too that like your sister, I would have asked too to die after all those men raped me. But no one should ever be put in the position you were put in. They do that to break people, to break families. I told you. Your brother, Malik, even me, we have fought in the war. It is not that we know more, we don't, it is just that killing gets easier than at the beginning. I think with time, we become more and more like those we fight. If not, we could not fight them. You cannot have good moral values and fight in a war. Once you take someone's life, you are changed forever. Your brother is in pain. You are in pain. We are all in pain. He has taken this decision from a place of pain and suffering, from a place of anger not reason. You are right, he has made the decision without even speaking to you, without even asking you or wanting to know more. But like you he is in pain, and he feels responsible. It is not rational, but he needs this. You left before the war really started. I am not defending your brother, Ria, I am just explaining something." Naira paused.

"I know I am not a fighter like all of you. I did not get the chance." Ria snapped. "I was taken by them because of Jamil before I even knew there was going to be a revolution or a war!"

"I know. Ria our country is very good at torture, but so is every other country. They just hide it better than ours. This woman is not even from our region, she is a European. In torture, they can beat you, they can inflict pain in a thousand ways, they can rape you and make you do terrible things to others. But I know from all of that, as I think you do too, that the beatings are not the worst thing they do to us. What never heals is what they do to our souls." Naira said.

Ria looked at her. "You are right. Our bodies hurt when they beat us over and over and our bodies never seem to forget what has been done to them even though the scars heal. But you are right, it is what they do to our souls that is the worst and where the true power of torture lies. Once they have slayed our souls, and murdered who we *were*, what is left? It is a fate worse than death itself. I am sick of my body keeping me alive in this way. I know there is no soul in there now. I am tired of bearing such a heavy burden. It is mine to bear, I know that, but I cannot. There was just one more purpose for me left in this existence of nothingness, and now my brother has taken it from me. My soul has gone forever Naira, that woman made sure of that. I feel bad because I think deep down that Hana is lucky to not be alive. This is not living. But it is that terrible woman who must pay for what happened to Hana and my mother if anyone is to pay, not her sister. My mother wanted that woman to pay!" Ria said.

Ria heard her own words too now and knew them to be true. She was completely disconnected from herself, just a body filled with rage and shame, no pleasure, no joy, no sense of any future. She inhabited a physical body that executed its functions of keeping her alive, but it could do little more than that. Ria was no longer Ria so who was she? What was she? She could not remember the last time she had even thought of the future with hope rather than dread. Before the massacre, she had just been a young girl prone to flights of fantasy, disconnected from the reality of things in her own country, happy in her ignorance. But that was then. That person had long gone.

Still staring at the wall, she took Naira's hand in her own, feeling just how cold Naira's hand was, like her own, despite the warmth of the room. Perhaps without a soul you cannot feel warmth. They sat there in silence, each immersed in their own thoughts and pain.

55

Ria couldn't tell how long they sat there like that on the bed. The flat was in silence. She turned to Naira.

"Naira. What Malik is asking me to do. No. What Jamil is *ordering* me to do, is wrong. Surely you agree. If I do this thing my brother demands, then I will have taken a second innocent life. I can never forgive myself for what I did to my sister, never, but it was a different situation to this. None of us believed we were going to get out of there alive. That is what I believed. My mother believed that too. We could not have imagined surviving. Yet, I did but I wish I hadn't." Ria said.

Naira looked as if she was going to say something, but Ria continued to speak.

"If I do what my brother asks, a mother of two young children will die for something she probably does not even know happened. She will die for something her sick, twisted sister has done. What that woman did to us is not her sister's fault. It's not right. I can't do it. That is not vengeance. My brother thinks that this woman, this Black Snake as they call her, will suffer at her sister's death, but he is wrong. I have spent time with this woman, she feels nothing. If her sister dies, she will feel nothing, but rage and that rage will drive her to harm even more people like us in even worse ways. It will become her justification. Do you understand Naira?" Ria asked.

Naira nodded.

Ria continued "This is something I know about her from being in a room with her for many hours and seeing how she reacts. My brother has not seen her, he has not seen the pleasure she takes in the pain and suffering of others, but I have. My mother wouldn't want an innocent woman to be hurt. She wanted this woman to suffer, to die! She vowed it to the woman face! I want to respect my mother's wishes more than my brother's. My mother's words to that woman back there in that base were as clear as water Naira, believe me. I am terrified of this woman and there is nothing I can do to control that terror, but even so I will gladly seek her out and put a bullet in her head. There is nothing I want more." Ria said and knew it was a lie as she said it.

What she wanted more than anything was to cease to exist. She wanted to carry out her mother's wish, but she was so terrified of the woman she doubted she was capable of it. She was too much of a coward, too weak.

She paused to breathe, and then said "They may have murdered our souls as we have said Naira, but this woman who tortured my sister, my mother, and me, she is not like us. She is worse than soulless, she is heartless, cruel, and dangerous. She enjoys the suffering of others. I know you don't, and I know my brother doesn't and I certainly do not. I could feel it when I was with her. She is, as Malik said, an experienced soldier. They called her captain, her men, and she is a woman, and they never questioned her orders once. It cannot be easy to gain that respect from men who are violent mercenaries. Imagine, what she must have done to earn it. It is fear I am sure that drives her men's 'respect' of her." Ria said scornfully as she remembered back.

"Naira, you know that I have no training. I do not even know how to use a gun. What Jamil asks of me is too much. Malik is trained and obviously has fought so why does he not just kill the woman snake? Why the sister? If I could just speak to my brother and explain it all to him, explain what this woman is like, and what our mother said to her, he would understand and change his mind. I will die before taking another innocent life." Ria said.

Naira looked sad. "Maybe your brother would understand Ria, but maybe not. He wants an eye for an eye, it seems, and he has a lot of information about this woman Malik said, so he knows what she's like, her reputation, what she does. The Jamil you knew before Ria, may no longer exist. You and I, we are no longer who we were before, and neither is Malik or anyone who was in that detention centre with us. We are all in pain and doing whatever we can to stop it from taking over. It is only anger that keeps our despair and desolation manageable, it is only our anger that gives us enough energy to go on. I did not take a knife and cut my wrists because I am a coward Ria. I did it because I could no longer tolerate the pain inside, a pain that just grew bigger and bigger every time I had to look at that child. That child that is not mine. He never was. We do whatever we can to stop the pain from becoming everything and we make mistakes." Naira said. "Try to understand your brother, Malik, and yourself Ria."

"Naira, I wish I could go home, and that everything would just go back to how things were." Ria said. "I know that is impossible because things are no longer the same."

"Ria, I understand, I really do. I want to go home too. But there will be no happy ending to this story, not for any of us. I'm going back because there is nowhere else to go and no reason to go anywhere else. I would rather die with the people from my region who refuse to give up and die with them for what I believe in than just exist unhappily here day to day, safe, but broken." Naira said.

Ria was very still now, not just her body, but her mind. Naira was right. What had she been thinking? Had she imagined that she would just arrive home and that everything would be like it was before? She was no fighter. She was not like Naira. She did not even want to fight, but she could learn.

She turned to look at Naira, who was looking at her with a worried expression.

"Naira, you are right. I have been so naïve and stupid. Despite everything that has happened I am still acting and thinking like the immature person I was before the massacre. Jamil may not be right, but he is asking me to take responsibility for what I've done. I have been sitting here with all this self-pitying talk of morals, forgetting the situation at home. He wants me to take revenge for our family, my mother wanted that too, so I will do it, if I can't even do that for Hana and my mother, then I am good for nothing at all in this life."

"Are you sure Ria" Naira said looking at her surprised.

"Yes Naira, but I will do it my way and on my terms." Ria said firmly.

"Ria, are you sure? Don't talk like that to Malik. I am not sure he trusts you yet. What happened back in that base Ria, please, you have to understand that is it not your fault or your responsibility. We are powerless in there. You will find no relief by carrying out your brother's plan. It is yourself you have to forgive. But if it is what you want to do, then I will help you no matter what Malik says. We have got this far together. He cannot force me to leave, and he cannot force you to do anything you don't want to do. Whatever you do must be your decision and it matters little whether you can live with it or not. Believe me." Naira said emphatically.

"I know. But it's too late for redemption, is it not?" Ria said.

"It is, but it is the same for us all, it's not just you." Naira said and smiled.

Naira stood up and reached out her hand.

"Come, let us speak with Malik. He will need to explain more details of the plan he has if this must be done tomorrow. He is a man of few words Ria, and he may seem hard, but I can see that underneath, he suffers a great deal too. He is a good man I think, and loyal to your brother. Do not let his distrust of you fool you into thinking that he is any different from us. He is a proud, young man, so he will not allow us to see his suffering. He probably rarely even allows himself to see it." Naira said.

Ria nodded and stood up. She took Naira's hand and moved towards her to hug her. They hugged each other and for a fleeting moment Ria felt better.

When they emerged from the bedroom, Malik had not moved. He was just sitting in the same place staring into space. He did not even look up when they walked back in, though he had to have heard them. Ria sat down where she had been before and so did Naira.

"I have had some time to think. I have some things too that I want in all of this. But first, tell me, what is it you and Jamil have planned, Malik?" Ria asked, afraid to hear his response.

Malik met her eyes. She looked into his and saw some warmth there. He looked relieved. Then his expression hardened, his eyes like steel bolts.

"Ria, you are wasting my time. You are still too immature despite what you have been through, I think. Are you going to do it or not?" Malik asked.

Ria paused. "Yes. But only if you let Naira help me, if not, I will not. Jamil can go to hell. What are all these conditions anyway? Is he trying to punish me? Has he forgotten that all this started with him? I do it with Naira or not at all. We all go. You too." Ria stopped and waited.

Malik's only reaction was an ironic smirk and a quick glance to Naira who nodded.

Then he said, "You are nothing like your brother, if only you knew him now." he paused, "Ok then. If that is your *condition,* fine. I have no more time to waste on all this. We leave tomorrow after it is done. It is already set up. I have called the mover about you Naira, it's not a problem." He said "Now. Let's go over the plan."

"Wait!" Ria interrupted him, he looked visibly annoyed. "There is something else."

"Something else? Have I not conceded enough and gone against the wishes of your brother already, something that will cost me when he finds out no doubt." Malik snapped at her.

"The woman, she goes too. But I won't be able to do it. I want you to do it." Ria said.

"No, that is not in the plan. The Black Snake stays alive." Malik said.

"Have you ever met her, Malik? In person? Has Jamil?" Ria asked, feeling more in control now.
Malik didn't respond.

"I have Malik, I spent a lot of time with her. She will not suffer from her sister's death. Believe me. but she will be angry, very angry. She will use it to justify harming more of us in even worse ways. She will make that her life's mission. She is a monster." Ria said with so much force that Malik looked surprised.

"NO." he said.

Ria folded her arms across her chest. "Then, I will do it without you."

"I have instructions to bring you back alive." Malik said. "You cannot go up against that woman, none of us can, she is an expert fighter, highly trained. She may be a monster, but she would swat you, Naira and me away like mosquitos." He laughed contemptuously "Don't be stupid,

Ria, this is not a game. We cannot afford to lose fighters. There are two fighters at this table."

Ria flinched. What was she then? Nothing.

He ignored her and started to speak.

"This is the plan Ria so listen carefully. I saw the woman arrive at her sister's house from the airport by taxi with my own eyes last week. I sent you the photo of her that same day. I have observed their routine, it seems very predictable. They don't go out much from what I have seen. This woman will be careful and alert no matter where she is. There are probably many who would like her dead. You can't be in that kind of work and not have enemies." Malik paused, looking down at some papers and a notebook in front of him.

"There does not seem to be a man living with the sister. When I checked her social media, I couldn't see anyone. Maybe she is divorced. Or maybe he is dead. I don't know. She lives alone with the children in a very big house near the park we met in yesterday. It's a rich area as you probably noticed. Since the woman arrived, it is the woman who has taken the children to school instead of their mother. So now that the Snake takes the children to school, the sister leaves the house a little later." he said, then Malik paused. The girls sat waiting.

"So, this is what happens every morning so far since I've been watching them. The Snake leaves the house with the children, then she takes about fifteen minutes to walk the kids to their school. She stops at a café on the way back and gets coffee to bring with her and returns to her sister's house. Because of the coffee stop, it takes her a bit longer to get back and it depends on the length of the queue. But so far it has never taken her more than twenty minutes to get back as she walks much faster without the children. Then, once she gets back to the house, her sister leaves for work." He said.

"How long after does she leave?" Ria asked.

"About ten minutes. Not longer." Malik answered.

"After that the Snake keeps out of sight most of the morning until she leaves for a very long run at midday. That takes an hour and a half in the days I have seen her. She is fit and fast. After that she stays in the house. I cannot see what she does. She does not leave again. Her sister brings the children home with her. Then, they stay inside all evening. I can never see them. The blinds are always down, which is good. You can't see the back garden from the road. The fence is a little high. I didn't go back there more than once in case anyone saw me." Malik stopped.

"But, if the woman is alone in the house all day, and the sister is not, does it not make more sense to kill her instead?" Ria said. "There are three of us, and only one of her."

"No!" Malik retorted. "The woman may be alone, but the house not only has an alarm system but as I already told you the Snake is highly trained, dangerous and will never let her guard down. It doesn't matter that she is visiting her sister. She's still dangerous and will have a weapon close. You Ria, are not trained at all. Naira is out of practice, and the Snake is better trained than me and with decades more experience than I have. She would have us all again to play with and a whole day to do it. Is that what you want? She is at a much higher level than us. It's not about numbers. There is a reason she is still alive after all her years in combat zones. We would not stand a chance, and our deaths would be slow, as you well know Ria." he said.

Ria shuddered. Surely, she would not do things like that in her sister's house, in her own country! One thing is going to wars in other countries for money and doing terrible things, but it was another thing to do them in her own country.

"You will kill her sister. We keep to the plan. The sister is an easy target, and it is the sister who must pay for what *her* sister has done." Malik continued.

"So, what is your plan?" Naira asked after a quick glance in Ria's direction.

Ria looked up now and flashed a sharp glance at Naira, she seemed very interested in this mission that had little to do with her.

"The only window of time we have to do it is when the Snake leaves the house with the children. That is the only time that the sister is on her own. She is on her own for almost thirty minutes. She waits for her sister to return, then she leaves. The plan is to get into the house just after the Snake leaves with the children and she can no longer see the house. We do it quickly, and then we leave out the back garden and out over the fence at the back of the house. There is a small lane there. The fence is high, but it is possible to climb over it. But we will have to be quick. The Snake only takes about thirty minutes in total, some days, a few minutes less and we still have to wait until she drops out of sight with the children before we can go in the house. Time goes quickly under pressure. You will have to act fast. We don't know if her sister has any training, but we should be prepared in case. We will only get one chance." Malik said. "Then, we will leave for home straight after." He smiled.

"But how will we get inside the house? You said there is an alarm. She will not let people like us in!" Ria said.

Malik looked at her and nodded.

"I know, that is the weak part of the plan. You will have to knock. Show her the gun." he said.

"Gun? What kind of gun?" Ria asked.

Malik reached into his bag and took out a gun. He then picked up a long barrel and held it up.

"A silencer." Naira said.

"Yes. If not, we would not stand a chance of getting away. The shot would be heard by neighbours." Malik said.

"Can you show Ria how to use it?" Malik asked Naira.

Naira nodded.

Malik looked back at Ria. "Anything else. Are you ready for this?"

Ria stared at the gun in his hands. "No, but I will be."

Malik nodded. "Naira will show you what to do with the gun. Then, get some rest. Tomorrow is a big day, and we must leave well before dawn." He said and got up to leave.

499

Soon they heard the shower.

Naira and Ria looked at each, got up, did the dishes.

Then Ria picked up the gun.

"Teach me everything I need to know about this." Ria said to Naira who nodded.

It was going to be a long night Ria thought.

56

They stayed up late practising until Ria felt comfortable holding and pointing the gun. Naira had even made her take it apart and put it back together again, just the main parts. She felt more confident and noticed how having the gun in her hand made her feel stronger. It helped her fear.

Ria now lay on her side of the double bed, thinking about Malik's plan. It was a ridiculous situation to be in. Malik and Naira were the ones with all the experience. It wasn't Naira's responsibility but how stupid was it to force the least experienced person, the least fit person to execute something so difficult.

"Are you okay Ria?" Naira asked from the other side of the double bed.

"I can't sleep." Ria said.

"Me neither." Naira said.

"Will I be able to do it?" Ria asked Naira.

"You will only know that tomorrow, Ria." Naira said.

"If I do it, how will the Snake know it was me, that it was us? How will she know that it was our family who did it and not someone else If she has so many enemies as Malik said?" Ria asked.

"I am sure Jamil has a plan." Naira said.

"I hope so." Ria said. "What is the point if she doesn't know who did it?"

Naira didn't answer at first but then she said "You know, people like this woman. When you see them do the terrible things they do when they torture people. Such acts of depravity and cruelty it is very hard to understand, you think they must be monsters, not right in the head, like with this woman, a person who does horrific things to people, even to children. But then she comes back and takes her sister's children to school. It's so incredible, isn't it?"

"It is." Ria said. "It is too easy to believe that these people are sick or not right in the head but maybe it is the only way we can explain the horror and cruelty they inflict on others. My mother called her sick many times, she didn't like it. If we thought that we were all capable of that, you know of taking such pleasure in doing such terrible things, all that cruel violence, I think we would not be able to survive. We need to believe that there is something wrong with people like her. This woman is probably a loving sister and aunt when she comes here, but she never stopped smiling when we were being beaten or Hana was being raped."

"Yes, I believe you. But not all of them are like her. I have seen others who torture, and you can tell they cannot stand what they have to do but I think they are so afraid of what will happen to them if they don't do it. Then that resentment makes them even more angry and cruel. But as you say, it is the ones who enjoy it as much as this woman that are the most dangerous, they have no limits. We should not underestimate her. If she makes any connection to you or your brother, she sounds like a person who would not hesitate to spend the rest of her days hunting you and your brother down. With her kind, revenge is always the first priority, not mourning. She lives for all that violence and terror, the thrill of the hunt. She will come for you and your brother if she knows it is you, but especially you Ria, you have history together. Consider that Ria before putting your name to any note."

Ria listened, Naira was right of course, but what was the point if the woman did not know it was revenge?

Naira continued "You said before you feared her reaction on our people. I think you are right about that. If she knows it is you, or Jamil, she will unleash even more violence against our people in general and in your area in particular. She will come back in a rage and do even worse things. There can be no connection to our people. It must look like one of her own did it."

"But how?" Ria said. "What if we get in, and wait for her to return, then we have both of them! Then she will know what it is like to see her own sister die, then she too can die! We can even make *her* pull the trigger like she did to me" Ria said, all reason leaving her as her anger developed a nasty taste for revenge.

"No, Ria, you are not thinking clearly. She is too well trained as Malik said already." Naira said.

"Anyway, she would not do it Ria." Naira said. "There is no reason for her to do it. She is not being held in a prison like you were. She has nothing to lose because if she refuses and you kill her sister and then her, that is it. She has no reason to pull the trigger herself. No ultimate choice. You have no leverage over her. You had your mother's life to preserve and Hana's. She put you in a situation with impossible choices. What you are thinking is not the same. Do you not see that?"

Ria saw it and calmed her racing thoughts.

She nodded. "I do. I see that. Let's get some sleep." Ria said but was wide awake, she needed to think, to prepare mentally.

57

It was almost time for them to leave. Ria finished her tea. She had not eaten a thing and she had been awake all night. Naira hadn't slept much either. It was still dark outside.

Ria glanced at Malik who was chewing on a piece of bread. He looked really tired as well. They were all going to do this very hard thing tired. Not ideal.

But despite her lack of sleep Ria felt adrenalised. She could however feel the effect of her nerves and the constant doses of self-doubt. A lot needed to go right today for things to go according to plan. She needed to get things right.

Malik sat and took the tea that Ria poured him.

"Tell me about my brother." Ria asked looking at him. "What is he like now?"

Malik looked taken aback by the question.

"What is he like? Malik said and frowned.

"Yes." Ria said, smiling at him.

"He's your brother! You have known him for longer than I have!" Malik said.

"I know, but you know him in a different way, in a different world. To me he was my big brother, I didn't know that much about him. I suppose I never took the time to ask. I wish I had." Ria said.

"I was not well when I met Jamil. My brother had just been tortured and killed. He took me under his wing. He trained me in everything, not just, how to fight, but he spent hours and hours teaching me. I owe my life to your brother and Alana, to everyone in the group really, but especially to your brother. He replaced my older brother for me in a way. We have been fighting together since that day. Your brother is a strong and courageous fighter and leader. He is intelligent and dedicated and he can take the hard decisions you know, the kind no one else wants to take but then he is also very kind and compassionate. Alana, our leader, well, she is also incredible, tough but fair. You will be happy in the group Ria. Things will change for the better once you get home and start training. It is like a family." Malik said and smiled.

Ria had tears in her eyes, for Malik and his loss and his pain, but her tears were more of pride in her brother. He was only twenty-two yet and already a revolutionary leader and a good man. She was relieved to hear that he was nothing like the woman who hunts him, their adversary. She had been afraid of that when she had heard what he wanted her to do.

"Thank you." Ria said.

"Sorry about what happened to your brother Malik." Naira said. "That must have been terrible."

"No more terrible for me than for anyone else in our country but thank you." Malik said. He looked at his watch. "let's go over the plan again step by step then we go."

Ria and Naira nodded. They went over the plan again. Ria would be like her brother. She would let him guide her like he had done with Malik when she got back. She could not fail today. She knew that she was not ready for this. But despite all of her doubts in herself, surely after all she had been through so far, this was the easiest thing to do.

Ria paced back and forth, glancing at the time constantly on her phone while the others finished their tea, and Malik checked his stuff, glancing at her in disapproval.

"I'm sorry." Ria said. "I'm just nervous."

"Well, pull yourself together Ria, this is no time for nerves." Malik snapped and went on checking his stuff.

"How did it go with the gun?" Malik asked looking at Naira.

"Great, she's an expert now." Naira said and smiled at Ria.

"Where is it?" Malik asked.

"It's in my bag. When I get nearer the house, I'll put it in the outer flap." Ria said.

"No, when we get nearer, put it in the back of your jeans like this, safety off." Malik said and stood up and showed her using his knife.

"You don't think I can do this do you?" Ria asked him.

He averted his eyes and started fiddling his bread.

"Answer me!" Ria said.

"NO!" Malik said raising his voice, "I don't. You are not ready."

"I am ready Malik, more ready than ever."

He stared at her. She stared back.

"Malik, she can do it, believe me. She is stronger than you think." Naira said.

Malik glanced at Ria and said. "She's still injured. She's obviously terrified. I hope you're right Naira. We leave in ten minutes."

Naira nodded. Malik got up and went into the bathroom

"Come on Ria. Look, I know this is hard. Very hard. But it will be over very quickly if we all do our part. Okay? But when it comes to the most difficult part with the sister, you cannot hesitate or have any doubts or get confused about where you are. I see that sometimes you go to another place in your head, maybe back to the base. This is a different situation, Ria. To shoot this gun you must be calm and breathe gently. You cannot shoot when you are tense and terrified. It is harder than it looks. I know this will reminds you of what happened with Hana but it's not the same. Remember, you will be the one in control. No-one else. The Snake will not be there."

"I can do this! I know I can!" Ria said, feeling so much more confident now, despite Malik's opinion.

"I know you can Ria." Naira hesitated. "Look Ria, now that Malik isn't here." Naira lowered her voice. "I think I know what happens to you, I have seen it before. It happens to me a lot too. Our minds return to other places, they go back, the body too. When we get to the house today, you are going to see the Black Snake woman for the first time since you saw her in that base when she leaves with the children. Seeing her is going to affect you greatly Ria, and your body and your mind will go back to how you were felt back there in the base with her. But you must try with all your strength to not let all that into your mind. You must do all you can to stay in the present. You will see her, and it will be a shock. There is nothing you can do to prevent that. Do you understand? That is why I think it would be better if you didn't see her. You know when she leaves the house. What if you don't look and when she's gone, I'll let you know. I think it is less risky. What do you think?" Naira asked.

Ria had not considered the effect of seeing the woman in real life would have on her. She had been so wrapped up in her disagreement about the plan, and processing all her newly installed memories, not to mention her doubt about her ability to carry out the plan. Now, she realised that Naira was right. She would freeze. She could not risk that happening. At the same time, she needed the anger of seeing the woman, to do what she had to do.

"I have to see her Naira. If not, I won't be able to do the rest. I need to feel the rage of seeing her. Just make sure that you are beside me, and if you see that I do go back to another time that you will bring me back. Slap me if necessary. I give you permission." Ria said and smiled.

Naira nodded. "It might not be rage you feel Ria, but terror. That is what I am worried about because terror paralyses. But okay. I will slap you if needed. Let's get ready. It's time to go.

Ria nodded and put the gun carefully into her bag. She threw on her coat, hat, and scarf and waited while Naira did the same. Malik was already at the door ready to go. They left the warm room and headed down the stairs and out into the dark, cold street.

It was time.

58

It was a brisk wintry morning as they walked out of the building and down the empty streets, just getting lighter as it neared daybreak. The faint outline of an empty sun rose ahead of them in the pale grey sky. Ria wished she had brought her gloves with her. She shoved her already cold hands deep into her jacket pocket out of the freezing cold. She wouldn't be able to shoot anyone with frozen hands! There was hardly anyone around except the odd dog walker, but traffic was steady despite the early hour. On they walked, the three of them, heads down in silence.

After about fifteen minutes Malik said "It's just up here on the other side of that park. It's a residential area where the wealthy live so we will have to be more careful, there are plenty of cafés around, just like the place where we met yesterday, but there won't be much movement yet. I don't think people like us are a usual sight in these places. With all the terrorist attacks being reported in the news every minute of the day, if anyone sees us hanging around, they will notice and maybe even call the police. We must make sure that doesn't happen. Keep those scarves up and hoods pulled down. Okay?" He said.

Ria nodded and they all walked over to a picnic bench Malik had pointed to. Ria's heart was pounding already, and her legs were playing up again. She wished she could be as composed as Naira and Malik seemed. They sat down on the bench.

"See over there, the big stone house with the black car in the driveway? That is the sister's house." Malik pointed. They all looked.

"It's a big house!" Naira said.

"It will look strange if we sit here with no coffee." Ria said.

"She's right." Naira said looking around.

"Stay here. I'll go. There's a café opening up over there." Malik said getting up. He walked in the direction of a small café.

Ria couldn't pull her eyes away from the house. It was a beautiful house. She thought of her own house burnt to the ground and felt angry. The house had a lot of large windows but as Malik had said all of the blinds were pulled down. The house had a small front garden and there was a large garage. Ria didn't know much about houses or gardens in this country, but it looked like a house that someone with a lot of money would have. The black a car parked in the driveway was big and new looking. The sister must have a good job Ria thought, or maybe it was mercenary money that paid for all of this. This situation felt unreal to Ria. She could not fully believe that the woman who had tortured her and her family in that military base was inside this lovely house, living a nice life with her sister and her children. She tried to picture the woman out of uniform, unarmed, but could not. It seemed a lifetime since they had last met but it had only been a few months. The woman will not have changed, but Ria was no longer the young girl she had been in that cell when the woman had erupted into her world. Now Ria would erupt into hers. She could not understand how this woman could do what she did and then come back here and pretend to be normal and play with her sister's kids. Was there some sort of switch this Snake flipped? A monster when she walked in countries like Ria's but a model aunt and sister when back in her own country. She wondered what her mother would think of this plan. Or Hana. Would they approve?

Ria could hear her own breathing. It was embarrassingly loud. She was breathing much too fast. Had Naira noticed? She tried to slow her breathing down to match Naira's but couldn't. She looked at Naira.

"It's okay." Naira said. "It's normal, just try to breathe more slowly, take control of your body. You are in control."

Easier said than done. Ria thought about all those American films she had watched. She had never seen a hero get panic attacks before the 'mission' or feel a strong urge to urinate or run away. No, they always seemed so confident about how things were going to turn out. She almost laughed. What was she doing comparing herself to a hero? She was no hero, more like the villain and even then, she wasn't that good at being bad.

As she sat there thinking and watching, her body suddenly tensed even more. Was that someone moving near the window upstairs in the house, a woman? She thought she had seen a face look out for just an instant. Her heat raced. Had it been her? Her eyes searched all of the windows, but she saw no one. The blinds were still pulled down. It must be just her mind playing tricks on her again.

Malik returned with three coffees and placed them on the table. He stood behind Ria and Naira.
She felt Naira move beside her and Naira nudged her with her elbow. "Malik!" Naira said.

"I see it." Malik responded.
Ria watched as a small white van pulled up and parked outside the sister's house. Two small women got out, opened the back door of the van, and unloaded mops and buckets filled with what looked like cleaning products. They watched in silence as the women walked up the driveway to the sister's house.

Naira gasped "Shit. They've got cleaners today. That's a problem!" Naira said, alarmed, looking around at Malik.
Ria heard Malik swear and turned to look at him as well.

He frowned and said "They must only come once a month or every two weeks or something. In the days I've been watching I have never seen them. How could I have known!" Malik said, tense and on the defensive. "Damn it" he said, frustrated.

"So now what?" Ria asked. "We can't go ahead with the cleaners in there." Ria felt a part of her wanting the plan to be abandoned, but another part that did not want that.

"It is not ideal but …" Malik said. "We must proceed as planned. We can't wait another day because the transport plans can't be changed with the movers. We are leaving straight after this. The woman could leave any day too."

"But the sister will leave for work while the cleaning people are still there, and by then the Snake will be back. They could be there for hours. " Naira said. "It's not possible Malik. Let's just go. Leave it alone and go home. Our fight is not here."

"I can't do that Naira. I promised Jamil. It doesn't matter about the cleaners. We will proceed as planned, it's our only chance. The time we planned it for is the only time the sister is on her own." Malik said.

"Yes, but she's not going to be on her own, is she? The cleaners will be there!" Naira replied.

"We could come back tomorrow. The cleaners won't be here." Ria said. "It will be safer."

"No! Naira if you want to wait here for us, you can. I don't expect you to do this now it is more complicated. But we leave today, that can't be changed. You know how hard arranging all that is, and we can't afford to wait another month." Malik said. "It has to be now. Ria and I will go."

"No Malik. I will do it." Naira said.

"Quiet! Look!" Ria said.

A woman was opening the door to the cleaners. She was wearing a tight tracksuit and t-shirt, she had long black hair and was smiling. It was strange to see the woman's sister. The cleaners went inside.

"Look, she doesn't look ready for work at all. Let's wait and see, maybe the sister waits until the cleaners leave. You know what these people are like, they wouldn't trust those cleaners, they look as if they are from the Maghreb." Ria said.

"No one trusts their cleaners here." Naira said. "Fatima told me so many things."

Ria looked sharply at her. "You know we are as racist back home about people from the Maghreb as the whites are! We need to change! We think we are the real Arabs, and they are just black Northern Africans, inferior to us because of their skin colour. The well off in our country have them as cleaners too and treat them like crap. The same way as white people treat us."

"Now is not the time for a racial debate Ria" Malik snapped. "In five minutes, the Snake will leave with the children. Get ready to move, and we need to be more careful now with this... complication."

"But what about the cleaning women?" Ria asked.

"We will have to pay them off or something or keep them quiet. They must not scream so we have to get in quick without them alerting the neighbours." Malik said.

"We are not going to hurt them, Malik. I refuse. Promise me that nothing bad will happen to them. They have nothing to do with all this." Ria said.

"Of course we won't hurt them! What kind of person do you think I am Ria." Malik snapped. "But we will have to improvise, and I don't like improvising."

"I am sure they are not loyal to these women." Naira said.

"You never know. They pay them, don't they?" Ria said. "They'll want to keep their job."

"I can give them more money than they will get paid in a month. I'll give them some money. We are doing this today so get ready." He checked his watch. "It's almost time for the Snake to take the children to school." Malik said staring at the house, frowning.

Ria and Naira stood up.

"When we get up to the front door Ria, have the gun ready to show. We need to get in and close the door as fast as possible so no one from the street notices. Everything needs to be fast. Malik, you need to get in quick to help with the cleaners while Ria deals with the woman." Naira said.

"Here Naira, take this." Malik said.

Ria turned to look and saw Malik hand Naira a long knife.

"What about you?" Naira asked.

"I have another one. Don't worry." Malik said.

Ria watched Naira take the knife and hold it up her jacket sleeve. She tensed visibly. Ria turned back to the house and braced herself for the woman's appearance with the children.

"I'm here Ria." Naira said. "We both are."

Ria glanced at her gratefully and then turned back to watch the door. She was tense and cold and terrified as she waited for it to open again. She could not do this. She reached her hand back and touched the gun where she had put it in the band of her jeans. It reassured her, knowing it was there.

"Remember, we have to wait a few minutes until she has turned the corner down the road, if not she could look around and see us. So even when she comes out with the kids we still have to wait. After that we don't have much time. Are we all ready?" Malik asked, his voice sounding higher pitched than usual to Ria. Perhaps a few cracks had appeared in his composure with the unexpected cleaner problem.

"It's messy with the cleaners Malik. I don't like it." Naira said.

"I know, but what else can we do?" Malik said. "Let's just focus. One minute and she'll be out, she's never late." He said moving up to stand in line with Ria and Naira who were still seated.

One minute was nothing but it was also an age. Ria's body tensed even more.

Then as she stared at the door, she saw it open and there she was. Despite the distance, Ria knew immediately it was her. It wasn't that Ria could see her clearly, she couldn't really, it was the way she moved, and above all it was how Ria's body reacted at seeing her that confirmed to Ria that it was indeed her. She didn't need any more proof than that. She watched in disbelief as the woman stood there smiling, waiting while her sister hugged her children goodbye. The woman then took their little gloved hands in hers and with one child on each side of her, walked down the driveway, chatting happily with the children. Ria held her breath. She could see her face clearly now.

"Ria." Naira said and nudged Ria in the side. Ria started. "Remember, we are not there. She won't see you, don't worry. She's leaving. "

Ria could not keep her eyes of the woman and two children as they walked child speed out of the driveway and down the road.

"Three minutes starting now. That's how long they take to turn off this street. Then you go to the front door." Malik said. "I'll make sure first that she has gone round. Wait for my signal. I will nod if it's okay, and if not, I'll raise my hand. Then I'll follow you in. Okay? Everything needs to be fast. Twenty minutes sounds like a long time but it's not. Not at all."

"Ria, did you hear Malik?" Naira asked.

The women and children had now passed out of Ria's view. She let out her breath, she felt her whole body tremble. Her mouth had gone completely dry. The fear was absolute, more than a shock. Her body remembered it all.

"Ok, let's get ready. Two minutes. Look this is harder with the cleaners but just remember what the task is. The Black Snake is very dangerous, so we have to get out before she returns. I will keep time. When I say go, we go. Naira first, then you Ria. I'll help you both over the fence." Malik said. "Let's keep everything calm, simple, and fast. Ready? One minute. I'm going to make sure she has gone." Malik said and walked forward.

Ria said. "This is it Naira."

Ria took the gun from the back of her jeans and held it in her hand, hidden by her bag. Naira looked at it, then at Ria. She squeezed her arm.

"You can do it Ria." Naira said and stood up.

Ria stood up too, her legs shaky foundations beneath her.

Ria saw Malik nod from his position and Naira and Ria began to move. They crossed the remainder of the park, walked over to the house, checked no one was looking at them and walked as casually as possible up the driveway. Ria felt sick. She had no idea how she would react when the sister opened the door, or even what she would say. They were at the front door. Her stomach was churning. Ria looked for the doorbell. It was time. She found it and pressed it hard, fingers clammy. She steadied her grip on the gun and readied it behind her bag.

They waited. It was a strange-looking door. Ria peered at it. It was blue. That was Hana's favourite colour, wasn't it? She struggled to remember now. Ria was sweating profusely, now in the grips of terror, clinging to the gun for the false sense of courage it gave her. Nothing was happening. No one was answering the door. Ria looked at Naira who just shrugged. Ria rang the bell again and looked for Malik. He was just behind them, frowning.

Ria waited what seemed like an age and then from inside she heard the slam of a door, voices and soft footsteps coming towards the door. The door opened, not fully, but far enough. It was not the sister who opened the door. It was one of the cleaners. Caught off guard by the unexpected Ria hesitated.

"Now." Naira said loudly, jolting Ria out of her frozen state.

Ria took the gun out from behind her bag and took a step forward pointing the gun at the cleaner who made an audible gasp and stared wide-eyed but didn't scream.

"Silence" Naira said to her in Arabic and pushed in past the cleaner holding the cleaner by her arm letting her see her knife.

She pulled the cleaner out of street view.

"Ria in." Malik said and pulled her in with him and closed the door.

Ria stood in the hallway pointing the gun at the cleaner, unable to take her eyes of her.

"Time!" Malik glared at Ria.

"Where is the other cleaner and the woman." Naira asked the cleaner in Arabic who was visibly shaking now. The cleaner pointed forwards towards the back of the house, and then upstairs.

"Who is upstairs. The woman?" Naira asked.

The cleaner nodded.

"I'll take care of the cleaners! You go upstairs and quickly. The clock is running." Malik said and making sure the cleaner saw his knife, he pushed her towards the living room area.

Ria looked after him.

"Let's go!" Naira whispered in a low voice.

Naira pulled on Ria's sleeve. "Come on. You have to go first." Naira said.

Ria walked up the stairs, pointing the gun, her legs shaking so much she was sure she would slip and fall back down. Naira was behind her. Ria went slowly up the carpeted stairs. She heard loud sounds like a television coming from one of the rooms. She could also hear every sound she and Naira made, their feet touching the carpet, the sound of their jackets moving, their breathing. Everything seemed as if it was happening in slow motion.

At the top of the stairs Ria stopped and strained to hear. It was hard to hear anything with the blaring noise from the television. She moved along the hall towards that sound, Naira now beside her. She stopped suddenly, she could hear someone, she was sure of it. She looked at Naira and Naira had heard it too, she nodded. They stood outside the door all the noise was coming from. It was half open. She knew she was in there. Ria didn't move. She couldn't do it. She just stood there.

Naira looked at her, pushed the door open and walked in pulling Ria in with her. The woman was standing in front of a tv screen. She was wearing shorts and a t-shirt now and looked sweaty. She turned around at the sound of them entering and Ria watched her expression of confusion.

Ria raised up the gun and pointed it at her. The woman's eyes widened, and she looked as if she was about to scream. Naira got there first, but she still managed a half scream, partially muffled by Naira putting her hand over her mouth and twisting her arm behind her back.

"Don't make another sound." Naira said in English, her hand now covering her mouth.

Naira looked at Ria gesturing her to come forward. Naira pushed the woman onto the bed.

Ria stepped forward, really close now. She could see the woman's face clearly. Her hair was different but those eyes, that face, they could have been twins. She looked terrified.

"Please, don't hurt me. I have two children. Take whatever you want. I won't even report it. Just take everything." The woman said rushing her words.

"Stop talking!" Naira commanded, putting the knife tip on the woman's neck.

"Time" Naira urged Ria.

Ria couldn't take her eyes off the woman. Ria attempted a laugh, but it came out wrong. "You think we have come to steal your things?" She tightened her grip on the gun. "Naira, move away."
Naira moved to stand away from the woman but remained near enough.
The woman said nothing, just sat there poised, not taking her eye of Ria and the gun.

"Do you know who we are?" Ria asked.

"There's no time for this." Naira warned.

"We are friends of your sister."

"My sister?" the woman was crying now, afraid. Ria could see her fear. Was she as terrified as she was?

"Do you know what they call your sister?"
The woman stared at Ria, shaking her head.

"No, come on." Naira said glaring at Ria.

"The Black Snake, that is what they call her. Do you know why?" Ria asked her.

"There is no time for this, come on!" Naira said, turning up the television sound louder.

"Your sister is a monster. How could you let her near your children? What kind of a mother are you?" Ria

521

said moving closer to her now with the gun pointed at her head.

Ria heard a noise behind her.

"What the hell. Ten minutes! Naira go down and watch the street for the sister, she won't be long. I've locked the cleaners in a room. They won't scream, I've paid them." Malik said.

Then he came up and stood to the side of Ria. "

What are you waiting for? We don't have time for chats!" He shouted at her.

"She has to know why." Ria said in a wooden voice, not taking her eyes of the woman.

Naira left to go downstairs. At seeing Malik with his knife, the woman sitting on the bed looked even more terrified. Ria could imagine the effect seeing Malik with his knife out had on her, and her realisation that they weren't here to rob her.

"Do it." Malik said.

The woman kept pleading in English.

"Shut up!" Ria shouted. "Your sister had my sister raped many times. She cut off two of her fingers, and then she forced me to shoot her. To shoot my own sister. Do you know what that feels like? Can you even imagine such a thing? Yet, you let her take your two children to school every day. That is what your sister does, that Black Snake. She is a MONSTER!" Ria's anger took over from her fear now. Ria saw her shocked expression, then her expression changed to fear as she realised that she was going to pay for her sister's sins.

"You have to do it now. We have to go. NOW!" Malik shouted.

Ria steadied her arm.

"I can see her coming, she's only about three hundred metres away." Naira shouted up to them from the bottom of the stairs. "We have to go."

Malik moved towards Ria to take the gun from her.

"You have wasted time." he snapped.

Ria moved away from him.

"No. I'll do it. Leave now. I'll be behind you." Ria said calmly.

Malik glared at her but stepped away. But he did not leave. Ria moved her arm and fired. She was surprised at how easy it was to pull the trigger. Not like that other gun. She fired again.

"Let's go." Malik said. "Now."

He left the room, grabbing Ria by the arm but she didn't need to be pulled. She stopped and pulled away from him.

"I'm right behind you. Go. There's not much time." Ria said.

She ran quickly after Malik who was already running down the stairs.

Naira was there looking out of the glass pane of the door. "She'll be here any minute. We have to go."

Naira looked anxiously at Malik and Ria. Ria saw that she was afraid.

"Let's go." Malik said.

Ria watched as Malik and Naira ran forward towards the patio doors. She followed them a few steps forward. Malik slid the doors open, waiting for Naira and Ria to go through first into the garden. Naira sprinted though and was halfway to the fence in the garden. Ria watched her from the patio doors and then Ria turned and walked back towards the front hall.

"What are you doing Ria, she's coming!" Malik said, looking out to the garden anxiously. "Come on, someone will see us!"

Ria ignored him. She stopped midway in the hall a few metres from the front door. She raised the gun and held it steady, trying to calm her breathing like Naira had shown her.

Ria could hear footsteps approaching the front door. She tried to control her terror. Her hand felt clammy on the gun grip, so she put her other hand up to help her steady it. She kept her eyes on the door. She heard the key being inserted in the lock and turned and her heart exploded in terror. The door opened. Her finger pressed the trigger slightly.

The blond-haired woman stepped into the hallway. She was holding a coffee in her hand. Ria saw those cold blue eyes see Ria standing there, and the look of confusion on her face as she saw the gun. Ria squeezed the trigger, then again, then again. The woman fell heavily to the floor, coffee spilling everywhere. Ria lowered the gun and kept squeezing the trigger until there were no more bullets to hit the body on the floor in front of her. The woman had fallen with her face to one side, one of the bullets had hit her cheek, the other bullets, Ria did not know or care. She looked down at the woman and saw that those cold blue eyes were now unmoving and fixed just like those of the dead students she had seen at the campus.

She was dead.

She felt a hand on her shoulder. A hand taking the gun from her shaking hand. She kept staring down at those eyes, at the strange mix of coffee and blood spreading out on the hallway floor.

"Come on now Ria. You have done well, but we must go now." Malik said gently pulling her away from the woman. "It's over now" he said.

She let him pull her and then she walked with him out into the garden. He lifted her up onto the fence and Naira helped her down the other side, then Malik jumped down.

"Did anyone see you?" Malik asked Naira.

"I don't know. Maybe from the houses, no one here in the lane. But we have to go. Anyone could have seen us go in or come out the back."

"Yes. Let's go. The front door is still open too. Let's go across the park, it takes us through the town, there will be more people there, then we can cut to the flat. I'll go slightly ahead, you two come behind me like yesterday. Naira! Stay close and cover your faces. Look as normal as possible. There are no sirens yet, but we can't be too careful. Let's go" Malik said.

Ria just stood there, not reacting.

"You'll have to help her." She heard Malik say.

"She's got blood all over her." Naira said.

"We have to get out of this lane. Here take this and wipe her face." Malik said handing Naira something

"When we get to the park, she can turn her jacket the other way. Let's move."

"What about the gun" Naira said.

"I have it. I'll dump it, but not here." Malik said.

Ria felt Naira take something and wipe her face.

"She's in shock or something." Naira said.

"She's fine. Let's go." Malik said.

Malik walked off along the lane towards the park. Naira pulled Ria with her.

"Ria cover your face." Naira said.

Ria pulled down her hood and pulled her scarf across her face. She had done it. It was done.

As they reached the park it started to rain.

"Ria, stop a minute and turn your jacket the other way." Naira said.

They stopped under a tree and Naira helped Ria take off her jacket and put it on the other way round. She checked Ria's face again for blood, then they moved quickly off after Malik.

"There's blood on my hands." Ria said, showing Naira.

Ria just stood there staring at her hands.

"Here, take my gloves, put them on." Naira said. "We have to go."

Naira pulled Ria gently by the arm and they moved off behind Malik.

"Are you okay?" Naira asked her.

"I can't feel my legs." Ria said.

"It's just the adrenaline, it will go soon, just keep walking." Naira said.

Ria said nothing else. She just kept walking, staring straight ahead. It was done. She felt no triumph, no exhilaration, no pride. No nothing. But what her mother had wanted done was done. That was all that mattered. Her mother's wish granted. Ria only hoped she would know somehow.

Ria and Naira walked slowly up the pavement, which gradually got more crowded with people. No one even looked at them. Everyone was busy with their own day. Ria kept her eyes firmly on Malik's hat covered head in the distance. He wasn't rushing, just walking at the same speed as others.

"Will we make it out?" Ria asked Naira.

"I don't know. It depends if anyone saw us." Naira said, sounding nervous. "But the flat is not that far, we should be there soon."

Ria nodded. She felt empty, and sad. But she knew her mother would be happy. She felt more worthy now. She had rid the world of a monster, her family's monster. Those children and the Snake's sister would be better off without that evil presence in their lives. The sister would recover, she had only shot her in the arm and maybe in the leg.

"She'll call the police. We have to hurry." Ria said that piece of information only now clicking.

"Who will?" Naira asked.

"The sister. I shot her, but I didn't kill her." Ria said. "She'll call. The police will go there. We have to hurry." Ria felt her panic return now. But why was she panicking? She did not know.

She no longer cared about anything. She had done her duty to her mother, and to her sister. There was now nothing more for her to do. She didn't want Malik and Naira to get caught, all of this had nothing with them. Maybe that was why she felt panicked that they would be caught and punished for something that was not theirs. She felt numb and her hands were shaking uncontrollably. She looked down at her gloved hands.

"It's just the adrenaline, like your legs, it will pass. Don't worry." Naira said.

Ria nodded, and just kept her eyes on Malik. She heard a siren and jumped. She wanted to look behind her, to check that here were police coming up behind them. She looked. There was no patrol car screaming up behind her, just everyday life, everyday traffic on a day she would never forget.

"We're almost there." Naira said.

Ria saw Malik fumble with the door, and hurry inside. They followed him in.

"Come on. Quickly. Close the door, Naira." Malik urged. "They will be looking for us soon. Thanks to you Ria, now they will know what we look like!" Malik said angrily.

He took the steps two at a time. Ria followed him ignoring his accusation. She moved slower on her jelly legs and Naira quickly caught up behind her. The three of them made it to their floor panting hard. Malik opened the door of the flat and in they went. Malik started pacing back and forth, obviously very angry.

"What's wrong Malik?" Naira asked him.

Ria sat down; her legs too shaky to stand. Naira went over to the sink, placed a glass under the tap, and then passed Ria the glass of water. She took it gratefully. Her mouth was so dry. She drank it all down.

She looked at Malik who was glaring at her, got up and walked into the bathroom. She looked at herself in the mirror and removed her hat, scarf, and jacket. She examined her face, searching for more blood. She could see some small spatters here and there on her face, tiny, dried specks on her hair. It disgusted her to think she had that woman's blood on her body. She took off all her clothes and turned on the shower. The water was tepid and soon ran cold but she didn't care. She scrubbed herself as hard as she could for a very long time. She finally turned off the water and shivering badly stepped out of the shower. She reached for the only towel she could see. She wrapped it around herself tightly, and sat down on the toilet seat, crossed her arms against her chest and just sat there rocking gently back and forth, staring at her reflection in the mirror.

Who was it now in that mirror? Not the same person as yesterday even. It was no one she knew that was for sure.

59

The bathroom door opened. It was Naira. She was holding a pile of clothes.

"Here Ria, put these on. We must go soon. You'll be okay. Maybe you don't think you will, but in time you will be okay. Being home will help. Soon we'll be out of this damn country and on our way home. You just need to rest." Naira said, placing the pile of clothes at her feet.

Ria said nothing. She just wanted to stay on that toilet seat, rocking back and forth. It was comforting. But she was cold.

"Ria? Did you hear me?" Naira asked. "The van will be downstairs in fifteen minutes. We can talk later. There will be time once we are out of this place."

"Wait with me, will you?" Ria asked.

"Of course." Naira said and picked up the clothes to help Ria dress.

Ria's hands were still shaking but with Naira's gentle help they managed to get her into a tracksuit bottom, a long-sleeved t-shirt, and a thick, hooded sweatshirt. The new clothes felt soft and comforting. Naira went to get her boots and helped Ria haul them on over clean socks. Ria felt like a small child.

"Let's go." Naira said.

Ria nodded catching one more reflection of herself in the mirror as she moved forward and flinched.

Malik was ready and packed, he hadn't even taken off his coat or hat, he was speaking into a small, old looking mobile phone, the kind Omar that had bought her. He seemed anything but calm. She had never seen him like this. He was always so, well, non-expressive and in control of himself. He still looked angry.

Malik hung up and turned towards them.

"We have to go down now. The van will stop and pick us up. They don't know what it's like at the city exits, there might be checkpoints. But the driver is white, so that is good at least." He paused and stared at Ria. "You shouldn't have done that Ria. We have lost the advantage of time, and she knows what we look like. She saw all of us. Now they will be looking everywhere for us and calling us terrorists!" He said loudly.

Ria heard him but said nothing. She did not even look at him. She was not going to apologise for what she had done, for what had to be done. Out of her peripheral vision, she saw him look at Naira and silently gesture with his arms out 'what to do' question.

"Let's go." He said.

They left the flat again, walking down the steps as quietly as possible. They waited in the foyer, Malik waited at the door to the street, looking out for the van.

After a while he nodded.

"He's here, come on. One by one, no rushing, don't do anything to make people notice us. This is a busy area, but still. He will deliver packages back and forth from the van for a few minutes while one at a time we get in the front of the van. Once you get in, check that no one is watching and then step into the back part of the van, once you are in the back, slide the compartment shut. Naira, you go first." Malik said.

Naira nodded and left. Malik watched.

After a few minutes he beckoned Ria. "Now, you, it's that big white van over there, see it?"

Ria saw it. She left. Walking slowly, not trusting her own legs, she left the building. She went over to the passenger side of the van, which was parked half up on the pavement, and with difficulty climbed up into the front seat. She looked around to see if anyone was paying attention, no one was. She looked back, Naira was there, beckoning her back. She moved between the gap in the front seats into the back that was filled with packages. She slid the compartment shut.

They waited there. Soon Malik was in the back with them. Malik closed the compartment shut and they sat there in the dark, the only audible sounds, their breathing and the traffic.

"We're vulnerable here. He needs to get moving." Malik said, looking at phone. "They must be looking for us by now."

After a while, they heard the driver door swing open and felt the van lurch a little with the weight of someone getting in. The engine started, and the van moved off slowly stopping every now and again, the driver getting out to deliver packages that Malik passed to him from the back and then moving off again. This went on for quite a while.

"It's time now." The driver said.

"Okay." Malik said, looking nervous.

The van moved off, and gathered speed and didn't stop again to deliver any more packages.

"It looks all clear." The driver shouted back after about an hour.

"Good." Malik said.

Ria saw him relax a little.

"How long are were going to be in this van?" Naira asked Malik.

Ria listened absently.

"A few more hours, then, we will change to a bigger truck. Then we will make some a few more changes between different trucks until we reach Turkey. There, it is a little more difficult, as you know. But Jamil has good contacts, it was not hard to get out, so it should be easier to get back in. No-one in their right mind will be trying to get in where we are going. But we have safe passage there." Malik said.

"Where are we going?" Ria asked.

"Home, Ria, home." Malik said. "We will enter at a point along the border about one hundred kilometres from your town, it's a black flag zone, but friendly for us."

Ria looked at Malik "Once we are out of this country, I want you to leave me behind. Not in this country where they will be looking for us, and for me. I want to stay behind in the next one. I don't care which one it is." Ria said.

"No. That's not happening. We cannot speak about that now." Malik said.

"Why not?" Ria countered.

Malik glanced towards the driver.

533

Ria looked away, irritated.

Malik looked at her "Ria. We are not out of danger yet. They will be looking for us everywhere. If we are lucky enough to cross the border at all, then, we can talk about why you would even suggest such a thing. But not now. Don't forget that we are in danger because of what you did. Or, more what you didn't do." Malik said in a tone that silenced any further talk and Ria, like Malik and Naira, just sat there in the dark trying to keep calm as the van trundled along.

60

They had just changed into the second truck. Ria thought it must be night by now, but her brain wasn't working very well, so she couldn't be sure. The truck was similar to the one she and Naira had travelled on. The light was dim and there were a few thin plastic-covered mattresses slung along a wall of high crates. They were all very cold and sore from all the bumping around in the back. To Ria the whole thing was still surreal. It had all happened so fast.

She was on the run again, but this time it was different, she was a criminal on the run this time. She was no longer the young girl who had escaped from the detention centre whining all the time about the unjust accusations levelled at her. It was cruelly ironic that what she had just done would actually be deemed an act of terrorism. Those charges that had seemed so unfair to her just a few days ago had become true, fair, and accurate. They had been prophetic. But it was not an act of terrorism that she had carried out. It had been an act of vengeance.

She was no terrorist. She had not bombed a marketplace full of innocent shoppers or slashed some innocent people on a train with a knife. It was true that she had taken someone's life, but that person was not innocent. She had done something good. She had rid the world of a monster. That hardly made her a terrorist.

She had shot three people now and killed two of them. She was a murderer. Not a terrorist. She had seen the terror on the sister's face. It was not the same look that had been on Hana's face. Horror, terror, desperation, what was the difference? Ria didn't know. She could feel the cold horror of what she had just done, but she felt no regret. Instead, she felt a certain release. That ever-present feeling of guilt and shame remained strong inside her and would always be there, she knew that. But it was not caused by what she had just done. Those feelings were why she used to go to the bridge every evening in the other city. It was why she had always had such a terrible feeling inside her. It was all because of what she had done to Hana. Malik had told them a couple of hours ago that they had crossed the border and were finally out of the country and were crossing into The Netherlands. Malik had explained already that they would have to go the long way home. It was too dangerous to go the other way, too predictable and not possible.   Malik and Naira had cheered when they had been told they had crossed the border and left that place behind. Ria could see they both looked visibly relieved. They were now in good spirits. Malik's anger had dissipated.

Ria had not spoken since she had asked to be left behind once they had crossed the border into a new country. She bided her time.

"Are we just going to keep staying in trucks all the time, without ever getting out? Now that we have left that country, surely, we can stretch our legs. I need to go to the bathroom. Don't you need to eat?" Naira asked.

"In about an hour they will stop. If they are looking for us, they will be looking on the eastern route, not on this one. They won't expect us to go backwards or to go the long way around and even if they did, they can't possibly have enough resources to monitor every route. But we will still have to be careful. Just in case. The police here will have been warned and informed. They know what we look like, and they know who you are Ria." Malik said.

"Have you told Jamil?" Ria asked.

"No. It's too dangerous to contact. There is no rush, is there?" Malik said.

Ria shook her head. "No."

"Ria, he will be proud of you. Now, put a smile on that face. You have just done a very brave thing. I am so proud of you. Hana would be proud of you, and your mother too." Naira said smiling at her. "Stop being so grumpy Malik, it all worked out. You said she couldn't do it, but she faced her greatest demon. It's more than a lot of us manage to do in a lifetime."

"Yes, you are right. I'm sorry Ria, it was just you know, all a bit close, and I suppose I was so afraid myself of having to face the Black Snake, and I didn't want to fail Jamil, or you." Malik said. "I understand why you did what you did. It was very brave. I know I could not have done what you did. You faced the person who you fear the most. Only the truly courageous can do that. I take back what I said about you not being anything like your brother. You are just like him. You should be proud! You are a courageous warrior who has avenged her family!"

"Proud? What is there to be proud of? I have murdered two people and shot another in less than six months. I murdered my own sister. I am not yet twenty years of age. Once we stop at this place, you will continue on without me. I am not going back to the war. I am tired of running and hiding and of all the violence. Let them catch me, I don't care. I will shout out to the police that I am here. You and Naira, you can go home, it will be easier for you without me, they are looking for me mostly, or all three of us, not two. I cannot go home. Do you not understand?" Ria said looking at Naira.

She saw sadness in Naira's eyes but there was understanding there too.

"Of course, I understand Ria. I understand. But don't just give up and hand yourself over to the police! You can't let them imprison you. You won't manage in prison, and they have no right. Come home and join your brother's group, you'll have a purpose."

Ria shook her head.

"Ria you cannot just give up. You have done nothing wrong. These people like the woman you have just killed come into our country as if they own it. Foreign soldiers from other countries come into ours without knowing anything about us, and just start killing us for money or for power or for whatever agenda. It doesn't matter if it is the West, the Russians, the Turks or the Gulf States who does the killing, they are all the same in the end. So don't feel bad about killing this woman, Ria! They just walk around in our country, their spies, their soldiers, their torturers like they have the right to be there, telling us what to do in our own country but when we dare come to their countries for refuge, for safety, or in search of a life without conflict, conflicts mostly of their creation, they don't want us there. It doesn't matter whether it is people like us, people like Fatima, or even people like those cleaners who we just frightened to death. They treat us all like inferior beings or potential terrorists." Naira said, passionate now perhaps as she neared her country again.

She was getting carried away it seemed to Ria, Ria didn't feel bad about the woman. She just wanted to leave.

But Naira continued. "What would they even put you in prison for Ria? After everything that has been done to you by their own people. Everything that you and your family have been through at the hands of this woman and her men, and our own pathetic, psychopathic military and they put you in prison? No! It is not right. Instead of treating you well after being tortured you were almost beaten to death by a group of young men and then labelled a terrorist when you are the furthest thing from that. But that woman you just killed, that Snake, she can do her killing in our country, even get paid well for it and then come back here to rest, walk free, and there is no prison for her! Such double standards! Torturing and killing one week and then free to walk her sister's children to school while she has young girls raped in our country! Where is the justice in that? You have brought justice finally to the equation Ria!" Naira was speaking low but with such passion, she had grown louder.

"Quieter Naira, please!" Malik said.

"I know Naira, but I feel no elation or relief. Just exhaustion. I am sick of all the violence and my own hypocrisy. I can't go on. I have done my duty to my family, but I will make my own decisions now, for once. I did what that woman told me to do in the military base and I killed my own sister and for that I am forever damned. I did what my mother wanted done by carrying out her promise to that woman and taking her life. I did all of those terrible things. That is the truth. Jamil does not own me. I owe him nothing. It is time for me to make my own choices now for once. Until now, all the choices have been made for me or about me. I will never let anyone have that power over me again. I will stay here in this place and that is final. You have each decided how to live your lives. Naira, you know you have. You want to go back and fight for your region. Malik, you want the same. That is noble, honourable, and whatever, but it is your choice, if there is even such a thing in war as choice. I do not judge your choices so please do not judge mine. I am no fighter and I have no desire to learn how to become one. This is a war we have already lost yet it is only just beginning. Our country will never be the same again, but the same people will run it. Nothing will change. There is no sense to all this violence. All these wars and for what? Maybe you see me as young and naive, but I certainly do not feel young anymore. If there is even a tiny piece of my soul still in there somewhere, then it has already lived a thousand lives. That is long enough." Ria said.

Malik looked at her and nodded.

Ria saw it in his eyes, he understood.

"Jamil will not be pleased." he said.

"You sound dead Ria. I know you. You are not someone who just gives up, do you not want to see your brother again?" Naira said, frowning and looking concerned.

Maybe she felt let down too, after all they were supposed to make this journey together.

"You were right when you said it to me before. Without souls, we are dead inside, Naira. When you kill, your soul dies." Ria responded, unmoving, she felt so heavy.

She knew Naira would be just fine with Malik. She also knew that Naira too felt dead inside and that her only way of surviving was by returning to fight. It was the only way she could feel alive after all she had been forced to endure during her own long torture. Without fighting, Naira would only have a long black abyss to stare into like Malik who no doubt fought to keep his own demons at bay, caused by the torture and death of his brother.

"Naira, you have been a great friend to me. I do not deserve you, I would not be here today, alive, if not for you, and for you Malik. But I have come to the end of my journey. I cannot look my brother in the eye or anyone else in my town for that matter. They all know what I have done. But even if they didn't know, even if they had more important things to worry about and surely, they have, I will always know that it is me who pulled the trigger and murdered my own sister, my own blood. No words, no deeds, nothing can ever make that right, it is too big a stain. A stain that never stops spreading inside me. My brother would never be able to forget it either. Every time he would look at me, that is all he would see. The person who killed his youngest sister and he will never stop asking himself why I did what I did to Hana. Deep down he will always believe there was another decision I could have made. The decision to not pull the trigger." Ria said then paused.

Malik looked at her with kind eyes. "There was no real choice in that situation Ria. In torture, the only choice is to comply or die, and we die anyway, one way or another, no matter what promises they make. When I started to train as a fighter with Alana and your brother, they taught us about all the torture techniques used by our regime, by the Americans, by the Russians, by these mercenaries in case we got captured. When I heard about how they break people to get information or just to frighten others, I remember thinking to myself, that I would never break. Not me. I was new and stupid. I thought nothing would get me to turn on my comrades, or on my family. But when they have you, they break you without effort, no matter how strong you are." He said.

"That's true Ria, we have had many tortured by the Americans, it is their speciality. We do not blame our comrades, but each time they torture one of us, we have to change everything, and we cannot let them come back and fight because they are never like they were before ever again, and we know they were forced to give up information. That is understood by all of us from the beginning. Malik is right." Naira said.

"So how will you fight then?" Ria asked her.

"I don't know. I will have to persuade them to let me." Naira said.

"This hand of mine." He held up his fingerless hand, "that happened when I was shot in one of the attacks. It hurt a lot, not so much the pain of the injury but the shame of the mutilation. It took a long time for me to get over it. But I did and I am alive but that is nothing compared to what they did to my brother, or to you Ria. Some nights I cannot sleep worrying that someday the same thing will happen to me." Malik said, now, dropping his hard composure and looking young and vulnerable again. "I pray I die by a bullet, or even a bomb, but not in some prison, tortured like my brother and so many more of us."

This was the most Ria had ever heard Malik say and she looked at him. He looked so very sad now as he talked about his brother and his fears. Ria had not been kind to him, she had treated him like an enemy. Now, she stood up, and walked shakily over to him. She sat next to him and put her arm round him and hugged him. Then she took his damaged hand in hers and they sat like that for a while, saying nothing.

She looked at Naira and saw that she was crying. It was a nice way to part Ria thought, no matter how sad and damaged they all were, they were finally being honest about their pain.

She knew he would let her go.

61

The driver pulled back the sliding compartment door that separated him from them.

"Here, you can get out here." The driver said. "You have thirty minutes. No longer."

They got up, rubbing their cramped muscles. Ria really needed to go to the bathroom, she had been doing her utmost to hold it in, she was not going to pee in the bucket that had been provided for them in front of Malik, or even behind him. They all seemed relieved to be getting out.

"Have you checked the area?" Malik asked the driver.

"Yes, all clear. It is not the usual time for police patrols. Try to look as clean as possible. Go to the bathroom first, clean up, then if you are going to get food or coffee, you will not stand out. Then be sure to have it outside."

Malik slid the compartment back.

"You heard him. Let's get cleaned up and have a last drink together." Malik said, smiling at Ria.

Ria smiled back and nodded. Naira put her arm around her friend's shoulders, and they made their way to the back of the truck and waited for the driver to open it so they could jump down.

It was daylight. Ria felt the cold breeze on her face and smiled. It was sunnier than usual. She felt lighter somehow, knowing that soon all of this would be over. She jumped down after Naira and Malik and they made their way to the bathroom area. They would meet outside when they had all freshened up.

Malik was there when Ria and Naira came out. They all looked much better. They might still smell a little, but not as badly as before. Ria felt they looked a bit more like travellers and a little less like criminals now.

"I'll go and get us some coffee and something to eat and we can have it over there." Malik said pointing to a nice picnic bench far from the car park, but still not too far from the truck. They could talk freely there and get some fresh air. It was in the sun.

"Good idea. Yet another picnic bench" Naira said and smiled.

Ria laughed.

Malik laughed too and moved away towards the restaurant to get the coffees.

Ria and Naira walked over to the picnic bench and sat down. It was a bright winter's day. A nicer day than Ria could remember experiencing in months. It was nice to see the sun again and a blue sky. She had missed that. It felt good to be outside after so long cooped up in the back of a trailer.

"I'll miss you, Ria." Naira said and looked sad. "I wanted us to go home together. You know you could come with me to my region. I understand what you mean about your brother and the people in your own home town, knowing what happened."

"Thanks Naira, that's very kind of you. I'll miss you too, and Naira, I can't thank you enough for everything you've done for me." Ria said. "I'm sorry you got mixed up in my family mess. It can't have been easy for you." Ria felt awkward mentioning it, she had never asked Naira how she had felt after what had happened at the house. She had made it all about herself, as usual. "Are you okay? I didn't even ask you." Ria said looking concerned.

"I am Ria, I was nervous. But I didn't do much. You did it all. It was a brave thing you did Ria, dangerous, but I understand why you had to do it. But she could have killed you." Naira said.

Ria nodded and smiled.

"I know. But she didn't. She probably didn't even recognise me before she died." Ria said. "That's the sad thing."

"You don't have to be sorry for me. I am happy to have helped and glad to have met Malik. You know, I think I like him." Naira said and reddened.

Ria laughed and said. "I knew it! I noticed how you would always change when he was around. I see how you look at him." Ria laughed. "And you were jealous when I went to sit near him before!" Ria joked.

"I was not! Stop it! He'll hear." Naira said. "Seriously, I am glad you finally saw that side of him. You always seemed angry at him." Naira said.

"Not really at him. I was and I still am angry at myself, angry at my brother, angry at everything that has happened. I suppose because Jamil wasn't here, I just took all my anger out on Malik instead. He wasn't exactly charming to me at the beginning either! But I can see now that he's a good man. A very good man for you." Ria said and smiled.

"You must tell him how you feel about him when I have gone. Naira, promise me." Ria added.

"I can't. The journey is long. If I tell him and he gets all strange like men do because he doesn't feel the same way, we will both feel uncomfortable for many, many days." Naira said. "So, no."

"Well, you will be together now for a couple of weeks so you will know how he feels. Something tells me you will not be disappointed." Ria said. "I wish you well with the rest of your journey and thank you Naira."

"So how will we stay in touch?" Naira asked.

The question hung there but to Ria's relief, Malik was back with everything, and the rustling of paper bags began as they dug into the food first and then the coffee so Naira's question remained unanswered.

"So, is it here you will stay Ria?" Malik broke the silence.

"Yes, for the moment." Ria said and looked down at the green grass.

Then as Ria fiddled with her sugar and coffee, Malik started to hum. Ria recognised the song immediately. Malik was humming the song *'Yalla Erhal Ya Bashar'*.[2] He was humming it more slowly than it was usually sung. Naira joined in with him singing the words and they sang it softly together. It was the most beautiful thing Ria had heard in such a long time. Goose pimples sprang up all over her skin and she wanted to cry. Finally, she let

---

[2] This is a Syrian song that translates as: "Come On Bashar, Leave". It was a protest song first attributed to Ibrahim Qashaoush who was found murdered with his vocal chords cut out. It was later attributed to Abdel Rahman Farhood. It was directed at the President of Syria, Bashar al-Asaad

herself. The song brought back so many memories for them all, happy memories of the days when all of the students in their country were singing this song together at the protests. It was a song of hope and determination.

She felt a huge lump form in her throat, but unlike before, the lump was from happier feelings, though the situation was sad. She looked up at them both, her only friends now. There could be no better farewell. The tears kept on coming, welling up inside her like a huge torrent that she could longer contain. She cried for Hana, for her mother, and for all of them. As Malik and Naira sang, she smiled through her tears. When they finished, Naira moved over to her and hugged her. Malik stood up and hugged her too.

"Goodbye Ria, you have fought well. I will tell your brother how brave you are. He will be proud, but not happy that you have stayed here. But he'll get over it." Malik said and smiled. Then he turned and walked away, back in the direction of the truck leaving the two girls together.

Naira was crying too. But it was time, they had to go. The thirty minutes was up. Ria hugged her tightly. No more words needed to be said. She could feel Naira's cold, wet cheeks against hers. Then, Ria pulled away, and let Naira go. They looked at each other and smiled. Naira turned and walked after Malik.

Ria sat down again, turned towards them, and waited until they were closed up in the truck. She watched as the truck drove away and sat there alone for a long time after, sad but enjoying the sun and the cold breeze on her face. She realised it was the first time she had been alone in a very long time.

She picked up her coffee to finish it and as she picked it up, something blew across the table. She picked it up, it was a small envelope. She opened it and there were some folded notes inside. She searched for a note, nothing. She counted the notes, three hundred euros. Malik must have put it there when she had not been looking. She would need it all. She was grateful to him. What had been her plan for money? She hadn't had one. All she had had was the decision to no longer proceed.
The money gave her options though.

She went back inside, covering up well and keeping her head away from any cameras. She looked around in the shopping area for a smartphone and picked out a cheap model. She went back to the serving area and got herself a tea and took it to the seated area searching for a plug. She had seen the signs for free wi-fi. She just needed to charge the phone. She found a table near the window towards the back, well out of sight and plugged the phone in. While she waited for it to charge, she sipped her tea, just observing the comings and goings of people in this new country that she did not know and for once thought of nothing.
The phone did not take long to charge. She turned it on and connected to the wi-fi. She first checked to see where she was, and where the nearest town was, then she spent a long time on the internet, searching. She didn't know what she was searching for until she found it.
She smiled.
Now, for a taxi.

62

15 months later, The Netherlands

It was a beautiful spring day. Ria could not see a single cloud in the sky. Ria looked at her watch and saw that it was almost time. She felt a slight twinge of nervousness as she looked around the beautiful garden area from the white wooden bench on which she sat. She smiled. It was like a scene from a film. But it wasn't, this was real life. She got up and entered the modern-looking building that had been her home for almost a year now. She nodded to the receptionist and smiled. He smiled back, and she walked down a long corridor to stand outside a heavy, wooden door.
She knocked.
"Come in." Ria heard a woman say.
Ria opened the door quietly and went in. Quietly was how everything was done here, and she liked that. It calmed her. The woman she had come to see stood up to greet her.
"Ria, come in, please. Isn't it a beautiful day!" The tall dark-haired woman said as she smiled warmly at Ria.
"Hello Martina. Yes, it is! So nice." Ria said.
The woman gestured for her to sit.
"This must be a very important day for you, Ria. You have been so patient. It has all taken such a long time. I know how hard it has been. All the waiting. The constant questions." Martina said.

"Yes, it has been hard, but being here has helped. The team is so wonderful. Everyone is so compassionate and kind. I consider myself lucky. Others like me are not so lucky. You do such important work here. I am more grateful that you will ever know" Ria said.

"I am so glad Ria. You have worked very hard. Coffee?" Martina asked.

"That would be great. Thanks." The woman strolled over to a small cabinet where a capsule machine stood and popped in a coffee capsule. Soon the gushing, gurgling machine spewed out a coffee.

The woman handed her the coffee, made one for herself and sat down. They were seated opposite each other, as they had often been over the last few months.

"So, as you already know, the court has finally granted your petition." The woman said.

Ria nodded.

"I have to say we were surprised when the lawyer called to tell us the news, as the court had refused it the first time. The lawyers think they were concerned about setting a dangerous precedent, and of course, they are very worried about public opinion. But fortunately, they accepted all the counter arguments so this time they granted your petition although with some conditions that I will now explain."

Ria sat forward in her seat.

"As you know this is still a relatively new law, so the legal and ethical territory is still a bit blurry when it comes to cases like yours. You are the first person to petition for assisted suicide on the grounds of intolerable

553

suffering without having an illness with a terminal prognosis. So, in terms of human rights, it is a big deal and something to celebrate because until now what you have achieved was impossible. Even with terminal cancer, it is not easy. Someday I hope that suffering will be looked at with more compassion. The challenge with cases like yours has been that unlike a terminal illness, it is impossible to objectively or medically establish the degree of human suffering at which life becomes intolerable for euthanasia to be a legal option. This is ridiculous because almost a million people die by suicide every year not to mention the huge number of attempted suicides every day. Then, as you also know, anything related to torture is so, well, blurry. States and courts get nervous when torture is tabled. So, in your case, you having the courage to share your therapy transcripts, and be prepared to go on record about things that are so hard, and the fact that it could be corroborated made the difference. I know that all that was not easy for you." Martina stopped and smiled at Ria.

"No, it was not. But I understood the need for caution with these cases. The lawyer explained it all to me. There are so many things that we feel on a human level, suffering in particular, but we just don't have the words to describe the depth or quantity of the pain. Maybe we have the words, but we don't use them often enough or they fall short. Perhaps it is only the language of poetry that can express them well enough." Ria said. "That is what I have discovered these last months."

"That is true, we lack emotional range in language, on a human level but especially when it comes to legal language and understanding. Law is often the opposite of emotional. We have had cases here of people who have been tortured beyond belief and are unable to express what they have gone through or how they feel. Some stop speaking for years. People retreat away inside of themselves and many never come out again. Torture breaks us, usually for ever. The tragedy is too that ill treatment and torture are rarely spoken about. Not one government will engage on the topic in any serious way, yet ill treatment and torture thrive in practically every corner of the world, despite all the denials and platitudes. It makes me so angry. Maybe I've been doing this work maybe for too long!" Martina laughed at herself, and her tone changed.

"You should be proud of yourself Ria for having faced your suffering and had the courage to do what you are doing. It shines a light on a very dark subject." The woman said. "You should feel proud of yourself."

"Thank you, but it would not have been possible without you and your team's help, really. Each and every one of them has shown me the difference human compassion and empathy can make. The granting of my petition for assisted suicide is a sign of hope in a very dark world. As you say, we are on a very slippery slope in our world today, not just in my country." Ria paused. "I do not deserve to live after what I did, so this is the best way out for me, as I can also speak about the things that really happen. There are so many people in here who deserve to live better lives, but I am not one of them. This is my way of taking responsibility for what I did."

"I know you believe that Ria. We have talked of this many times." Martina said. "But please, try not to judge yourself so harshly Ria. You have seen many others here in this centre who have been through things like you even though they will never speak of it. Try to show some compassion to yourself." Martina looked at Ria.

Ria looked away, embarrassed.

Martina continued "Ria, even though you have been informed already about the procedure, now that your petition has been granted, I am obliged by law to talk you through the next steps and a couple of the conditions the court has set. Is that okay? Then you must sign a document saying that I did that." The woman rolled her eyes and smiled.

Ria nodded and smiled too.

"We have received the official permission. I will give you a copy when we finish. So, first of all, you must state on this form here that you still intend to go through with this, you must sign that today. This is so the court can be sure that you still wish to do this. Then there are more reconfirmations checks. These checks are in place to make sure that the person, you in this case, has time to reflect and understands what they are doing. You can roll all of this back any time you want. You can change your mind at any moment. From now until you check in to the clinic you must see a court appointed therapist specialised in these types of petitions once a week."

Ria nodded. "Yes, I understand, but I won't change my mind. No problem about the therapist."

"Then, if you reconfirm in a month's time, you have a face-to-face confirmation process with a specialised judge, and a report is submitted to the court by the appointed therapist. Their job is to ensure soundness of mind and that you are fully aware of what your decision implies. If there are no issues, you will hear back a few days later. Once that happens, if you still wish to proceed, you can make the appointment at the clinic for the day of your choosing. So, all told, it will take another six to eight weeks, give or take." Martina said, and looked at Ria to see if she had any questions.

"That is all okay. Thank you." Ria said.

"Are you sure there is no-one you want us to contact for you? Back home perhaps? I know you said that there was no one, and I know things have become even more complicated there but perhaps now that they have granted your petition, maybe you think differently about that?" The woman let the question hang there a second.

"No thank you. There is no-one I want to inform. I am sure about that." Ria said. "But thank you for offering."

"Do you want anyone to be notified afterwards?" Martina asked.

"No. There is no need for that either." Ria said.

"You are the first person of your age, who is a victim of torture to avail of euthanasia granted on compassionate grounds because of intolerable suffering. We are legally bound to respect the court's gag order so don't worry the press couldn't print anything even if they found out. The clinic has the same restriction. No one will know. One of the conditions apart from everything else, is that you are not allowed to speak to anyone about this." the woman said.

"I won't. I understand. Will there be any problems with my terrorist allegation problem?" Ria asked.

"No, the human rights people have dealt with that. The country in question didn't want any information about the mercenary who tortured you coming to light. Mercenaries are supposedly illegal. We have informed them that your petition has been granted so that matter is now closed. You don't need to worry about that anymore" the woman said.
Ria nodded.

"That is a relief. Perhaps, this should be made available to more people like me." Ria said.

"Now that Ria is above me! I do think it is a question that should be discussed and addressed from other perspectives other than medical or legal perspectives only. It is important to have healthy discussions around euthanasia and include considerations from ethics, philosophy, social psychology and not just let lawyers and doctors decide things!" the woman smiled at Ria, her eyes twinkling.

"Will I see you again?" Ria asked.

"Yes, of course, once you sign the confirmation document today, I'll see you for the next confirmation and then once more the day before you go to the clinic. I can come with you if you'd like. Have you thought about who you want to be there with you?"

"Yes, I think it's something I need to do on my own but thank you Martina. It's so kind of you to offer." Ria said firmly.

"Okay. You are staying here so we will still see each other anyway. Jonas will be in touch about the dates for the other procedures, don't worry about them, they are mere formalities to make sure you are still sure. If you are still sure, nothing will change." The woman said. "You can change your mind at any time. Remember that, Ria."

"I know. But I am very sure." Ria said and smiled.

"And you understand how it will happen once you go to the clinic, yes, you are sure?" Martina asked.

"Yes, I have read all the information. It is nice how they do it. I am fine with it, I admit I am a little nervous, but I am not afraid. I would be more afraid if I had to continue living." Ria said.

"That is the real tragedy of torture, is it not?" Martina said.

"It is." Ria said.

"Okay then, anything else you would like to ask me?" Martina asked.

Ria shook her head and stood up. The woman stood up as well and hugged Ria. Ria hugged her back and left the room. She walked back out into the sunny spring day and returned to the bench she had been sitting on. She took out her notebook from her bag and looked at the list of things she wanted to do before the time came. There weren't many things that weren't already ticked off. She had been receiving a small amount of money from the government every week and she was staying in this beautiful, compassionate place where she felt accepted and understood. She didn't need much else. She had already done the most important things on her list. The few remaining things cost nothing. She revised her list one last time, and satisfied there was nothing else to add, she closed the notebook and tilted her face up towards the warm sun.

Soon it would be over. She smiled.

THE END

A Note from the Author

This novel is dedicated to all those who have suffered and continue to suffer ill treatment, torture and abuse across the globe. It is convenient, but incorrect to think of ill treatment and torture as being things of the past or things that only happens in 'backward' countries. Nothing could be further from the truth.

No one can know the exact number of people tortured each day. There is no register and no statistics. Specialised organisations working in ill treatment and torture only see a fraction of those who have actually suffered from it and there are not enough organisations in the world with the skills and resources to support those who do manage to get away. Only a small minority will ever receive support from organisations like these, but far too many sit with no help at all in detention centres, prisons, and camps across Europe or travelling along the myriads of perilous migrant routes, already suffering.

Imagine all of those who remain unseen, unsupported and broken! It is truly heartbreaking.

Ill treatment and torture are used by both state and non-state actors alike. States ignore the agreements they have signed and the laws that prohibit ill treatment and torture. The lack of records and statistics is deliberate. Ill treatment and torture are often framed as being politically or state motivated and this framing conveniently ignores some of the worst types of violent ill treatment and torture. Or we tie ourselves up in useless knots trying to agree on definitions and set criteria for the worst kind of human suffering instead of putting an end to it and providing more resources to those affected.

We must never forget that horrific ill treatment can be happening just down the road from where you live behind the closed doors of so called 'respectable' citizens, not only in dark, dingy prisons.

Ill treatment and torture are not exceptional events. Sadly, they are all too common, yet we find comfort in our denial of its existence and our lack of curiosity. It is easier to believe that the people who flee their countries are just after jobs, unless those fleeing are white. If they are white, they are not sent to the camps on Lesbos.

If only you knew what really happens to the majority of people who flee their own countries. If only you knew what horrors, they go through on their way to another country where they hope they will be safe. Many die trying, their bodies rotting in some desert, or bloated at the bottom of the Mediterranean, or in some ditch, or just thrown in some wet concrete at the back of a construction site, their families never finding out what ever happened to them.

Or maybe you do know about all of that, and it does bother you!

If against all odds they make it, we disbelieve them, we distrust their stories, we fear them, so we keep them confined in terrible cages like on Lesbos. Developed countries channel funds to underdeveloped countries with dubious human rights records to keep them out, far away from our borders. Or some people support and even elect people who want to build huge walls to keep people off land that white people stole.

We have made the people fleeing the problem and not what they are fleeing from. They are fleeing from the violence often created, sustained, maintained, or encouraged by the countries they flee to.

I am worried about all of those people, aren't you? I have been to many of the places they flee from. I would flee too if I lived there, and I believe you would too.

But I am also very worried about the increasing indifference to human suffering that I see in the world today, indifference directed especially at those people suffering who do not look like us.

What you have read is a work of fiction, or is it?

I'll let you decide.

Teresa Murray

Printed in Great Britain
by Amazon

ISBN 9798329710045

90000